continued . . .

TWIN
PEAKS

SUSAN JOHNSON
JASMINE HAYNES

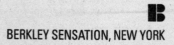
BERKLEY SENSATION, NEW YORK

THE BERKLEY PUBLISHING GROUP
Published by the Penguin Group
Penguin Group (USA) Inc.
375 Hudson Street, New York, New York 10014, USA
Penguin Group (Canada), 90 Eglinton Avenue East, Suite 700, Toronto, Ontario M4P 2Y3, Canada
(a division of Pearson Penguin Canada Inc.)
Penguin Books Ltd., 80 Strand, London WC2R 0RL, England
Penguin Group Ireland, 25 St. Stephen's Green, Dublin 2, Ireland (a division of Penguin Books Ltd.)
Penguin Group (Australia), 250 Camberwell Road, Camberwell, Victoria 3124, Australia
(a division of Pearson Australia Group Pty. Ltd.)
Penguin Books India Pvt. Ltd., 11 Community Centre, Panchsheel Park, New Delhi—110 017, India
Penguin Group (NZ), Cnr. Airborne and Rosedale Roads, Albany, Auckland 1310, New Zealand
(a division of Pearson New Zealand Ltd.)
Penguin Books (South Africa) (Pty.) Ltd., 24 Sturdee Avenue, Rosebank, Johannesburg 2196,
South Africa

Penguin Books Ltd., Registered Offices: 80 Strand, London WC2R 0RL, England

This is a work of fiction. Names, characters, places, and incidents either are the product of the authors' imagination or are used fictitiously, and any resemblance to actual persons, living or dead, business establishments, events, or locales is entirely coincidental. The publisher does not have any control over and does not assume any responsibility for author or third-party websites or their content.

TWIN PEAKS

A Berkley Sensation Book / published by arrangement with the authors

PRINTING HISTORY
Berkley Sensation trade edition / August 2005
Berkley Sensation mass-market edition / October 2006

ISBN: 0-425-21110-X

BERKLEY SENSATION®
Berkley Sensation Books are published by The Berkley Publishing Group,
a division of Penguin Group (USA) Inc.,
375 Hudson Street, New York, New York 10014.
BERKLEY SENSATION is a registered trademark of Penguin Group (USA) Inc.
The "B" design is a trademark belonging to Penguin Group (USA) Inc.

PRINTED IN THE UNITED STATES OF AMERICA

10 9 8 7 6 5 4 3 2 1

Contents

WEDDING SURPRISE

Susan Johnson

ONE

It was a warm, sunny afternoon, the autumn leaves were at their brilliant peak, and half the population of the Twin Cities had clogged the roads to Cutterville, Minnesota, like they did every October to see the awesome color in the river valley.

The two occupants of Room 206 in Mill Valley Inn, however, were indifferent to nature's splendor—indeed to anything outside the confines of the canopied, four-poster bed that took up a major portion of the room.

Although, even had they been predisposed to take a break from their current activities and view the autumn leaves, they couldn't have seen anything. The windows had steamed over.

"Oh, oh, oh, oh, ohhhhhhh, *God!*"

The high-pitched scream echoed in the faux English country house hotel room, bringing a smile to the dark-haired man.

It was his turn—again.

But he wasn't a screamer.

Not that his orgasm a few seconds later wasn't right up there in the Top Ten category.

And he should know.

Fucking A, this lady was hot.

Exhaling softly a moment later, he kissed her, and rolled away, stripping off his condom and dropping it in the wastebasket with the finesse of considerable practice. "Give me a minute," he said, exhaling softly, turning to smile at her. "And we'll try that again."

Sofie smiled back. "No argument here."

Sofie Piper had been lusting after Jake Finn since he'd first walked into the teachers' lounge in August. The new football coach, who had been hired at a princely salary to bring Cutter High to the play-offs, had made her heart go pit-a-pat, not to mention racheting up her primary pleasure center big time.

When she'd seen him alone in the bar downstairs, freshly spiked hair and ripped body as usual, she'd cranked up her courage and gone to talk to him about more than the gossip at school. It wasn't as though they hadn't been flirting with each other in a quiet sort of way for a while, but, with football season in full swing, he didn't hang out in any of the local watering holes, and she never saw him outside the teachers' lounge.

Okay—to be perfectly honest—another factor had also been in play. She and her friend Camille had had a two-martini lunch after they'd checked in, which had made it a whole lot easier to go up and make a pass. Jake had been more than receptive, too—really endearingly eager. And *voilà*—forty minutes later—all her wet dreams had come true.

"I would have shown up for this wedding earlier if I'd known I was going to meet you in the bar," he said with a lazy smile, stroking her fingers as he lay beside her. "Most definitely."

"Then I'm glad I came up and talked to you."

"Me too," he said with a grin. "Way glad. When you said, 'Don't you think small talk is overrated? Why don't you come upstairs,' you made my day. In celebration of our meeting up," he added, twisting around and reaching for the champagne bottle on the bedside table that he'd grabbed from the bar, "how about some bubbly? I haven't felt this good since the winning goal at Madrid." After ripping the foil and cage in one swift motion, he pulled out the cork and held out the bottle. "First chug?"

She was only half listening, focused instead on the really impressive display of sleek, honed muscle in motion, *and* the tantalizing resurgence of his arousal that was stirring and swelling with each beat of his heart. Lordy, Lordy, that kind of stamina was impressive.

"Yes—no?"

His dark brows were raised in query. He'd obviously asked her something. "Sure," she said, winging it, taking the bottle from him and gulping down some champagne. Not that she needed alcohol when her life couldn't get any better than this. Glancing at the bedside clock, she was hoping they had hours yet before the strains of the wedding march put an end to her voluptuous pleasures.

"The wedding isn't until five. Plenty of time," he said, reading her mind, or maybe confident enough to know women were never in a hurry to leave. "And we're back in the game," he added with a grin, glancing downward at his rock-hard cock. "You're damned inspiring."

She was tempted to say he'd inspired weeks of wet dreams for her. As for his towering erection, *inspiration* was too tame a word for what she was feeling; her vagina was practically liquid with longing. Not that she was about to divulge her over-the-top horniness. Men liked casual. And the sex was way too good to jeopardize by coming on too strong. "Speaking of inspiration," she said instead, "that last orgasm was about as good as it gets. If you don't mind, I'm feeling greedy."

He smiled. "I'm with you there. More?" He swung the bottle in her direction.

She shook her head, intoxicated enough by having Jake Finn where she most wanted him. In her bed with his huge dick primed to take care of business again.

"I'm good too," he murmured, setting the bottle on the floor, pulling her close so she was snuggled against his body. "Tell me what you want next—top, bottom, sitting, standing, or something more creative?"

The word *creative* struck some lecherous gong in her head and she was quickly sifting through her repertoire of recent fantasies when the phone rang.

"Don't answer," he murmured, dipping his head to kiss her.

Easy for a man to say. They didn't understand phones required answering. "It's probably Camille," Sofie said, pushing up on one elbow. "She was going to call me when she was unpacked."

"So?"

"She'll come and bang on the door if I don't answer." Already reaching for the phone, Sofie murmured, "I'll tell her I'm busy."

His smile was sweet, understanding even. She'd definitely made the right choice finally asking Jake what she'd been dying to ask him for weeks. Was life good or what?

"Jenny's hysterical," Camille said without preamble, her voice brisk like it was when she was in her take-charge mode. "Charlie's old girlfriend—the diva Brittany— showed up with some relative of his. Jenny's talking about canceling the wedding. We have to talk her down. Come get me. Room 202."

"I can't right now. Go without me." Sofie turned to give Jake one of those I'll-be-with-you-in-a-minute smiles.

"What do you mean you can't? Just hurry. Jenny's practically going ballistic."

Why was she getting the feeling she was talking into a black hole? "I can't—really—no," Sofie said firmly.

"I'm coming to get you."

And on that curt declaration, the phone went dead.

"Jeez, Camille's on her way over," Sofie muttered,

scrambling out of bed and reaching for her slacks. She shot a glance over her shoulder at the buff centerfold lying in her bed. "Don't you dare move. I'll get rid of her."

He stretched lazily, smiled, and reached for the bottle of champagne. "I'm not going anywhere."

Was he sweet or what? She couldn't believe her luck. Gorgeous, agreeable, spectacular in bed. That Zen stuff she'd been practicing must be paying off. Like: Through our senses the world appears. Oh, yeah—big time with regard to her senses that had been doing an over-the-top, happy dance ever since Jake had followed her into her room.

TWO

Racing down the hall, barefoot, pulling her T-shirt on as she ran, Sofie suddenly caught sight of a much too familiar figure coming up the stairs.

Her eyes flared wide.

Oh, fuck.

It can't be.

Her head felt like it was spinning like that girl in *The Exorcist*.

JAKE FINN WAS WALKING UP THE STAIRS BIG AS LIFE!

And his hair wasn't spiked. It was the same as always. Just like the football jersey he wore.

Oh, shit. She was *so* fucked!

Hunching over to stay below the balustrade, she sprinted ahead, hoping to make it around the corner before he reached the top of the stairs.

She probably broke the record for the fifty-yard dash, and completely out of breath, shot inside Camille's room, slammed the door shut, and fell to her knees, gasping for air.

"What the—?"

Sofie thrust her hand out like a traffic cop, and completely out of character, Camille let the shoe she was holding drop to the floor and actually shut her mouth and waited.

"Something really—weird . . . happened," Sofie panted a moment later. "I'm not sure what, but—I'm screwed . . . royally. And I don't care if Jenny is contemplating suicide. My problems are—ten times . . . worse."

Even Camille, who wasn't known for her empathy, understood something of catastrophic proportions had occurred. "Let me help you up," she said, offering Sofie her hand. "Come, sit down. Tell me what happened. You look like you've seen a ghost."

"I might have." Sofie took a few steps and dropped into a chair. "Or I—hope like hell . . . I did."

"Who did you see?" Camille spoke in her best fake-therapist smooth-as-silk murmur.

"Jake Finn." Sofie shut her eyes, opened them again, her expression pained. "Maybe . . . probably . . . oh, hell"—she grimaced—"it was him."

"So you saw Jake Finn. Is that a problem?" But Camille's voice was extra soft and she was watching Sofie like she might detonate.

"Pretty much—because there's a man waiting in my bed. A man I just had the best sex of my life with. A man I thought was Jake Finn. Obviously I was wrong—or else I was hallucinating."

Camille smiled, sat down beside Sofie on another beruffled, chintz-covered chair that went with the excessive chintz overkill in the room's decor, patted her friend's hand, and said, gently, "Let me explain, sweetie. You're not hallucinating, so rest easy. That man in your bed must be Jasper Finn, world-class soccer player, bed partner to starlets and celebrity beauties at home and abroad. He's Manchester United's superstar and most women would sell the family farm to go to bed with him. He's also Jake's twin."

Sofie groaned. "How do you know all that?"

"You must live in a cave. Everyone who reads the scandal sheets knows Jasper Finn, and if you weren't so starry-eyed about Jake, you'd pay attention when he talks in the teachers' lounge. The subject of his soccer-playing brother has come up more than once." Camille grinned. "So was Manchester United's star player as good in bed as his publicity proclaims?"

"Oh, yeah." Sofie sighed. "But I'm still screwed."

"Scale of one to ten?"

"Who cares when my life is in the toilet?"

"I do. Give me a number."

"Okay. A fifteen."

"Jeez! Some people have all the luck. Why couldn't I have bumped into him?"

"I wish you had—okay?—cuz he's turned out to be a real fucking problem for me, starting with the fact that he's still in my bed. What am I going to *say* to him?" Sofie wailed.

"Thanks for keeping my bed warm. Give me a minute to get my clothes off?"

"But it's Jake I'm enamored of—not what's-his-name," Sofie said with a pained look.

"Hello. What's the difference. They're twins. And if the soccer player is a fifteen, I'd say count your blessings. Unless you're a gambler."

"Look, everything's not about sex."

"It isn't?"

Sofie frowned. "We can't all be into record keeping."

"I hope that wasn't an insult."

"God—sorry." Sofie offered Camille a rueful smile. "My brain is wrecked. I'm jumpy as hell, mega-confused, and *sooo* embarrassed." Sliding down in her chair, she contemplated her painted toenails as though life's solutions were reflected in Revlon's Crimson Tide Gloss. "If Jake finds out," she muttered, "it could screw up whatever chance I might have to—you know . . . make a connection with him."

"Melissa might get him after all," Camille said with a grunt of displeasure.

"Jeez, don't say that. Not our evil genius vice principal

who sucks all the good-looking men into her sexual force field."

"She's been working him hard. Maybe he'll give in to those big boobs and sultry glances."

"Now I'm really depressed."

"Do you want me to go and explain to Jasper?" Camille grinned. "I might even be willing to pay you for the opportunity."

Sofie smiled wanly. "It's a nice thought, but I should probably go myself and explain. You know—act like an adult. Or try. Hell, I'll just lie."

"That works. But seriously, are you really going to give up a fifteen on the pleasure scale for maybe a forlorn hope? You've been mooning around for Jake since school started."

"He's busy with football season. You know how the coaches eat and sleep football till the season is over. I understand that. And it's not as though he hasn't been really sweet whenever we talk."

"Maybe he's too nice. He could be gay—have you thought of that? He hasn't dated anyone all fall—or at least anyone in town. Maybe that's why even Melissa's big tits haven't gotten a rise out of him."

Sofie scowled. "He's not gay."

"It's not out of the question. There's plenty of gay athletes."

"He's not, okay? Franny Graham knows a friend of a friend from his last high school, and she says he dates women all the time. He's just wrapped up in football now. I had a boyfriend in high school who barely had time to eat during football season. And remember, they're paying Jake a fortune to bring Cutter to the finals."

"I don't know. It still sounds odd to me. I'd never get so wrapped up in Shakespeare that *I'd* forget about fucking."

"You don't ever forget about fucking."

"You should talk, Miss Let-Me-Tell-You-My-Latest-Wet-Dream. I don't think I'm the only one who has sexual fantasies. And yours are probably better cuz they're in French." Sofie taught French and spoke like a native.

"For your information, my dreams are not in French. Jake wouldn't understand it."

"Okay, okay, so he's at the top of your list—in spite of everything. If you're *that* intent on having him, just tell his brother it was nice, but you have to get ready for the wedding. Give him a kiss and shove him out the door."

"Easy to say. He's really nice. I don't want to be rude."

"It seems like you might not have decided yet."

"Of course I have. I just don't want to hurt his feelings."

Camille's eyebrows rose. "A man who sleeps with the number of women Jasper Finn does probably understands the phrase 'It was nice. I'll call you.' He uses it all the time. Although, why you're even contemplating giving up a for-real fifteen for a possible is beyond me. I wouldn't take those odds."

While Sofie liked sex as much as the next person, she and Camille had never approached male-female relationships with the same mind-set. Sofie was into dating while Camille's preference was for hooking up. It was probably puerile for a woman of twenty-six to be into infatuation, but she was and Jake intrigued her for a ton of reasons beyond sex. She liked his really warm laugh that lit up a room and her heart. She liked how he always helped old Mrs. Haugen, the home ec teacher, with her coat and brought up her car to the front door when it was raining. And he hadn't fallen for Melissa's heavy-handed flirting—or at least, not yet. Did that show a discriminating character or what? He was really good with his students, too—he seemed to care about them with a well-meaning kindness rarely seen. They'd talked a lot about making school work for those students who weren't the high achievers or star athletes. Mostly though, she liked how he looked at her when they talked—like they were alone in the room or maybe the universe, like he really wanted to do more than talk. He had the bluest eyes, gray-blue, and cool—but not cold. Oops—not a good image; his brother had those same eyes.

Anyway, she wasn't about to give up on her fantasy about Jake Finn, despite his slowness in asking her out.

He'd said more than once how football season got in the way of his personal life. And that was good enough for her. As for the recent awkward—though highly pleasurable— incident in her bedroom, she knew what she was going to do. "I'll just tell Jake's brother that Jenny needs us; she's talking about canceling the wedding—which is true," Sofie said decisively. "If Jake's twin sleeps with tons of women, whether I do again or not won't matter to him."

"A word of advice if you're intent on your football coach. I'd suggest you make nice with him tonight, or the huntress, Melissa, might ace you out. She'll be wearing the lowest-cut dress at the wedding, and I guarantee, she won't let a second pass before gluing herself to Jake's side. When she can barely keep her hands off him at school, for sure, she's going to make her move this weekend with beds conveniently near. That said, I still don't understand why the soccer brother isn't turning you on. He's turned on most of the women in Europe."

"Call me picky."

"Or stupid."

"Maybe Jake's even better in bed. Have you thought of that?" Sofie said.

"And maybe he isn't."

Rising from the chair, Sofie spoke with the assurance of a true zealot. "I'm sure he is. I'd better get back."

"Whatever. Just play it by ear with darling Jasper, that's all I'm saying—you know . . . don't burn any bridges."

"Have sex again you mean," Sofie said, moving toward the door.

"Why not? A fifteen isn't to be rashly discounted."

"It's not a rash decision."

Camille shook her head. "I don't get it, but good luck, whatever you do."

"Thanks." Sofie turned with one hand on the doorknob. "I'll come back after I talk to him, and we can dress together. Those bridesmaid headdresses are dicey to get on."

"I've been thinking of losing mine. I don't look good with fruit in my hair."

Sofie grinned. "We're going to look like bushes walking down the aisle."

"And therein lies the problem."

"So Jenny likes cherries. There's no such thing as a decent bridesmaid outfit anyway. Speaking of weddings," she added, "do you know why Jasper is even here? He's a long way from Manchester."

"The same reason Jake is. They're friends of Charlie's. They're all from Iowa somewhere. If you grow up in Iowa and you want a job, you ultimately end up in the Twin Cities, Chicago, or St. Louis."

Camille and Sofie were both from small towns in Minnesota and had followed the same job trail to the Twin Cities. When Cutterville had been overtaken by urban sprawl a few years ago, the school district had grown so large, their teams had moved into the big-leagues. Which meant they needed big-league coaches.

Camille grinned. "It sounds as though you two didn't have a lot of time for conversation."

Sofie blushed. "If we had, I might have figured out he wasn't Jake."

"With that kind of chemistry, maybe you should keep your options open. A man like that who can turn you on that fast"—Camille jabbed her finger at Sofie—"he's a keeper."

"Uh-uh. My mind's made up. I'll thank him politely, lie about Jenny needing me, and send him on his way."

Camille grinned. "Give him a kiss for me."

"Give him your own kiss after the wedding." Sofie's eyebrows flickered up and down. "I have a feeling he likes women."

A moment later Sofie stood in the hallway, doing a quick check of the corridor to see that she was alone. No way did she want to run into Jake.

An empty hallway; thank you, God.

One small blessing in the train wreck of her life.

Silently running through her excuses, she walked to her room.

THREE

Jasper smiled from the bed as Sofie entered the room. "Crisis averted?"

Even in that short query, the faintest nuance of a British accent underlay his words. How could she not have noticed? "I'm afraid not," she said, trying to speak in a businesslike tone with the full glory of Manchester United's star footballer, nude and aroused, dazzling her retinas. "One of Charlie's old girlfriends showed up for the wedding, and Jenny is threatening to cancel the nuptials." Sofie didn't move from the vicinity of the door just to be safe. "So . . . that is—I have to go and calm her down."

"Brittany must have showed up," he said with a grin. "I figured she would."

"You know her?"

"If you lived in Cedar Grove, you knew Brittany. She liked to be noticed. Charlie never saw that side of her. He thought she really was a Sunday School teacher."

"Whatever she is, I have to convince Jenny she's not a threat."

"Seriously? Why can't Charlie do that?"

"The groom can't see the bride before the wedding."

"You're kidding. It's the twenty-first century."

"Yeah, well . . . I still have to go." She should have just left already, but his enormous appeal was really—well—enormous. There were valid reasons why he was in all those scandal sheets: The Colin Farrell of the soccer leagues—all male mojo and charisma—was a damnable eyeful.

"Stay for a few minutes more," he murmured, coming up on his elbows.

"No . . . I can't." She found herself pressing her palms against the door, as though the solid surface would serve as anchor to her good intentions. With a hard, muscular, clearly aroused male body available for her pleasure, she was finding prudence and self-denial increasingly difficult to sustain.

"Sure you can. What's a few minutes?"

If she were a woman of principle, she wouldn't have been experiencing the heated pulsing between her legs. If she had a modicum of restraint, she wouldn't have felt her pulse racing. "I gotta go," she whispered, curbing her wanton impulses with enormous effort, turning to open the door.

His reflexes were superb, honed on the professional playing fields of the world, and she'd no more than touched the doorknob when his hand covered hers, the leap from bed to door an awesome display of grace and power. "Why don't you come one more time, and then you can soothe Jenny's temper," he whispered, kissing the little dip behind her ear before turning her and pulling her close.

"I shouldn't," she breathed, his erection hot against her belly, her slacks notwithstanding.

"Jenny won't care." He was deftly unbuttoning her waistband.

"She—"

His mouth covered hers, swallowing her feeble protest, and as she responded to his kiss and her breathing quick-

ened, he understood no one was going to be making anyone do anything they didn't want to do.

Hot with shame, she felt him unzip her zipper, slip her
slacks down her hips, lift her away from the puddle of fab-
ric on the floor. She should push him away, shout an em-
phatic no, dismiss the salacious urges of her body, do
anything but moan softly under the cajoling pressure of his
lips and think of how he'd feel sliding deep inside her.

No, no, no, no, no, she thought, but never uttered the
words.

And what Jasper heard instead were breathy little
moans, voluptuous little sighs, and what he felt was the
soft friction of her hips rubbing against his cock. "Here?"
he murmured, lifting his head enough to look at her. "Or on
the bed?"

She didn't quite meet his gaze.

For a woman who fired up in seconds, her hesitation—
however minute—was a turn-on. "This won't take long,"
he murmured, sliding his hands under her arms, lifting her
up on her toes. "Stay there, now," he whispered, knowing
she wouldn't move, knowing she wanted what he wanted.

Crossing the small room, he pulled a condom packet
from his jeans pocket and ripped it open. "Spread your
legs, darling," he softly ordered as he walked back, slipping on the condom, his erection surging upward at her
ready compliance.

Right now he could ask her to do anything and she
would, he thought, the creamy rivulet sliding down her inner thigh indication of her feverish arousal. Her skin was
flushed, her breathing labored, her impatience for cock
every man's fantasy. He'd have to thank Charlie for inviting him to his wedding.

As he reached her, he slipped a finger up her slit. "Do
you want me to hurry?"

"No," she whispered, struggling against temptation, trying to ignore what he was doing to her clit with his finger.
"No," she gasped, "don't . . ."

But her voice died away at the last, and spreading her thighs with his knee, he forced her legs apart, adjusted the head of his cock against her hot, slick sex, and drove upward with swift, practiced finesse. She uttered a suffocated little cry, clutched his shoulders, then shifted her hips—asking for more, her cunt melting around him like liquid heat.

He gave her what she wanted, cramming her full, and urged on by her breathy sighs, flexed his quads and forced himself deeper still, impaling her, lifting her up off her toes. She screamed, her nails dug into his shoulders, and an instant later she came, her vaginal muscles strong enough to ripple up and down his cock even through a Trojan.

This tinder hot babe really stoked his fire, and he wasn't polite this time—no waiting until her last little spasm.

He came in a deluge, but then he'd been waiting for her return, anticipation fanning the flame, and moments later they were both trying to catch their breath. Withdrawing so she could come down from her tiptoes, he smiled and brushed her mouth with a kiss. "I'm glad you didn't run off."

Not sure whether she should be shamed by her wantonness or grateful for one of the better orgasms of her life, she stammered, "Yes, I mean . . . I probably should have—oh, hell—thanks . . . that was great."

He grinned. "The pleasure was all mine. And I guess you want me to go now."

Lord, he was sweet, picking up on her stammering discomfort, playing the gentleman. "I should . . . see—Jenny," she said, still seriously discomfitted. So much for adult composure.

"Gotcha. I'll see you at the wedding, then." Giving her a quick kiss, he moved toward the bed, discarded his condom, and picked up his boxers. He talked about Charlie as he dressed, clearly more at ease in postcoital situations than she. But if Camille was right, he'd been here a couple thousand times before.

Sofie answered, distractedly, overcome with guilt, mentally beating herself up for not having the willpower to resist the twin brother of the man she supposedly was infatuated with. God, she was hopeless when it came to self-control. Not that Camille wouldn't be happy with the outcome. If only she could be so cavalier.

Jasper gave her a hug once he was dressed, said with a wink, "Remember to save me a dance," and walked out of the room—no kidding—whistling.

There it was, clear as a bell.

That's how men dealt with sex. No guilt, only good times.

In the meantime, she would be rerunning the disaster of 1) her mistaken identity blunder, 2) her wanton libido, and 3) not being able to whistle off her indiscretions like world-class soccer players.

Crisis time. She needed someone to tell her everything was going to be okay. Better yet, make it all go away.

"I did it again," she said before Camille could say hello.

"Don't sound so glum. Way to go, baby."

"I need a therapist."

"Don't waste your money. I'll set you straight. Bring your stuff over and dress here. I'll give you some sterling advice on the ways of the world. You've had your head buried in the cultural world of France too long."

"It's not that cultural. Remember, the French probably invented dangerous liaisons."

"No, they didn't. It started with Eve and the snake. But let me reassure you, sweetie. Jake doesn't expect you to be a virgin."

"But, jeez, his brother!"

"Listen, if they were raised in the same small town as Charlie—they probably dated the same women. The dating pool is limited. I heard Jenny talk about a population of five hundred. Think about it—okay?"

"Jasper did say he knew Brittany—you know, that old girlfriend of Charlie's Jenny is going wacko over. Maybe Jake knew her, too."

"There, you see? You're not the first woman to screw someone's brother."

"Thanks—I needed that." Camille always saw the big picture.

"You can repay me by standing aside when I make my move on darling Jasper."

"Not a problem. Be my guest."

"You astonish me. Apparently you have no starry-eyed, hankering-after-celebrities impulses."

"'Fraid not." Maybe men were right. When it was just about sex, you could take it or leave it.

"Good. My field is clear—or semiclear. Once the other women discover the star in our midst, I'll be run over in the stampede. Not that you don't have Melissa to contend with."

"Uh-uh, you do. When she finds out we have a world athlete in our burg, she'll laser in on him instead."

"Sure, ruin my day when I have to wear a prissy brides-maid dress *without* a low-cut neckline. Oh, hell, come over and we'll figure out what to do to get our dream dates over a drink from the mini-fridge."

Click.

Not that Sofie wasn't familiar with Camille's disregard for phone courtesy. Bottom line, though, she'd been talked down from her guilty pleasures. Thank God, Camille could always be relied on to set her straight when she obsessed.

Now if she only didn't have to look like a cherry bush for the next couple hours, life would be swell.

FOUR

The wedding remained on schedule, thanks to Jenny's mother, who said she wasn't about to lose the thirty thousand this wedding cost because Jenny was jealous of some old girlfriend of Charlie's.

Jenny snapped out of her tantrum when faced with her mother's blunt fiat, and Mrs. Mercer knew enough to sweeten the pot with an offer of an extra week in Hawaii for the honeymoon.

Order was restored. Feelings were soothed. Charlie didn't even catch a whiff of trouble.

And when he saw his bride coming down the aisle, his love and pride was so achingly obvious, Jenny forgave him for having a girlfriend rude enough to show up at her wedding.

Sofie nudged Camille as they stood at the front of the church waiting for Jenny to walk down the aisle. "Is that love or what?" she whispered. "Look at Charlie's face."

"Maybe we'll have to see about catching the bridal bouquet."

"Maybe this time I might actually want to," Sofie said,

awash in a sugar-sweet sea of matrimonial empathy. "I'm thinking white picket fences and baby carriages."

"You're going off the deep end."

"So, it feels good. Did you see Jake walk in all dressed up? He looked fabulous."

"Just like his brother walking beside him," Camille teased.

"You have your fantasy and I have mine, thank you very much—hush, here she comes."

The wedding was lovely: the glow of candlelight and Mrs. Mercer's attempt to recreate some floral paradise, picture perfect; the quirky, personalized vows Jenny and Charlie had written that included their dog and cat, heart-warming; the minister who played the guitar for the vocalist, who sang Charlie's favorite song, "Interstate Love Song" by the Stone Temple Pilots, had the talent of a rock star under his vestments, and the tears in Jenny's eyes made Sofie cry. It was one of the nicest ceremonies Sofie had every seen. Or maybe she was in a wedding mood. Maybe love and marriage had taken on a new relevancy now that her heart had zeroed in on someone for real.

Not that she was crazy enough to jump from point A to Z without going through the requisite alphabet of getting to know Jake. But she was feeling wedding fever like nothing she'd ever experienced. It was all touchy-feely nice, but it was scary, too; she'd never felt this way before.

Worse. She'd never even dated Jake.

She hoped she wasn't losing her mind.

She was hoping she could chalk this up to that love-at-first-sight thing that had been around a lot longer than she.

Okay. Back up. *Love* was a pretty strong word. Could she call it something else?

Although, with sweet, tender *amour* perfuming the air, who wouldn't be in the mood for love?

While the organist played, the reception line zipped by in a blur, and immediately after, Camille and Sofie ripped off their headdresses, leaving them free to try to catch the bridal bouquet without looking through a tangle of green velvet ribbons and man-made cherries.

"Damn," Camille muttered a few moments later, a loser in the bouquet scramble. "I was already planning on living in England. Kyra doesn't even need the bouquet. She's engaged."

"I had it, but Kyra ripped it out of my hands," Sofie complained. "Although if the girls' volleyball coach can't outjump me, she might as well give it up."

"Anyone can outjump you," Camille said with an arched brow. "You come up to my elbow."

Since Camille had been an all-state center in high school, Sofie didn't take it personally. She considered herself more or less normal size. "I see a tray of champagne glasses coming our way. I'm thinking empty a couple of those, get Jake in my sights, and make my move."

"I'm gonna go and find my target before the pursing women surround him," Camille noted. "And if I'm lucky, I won't see you till morning."

Sofie was left in the milling crowd of guests, the decibel levels beginning to rise. Free champagne was to blame for the noise levels—a good number of two-fisted drinkers were getting their share of the Cristal. Plucking a flute from a passing tray, Sofie stood to one side of the colorful, artfully arranged canapé table, scanning the crowd for the nonpareil apple of her eye.

A string quartet was playing in one corner of the large reception room—background music to the food and drinks. There would be a band later for dancing, and then in the wee hours of the morning some blues singer was scheduled to tranquilize the crowd and send them off to bed. Sofie had heard about every detail of the wedding during the last year when Jenny—an obsessed bride-to-be— had talked of her wedding ad nauseam to all her fellow teachers. She even had file cards on top of file cards for every minute of the wedding festivities—color-coded to boot. *That* had been impressive to Sofie, whose idea of organization was one pile for bills, one for newspapers and magazines, and one pile for everything else. The everything-else pile always ended up on her desk, and once a year she cleaned it up—a task made easier by the fact that everything was pretty much out of date by then and no longer relevant.

Drinking her champagne and daydreaming her usual dream that involved a football coach in her bed, she didn't hear Jasper come up behind her until he whispered in her ear, "Long time no see. I missed you."

She jumped. Not because he'd whispered in her ear, but because Jake was making his way through the crowd toward her. And he was scowling.

Shit. She wasn't good at juggling two men at once.

She'd had limited experience—okay—none.

"I checked into my room." Jasper kissed her cheek, taking her near-empty glass from her hand, handing it to a passing waiter. "It has a fireplace. You'll like it."

His kiss was a light, brushing caress that could be one of those European greetings. She was hoping that's what Jake thought. Although Jake's scowl was still in place. She was guessing he wasn't buying into that European hello-kiss thing. People in the Midwest didn't do that. Maybe for your grandmother on her birthday, but otherwise a kiss was a kiss—period.

She backed away—or tried to. Jasper had taken her hand.

He pulled her against his chest. "We don't have to stay for supper," he whispered. "We'll call room service."

Jake was bearing down on them.

As though sensing his twin, Jasper looked up. "Hey, baby brother. Wuzzup?"

"Knock it off." Jake nodded at Jasper's hand. "Let her go."

Jasper shot a glance at Sofie, then back at Jake. "For real?"

"Yeah."

Sofie's heart practically jumped out of her chest when Jake said, yeah, like some caveman about to do hand-to-hand combat for his mate. Wow. She tried to look innocent, all the time praying that Jasper wouldn't snitch on her. Sleeping with him had been an honest mistake. No one could blame her for not knowing Jake had a twin. She shouldn't be penalized for not asking questions at a time like that—you know . . . in the heat of passion. As for the second time, she refused to think about it because she had no excuse.

Jasper released her hand. "I didn't know you two were an item." Jasper's gaze shifted from Sofie to Jake again.

"You don't know everything."

Thank God Jake had answered. What the hell could she have said? We are, but I like some on the side? Or the truth—we aren't, but I'd like to be? "We both teach at Cutter High," she said, deciding evasion was least likely to get her in trouble. A relative term when Jasper could blow her cover any second.

"You promised me the first dance." Jake held out his hand.

No one danced to string quartets, but this probably wasn't the time to point out the fact that there was no dance floor or dancers in sight. Taking his hand, Sofie felt an immediate warmth—tingly and rose-petal nice . . . a harpsichord should be playing in the background with troubadours singing. If she was mixing her centuries, she didn't care.

Jasper stepped back, his expression neutral. "See you guys later." But his probing gaze followed them as they walked away. He hoped his brother wasn't head over heels, because in this case love might be blind.

The lady liked variety.

FIVE

"Sorry about butting in," Jake said as they moved through the throng, "but you don't know my brother. He only shops, he never buys." No way was he going to let Sofie walk away with someone else; he'd had to rearrange his whole schedule to make this weekend happen. And he'd been planning on spending the weekend with her.

"I was looking for you anyway," Sofie said, not wanting to touch that statement with a ten-foot pole, ignoring the guilt assailing her. "I wanted to tell you how great you look all dressed up." A navy suit, white shirt, French cuffs, a lavender-gray tie in the softest silk, black shoes; he could have been an ad for Georgio Armani.

He glanced at her. "You look great, too." He smiled. "I like ballerinas."

She grimaced. "Barbie dolls are to blame for brain-washing susceptible young minds."

"It's not so bad. It's a good dress for dancing. Not that we can actually dance yet, but"—he shrugged—"I wanted to get you away from Jaz. He's not your type."

Uh-oh. Here's where a real strong streak of female independence would come in handy. You know—where the belief in absolute equality between the sexes is ingrained in one's psyche, and the ability to shrug off sexual peccadillos with élan is second nature. If only Camille—the original "I am woman" prototype—were here. Bereft of that support system, Sofie wimped out and changed the subject. "I'd like a drink."

"Champagne or something with hair to it?"

"I'll have a Cosmopolitan. Make it strong." These were desperate times.

He gave her a look.

"Bridesmaid stress."

Jake grinned. "One stress-relieving Cosmo coming up."

She watched him walk away, congratulating herself for having avoided any major pitfalls in terms of full disclosure. And apropos long-held fantasies, things were definitely looking up. Jake had come looking for her. Yay! She hadn't had to hunt him out. Now all she had to do was stay clear of Jasper—not too difficult a task in this crush—and she might survive her prewedding blunder.

Jake returned carrying her drink and what looked like a vodka rocks for him.

"I was planning on asking you out before—about a hundred times," he said, handing over her drink. "But football takes so much time, I figured I'd have to wait till the season was over. When I saw Jaz making his move"—he shrugged—"that plan got scraped." What he didn't say was that he'd damn near gone psycho. Which meant he'd been thinking about Sofie Piper for too long without getting with the program.

"I was thinking about asking you out, too." She lifted her glass. "To good intentions."

His smile was slow and sexy as he raised his glass, his world back on track. "To good times."

Uh-oh, the troubadours had stopped singing and her senses were heating up big time. It was as if she was cranked up on ecstasy because going straight upstairs suddenly seemed like a good idea. Again. Okay, so she'd made a mistake the first time. This was the right guy.

"Are you hungry?" Jake nodded at the buffet line.

"Not really." See—they both had the same idea.

"I'm starved, but if you don't—"

"No—no, the food looks great," she quickly said. Whoops. Never look too eager. She compensated by taking a casual sip of her Cosmopolitan, like she had all the time in the world.

"I left home without eating." He shrugged. "A couple of kids stopped by this morning and I was late getting out." He drained his drink. "Let's get in line."

He'd poured down his vodka without blinking. That much straight booze would have choked her. Not that she hadn't noticed he had major mojo a thousand times before.

"You finished?" He nodded at her martini glass.

She debated giving up the last inch of liquor, decided against it when she needed a modicum more female backbone, and drank it down.

He took the glass from her, handed it to a passing waiter, and putting his arm around her shoulder, drew her toward the buffet line.

He just oozed male assurance in a strong, silent, unassailably competent way, as though he were eminently familiar with taking charge. Of course, being a quarterback for a decade or shepherding five teams to state championships in as many years would bolster one's confidence.

She was trying really hard not to hyperventilate now that her daydreams were finally beginning to play out. Lordy, he smelled good—his cologne faintly sweet and musky; he *felt* good—his hard-muscled body up close and personal. And he had the nicest smile—Ohmygod, he was going to kiss her!

"I've been wanting to do that for a long time," he murmured as his mouth lifted from hers. His teeth flashed white in a grin. "You're blushing."

"You caught me by surprise." This probably wasn't the

time—here in the buffet line—to explain it wasn't embarrassment pinking her cheeks, but lust. That kiss had kicked her libidinous impulses into overdrive, as though she were some bona fide nympho when, in fact, she was the least likely woman to claim the title. Was it possible they were piping some aphrodisiac into the ventilation system at Mill Valley Inn? Or did the Finn brothers exude some devilish magic?

"When there aren't so many people around," Jake whispered, "I'll do it better. I'll take my time."

Witty replies were in short supply when her brain was flooded with speculation on what he might do when he was taking his time. She was about to murmur something certifiably inane when a sultry voice behind them murmured, "If it isn't darling Jake."

Sofie's first impulse was to thank God for the interruption. Her second impulse was to feign deafness. Even without turning around, she knew who was playing the resident sex kitten.

Jake must have been ignoring Melissa, too, because it took a tap on his shoulder before he half turned and acknowledged her.

"I've been looking everywhere for you," she purred, studiously ignoring Sofie, who was hard to ignore, nestled as she was in the curve of Jake's arm.

In her enviable one-upmanship position Sofie was immune to Melissa's rudeness. "Hi, Melissa," she said, sweet as sugar. "Did you like the wedding?"

The svelte brunette, wearing, as predicted, the plunging neckline of the night, gave Sofie a fleeting glance. "I've seen better." Melissa turned her thousand-watt smile and barely covered boobs toward Jake. "I bet Rutledge I could get you to play the drums later," she murmured, running her finger down his arm. "You're sooo good; he's never heard you perform." The words *good* and *perform* were X-rated whispers.

"Not tonight," Jake said blandly. He nodded in the direction of the bridal party seated at the head table. "Jenny has the evening's events arranged down to the last second. Maybe some other time."

"You have to promise to dance with me later, then."

Jeez. Sofie didn't know women actually did that breathy purr outside of phone-sex lines.

"Maybe some other time," Jake repeated, his voice middle-of-the-road neutral. "We're going to eat now. The prime rib's from Charlie's dad's farm and it's worth the drive." He smiled. "If you'll excuse us."

He turned away.

So Jasper Finn wasn't the only smooth operator in the family. Jake did that "Don't call me, I'll call you" with equal aplomb.

Which could be good or bad depending on whether she was the recipient of that put-down or not.

"Sorry," he murmured as Melissa flounced off. "She's not the shy type."

"You think?"

He laughed. "She's been intimidating students too long; attack mode comes natural."

Sofie didn't want to burst his bubble, but Melissa had been in attack mode with men even when she taught Minnesota history. "I thought the wedding was really nice." If you don't have anything good to say, etcetera, etcetera; her mother would have been proud. "All those flowers and candles were full-scale Hollywood romance."

"No kidding. I even got misty-eyed a couple times when they spoke their vows."

Sofie did a quick double-take in case he was kidding, but he didn't look amused. "Really?" she said before she could catch herself.

He shrugged. "Men think of marriage once in a while, too."

"Once in a while as in once every Ice Age?"

"You're too cynical, babe." He grinned. "Am I turning you on with this talk of marriage?"

"You've been turning me on from the first moment you walked into the teachers' lounge. Oops, sorry, that's the Cosmo talking. Strike that last remark."

"Hey, no way. You turned on is definitely on the agenda."

"Keep it up and Melissa will look tame as a nun compared to me." Sofie clamped her hand over her mouth. "Jeez, I shouldn't have said that either," she said through her fingers.

Pulling her close, he nuzzled her ear as though they weren't in line with a hundred other people. "Don't worry about it and if I wasn't starved—for food," he clarified, his mouth warm on her skin, "I'd have you show me that nun stuff right now."

She giggled, half drunk or punch drunk with giddy delight. "So I'm losing out to a slab of beef."

He eased back enough to smile at her. "I'll eat fast."

Was that charming or what? Not that seductive charm didn't run in the family. Which thought caused her to flick a quick glance around the room, checking on Jasper's whereabouts. With her much-imagined paradise within reach, she wasn't looking for any screwups.

As they finally reached the food, conversation was curtailed while Jake filled his plate and Sofie selected a few scraps of salad, some shrimp, and numerous chocolate desserts because chocolate was good for the heart, as every health-conscious person knew. Jake pretty much concentrated on Iowa-raised beef and potatoes, and then they made their way to one of the Martha Stewart-type decorated tables.

They ate, or rather Jake ate while Sofie pushed her salad and shrimp aside, spooned up her desserts and allowed the waiter to keep filling her glass with champagne. Perhaps the festive atmosphere inspired more effervescence, perhaps she was slightly nervous, or maybe turning down Cristal champagne seemed ungrateful. More important, perhaps, she'd been awaiting this occasion for a very long time.

Then the band started playing and Jenny and Charlie had the first dance—cause for another misty-eyed moment in an evening of exceptional sentimentality.

Jake touched her hand. "Hey—are you all right?"

She sniffled and nodded, not about to mention she was seriously thinking about love—you know the kind in eight point caps with garlanded roses—when she never had before. When it was stupid and juvenile and completely bizarre with a man she hardly knew.

Pulling out his hankie, Jake wiped away the tears running down her cheeks. "It gets to you, doesn't it." He half lifted his hand. "All this love and romance."

"Or else I've had one too many champagnes."

He chuckled. "Or that. Come on, dance with me. Let's take advantage of this feel-good moment."

She would have gone to the moon with him right then. Maybe they should put that in the Cristal ads. Not that she was going to scare him off by saying so. "I'd love to dance," she said instead.

He leaned over and kissed her as they sat side by side at a table of ten other people who unabashedly stared at them.

If only she hadn't opened her eyes at the end and seen Jasper watching them from across the room. A little shiver of dread raced up her spine.

Luckily, Jake was answering a man across the table—something about the name of the song being played and she was able to focus her attention on their conversation. Her panic over the possibility of being revealed as an oversexed trollop lessened.

Thank you, God, Camille had just come up to talk to Jasper.

She was saved.

"Ready?"

Jerked back to reality, Sofie smiled what she hoped was a smile of complete and utter innocence. "Ready," she said.

Jake was a great dancer, but then any man who could scramble behind a defensive line with three-hundred-pound gorillas trying to break through had to be nimble on his feet. The band was playing lazy ballads for slow dancing in keeping with the romantic mood of the evening, and just being in Jake's arms was right up there with shoe shopping and chocolate mousse. Just to add to what was fast approaching the enchanted evening of the century, not two seconds ago, Camille and Jasper had walked out of the room.

Sofie was thinking life couldn't get much better.

Discounting the possibility of having sex with Jake later that was in a whole other category—like, beyond perfection.

But he didn't seem to be in any hurry—you know . . . in terms of getting it on; they'd danced two dances already. For a fleeting moment she wondered if Camille was right and he was gay.

Ahhh . . .

Scotch that rumor.

The most glorious hard-on was currently swelling against her stomach.

"Sorry," he murmured. "I've been trying to rein in my libido."

How sweet. She could say, "Don't bother." She could play coy and pretend she was flustered. She could take charge and say, "Your room or mine."

"It's not a problem," she murmured, opting for ambiguity at this initial stage. "You're a great dancer."

"Thanks. You, too." Then he took a deep breath and said, "I'm not going to be able to keep this up—I mean . . . when I'm this excited, I'd rather not be on public display. So"—he blew out a breath—"would you care to go somewhere else for a drink . . . or—"

"Yes." She smiled up at him. "Yes—six weeks, five days ago."

His smile was pure sunshine. "You've been on my mind, too. Nonstop for weeks." And if the possibility of some psychic connection actually existed, he was feeling it.

"We can compare fantasies. I have a file."

He laughed. "If only the other teachers knew what I was thinking when I saw you in the teachers' lounge." He was dancing them toward the doorway.

"Oh, crap, Melissa's giving me the evil eye." Seriously. There she was not ten feet away.

"So?"

His blunt dismissal was highly erotic, as though she'd beaten out the Miss Universe of sex kittens and was eligible for the prize. Which in her case came in a tall, dark, handsome supercharged package. "So, nothing," she said as casually as she could considering Melissa was staring daggers at her. "Your room or mine?"

"Mine has some champagne cooling in the fridge."

"For me, I hope." She'd given up on coy.

"Oh, yeah. Definitely for you."

"Do you think it's too early to disappear?" She suddenly had second thoughts.

"If we don't, I'm going to embarrass myself. You'll have to walk in front of me as it is."

"What about the toasts?" She grimaced. "We bridesmaids have our duties."

He sighed. "I'll sit in a dark corner and wait."

Jenny had invited two hundred guests, all of whom were crammed into this room, and whether she was here or not probably wouldn't be noticed in the crowd. So she wasn't around when it was her turn to toast the bride and groom. She could have been in the ladies' room. And bottom line—weighing duty against sex—no way was she going to be dutiful. "Let's go."

He came to an abrupt stop. "*Yesss.* Now, stay close. That ballerina dress is going to come in handy." Lightly gripping her shoulders from behind, he guided her off the dance floor toward the exit.

Oh, Christ, he thought. There was Brittany chatting up her cousins. If God was on his side, she wouldn't see him in the crowd.

As if, he realized with an inner groan as her fat cousin Mae shifted slightly to grab a glass of champagne from a passing waiter and Brittany caught sight of him.

Her face lit up. "Jake! Hey, Jake! Over here!"

Waving and smiling, she left her cousins behind like day-old news. Same old Brittany. Always the opportunist. But there was no way out of it. She was on a collision course with them. "An old classmate from Cedar Grove," Jake murmured, dropping his hands from Sofie's shoulders.

An old girlfriend, too, unless she missed her guess, Sofie thought, the beautiful blonde in the silver lamé gown doing that eye contact thing with Jake that suggested shared memories. And those memories weren't about choir practice.

Man, she had competition on top of competition tonight.

First, Melissa's plunging neckline and now Hollywood-style silver lamé. This lady wasn't the usual Midwestern type. She could have been on the cover of some magazine.

"Hello, darling," Brittany said as she reached them, her intonation so beautifully lyrical, it screamed professional singer. "I hear you're doing extremely well." Her smile was professional, too. "Winningest coach in the Midwest, four years running. Not bad."

"Thanks. Brittany meet Sofie Piper, Sofie, Brittany Olsen. Sofie and I teach together."

"Nurturing young minds. How virtuous." Her gaze never strayed from Jake's, Sofie relegated to the last row in the balcony.

Although anyone wearing a hideous ballerina gown couldn't compete style-wise against designer silver lamé. That Jake's lovely hard-on was pressing into her back was consolation, of course. Not that she didn't consider the fickleness, and/or inconstancy of men as well, but at the moment, she was feeling pretty secure.

"We *have* to find some time to catch up," Brittany murmured. "I haven't seen you in ages. Remember all those parties down by the river." She winked. "Sultry nights and teenage hormones . . ."

"Yeah, well—that was a long time ago."

Brittany smiled, every perfectly capped tooth glistening white. "Fun times—you have to admit."

"Mom tells me you're on Broadway," Jake said, deliberately changing the subject. "Congratulations."

"Off-Broadway, but hopeful," she said with a lift of her brows.

False modesty, but Brittany's acting was getting better, he thought. "You'll make it. I'll read about you in the *Times* someday. Look," he murmured, "we're going to get out of this crowd for a minute. I'll see you around later."

"I'll round up Jasper." Her laugh was a light, silvery trill that smacked of the stage. "We can all take a trip down memory lane."

"Sounds good." But Jake was already nudging Sofie forward, a trip down memory lane with Brittany not on his calendar. Brittany and Broadway were a perfect fit. The Great

White Way of Make-Believe and Little Miss Vanity. As for the parties down by the river—that was ancient history.

He was quiet as they made their way across the foyer to the stairway, the awkwardness of running into old girl-friends always embarrassing. He wasn't a scrapbook kind of guy. Life went on.

Sofie debated whether to mention the gorgeous platinum blonde or not. Brittany was a woman not easily dismissed—all that bold prettiness made a real impression. Not to mention, Brittany looked as though she was a regular at the gym. Aargh . . . why couldn't *she* bite the bullet and exercise. Especially when she was trying to impress the buffest man in town.

Maybe she'd tell Jake to turn off the lights when they reached his room. Really—after both Melissa and Brittany, she was a distant fiftieth in the run-off for Most-Toned Female. She wondered if playing with the neighbor's dog counted as exercise? Or the bike ride she took two months ago? Damn, it was hard to compete with gym-rats when her physical activity consisted of walking from her car to the nearest door.

Although, disorganized as she was, she went to the grocery store every day because she was always running out of something. And the aisles were long.

There. A small sop to her conscience.

Jake kissed the nape of her neck as they reached the stairs. "You're the hottest babe in the universe," he whispered.

"Back at you—different gender," she said, turning to smile at him, any further self-criticism and doubt effectively obliterated by hot-babe references. "Don't you just *luuuuv* everything about weddings?"

She was walking on air or flying to the moon or any number of other sublime enterprises generated by romance, lust, and a handsome man who wanted her. She was probably a prime example of overwrought desire suspending disbelief, but what the hey—life was short. And she'd been wanting Jake Finn for six weeks, five days, and ten hours, give or take. She was allowed.

When they reached the top of the stairs, he swept her up in his arms as though he, too, might be high on romance and lust, and kissed her all the way down the hall to Room 218. Bending slightly, he turned the knob, shoved the door open, and walking into the room, kicked the door shut. "Now then, Miss Piper, I feel I have to warn you," he said with a grin. "This could take all night."

"Lucky for you, I left my schedule open."

"I would have opened it even if it wasn't open," he said, husky and low.

Ohmygod, she was going to come just listening to that deep voice of authority. "What if I said you had to wait?" Oops—she could mouth off at the worst of times.

He looked at her.

She could see the wheels clicking.

"Don't be a wiseass." His eyes locked with hers as he moved toward the bed. "Or I might have to spank you," he added with a grin.

Wow. He had her going there for a minute, but that sexy grin shifted everything into the fun zone. Was that fabulous or what? He knew how to play. Not that it was a requirement, but he'd generated so many sexual fantasies for her, she liked that kismet moment when he seemed to intuitively know. On the other hand, he might be so accomplished, he'd played this game a thousand times before.

Not that she was going to contemplate any thousand times before—no way.

And since disassociation was one of her most useful coping mechanisms . . . there. He had no past.

Less introspective, Jake was pretty focused on getting off as soon as possible. The only question was whether Sofie liked foreplay—or how much she liked foreplay. He'd have to play it by ear, curb his enthusiasm, and in general act the gentleman when he would have preferred something more Neanderthal.

Depositing her on the bed, he followed her down with

the supple grace of a conditioned athlete, easing her legs open enough to settle between them. Resting his weight on his forearms, he held his body bare inches above hers, his erection poised at the juncture of her thighs. Almost immediately he knew it was out of the question to make this last. She was breathing almost as fast as he was; her fragrance—and not just her perfume—struck every olfactory receptor in his body. His cock was aching it was so hard. Playing the gentleman wasn't a real option. "How polite do I have to be?" he murmured, moving his hips faintly.

It took her a moment to reply, the jolt to her senses when his enormous erection rubbed against her throbbing sex leaving her momentarily breathless. "I don't know," she whispered, not even sure any more what he'd said, every give-it-to-me nerve in her body strumming at Mach 1.

Her flushed face and half-lidded eyes, the way she suddenly clutched at his shoulders and moved against his cock were answer enough. He reached for his zipper.

"Hurry."

He must have died and gone to heaven, he thought, the single whispered word a perfect match for his own feelings. Coming up on his knees, he shoved her skirt upward, and had her shoes and panty hose off a second later.

She watched him pull out his erection, the enormity of his upthrust penis breathtaking, better than any fantasy. She was speechless. Not a common occurrence for Sofie Piper, who was known to run off at the mouth.

But baby, baby, she didn't even think about talking.

She only wanted to feel.

"Now," she managed to exhale, the single word invitation, command, lush promise—the 911 of hot and bothered.

They were definitely on the same wavelength . . . or maybe he'd thought about this so many times, he was running on pure memory. Pulling out a condom from his pants' pocket, he slipped it on.

On that first instant of contact, when the head of his dick eased into her slick, hot sex, he gasped, she gasped, and their eyes met like they'd found each other in the blackness of the universe.

It can't get any better than this, she thought, arching her hips upward to draw him in.

And then he made her a liar.

Because it got better and better still with each gentle thrust, her vaginal nerves welcoming the biggest cock she'd ever felt with rapturous ripples of gratitude.

But he took his time.

Size was an issue. He didn't want to hurt her.

But ultimately he was buried to the hilt in the sweetest of cunts, his heart was beating like a drum, and he was hoping she didn't take hours to come because he wasn't feeling particularly in control. Maybe it was having to wait so long for her, maybe it was all the wedding sentimentality screwing up his brain, maybe this was what sex was like when it wasn't just for recreation. It felt as though his head was going to blow off.

"I'm really sorry," she gasped, hoping he wouldn't think her a nympho, because she was going to come before he even moved. "Jesus Christ . . ." And she came—just like that—affirming what all the women's magazines always said: Sex was primarily an intellectual function with women.

Who would have known?

It took him a heartbeat to follow her in climax and he didn't apologize. It felt too damned good.

"Jesus, you'd think it was my first time," he muttered, once he found the breath to speak. "I promise to do better next time."

"I'm not sure better's possible," she whispered, biting back an impulse to tell him he was the best of the best of the best. This wasn't the time to look like a love-crazed stalker when he was promising her more hot sex.

"Hey, Jake!"

A shout, a knock on the door.

A much too familiar voice, Sofie thought, going rigid

beneath him, imagining all her dreams evaporating into the ether of deception and deceit.

"Go away!" But Jake pulled out, ripped off the condom, and swung onto the floor in three seconds flat. He'd forgotten to lock the door. Zipping up, he tossed the condom in the wastebasket, strode to the door, flipped over the security bar, and only then eased the door open a small distance. "Seriously, go away," he said to his brother. "I'm fucking busy."

"Brittany thought you two might like to have a drink with us." Jasper did one of those I-tried-to-talk-her-out-of-it flickers of his brows.

Jake glanced past his brother and saw Brittany smiling innocently, as if she didn't know she was interrupting something. He didn't smile. "Maybe later."

"You sure?" Even though he was here running interference, keeping Brittany at bay, Jasper played his part. "Charlie's doing party tricks."

"Yeah, I'm sure." Jake tried to sound polite when he damned well didn't feel like it. "Have a couple drinks for us." Shutting the door, he turned the bolt lock. "Sorry about that. Brittany can be persistent. Missing the party stuff isn't a problem, is it? I suppose I should have asked."

Sofie was trying to get over the terror of Jasper outside the door and the groundswell of guilt he engendered. Next to that, Brittany's butting in was a paltry trifle. Jake was looking at her, obviously waiting for a reply. Get a grip. "No—no . . . it's not a problem," she stammered. "I've heard Jenny obsess over this wedding for a year. I'm good."

"Charlie said she can be compulsive." He kicked off his shoes. "Although maybe weddings do that to women."

Sofie lifted her brows. "Jenny puts her spices in alphabetical order."

"Okaaay. Charlie used to only wash clothes once a year in college. I hope they make it."

"We probably shouldn't be having this conversation on

their wedding day." Sofie felt disloyal. "Opposites do attract, they say."

"There you go." Jake smiled. "On the other hand, I don't give a shit one way or the other."

Sofie didn't have real strong feelings either—what with the major discrepancies in personality between Jenny and herself. But she preferred a hopeful tack—as if she might be punished for currently living her fantasy if she didn't show more compassion. Camille would call her a wimp for even thinking such thoughts. Then again, Camille didn't have a grandmother who worried about propitiating the gods. Knock on wood was not just a casual phrase with Grandma Berg. "I guess I'm relatively indifferent, too," she replied, going for broke, figuring she had some serious backup should a thunderbolt come down from above.

"I'm glad that's settled," Jake said sardonically, giving Sofie a smile.

"Definitely. I'm done talking about it." Propitiating the gods was not to be taken lightly.

"How about we talk about giving this another try with less clothes on?" he suggested, beginning to strip off his suit coat. He grinned. "And see if we can keep it going longer than twenty seconds."

"I do apologize."

"Forget it. I was right behind you." He tossed his coat on a chair and untied his tie.

"I've been thinking about this too long, I suppose."

"Amen to that. So would you like some champagne— you know . . . pace ourselves." He pulled his tie loose and dropped it on the end of the bed.

Why not on the chair with his suit coat, she thought, a little anticipatory shiver racing up her spine. And then, because she lived her life on impulse more than she would like, she asked, "What's with that?" and pointed at the tie.

"Might need it later," he said, unbuttoning his shirt. "Want a blueprint?"

She shook her head, but really—that sexy look in his eye was doing disastrous things to her self-control. She wasn't so sure she'd make it past the twenty-second record if he kept it up. "Maybe I should have some champagne," she murmured.

"Need some brakes on your libido?" He pulled his shirt from the waistband of his slacks, let it fall off his shoulders and slide down his arms onto the floor.

"Yeah, definitely," she whispered. She'd never seen muscles like that; he could pose for a workout-machine ad—you know those photos where the model looks like he could lift a car.

"Champagne coming up. Want a fire?" He nodded at the period fireplace that dominated one wall.

"A fire would play into my fireplace fantasy."

He laughed. "I can't provide a fur rug, but I have the champagne. Did I get it right or is your fantasy less conventional?"

"I have several with and without fur rugs."

"You should write fiction."

"I prefer reality." She glanced at his crotch. "Particularly yours."

"Speaking of reality—your pussy fits me to a T. I must live right."

"We, if you don't mind," she noted, wiggling off the high bed and landing on a needlepoint carpet covered with cabbage roses, deciding the circumstances really made self-restraint impossible. "You've got the touch, Finn."

His brows rose. "I wish I could take credit; it doesn't take much for you."

"The credit's all yours—or his," she murmured, nodding at the rising bulge in his trousers. "Nice powers of rejuvenation."

"I'm highly motivated. Come here so I can take that dress off. I'll light the fire later—after I light yours."

At his softly uttered words, Sofie felt a little tremor travel downward, triggering a lush cascade of desire. There was something visceral and hot about a man who expected compliance. There was something equally nice about a guy who wanted sex as much as you.

"Maybe we can do the fire next time," he murmured, watching her approach, her gaze on his dick. "Hey, babe, you have to look at me."

Her gaze slowly lifted and met his, her smile only inches away. "Better?"

"It's all about cock for you, isn't it?"

"It is right now." She glanced down again.

"Look at me or I won't give it to you," he whispered.

Her eyes met his once again, spring green and amused. "Yes, sir."

He grinned. "Just checking."

"On the power of your dick?"

"On the extent of your horniness."

"No contest, there. I'm more than willing to defer to your dick, provided I don't have to wait too long."

"Not a problem. I'm on a short fuse. Turn around so I can unzip your dress."

She immediately complied. There was something about the term *short fuse* that was outrageously arousing. Along with his centerfold body, nude from the waist up, and the very real promise of that glorious cock stirring beneath the navy wool of his trousers. The reward was well worth any degree of acquiescence. Call her easy. Right now, she was—in spades.

All she could think about was feeling him slide inside her.

All she wanted was a superfine orgasm like the last one. The sooner the better.

He deftly unhooked, unzipped and seconds later lifted the bouffant, Swan Lake confection over her head and threw it on the small sofa. Then he lightly gripped her shoulders, turned her around, and smiled.

"You like white lace?" That he did was evident, she reflected, his impressive hard-on rising even higher.

"Oh, yeah," he murmured, his gaze traveling down her body and then up again. "You look good enough to eat." Her white lace bustier barely covered her full breasts, the mounded flesh balanced on ruffled, lacy half-cups, the technical hydraulics in danger of being overwhelmed by the opulent weight. He ran a fingertip lightly over her plump breasts. "Is all this for me?"

She nodded, his touch igniting a carnal fire, the imminent possibility of orgasm trembling through her senses, every sexual receptor in her body shuddering on the brink.

Slipping his fingers under one breast, he lifted it free of the lacy cup, weighing it in his hand. "Talk to me," he murmured, rubbing her taut nipple with his thumb.

She softly moaned, holding her thighs together to constrain her arousal.

"Tell me if you like this. If you'd like me to suck on your nipple."

If he sucked on her she'd come in seconds; she wanted more. She wanted him inside her. "Don't," she whispered.

"Sorry," he said, in a brusque tone that wasn't sorry at all. That was instead, male prerogative in action.

She could feel the wetness between her legs, the hot fluid oozing downward, the ache of desire so intense, she tried to pull back.

His fingers closed on her nipple, holding her in place.

And the streaking pleasure rushed downward from her nipple to her throbbing vagina like molten gold. "No, no, no," she breathed.

But his head dipped, he drew her nipple into his mouth, gently bit the turgid crest, rolled it on his tongue, teasing her for a moment before his mouth closed on the elongated tip and he sucked in earnest.

The waves of sensation rolled downward, one after another, hotter and hotter, harder and harder, each tug of his mouth a direct conduit to her throbbing, impatient cunt.

She was panting and squirming; she wanted cock. And he'd give it to her just as soon as she came. But first things first. This wasn't the time to make major adjustments.

She suddenly went still and screamed, the breathy orgasmic sound muffled by the chintz—drapes, slipcovered furniture, canopy, coverlet, pillows by the score. They could have been in a bomb shelter for all the outside noise.

He held her close a moment later as she went still, mute now and clinging to him. And he thought he was going to have a damned good wedding night by proxy. Sofie Piper was one hot babe.

And once she had time to rest, he'd see about balancing the orgasmic equation.

He carried her to a chair. "Take it easy," he said, well-mannered and well-behaved, as though he didn't care if he got any or not. "Watch me start the fire."

She leaned back into the chair and smiled, willing to watch him anytime. And with her body still strumming faintly in blissful memory, observing the man of her dreams, clothed only in his trousers, wasn't a hardship. Tanned and muscled like a god. "Ummm . . ."

"You okay?"

She hadn't realized she'd softly moaned out loud. "I'm still a little bit out of it."

"I'll get you some champagne. Cookies?"

She grinned. "You're better than a butler. You serve up sex as well."

"Maybe butlers do, too."

The way he said it made her wonder if he knew something she didn't know. "I've never seen a real butler."

"I've seen a few," he said over his shoulder as he moved toward the mini-fridge.

"You must run in different circles."

"I was wooed by the NFL after college. The owners of those franchises live large." Pulling out a half bottle of champagne, he stripped off the foil, opened the bottle, and reaching over, handed it to her. "Bottoms up." He took out a small bag of Famous Amos cookies from the mini bar and tossed them at her. "Now watch and learn, babe. I was a Boy Scout."

He still was, she thought; he was always prepared, his erection making her drool. Not that she was deterred from eating a handful of Famous Amos cookies while she surveyed her live-in butler arranging a nice blazing fire in no time flat. She was going to need some sustenance to last the night.

Pulling the quilt from the bed, he spread it on the floor before the fire, took out a beer from the mini-fridge for himself, and sitting down, beckoned her with a smile. "Come join me." He unbuckled his belt, stripped it off, and tossed it aside. Then he leaned back on one elbow and watched her approach, his gaze trained on her strawberry-blond curls just below the lace ruffle on the bottom of her bustier. "You're nice and wet," he murmured, his eyes lifting to hers. "Ready for action."

"And you're hiding your equipment," she said with a smile. "Are you bashful?"

"Yeah, that's me," he said, his grin wicked. "I undress in the dark. I've got a pocket full of condoms. I was just keeping them handy."

"You could put them there." Sitting down beside him, Sofie pointed to the bottom shelf of a table behind him.

Shoving his hands in his pockets, he pulled out enough condoms to make her heart flutter. Her brows rose. "It should be a memorable night."

He grinned. "I've got a good feeling. Want some help with that bustier?"

"What kind of help?" She had her plans, too.

"Taking-it-off help." He upended the beer bottle and drank half of it in a single gulp.

"Then yes. And I want the real thing this time."

"Don't worry. We have all night."

"I'm not worried. I'm just feeling really sexy."

"I'm pretty sure I'll be able to help you out," he said with a smile, moving with a supple ease, coming up off his elbow, quickly emptying the beer bottle, setting it down and reaching for her in a single silken movement. Pulling her between his legs, her back to his chest, he unhooked her bustier and threw it on the sofa.

Swiveling around, she smiled up at him. "Now it's your turn."

"Or yours." He slid backward slightly and swept his hand downward to his zipper. "Be my guest."

"Do you ever have anyone refuse an invitation like that?" she asked, turning around and coming to her knees.

"Have you ever had anyone say no to your hot little pussy?"

"You didn't answer my question."

"That's right." He glanced down and then up again, a faint smile warming his eyes. "Take it out."

Really, this was one of those times when you believed in wishes being granted because she'd wished for this in any number of fantasies. She almost felt like she was experiencing a déjà vu moment as she unbuttoned and unzipped his suit pants. "Lift up a little," she said.

She wouldn't have been able to move him, so it was nice of him to so readily comply. His trousers came off with a little help.

He was tanned everywhere; he might have been one of those *Survivor* contestants from TV. Or maybe his swarthy skin was Finn genes, like the dark hair on his legs and pecs and the light dusting on his arms. He was all hard-as-nails brawn and muscle and quietly looking at her with those cool gray-blue eyes as though unaware of the brute strength he exuded. "I suppose everyone tells you what a great body you have." Oh, God, now she sounded like some sycophant or groupie. She could feel herself blushing.

"I suppose they tell you the same thing," he murmured, reaching out to run his palms over her plump breasts. His gaze met hers as his hands dropped away. "I like when you blush."

Cedar Grove had produced two brothers who knew how to put a woman at ease with charm and grace. She didn't feel like a groupie anymore. Slipping her fingers under the waistband of his blue-and-white striped boxers she said, "One more time."

He must have heard the small impatience in her voice because he quickly pulled his boxers off himself.

His body was warm to the touch—warmer than hers, his

scent of arousal triggering some primal olfactory nerves in her; she found herself wanting to rub herself all over him. And taste him. "Do you mind?" she whispered, touching the swollen crest of his grand, upthrust penis, tracing her finger downward over the distended veins, stroking the fullness of his testicles resting on the quilt.

"Do you think I mind?" he said, amusement in his gaze.

She smiled back and almost said, "Thank you a thousand times for making all my fantasies come true," but she didn't want to sound like some nut case. Not now. Not when she was about to go down on that showy cock and assuage weeks of wishful thinking.

She was gratified to hear him gasp softly as she drew the shiny crest into her mouth, she was more gratified to hear his breathing change as she dipped her head lower and absorbed more of his length. Although it was going to be impossible to take more than half without choking. Which, selfishly, was a very nice thing for her in terms of fornication later.

He slid his fingers through her hair a few moments later, his touch light, guiding her deftly, not imposing his will— just directing the rhythm from time to time, slowing her down when he wanted to, easing himself in more deeply when she didn't think it was possible. Settling her into a pleasurable rhythm.

But selfish motive eventually overcame her—she wasn't as diplomatic as he—and suddenly pulling away, she sat back on her heels. "I want you in me," she said.

He took two really deep breaths before he opened his eyes, and then in a voice that could have been ordering at McDonald's, he said, "Sure." Reaching behind him, he pulled a condom from the stack, ripped the package open, slipped the condom on half way, shut his eyes briefly as he paused and then having gotten himself under control, slid the condom down the rest of the way.

She was already moving toward him, and he helped her onto his lap, slid his hands under her bottom, and lifted her enough to position her cleft over the head of his penis.

Then, past preliminaries after the sudden change of plans, he grasped her hips and pressed downward. Although old habits die hard and while he would have preferred ramming speed, he took care not to rush, although he was gratified a moment later to feel her wriggle her hips—asking for more. Not a problem, he thought considering he'd just about been ready to come when she'd changed the deal.

As she came to rest on his thighs, crotch to crotch, impaled, ready to go off the deep end without so much as a single movement, she understood she was in big trouble. She was capable of coming just looking at him.

The least impulsive person on the planet, Jake was surprised at how little restraint he had with her. He wasn't sure he liked the feeling.

Sofie eventually came three times to his one—the first two times without him lifting a finger. At the last—perhaps turned on by her wild abandon—he climaxed precipitously when he hadn't planned on it.

He blamed his recent celibacy; he'd been too busy putting together this new team to think of women. He was fucking supercharged.

Sofie, on the other hand, didn't concern herself with motive or cause; she only basked in the blissful glory. She had no intention of taxing her brain about whether she came too fast or too slow or too often. The parts of her body involved in the action tonight had zero intellectual aspirations.

Taking a short break, they lay on the quilt and kissed like teenagers. It wasn't as though they hadn't thought about kissing each other before; they could have exchanged fantasies in that regard.

Jake kissed Sofie everywhere—taking his time: her lips, cheeks, eyelids; her silken shoulders and small hands; each finger and toe; the dip behind her ears and the heated spot behind her knees.

And she returned his kisses, trying to mimic his casual

caresses, failing miserably, wanting him more desperately, so desperately she finally pleaded, "Let me come again right now."

"In a minute," he said, looking up from between her legs, which was the major reason she was pleading with him. He'd been kissing her in all her happy places as if he had all the time in the world. "Give me one of those cookies."

"How can you be hungry at a time like this," she panted.

He snapped his fingers and gave her a look that translated: Do it my way and you'll be rewarded.

She handed him a Famous Amos cookie.

Holding the cookie between his thumb and forefinger, he separated the outer and inner lips of her vulva with his middle fingers and gently inserted the Famous Amos cookie between the plump lips. As he slid the cookie into place, he gave her a smile of satisfaction. "Can you feel it?"

"God, yes," she whispered, not sure whether her quivering tissue liked Famous Amos cookies or Jake Finn's caresses. The hard, pulsing rhythm between her legs was sending wild, raging signals of arousal to every cell in her body.

"It fits perfectly," he murmured, running a fingertip around the bordering flesh.

"I don't care if it fits," she wailed.

"Maybe you'll care about this," he whispered, dipping his head, licking the cookie first, then the swollen, throbbing tissue holding Famous Amos in place, then her half-hidden little clit buried now that she was dying of longing, then everything in reverse order again, repeating the virtuoso dance of his tongue over and over again until she climaxed in a frantic, seething orgasm.

At which point, he ate the cookie, put on a condom and moved into position.

"Wait, wait, wait," she whispered, not entirely sure she was breathing yet.

"I'll go real slow," he whispered back. "Trust me."

He turned out to be really trustworthy, and before the night was over, she realized he was not only a man you could trust, but a man who had the ability to make pleasure user-friendly.

He'd also become her bona fide, Grade A, tied-up-with-a-red-ribbon, gold standard for sexual pleasure.

SEVEN

Sofie heard the knock on the door through a sleepy haze. Then half-awake, she heard the shower going—and another louder knock, followed by Camille's raised voice. "Are you there? It's me."

Since Jake was obviously in the shower, either she had to drag herself out of bed or continue to be harassed. Deterring Camille the Bulldozer was not an option.

After another flurry of sharp raps, Sofie muttered, "I'm coming, I'm coming," and rolling out of bed, threw on the hotel robe and padded to the door.

Flipping the bolt and the lock, she eased the door open. "You woke me," she groused, rubbing her eyes. "What's so important? It's the crack of dawn."

"It's after nine o'clock and I had to tell you about my wonderful, fabulous, incredible night! I'm supposedly getting a latte for Jasper and me," Camille added, in a rapid-fire staccato, "so I'll just stay a minute."

"Congratulations. Can we talk about this later?" Sofie said, trying to keep her eyes open.

Camille grinned. "You look suitably dazed. It must have

been a good night for you, too. Did your dream man perform to your satisfaction?"

"Oh, yeah." Sofie half smiled. "I'm definitely satisfied."

"Jake doesn't know you slept with Jasper, does he? Oh, shit." Camille turned ashen. "I gotta go."

As Camille fled, Sofie braced herself.

"You slept with Jasper?"

The voice behind her was ultrasoft.

"Not exactly," she said, trying to jack up her courage. Inhale, exhale—okay, turn around.

Jake was more or less filling the bathroom doorway, a towel wrapped around his waist, his body still wet from the shower, his dark hair slicked behind his ears, his eyes cold as the grave.

"Not exactly?" he growled.

"Well . . . sorta—I guess," she stammered, wishing she could make that steely glare go away. "Let me explain."

"Christ, Jasper just got here yesterday." A muscle along his jaw clenched and unclenched. "You're a damned busy woman."

"It wasn't like that. I made a mistake. I thought he was you."

"We don't look alike." Clipped and cool.

"Of course you do."

"I'm forty pounds heavier."

Jeez, she hadn't thought to weigh Jasper. And even if Jake was right—he did have more muscle—by the time Jasper was nude, she wasn't thinking about DNA. Or that she was in some Twilight Zone of identical twins. "You've got it all wrong. I'll tell you how it happened."

"What's to say? You fucked him." A malicious smile twitched the corners of his mouth. "Maybe you'd like to try a threesome sometime. Jasper and I make a pretty good tag team."

She didn't need any holier-than-thou put-down from a guy who could fuck all night and not even break a sweat. "Screw you," she said.

"You sure now? You wouldn't want my brother?"

"Obviously, you're not going to listen or be reasonable about this," she snapped, grabbing up her dress from the sofa.

He snorted. "You might want to think about fucking one guy at a time if you're talking reasonable."

"I see the double standard is alive and well," she said tartly, snatching up her shoes. "For your information," she added, fuming at the age-old bigotry, getting madder by the second that a woman's sexuality required a different moral barometer than a man's, "I *did* fuck one guy at a time." She didn't need any righteous indignation from a guy who knew every position in the Kama Sutra.

"Maybe you should let the bed cool in between next time," he sneered. "So you don't lose score."

If it were possible for smoke to come out of her ears like cartoon characters in a rage, she could have been colored that way. Coming to a dead stop in her clothes gathering, she smiled ultra-sweetly. "I'm sorry. Did you want to be first? Is this about sibling rivalry? Is your sensitive ego bruised?" Her smile disappeared and a hurricane-level fury deepened the green of her eyes. "Ask me if I care, you self-important prick," she spat. "Better yet, let me give you some advice. Everything isn't fucking about you!"

Her rising shrillness registered through the haze of her anger, but she was so teed off, she didn't care if he thought she was a psycho. *Fucking bastard!* She'd made a mistake—a stupid blunder. She was sorry as hell she hadn't put Jasper on the scale. *But she hadn't—OKAY?* And if Jake didn't have the decency to give her a chance to explain, to at least listen to her, he could go fuck himself!

And if the vast scope of his sexual repertoire last night was any indication, he probably knew how to.

The sudden quiet in the room was absolute—like that hush after an atomic bomb detonates . . . before the impact begins to radiate outward.

"Take the robe with you," he snarled. "I don't want it." Then he took a step backward and slammed the bathroom door shut.

As if she was contaminating his frigging robe!

She almost ran to the bathroom door and threw it open out of sheer rage.

Then, she heard the TV come on, heard the water start running, heard him fucking *turn on his electric razor*! Asshole. He could blithely dismiss her and his life sailed on across an unclouded sea. No course correction, no change of plans. Time to shave.

Melanie could have him, the cold-hearted bastard.

Or silver lamé babe Brittany could have her turn.

None of them had a fucking heart anyway; they deserved each other.

Bundling up her clothes, she stalked back to her room, half-hidden by the puffy cloud of green tulle scrunched in her arms, the heat of her anger enough to fuel a rocket to the moon. Then *she* took a shower to wash away every last possible vestige of her night with Jake Finn. She didn't want to smell him, she didn't want the imprint of his hand on her skin, she didn't want any remnant of last night to sully her body. She stood in the shower so long her skin shriveled up like a prune. Then she threw his robe in the trash basket, put on the clean one in her room, turned on the news, and told herself there were people in the world who had it a whole lot worse than she did.

That rationale, while eminently true, only worked for about five minutes, and then she fell into a sprawl on the bed and sobbed her heart out. From fury mostly, but from wretchedness, too. And like every other person suffering adversity, she sobbed, "Why me?"

The phone rang, but she didn't answer it. No way was it Jake. He was too pissed. And she wasn't in the mood to even talk to Camille—although she probably wouldn't be calling after she'd shot off her mouth at what would go down in history as the worst possible time. Whomever was calling could damn well wait until she was in a better mood. You know, in about ten years.

What she needed right now to mitigate the slings and arrows of the world was some chocolate—although after last night she wasn't about to eat the Famous Amos cookies in the mini-fridge. But she could always eat the Toblerone and the plain and peanut M&M's and the chocolate-covered almonds. She immediately did, along with the jelly beans, and she didn't even like jelly beans.

She was surveying the few items left in the mini-fridge when the small chiming clock on her mantel struck ten, reminding her that the wedding brunch was beginning. After brunch, everyone was to gather in the solarium to watch Jenny and Charlie open gifts. Not that she had any intention of mingling in her current mood.

She was going to stay in her room and clean out the mini-fridge until it was time to go home. Too bad she hadn't driven, or she could have left right now.

Jake was still in his room, too, although he wasn't doing any crying or sublimating his anger with food. His frustration had been more explosive—taking the form of his fist slamming into the wall. He was sitting on the sofa now, nursing his sore hand, figuring he'd have to pay a bundle for that shelf with knickknacks and those two photos of England that had smashed to the floor. And as if he wasn't already bent out of shape enough, he felt a crunch at the base of his spine and, reaching back, pulled Sofie's bustier out from under the pillows.

Fuck. He shoved it under the sofa. As if he needed any reminders of her big boobs falling out of that white lace.

He'd tried to tell himself it didn't matter whom Sofie'd slept with. It wasn't as though they were a couple. Hell, for all he knew, she slept with two or three guys every day. Not that any such rumors were circulating around the teachers' lounge. Melissa for one would have loved to spread that kind of gossip if it existed.

So—maybe Sofie'd been telling the truth.

Maybe she'd thought Jaz was him.

Or then again, maybe she was a liar.

For the first time in his life he seriously questioned his

instincts, when in his line of work, you operated on split-second instinct more than anything else. In the middle of a play gone wrong there wasn't time to run through the playbook or ask for directions, you just winged it. And now he found himself wondering if he'd been all wrong about Sofie. Whether he'd fallen for someone who couldn't tell the difference between one guy and another when she wanted some action. Jesus, he felt like shit. Mad and sad and fucking disappointed as hell. It just went to show how stupid it was to get serious about any one woman.

He knew he was going to have to put up with some wisecracks from his brother he didn't want to hear. It wasn't as though they hadn't shared a woman or two in the past; Jasper wouldn't understand the difference. The problem for him this time was that he'd been thinking about Sofie Piper as maybe something more than just another woman.

How's that for bonehead thinking?

He must be losing his mind. All football and no play had made him flip out. Hadn't he always kept it simple before? He and Jaz both. Neither of them was ready for permanence. Both of them had always just had fun. This didn't have to be any different.

It was a relief when he figured it out.

When all the pieces fell into place.

Don't rock the boat.

Keep your eye on the ball—which for him was winning state this year for Cutter High. They were paying him enough. He couldn't afford to screw himself up over a woman.

He finally noticed the TV was still on in the bathroom—some talking head was arguing with another talking head about whether 527s were legal. Christ, he thought he had problems. Lots of luck guys, he thought, reaching for the remote.

Jesus, he was starved.

He glanced at the clock.

Yesss—brunch time.

EIGHT

Sofie would have been even more ticked off if she'd known that for Jake, brunch had displaced further deliberation on her, their argument, and life in general.

If Camille hadn't been so dogged, Sofie wouldn't have known. But personalities don't change overnight, bulldozers do not morph into dulcet honeypots, and Camille had come knocking on her door. She was slightly more well-behaved in her guilt-ridden state, but not completely cowed.

And she wouldn't go away.

Not that Sofie didn't ignore the first fifty times Camille knocked and shouted, "I'm not going away until you open this door!"

But Sofie's nerves were ragged as hell—what with the muddle of woulda, shoulda, coulda seething in her brain—and the fifty-first knock was too much.

"Okay, okay, I'm coming!" she screamed, just in case Camille still didn't understand the full extent of her anger. Opening the door, she just stood there, looking sullen and moody, seriously ready to commit murder.

"I know, I know, it's all my fault. I never know when to shut my mouth, and if I could take it back, I would. Do you want me to apologize to Jake? I will. I'll do anything. I'm soooo sorry. He really looked mad. Fire was coming from his eyes and it's all my fault."

"Never mind," Sofie said with a sigh, knowing full well Camille hadn't been the one that was bullheaded. "It's not all your fault," she muttered, standing aside so Camille could come in. "He could have at least listened to me. Screw the jerk. He probably would have heard about it from his brother anyway. You just moved up the timetable."

"I really am sorry," Camille said, giving Sofie a hug. "You can pay me back anytime. I deserve it."

"Nah. It was my mistake, anyway." Walking over to a chair, Sofie plopped down and slid into a sprawl. "On the plus side," she murmured, her mouth twitching into a grin, "at least I had some memorable sex."

Camille smiled as she sat down across from Sofie. "We can compare notes—or half notes. Jasper knows his way around."

"Tell me about it," Sofie said with a grimace. "Although, disasters aside, I wasn't looking for anything more than sleeping with Jake this weekend and I did. So there. Mission accomplished. End of story."

"Hey—you're talking to your best friend since second grade," Camille gently noted.

Sofie's mouth pursed into a moue. "Okay . . . so I'll get over the nightmare someday. Maybe in the next millennium. That was sooo embarrassing—*is* embarrassing. I'd really like to get out of here right now, go home, and eat a box of chocolates—make that two."

"You can tell me to go to hell, but I'll say it anyway," Camille declared, leaning forward slightly, meeting Sofie's gaze. "If you cut and run, it's gonna look as though you're a puss or demoralized or worse, in crisis over some guy or guys. You gotta look 'em in the eye and say—'What?' like a guy would do. You know—pretend like nothing happened that mattered any more than say . . . the price of tea in China."

Sofie groaned. "I don't know if I'm up to any 'in-your-face' attitude. Although Jake was such a colossal jerk"—she slid up in her chair—"just thinking of what he said to me might crank me up."

"That's the spirit. You're on the right track. And I promise to do penance for my awful timing. I'm not trying to get off the hook. I really will. But, right now, you don't want to skulk away. *Capish?*"

"Yeah, I guess." Camille was right, of course, not that it made the prospect of going downstairs any more palatable.

"We should make an appearance at the opening-gifts thing. Are you hungry? The brunch is still on."

"I'm *am* hungry, emptying the mini-fridge aside. You just can't get full on candy." The thought of real food was tempting.

"I'll wait for you to get dressed. Then we'll go downstairs and pretend nothing happened."

"What about you and Jasper? What with everything going so incredibly well last night, aren't you meeting *him* for breakfast?"

"Well . . . maybe, but it's not important," Camille murmured. "He's leaving for London tomorrow anyway."

"Then don't worry about me. Spend your time with him."

Camille looked sheepish, a rarity right up there with pigs flying. "Actually, he's going to stay at my place tonight. You know . . . so he's closer to the airport."

It took every shred of charity Sofie could dredge up to say, "I'm really glad for you. He seems like a nice guy."

Camille shrugged. "Not nice so much as having the stamina of the Energizer bunny." She grinned. "You and I have never been looking for the same thing, sweetie. I'm more practical. Now, let's get you dressed and make an entrance downstairs. What are you going to wear?"

NINE

Jasper met Jake at the entrance to the dining room.

"You got hungry, too, I see."

"Yeah," Jake said. "More like starvation."

Coming downstairs at the same exact moment was like ESP across continents—a twins thing; they were even known to pick up the phone at the same time to call each other.

"After brunch, duty calls," Jasper noted as they moved into the room. "We have to look interested while they open gifts."

Jake rolled his eyes. "Do we have to? I'd rather go home."

"We have to for Charlie."

The three men had been friends since childhood, living next door to each other or as next door as you can get on several-thousand-acre Iowa farms. And the only reason the Finn brothers hadn't been groomsmen was that Charlie had six brothers. The twins while silently relieved had both said the same thing to Charlie when he'd apologized: "Not a problem. Don't worry about it."

"Charlie seems happy." Jasper nodded at the newlyweds across the room.

"She alphabetizes her spices."

"No shit," Jasper murmured. "Christ, maybe we'll be doing this all over again in a few years. And speaking of screw-ups, Camille says it really was a mistake—you know . . . for Sofie."

"Or not."

Jasper lifted his brows.

Everyone knew men fantasized about twins, but women liked twins, too. On more than one occasion, Jasper and Jake had met those women.

"It could be true," Jasper offered, making the conciliatory effort. "She could have made an honest mistake."

"I doubt it."

"I think she called out your name, once," Jasper lied, wanting to make his brother feel better. "I'm pretty sure she did."

"Christ, Jaz, don't snow me."

"I'm not."

"Good try, man."

The tick in Jake's jaw was unmistakable.

"Want to talk about it?" Jasper asked gently.

"Fuck no," Jake snapped. "I want some ham and eggs."

In typical male fashion, matters of the heart took second place to digestive considerations.

Which meant there was a reason why the phrase "The way to a man's heart is through his stomach" had been coined centuries ago.

When Sofie and Camille entered the dining room, Sofie made sure she stayed as far away from the Finn brothers as possible. But taking Camille's advice, she put on her happy face, going out of her way to chat with Jenny and Charlie, exchanging banalities with the other bridesmaids, joining a discussion with some of the other teachers from Cutter High that segued into agreement over the football team taking state this year.

Not if she murdered the coach, she thought.

But she smiled instead and listened to old Rutledge run down Cutter High's football stats since 1986 and only then, said, "All the players are really good this year. Especially Bobby Bratski." It was the closest she came to a personal slam against the winningest coach in the Midwest.

"You're doing very well," Camille whispered as they sat down to eat. "I'm thinking Oscar for best performance of the year."

"When you're hungry, you'll do anything. And these popovers are worth being in the same room as Jake."

"That must be why you took six of them."

"That's exactly why I took six of them. Is that a problem?"

Camille laughed. "Not for me, babe, but it might be for those tight jeans you're wearing."

"Carbs elevate serotonin. They make you happy."

"That explains the three desserts."

"It's my short-term fix for purely psychological reasons. Once I get home, I'll eat properly."

Camille gave her a look. "I've seen your refrigerator."

"So I'll eat properly after I go to the grocery store. Don't knock me when I'm down."

"Sorry, sweetie." Camille patted her hand. "Want me to get you another slice of chocolate cake?"

Sofie smiled. How sweet was that from a carnivore whose plate was filled with ham, bacon, and sausage? That was true friendship, not that she hadn't held Camille's hand more than once when her sex life had gone south. Sofie waved off Camille's offer with her buttery knife. "This'll do, but thanks. Just tell me when we can leave and my happiness scale will go off the charts."

"The minute the gifts are all opened."

"Okay, it's twelve-fourteen," Sofie said, checking her watch, feeling like a kid in grade school waiting for gym to be over. With luck, she'd soon be getting into Camille's black SUV and they'd be on the road back home.

Life was about hope.

Sofie didn't know if she should be grateful or irritated by the fact that Jake kept his distance from her as much as she did him.

She was mostly grateful.

But in the less rational part of her brain—the pissy part—it irritated her that he could ignore last night without so much as a glance in her direction.

And in the portion of her brain that didn't even give a nod to reason, she found herself seething at the sight of Jake holding court with his brother, the two men totally surrounded by flirtatious females and obviously enjoying themselves.

Christ, she didn't know so many single women had been invited to the wedding.

Finally—thank all the saints in heaven—the last gift was opened, the last glowing thank-you was offered, and the newlyweds were being roundly applauded for putting on such a great wedding.

Jenny and Charlie looked so happy, it almost made Sofie cry.

And why not, she rationalized. Weddings always made her cry.

Or more pertinently, over-the-rainbow newlyweds made her cry when her own life was in a nose dive—happiness wise.

And that was the sad, pitiful truth, Camille's in-their-face advice notwithstanding.

She had never been much of an in-your-face kind of person anyway, unless she was really, really mad. And even then her anger never lasted. Which might explain her missing Jake already—despite everything he'd said. Maybe he'd just been mad that she'd slept with his brother. You know, like jealous.

Whoa.

It really wouldn't pay to go down that road to nowhere after a one-night stand.

He hadn't left one single door open.

In fact, he'd slammed the door shut.

Literally.

This probably would be a good time to think about moving on to a entirely new fantasy. Not that Cutter High offered any good prospects. She'd have to range farther afield—like Grange, ten miles away. The Silver Dollar Bar had a country-western band on weekends.

Now she really was depressed. Not only didn't she own a pair of cowboy boots, she and country music weren't a good match. "I'm going up to pack," she announced, getting up and walking away before Camille could offer any more advice. Or before she burst into tears. "See you in the car."

While Jake may have appeared fully occupied with the crowd of women around him, he'd found himself searching out Sofie in the crowd more than he cared to admit. It wasn't very sensible, considering the state of their relationship. She'd ripped into him, chewed him over, and spit him out. And more important, he reflected with an inner sigh, the football season had a long way to go yet, not counting the semifinals and finals, God willing. Even if he wanted to revive what may be an as-good-as-dead relationship, he wouldn't have much of an opportunity. Football consumed nearly 24-7 of his time. He'd had to plan for this weekend for months. He was lucky if he was in bed by midnight every night; when practice was over, he went over scouting reports and planned scrimmages for the next day. He more or less ate and slept football and had for nearly fifteen years. But at times like this, when his life could be better, he felt the grind.

On the other hand, football had been good to him— college scholarship, Big Ten title his last three years, Most Valuable Player those years, too. And now, high school teams that had made him the winningest coach in the Midwest.

So suck it up.

He could be nursing NFL injuries that would have made him an old man at thirty. One of the reasons he hadn't taken the NFL offers. Although the major reason had been Coach Thurgood, his mentor and friend in high school. He'd always wanted to be like him—a kind, decent man, not an asshole drill sergeant. A coach who let all the players participate, not just the stars—a coach who could make football fun and still win games.

So his love life wasn't so great right now.

He'd get over it.

He had football games to win.

And no way was he going to let down his players.

So bottom line, he didn't have time to think about Sofie Piper even if he wanted to.

A short time later, her suitcase in her hand, Sofie came to a sudden stop on the staircase. Jasper was standing in the lobby, talking to a group of guests Sofie didn't know. Iowa people, she figured.

And if she wanted to get out the door, she'd have to walk right by him.

Fuck.

She wondered if she'd sworn out loud, because he suddenly looked up and saw her. And what was a million times worse, he excused himself from the group and began walking toward her.

Okay, act like a grown-up. Don't turn and run.

Although it was tempting.

Continuing downward, she met him where he stood and waited at the bottom of the stairs.

"Got a minute?" he asked, nodding to a corner of the lobby without guests milling about.

Was it possible to say no? But before she could even make a decision, he took her suitcase from her and guided her with a hand under her elbow to an out-of-the-way area.

"I just wanted to say I'm sorry for any trouble I may have caused you and Jake." Camille had been adamant about Sofie's unknowing role. He liked Sofie, so he'd give her the benefit of a doubt. He liked Camille, too, so he was inclined to believe her. But mostly he was hoping he could patch things up for his brother. "Jake can fly off the handle, but he'll get over it."

"He didn't sound like it, but thanks."

Jasper blew out a breath. "I don't know what to say. It was a real screwup."

"Yeah, well, I gotta go." She wasn't in the mood to do any postmortems. She just wanted to escape the debacle as quickly as possible.

He silently handed her her suitcase. "Let me know if there's anything I can do."

"Sure." As if, she thought, reliving the look of rage on Jake's face. "Thanks for being cool about this. Seeya," she said.

He watched her walk away, his feelings unsettled. Then someone called his name, and he turned just as the door of the Mill Valley Inn closed on Sofie.

TEN

The following week at school Sofie made a point of never going into the teachers' lounge—although she wouldn't have had to forego the stale coffee, Chips Ahoy cookies, and Melissa's snide remarks.

Jake was giving the teachers' lounge a wide berth, too.

Sofie spent her evenings reading Diderot's *Encyclopedie* in the original French, something she'd vowed to do since college. At the end of the week she was on page ten of the first volume, which didn't bode well in terms of completing her assignment before she died. She'd also sort of half-watched episodes of *Seinfeld* while she read because she needed cheering up.

Camille had called a bunch of times, offering her various going-out options. But Sofie wasn't in the mood. When she wasn't reading Diderot or watching *Seinfeld* reruns, she was eating ice cream or Chinese take-out from Byerly's or else she was in the process of driving to or from Byerly's.

So between teaching and all her other activities, she'd kept quite busy.

She could only think about Jake twenty-three and a half hours a day.

In terms of busy, Jake was in one of those damned-near-drowning levels of activity. Two of their toughest teams were coming up on the schedule; the kids knew it, he knew it, and everyone was keeping their noses to the grindstone. If they could win both those games, the rest of the season was more or less clear sailing. Knock on wood.

He'd been jacking off more than usual with Sofie on his mind, but that was to be expected. He hadn't been able to shake off the memories of their night together, and whenever he saw Famous Amos cookies in the grocery store, he got a hard-on. But late at night was toughest on him. He'd picked up the phone a hundred times to call her only to put it back down. You couldn't call people at three in the morning unless you were a stalker.

If only he'd known Sofie was awake most of those nights hoping like crazy the phone would ring.

There it was—unrequited passion in small-town America.

Cutter High won the away game against Green Lake, 21–7, even with the hometown fans screaming so loudly, Bobby Bratski's play calls were barely audible.

Their last strong contender was on the docket next week, and if they could take Wixon Prairie, he might think about having a beer to celebrate, Jake thought. He wasn't sleeping well, he was running on adrenalin and coffee; he needed a break.

Sofie had capitulated and was back in the teachers' lounge, missing the Chips Ahoy most. Melissa she could do without, although there was a certain satisfaction in knowing that *she* knew Sofie had spent the night with Jake at the wedding. Melissa's angry looks were the equivalent of little bluebirds of happiness flying her way. So call her petty. It felt good.

And it wasn't as though she'd been über-courageous in reentering the lounge. Camille had told her that Jake wasn't coming there anymore.

As another week went by, Sofie revamped her personal entertainment to include *Sex and the City* reruns and Mexican take-out. She was on page thirty-eight in Diderot and becoming more well-informed—eighteenth-century wise—by the day. She'd also accumulated a fantasy wardrobe, thanks to *Sex and the City*, and was now cognizant of every major U.S. designer.

Sitting at home and moping was very educational.

On Thursday night at nine o'clock, Sofie discovered she was completely out of Ben & Jerry's ice cream. How something so shocking could have occurred could be laid at the door of Carrie's approaching reunion with Mr. Big. The last two episodes had been leading up to the moment when Mister Big returned to Manhattan from Napa, and Sofie simply hadn't had time to break away and drive to the grocery store with true love in such peril.

She would definitely need a fresh supply of ice cream before the concluding episode that ended happily—she'd already watched the show three times before, so she wasn't real worried. But you had to give those screenwriters credit; they knew how to hold an audience.

The night was cold and windy as she walked to her car parked in her driveway. October in Minnesota—what could she say. She turned the heater to high and drove to the grocery store, mentally going over the various flavors she'd buy. Tomorrow was Friday. She'd need a supply for the weekend. Any thoughts of looking farther afield for fresh dating prospects were more or less in abeyance at the moment. She was busy with Diderot. She'd look around later. And so she'd told Camille, who had been nagging her to go out something fierce lately.

Buttoning up her nondesigner, outlet mall jacket, she

stepped from the car in Byerly's parking lot. She should have worn socks, she thought, her bare feet in her mocassins instantly feeling the cold. Racing to the entrance, she rushed through the sliding doors into the warmth of the store.

Ah—Ben & Jerry's only a few short yards away.

She could feel her gloom lifting already.

Jake was standing in front of the cereals with a carton of milk in his hand, looking for Frosted Flakes, when he saw a flash of blond curls out of the corner of his eye.

Now, half the population in the Midwest has blond hair, but that particular shade of strawberry blond—not so many.

And women with short, curly strawberry-blond hair in this small town—even less.

And women with that sexy, tousled, I-just-got-out-of-bed style strawberry-blond hair—the possibilities were dwindling fast.

He turned and looked—just to make sure.

It *was* Sofie, twenty yards away in front of the freezer section. Since her back was to him, he had a moment to sort through the tumult in his brain. Not that he needed much time when his dick was pretty much in charge of the game plan.

Fuck it. He was going to go up to her, say hi, apologize, and if she shot him down, she shot him down. Nothing ventured, etcetera, etcetera.

You win some, you lose some, but if you don't even try, you never have a chance.

Quickly scanning the cereal shelves, he spotted the Frosted Flakes, grabbed the largest box, and started up the aisle to cross his personal Rubicon.

Crap. She was gone.

How had she disappeared so fast?

Moving forward quickly, he reached the freezer section running the length of the back wall, looked left and right.

Nada. Christ, she couldn't have gone far in mere seconds. He'd check out the next aisle.

Wheeling around the end cap display of Ritz crackers, he jammed on the brakes and screeched to a halt.

Yessss. There she was, squatting on her heels, surveying a row of Malkins jams.

"Need some help?"

She half turned at the familiar voice and found herself at eye level with Jake's crotch. "Not really," she said, trying to sound cool and not succeeding with his erection swelling before her eyes. Coming to her feet quickly before her libido took over, she said, "What are you doing here?" Although she shouldn't have asked; she should have blown him off with some cutting remark.

"Getting this." He held out the box of Frosted Flakes and carton of milk, inhaled, met her gaze, and exhaled softly. "Look, I'd like to apologize for what I said at the wedding. I was a jerk. I never should have said any of it."

Wow. If she'd wanted abject atonement, she'd pretty much gotten it. "I don't know what to say." Maybe it was all her dreams coming true at once that made her more or less speechless for the first time in her life. Or maybe she was trying to sort through all the double-standard bullshit he'd thrown at her that weekend and trying to decide if his apology was enough. Like did she still need a pound of flesh?

"I'd like if you'd say you forgive me. I haven't been sleeping much."

"Because of me?" Okay, that was way too good to pass up. Her powers of speech had returned.

"Pretty much."

"*He* probably gets a vote, too, though," she said, glancing down at the bulge in his jeans. "If I know you."

"You don't know me—not really. That Jasper thing caught me off guard. I'm not usually such a prick."

"You want me to forgive you?" She was rubbing it in, but hey—she was allowed after what he'd said.

"Yeah, I would."

"And then what?"

"It's up to you. But you've been on my mind." He exhaled. "A lot." It was a concession of considerable magnitude for Jake Finn, who didn't get serious with women.

"Really. Is that so?"

He smiled tightly at her arch look and cool tone. "Look, I'm not good at groveling, so say yes or no. That old lady over there is way too interested in this discussion."

Sofie shot a glance at the woman halfway down the aisle. "Maybe she's looking at your crotch."

"Okay, that's it—have a nice night." He started to move past her.

"Wait."

He stopped, met her gaze, his gray-blue eyes wintery. "For what?"

"I never know when to quit," she said with a faint lift of her brows. "I'm sorry, too."

His smile was instant and dazzling. She was immediately jealous of every woman who'd ever seen that smile.

"What say we start over," he said, tactful as hell. "Nice to run into you tonight. I see you're stocking up on ice cream," he added, glancing at the basket on the floor.

"I've been feeling kind of lonely lately." She didn't have that celebrity coach finesse. "The ice cream helps."

"Maybe I could help." His voice was neutral; they could have used that nonpartisan sound in the polarized congress.

"Maybe you could," she said, trying real hard to appear as mature and grown-up as he.

He grinned. "Wanna give it a try?"

She nodded. "Yeah."

"Clean slate?"

"I'd like that."

He gave one of those quick, male double nods. "Done."

"So now what?" Really, when it came to subtlety and maturity, she was hopeless, or maybe just looking at his erection made delicacy and tact impossible. Not that she was going to jump right into bed with him. Not after the wedding fiasco.

"Care to come over to my place?" He smiled. "I'll share my Frosted Flakes with you. You can put your ice cream in my freezer."

· Really, she must have gone way too long without sex. She was reading sexual innuendo into words like Frosted Flakes and ice cream. Or maybe it was words like *share* and *put in*. Or maybe it was his absolutely gorgeous cock that seemed to be getting really enormous. "If I come over, I can't stay long. Tomorrow's a school day." She had to at least attempt some rudiment of self-control.

"And game day."

"So, is Cutter going to win?" She was relieved at the opportunity to change the subject; her treacherous libido was giving her trouble. "Wixon's supposed to be good."

"All the kids are pretty psyched." His gaze shifted down the aisle and then back again. "Could we talk about this at my place? That old lady's making me nervous."

"It's your hard-on—and I'm not being cute." It was the truth; you couldn't miss it. "Maybe she's a member of the morality patrol."

"Christ," he muttered. "As if I need that. Here." Pulling a wad of bills from his jean's pocket, he shoved it into her jacket pocket. "Buy these for me." He dumped his cereal and milk into her basket. "I'll go out the back door and meet you in the parking lot."

As he strode away, Sofie chose an alternative path as well, preferring not to pass by an old lady who might support Chastity for the American Way or something. You never knew. Even Sponge Bob was coming under attack these days.

Approaching the checkout lanes, she scanned the area for any suspicious-looking older women. Now that her life was going pretty darn good, she didn't want any trouble. Luckily the coast was clear.

Rose Capeletti, one of her homeroom students, was

manning the cash register. They exchanged small talk while Rose ran the items through and packed them. As she handed Sofie the two bags, she smiled with her mouthful of braces. "Coach Finn's hot, isn't he?" Her gaze flicked upward, and Sofie saw the bank of surveillance monitors above them.

"He sure is." There was no point in playing coy when Rose was giving her the thumbs-up. "I hope Cutter takes state this year." An attempt to portray their conversation in broader terms might be fruitless, but Sofie decided to give it a try. "Coach Finn tells me the players are psyched to win."

"You have yourself a nice time," Rose said with a wink, apparently not to be deterred by conversational segues. "That's his truck out there waiting for you."

No way was she going to respond, and while Sofie understood small towns allowed one little privacy, she walked away with more than a few misgivings. By morning, half the school would know that she and Jake had met at the grocery store.

His cherry-red, full-size, extended-cab, four-by-four pickup truck with KC lights on the roof and fancy chrome rims idled outside the door with a low, throaty resonance that testified to after-market mufflers.

Detroit's answer to testosterone.

Glistening testament to Jake Finn's male mojo.

As she reached the truck, Jake shoved the passenger door open and leaned across the seat to take the bags from her. "Thanks for running interference," he said, placing the two bags in the backseat with one hand and holding out his other to help her up into the cab.

"Apparently, we were on *Candid Camera,* so I don't know how much good it did. Rose Capeletti gave me a suggestive smile and told me to have a nice time with you."

"Who cares." Reaching past her, he pulled her door shut. "Hey, Rose, take a look, I'm kissing Miss Piper," he called out. And then he kissed her right there in Byerly's parking lot for all the world to see—or more pertinently, for Matt Richie the bag boy who stood open-mouthed to see. As Jake raised his head a moment later, he whispered, "God, I missed you." That he saw Matt out of the corner of his eye was irrelevant.

"I missed you twenty *Seinfeld* episodes and the entire last season of *Sex and the City,* not to mention a couple dozen pints of Ben and Jerry's."

"Good thing I caught up with you before you ran out of reruns." He'd turned slightly, blocking Sofie's view out the windshield.

"And before I gained another ten pounds."

"You look great, better than great."

"I'm feeling great—thanks to you."

He dropped a light kiss on her nose. "I could make you feel better."

She smiled. "I'll think about it over a dish of ice cream."

He knew better than to press the issue; she was calling the shots. "Then buckle up," he said, pulling her closer, snapping the center seat belt across her lap. "I'm not taking any chances with you. It's been a tough week and a half."

"What about my car?" She lifted her brows. "I worry about Rose's gossip line."

"Screw it. We're not doing anything illegal."

"That's reassuring," she teased as he made a sharp left away from the store. "Maybe I should ask you what you *have* in mind, Coach Finn?"

He liked the tantalizing purr in her voice, the way she leaned into his body. "You want me to spell it out?" He exited the parking lot onto the highway running through town.

"Would you?"

He shot her a look. "Think I can't?"

She held his gaze for a heated moment. "I think you can do anything you want."

Taking her hand, he placed it over the bulge in his jeans. "Then why don't I give you a rundown." The speedometer leaped from twenty to sixty as they left the town limits behind. "For starters, I'm not planning on sleeping tonight.

And you'll have to eat your ice cream in bed. I don't feel like waiting."

His gruff impatience turned on all her sex-starved body systems in two seconds flat, or was it the pulsing hardness under her hand that sent her libido into overdrive? "And then what?" she whispered, tracing the length of his erection with her palm.

"Then I'll take your clothes off and put this"—he placed his hand over hers and pressed downward—"into your tight little cunt and make you come until you can't come anymore. And when you beg me to stop, I'll say, *Just once more,* and make you come again."

"What if I won't let you."

"You won't have any choice. And you'll be so wet I'll know you don't mean it." He lifted his hand, took her chin between his fingers, and turned her face to his. "You like to fuck," he said, husky and low. "You like it every which way." His gaze flicked to the road and back again. "Don't you?"

"I like it with you," she said, holding his gaze.

There was an edgy ferocity in his eyes, reminding her that this was a man who had powered his way to gridiron fame in a sport that sanctioned brute force. She wasn't sure whether she should be intimidated or not.

He suddenly laughed. "Hey, music to my ears," he said with a grin, that moment of wildness gone from his eyes. "Hang on, I'm punching it."

He burned north on the county road, his truck's four hundred horses coasting at eighty. He slowed as his driveway came into view and cranked a left, turning onto a gravel drive. His farmhouse sat up on a hill, at the end of the long drive, the large white structure silhouetted against the moon.

She should have known he'd live on a farm.

"Home, sweet home," he murmured as he braked to a stop by the back door. "Come in and I'll get you that dish of ice cream." He shot her a grin. "Or whatever you want."

Carrying their groceries, he ushered her into a large

kitchen, equipped with every appliance known to man, including an almost empty wine cooler.

"Fancy," she said, thinking of her two-bedroom condo with a galley-sized kitchen. "I like that," she added with a wave at a bright yellow curved banquette and table in a curtained alcove.

"The people before me did all this. I've barely unpacked. Don't look in the living room. It's nothing but boxes. Take a seat," he offered. "I'll get you some ice cream."

He walked to a large stainless-steel double-door refrigerator, pulled open the freezer door, and turned. "What kind?"

"Chocolate chip cookie dough," she said, sitting down on the cushy banquette, as he put the milk and ice cream away.

"Comin' up. Want a sandwich? I'm going to have one." He started taking things out of the frig.

For some reason, he'd changed his mind about being in a hurry. Not that she was going to look overly eager if he wasn't. Tell that to her pulsing clit, though, she thought, shifting on the seat. All she could think of was the delicious feel of his cock under her hand. Sneaking a peek, she noticed he was still obviously horny; maybe he was doing one of those Zen denial things—you know, testing himself.

"Sorry, I got hungry," he said, as though reading her mind. "I hope you don't mind waiting a minute. I'll eat fast."

"Take your time. I can wait another couple minutes."

He swung around, his hands full of sandwich makings. "This can wait."

"I'm teasing." How was that for polite. "Take your time."

"You sure?" He must have seen something in her face. "Come here," he said with a grin. "I'm ambidextrous."

No way she was going to say no, not with that sexy look in his eyes. And knowing him, whatever he had in mind was going to feel good.

Emptying the items he held onto the counter, he watched her walk across the large kitchen with the hottest look he'd ever seen.

Maybe she'd come before she got to him.

Then he could use both his hands to make his sandwich.

Obviously, the week and a half since he'd given her a new appreciation for sex had been a couple days too long because she was finding it hard to keep from panting. She stopped just short of him, controlling her breathing with effort, wondering if every woman who saw that look in his eyes instantly melted inside.

He flicked his finger at her Gap chinos. "Take those off."

"What if I don't?"

He smiled slowly. "You're gonna. Why even try?"

She didn't know if his assurance pissed her off or heightened her impatience. Both, she decided, but she said, "You're pissing me off." No way was she going to add to his irritating self-confidence.

"So? Do you want it or don't you?" He knew what turned her on, and it wasn't hearts and flowers.

Jeez, when he talked like that, like maybe she wouldn't get it, she got even hotter. Her gaze flicked to his crotch, the faded denim stretched to the max over one awesome erection. A greedy ripple shuddered up her vagina and she kicked off her mocassins. Quickly unzipping her chinos, she pushed them down her hips and stepped out of them.

"Those, too."

He did that one-finger thing and she took off her panties.

"That's a good girl. Come here now."

It was the softest, sexiest whisper in the world, in the universe. Like he knew he was going to make you feel good. Like you could count on it.

In two steps she came within reach and sliding his hands around her waist, he lifted her up on the counter. "Spread your legs."

She did of course.

He smiled. "I've been missing this," he murmured, slipping his finger up her wet cleft, then deep inside her. "Hot, wet cunt with my name on it."

There was no denying she wanted his name on it more than anyone else's. Along with something else of his inside her.

Turning her slightly, he eased her onto her back, his finger still inside her, gently stroking. Then he pulled two slices of bread from the package and laid them on her stomach atop her old flannel shirt, added a second finger to the first, forcing her wider, revving up her sharp-set cravings. "Do you like mayo?"

"I like . . . whatever—you like," she breathed, not entirely sure of what he'd asked her, his fingers having found the rough nub of her G-spot with incredible delicacy, with a precision that could only come from considerable exploration into little hidden G-spot entertainment centers. Her nerve endings in that teeny-weeny spot were highly concentrated and finely attuned to his touch or him to them, and she came the first time before he could get the mayo on the bread. He worked faster after that—on his sandwich; G-spots didn't as a rule like the overzealous approach. But when one was ambidextrous—one hand worked fast, the other slow, and both ultimately accomplished what they set out to do.

He even had her dish of ice cream ready when he lifted her up off the counter three orgasms later and carried her over to the banquette table. "As I recall, your little clit likes to be sucked, too," he whispered, lowering her down, lifting her legs over his shoulders, and bending his head. "How about you be *my* dessert."

At that point—faintly enervated by orgasms—she was beyond speech, but her hearing was excellent and she was wondering if you could love someone for their mind-blowing sexual congeniality alone. Because she was definitely floating in some nirvana of utter devotion and rapture. And at the precise moment, when his mouth closed over her throbbing clit, she knew without a doubt, she was in love. She screamed so loudly when she came that time, his gaze flicked upward, checking to see that she wasn't hurt.

No problem there.

She'd just gone over the edge faster than usual.

Whether he'd been playing some mind game with himself, or just pretending he didn't care too much, he finally gave in to the insatiable lust and desire she inspired in him every waking minute of every day. Slipping her legs from his shoulders, he pulled her into a seated position and held her shoulders for a moment to steady her. "Can you sit up by yourself?"

She didn't answer right away, so he gave her another moment and asked again.

This time, while she didn't quite meet his gaze, she nodded.

For a man who'd finally given up on restraint, it was enough.

Swiftly moving across the room, he picked up the dish of ice cream and his sandwich and returning to her, held them out. "Take these. I'm going to carry you upstairs."

She was sweetly docile in the wake of her orgasms.

And he was even more turned on.

As though he had been the instrument of that winsome submission.

Then she smiled and whispered, "Thank you so much," and he felt triumphant, as though he'd won some fucking prize.

He was in deep this time.

Fucking A he was.

But long-held practice thrust aside further contemplation of tender feelings, habits of a lifetime focusing instead on the more immediate possibility of coming in the next few minutes. He was done waiting.

Lifting her into his arms, he exited the kitchen and took the stairs two at a time, as impatient now as she had been a short time ago. Entering his more or less empty bedroom save for a bed, bedside table, lamp, and TV, he placed her in a seated position on the edge of his bed, took the dish and sandwich from her, set them on the bedside table, and stripped off his clothes like he was on fire.

And in a way he was.

A feeling Sofie shared. It was frightening, she thought, how simply looking at him could trigger her lust, as though he was her aphrodisiac, love potion, and mind vibrator rolled into one. He was too handsome and beautiful, or maybe she was so outrageously shallow he only had to stand before her in all his glory and she was lost to all reason. Whatever it was, she was in heat—big time—every carnal itch in her body waiting to be scratched.

She began unbuttoning her red plaid flannel shirt.

He looked up from shedding his boxers and smiled. "Are your motors purring again?"

"Every one of them," she whispered, sliding her shirt down her arms.

A second later he was unhooking her bra, swiftly, businesslike; he had things on his mind other than seduction. Pushing her back on the bed, he entered her seconds later, felt her arms wrap around his shoulders, heard her soft, rapturous sigh, and growled deep in his throat as though he were some wild beast who had finally found his mate.

And maybe he had, because he hadn't even thought of putting on a condom—this from a man who never, *never* forgot.

Wrapping her legs around his hips, Sofie gratefully met his hard pounding rhythm, in perfect tune with his fevered passions, matching each powerful thrust and withdrawal with a voluptuous little moan, feeling insatiable, flame hot—searching for that tantalizing moment of release.

As she suddenly began peaking, he took heed, watching, waiting . . .

And when she went still, when her tight, little cunt began fluttering and quivering in convulsive spasms, he indulged his raging impulses—a week and a half delay too long for the niceties of logic—and poured, gushed, ejaculated into her without thought or care or conscience.

A millisecond after her last orgasmic whimper, Sofie slapped him so hard, he almost lost his balance. "What the fuck?" he muttered, scowling.

"Are you crazy—coming in me!" she shrieked.

She might have a point, but his cheek was still stinging from her blow. He wasn't feeling real gracious. "You coulda stopped me."

"Oh, yeah, that was going to happen."

"I didn't see you trying."

"Get the hell off me." She shoved him hard.

He didn't move.

"What're you doing?"

"Nothing."

"I can see that. Would you get your cock out of me?"

"Uh-uh."

"Godammit, Jake!" Oh, no, oh, jeez . . . she could feel him getting bigger—fast . . . as though he didn't take orders well or only needed five seconds between fucks. Or liked where he was.

And what was ten times worse—she liked where he was.

Didn't she have a brain?

Couldn't she control her damned wanton libido?

Was she completely senseless?

"Look, I'm sorry," he whispered, kissing her, his lips brushing back and forth across her mouth in a lazy arousal—coaxing her out of her bad mood. Her greedy cunt was flexing around his cock, which meant her head might be mad, but her body wasn't. "It's not your fault," he murmured. "It's mine. But it's no major disaster. You're on the pill—right?"

"I'm allergic."

His head snapped up, his life flashed before his eyes. "For real?"

"Yeah. Sorry."

He gazed at her, clearly contemplating options. A second passed, two, three, then a smile slowly lifted the corners of his mouth. "What the hell. We might as well take advantage of the situation. It's a helluva lot better without a condom."

"Hello. Are you demented?"

"I already came in you. How can a few more hours hurt?"

"Easy for you to say."

"Think about it." He moved in her, already back in peak form. "We're only talking a few hours. . . ."

He was incredibly persuasive or Sofie's libido was a sucker for a flawless centerfold guy with a world-class cock.

He had his way.

Or maybe they both did.

And it was about a thousand times better without a condom, he decided—Sofie Piper's slick, hot, silky-smooth vagina was just about the best place in the world to come in. And he knew the difference. He hadn't spent all his time playing football.

Much later that night, enervated by pleasure, Sofie lay half asleep in Jake's arms.

"Hey," he whispered.

"Ummm . . ."

Her head was on his chest, her body warm against his. "Let me know if I'm crushing you."

"No way," she murmured.

She felt like an island of peace in his arms, her softness and warmth a blissful respite from the violent, rough-and-tumble world of football—from the never-ending pursuit of victory.

Although he hadn't realized he needed respite until now.

Or that he needed Sofie.

Not that he was averse to changes in his life, when those changes could make him feel this good. And for a guy who had spent years making split-second decisions as a quarterback, he didn't need a team of lawyers to lay out a case. He liked being with Sofie, so he'd be with her.

He fell asleep with a smile on his face.

When his alarm went off, he looked down at the blond

curls and flushed cheek resting on his chest and found he liked having her beside him in the morning even better. But there wasn't time to do more than kiss her awake and say, "I've got kids waiting for me at school. We gotta go in fifteen minutes."

She understood and was dressed and waiting when he came out of the bathroom.

"If there's any problems with last night—condom wise," he said, "let me know."

She smiled. "Don't worry. You'll be the first to get the bulletin."

He thought he might have felt some fear or remorse when she looked at him like that.

Nope.

Maybe this relationship wasn't exclusively about sex anymore, he thought. "Ready?" he said, because he wasn't much for introspection, especially at this time of the morning. "I'll buy you coffee on the way."

"No, thanks. I'm going home to sleep until seven-thirty. Unlike you, I don't schedule early classes."

"Unlike you, I don't have a choice. And thanks, I had a great time."

"You're welcome." She grinned. "Sincerely."

She knew better than to elaborate; she didn't want to scare him.

ELEVEN

Sofie insisted he drop her off at her car, not about to let her Volkswagen Beetle sit in Byerly's parking lot for the entire day for all to see. Gossip would be bad enough without adding fuel to the fire.

"You worry too much," Jake said as she buttoned up her jacket.

"I'm not a superstar coach who can do no wrong. I can be replaced."

He couldn't argue her point. It would take a major scandal for the school board to get rid of him, seeing how Cutter High had an 8-0 record after three years of not having won a game. "Eat lunch with me, then," he said.

"I'm not so sure I can be trusted within five feet of you."

"Sounds good. We could eat lunch at my place."

"Even I'm not that fast." Lunch period was only a half hour.

"I've got a nice backseat, tinted windows"—he grinned—"and hair-trigger responses."

"I know all about those responses, but no thanks. I can

just see the crowd gathered outside your truck as we get out of it."

"Scaredy-cat."

"I don't have your salary. I need this job."

He stopped teasing. "I know. How about you meet me after the game? We're going to win. I'll feel like celebrating. I'll save you and Camille a seat on the fifty-yard line."

"I don't know."

"It better not be about meeting me after the game."

"No—I mean about sitting on the fifty-yard line. Why don't I find a seat somewhere else?"

"Are you ashamed of being my girl?"

The sudden silence was thunderous.

He couldn't believe what he'd just said.

She couldn't believe she was wishing with all her heart that he wasn't kidding. "How about I settle for being your friend," she said, taking the polite-as-hell approach.

"I like girlfriend better." He didn't like her evasion. He realized he'd meant what he'd said. "Don't fuck with me." He grinned. "I'm sensitive."

"Okay. I'd like to be your girlfriend, but I'm still not going to sit on the fifty-yard line. I'm the-last-row-against-the-wall kind of person."

"As long as you're my girlfriend, what the hell—sit wherever you want."

"Hey!"

"And I mean it in the nicest, most benevolent way." He tapped his wristwatch. "Much as I'd like to continue this argument, I have my guys waiting for me in the weight room."

"You're serious." She thought he had papers to grade or reports to read or something. He taught social studies.

"Every day, babe. Five forty-five—we're in the weight room." He smiled. "We're dedicated."

That explained his perfect body, every muscle toned to the max. "How long do you train?"

"An hour, hour and a half. It's fun. I really gotta go,

though," he noted. "After the game, outside the locker room. Give me a half hour to thank my kids."

He was all business, when it came to his duties, she thought, watching him drive away, understanding why he was so successful as a coach. He worked hard, he worked as hard as his players did, he didn't slough off for a second. Jeez, it made her feel like a real lame-ass. She'd have to stop watching so much TV and read more, maybe even think about exercising. He probably ate nutritionally, too, although Frosted Flakes gave her some hope. Maybe he wasn't completely perfect.

Although when it came to sex, he was not only perfect, he was out of this world.

Rose Capeletti had spread the whole story—with explicit details as noted on the TV monitors—by ten o'clock that morning, so Sofie had had more than her share of looks and tittering in her French classes. She pretended not to notice. A pose less easy to sustain in the teachers' lounge when old Mr. Rutledge announced in front of everyone, "I hear you're shacking up with the coach."

"I certainly am not," Sofie had replied, fortunate that Rutledge had worded his comment in such a way that she could lie with comparative ease. Had he said, "sleeping with the coach," she might have had more trouble brazenly denying it.

Although it wouldn't have mattered what she'd said as far as Melissa was concerned. Her accusatory glances lasered Sofie with unremitting fury all day. And in Melissa's administrative capacity, she had considerably more time to hang out in the lounge than ordinary teachers who actually had to show up for classes.

Eventually Friday classes came to a close and Sofie escaped any further knowing looks or teasing comments. Camille had said she was more than happy to go to the game with Sofie, and they left early enough to find seats in the back row. Not that Sofie was incognito by any stretch since Camille kept waving at Melissa whenever Cutter High's vice principal looked their way—which was often.

Although Sofie had to admit, she felt like a winner if there actually was a contest between Melissa and herself. And if there wasn't, she felt like a winner anyway. This must be how Jake feels after every game, Sofie thought— elated, cheerful . . . flying high.

Once the game started, Sofie watched Jake more than the game. He stood on the sidelines, his hands in his jacket pockets, never shouting or pacing or calling his players names like Wixon's nasty coach who screamed the entire game. Jake would just dip his head when he talked to his players, say something, they'd nod and trot out on the field and make another dazzling play. If every football game was like this, she'd have to come and watch them more often.

Although Sofie wasn't the only one in town who had noticed the difference this year in Cutter High's team. The stands were packed—standing room only—the fence along the field lined six deep with spectators. That's what a winning coach could do. Fire up the town.

Cutter won against Wixon in a blow-out, 28–3, assuring Cutter High some headlines in tomorrow's big city papers. Wixon Prairie had been undefeated for two seasons.

As the crowd erupted in an earsplitting roar at the end, Coach Finn slapped all his players on the back, then walked about ten feet out into the field, scanned the crowd, found the person he was looking for in the back row, and blew Sofie a kiss.

Her face turned a hundred shades of red as everyone in the stands turned to look up. The kids all knew Jake was giving that kiss to Miss Piper—they'd heard the stories in school—and some of those parents whose kids actually talked to them at the supper table knew, most of the teachers knew, and by morning, probably even the big city papers would know.

"Ohmygod," Sofie breathed, trying to melt into the crowd.

"Hey, don't knock it. That was beautiful," Camille said, her eyes brimming over.

"Jeez, are you crying?"

"Fuck no." Camille snuffled. "It's the wind."

The crowd was beginning to exit the stands, Sofie's fifteen seconds of fame thankfully over. But the warm glow remained. "That was kind of sweet."

"Kind of?" Camille exclaimed. "In front of the whole town? I guess so. And if you let Jake Finn get away, I'm going to disown you as too stupid to be my friend. Those Finns are keepers. I told you so."

"I know. Jake's got a real nice farmhouse, too."

"So I heard. He can afford it."

"He asked me to be his girl. Is that too hokey?"

"Hello. Jake Finn and hokey aren't even in the same universe. I hope you said yes. Jeez, don't look at me like that. You said yes, didn't you?"

"Eventually."

Camille grinned. "See, that's my problem. I don't know how to play hard to get."

"I have to meet him at the locker room in a half hour."

"He's going to be in a mood to celebrate."

"That's what he said."

"Jasper's team won today, too," Camille said.

"You little sneak—holding out on me. He called you!"

"He's coming back for Christmas. Here, not Iowa."

"Does Jake know?"

"He was going to call him tonight. So what do you think?"

"I think you've got yourself a winner."

"Maybe."

"Me, too, maybe, but whatever happens, I'm going to enjoy every second of this dream."

Jake was pacing outside the locker room when Sofie arrived.

"I thought you forgot."

"The stands were so crowded, it took forever to get out. Congratulations. That was a great game."

"Thanks." He pulled her into his arms and kissed her, right there—with the players still coming out of the locker room, with mothers and fathers standing around waiting for their kids. "Let's get out of here," he whispered against her mouth. "I feel like celebrating."

"Everyone's looking," she murmured, trying to pull away, the players' whistles and "way to go, Coach" echoing in her ears.

"Let them. I'm kissing my girl."

"I don't know if I can afford the scandal."

"Do I have to marry you?"

His eyes were very close and sparkling with laughter.

She wasn't going to sound like an idiot and answer that one. "You don't have to do anything," she said.

"What if I want to?"

"Don't tease, Jake." Not about that, she thought, not when she was beginning to care too much. Not when even Ben & Jerry's wasn't going to be enough if he left her.

"I'm serious. Marry me."

"No, you're not." He couldn't possibly be.

"I'll ask you in front of all these witnesses," he said. "Is that serious enough? Hey, listen up!" he shouted. "I'm going to propose to Miss Piper!"

Maybe he'd lived his life in the spotlight, but she wasn't prepared.

Then he went down on one knee, like men did sometimes on the *Today* show in front of that crowd outside, and he looked up at her while the hall outside the locker room became so quiet you could have heard a pin drop.

"Marry me, Sofie. You make me really happy."

She shouldn't say yes when she barely knew him. What if it didn't work out and all these avid spectators would know they'd made a huge mistake? People didn't actually get married when they'd spent only two nights together, did they?

"Say yes," he whispered, careful to keep his voice down so no one else could hear. "Or I won't let you come again."

Now that was a terrifying thought. More terrifying than any speculation about short-lived courtships.

"I mean it," he whispered. "You've got five seconds. Five, four, three, two—"

"Yes," she said, bending down to kiss him, not caring who was looking or what they thought. She suddenly felt aglow with happiness as though she was lit up from within.

"Now we really have something to celebrate," he said, standing upright, tossing a quick smile at the crowd. "She said yes."

A cheer went up.

"Want to get married on the fifty-yard line next home game?"

"Jake, for heaven's sake," she murmured.

"We'll talk about it." He turned to the crowd. "She doesn't know if she wants to get married on the fifty-yard line next home game."

A low groan went up.

He grinned at her. "See, you're disappointing everyone. Including Melissa," he said under his breath.

The man was masterful. A strategist on and off the football field.

Sofie scanned the crowd and met Melissa's lethal gaze. "It's so fast, but—maybe," she said.

"I just don't want to wait," he whispered. "I just got hit over the head with love and it's pretty damned nice. But if the football field is too public, you say the word—anywhere is fine."

He was tall, dark, and handsome, talented as hell, sweet, loveable, full of sexy charm, and capable of going all night without missing a beat. Why was she even hesitating? "If it's cold, we could get married in the gym."

"Perfect." He met her gaze. "Can I tell them?"

She nodded.

"We're getting married next home game—on the fifty-yard line if it's warm, in the gym if it's cold. You're all invited."

The cheer was almost as loud as the one at the end of the game.

"Now if you'll excuse us, we have to make some wedding plans."

As he held her close, they made their way through the crowd of well-wishers, a swell of congratulations following them outside into the cool night.

"Do you think it was wise to invite everyone?" Sofie asked, as they walked to his truck.

"The kids will like it. I'll pay for it. Tell me how much when you've figured it out. But one request. Keep the ceremony short. And I don't want to write my own vows."

"What if I write them?"

"Fine. Great. It's your baby. Remember pop for the kids. They can't drink."

She liked how he always thought about his players. It made her all warm inside. He might look like he could tear down a house with his bare hands, but he was really kind.

"Shit, I forgot about my family," he said. "Oh, well, you can meet them at the wedding and I'll meet yours. We should probably talk to the cafeteria staff about catering. Get plenty of food. My kids eat like horses. I gotta call Jasper, too. Hey, babe, you're awfully quiet. Did I say something wrong?" Coming to a stop, he took her face in his huge hands and bent low to meet her gaze. "Everything's okay, right?"

Her eyes filled with tears. "Everything's perfect."

"Don't cry. I'll cry." He smiled. "Really, I will. I almost cried at Jenny and Charlie's wedding and those vows were really stupid."

She laughed—which was his intent.

"Ice cream first or second?" he said. "Your Ben and Jerry's is still in my freezer."

"First."

"How about we toss a coin?"

"I forgot to eat supper."

"Then Ben and Jerry's first." As they reached his truck,

he opened the door and lifted her into the cab. "Whatever my baby wants," he said with a smile.

Walking around the back of the truck, he got in, fired up the engine, and shot her a look. "Having you is better than winning any game." His criteria for happiness had changed.

"I want to say pinch me, I must be dreaming, I feel so good."

"Nice, hey?" He backed out of his parking space.

"Oh, yeah. *La vie est belle,*" she said, her Parisian accent flawless. "Life's beautiful."

"And I figure I must be going to Disney World, cuz I feel like I won the Super Bowl. Come here, babe. I need a kiss from my fiancée."

DOUBLE THE PLEASURE

Jasmine Haynes

Acknowledgments

I received so much help from so many wonderful people. I'd like to thank Linda Eberharter for giving me a shot, Moni Draper and Cheryl Clark for their expertise, Dee S. Knight for all her support, and most especially Jenn Cummings for being my miracle worker. For all their guidance, I'd also like to thank my agent, Lucienne Diver, and my editor, Christine Zika.

ONE

"I think, for your thirtieth birthday, you should seduce a man."

Kristin Prescott blushed and said a little thank-you prayer that the only other occupant of the steam room had vacated moments before Kirby's declaration.

Kristin tried to sound flip. "It's your birthday, too. You do the seducing."

"My darling sister, I have a vibrator, I don't need a man. You, on the other hand—"

"I don't need a vibrator or a man." Okay, so maybe she needed both, the man definitely more than the vibrator.

Sweat dripped off Kirby's nose, steam pumped from the valve, and the overpowering scent of eucalyptus made it hard to breathe.

Kirby went on. "You've got to repair your self-esteem."

"My self-esteem?" A nasty telltale squeak laced her voice.

"Kristin, you're sadly lacking in the confidence department."

"I've got plenty of confidence." Not.

"Sure, in your job, you do. But get you around a pack of hot-looking guys, and you let yourself fade into the wallpaper."

Kristin rubbed perspiration from her forehead. "You've got me there. I can't deny it."

"That's why you haven't been on a date since Blake . . . left."

"You can say he dumped me." Her fiancé had given her the heave-ho over six months ago. It wasn't that Kristin wasn't over him, she was, it was just . . .

"I haven't found anyone interesting."

Except Ross Sloan. Her boss. All he noticed about her, though, were her flawless memos and intricate spreadsheets. She didn't think he even knew her first name.

Kirby snorted, but didn't comment on Kristin's little evasion. "Did I ever tell you what an asshole your ex-fiancé was?"

The sisters thought differently about sex, career, marriage, everything, but Kirby was loyal.

"And I love you for saying that."

Still, Blake's final crack had slipped beneath Kristin's skin like a nasty sliver.

Why can't you be hot and sexy like your twin sister?

The answer was right beside her. Kirby, naked, stretched out on her stomach, her towel draped over the tile beneath her; Kristin, primly seated on the step above, her own towel wrapped tightly, covering her from armpits to thighs. They were identical twins, but in looks alone; their manners and personalities were completely opposite.

With his last words to her, Blake hit her smack dab in the middle of her biggest insecurity. That she didn't have what it took to be anything like Kirby, except on the outside. She wasn't sexy. She wasn't hot. But she didn't dislike sex the way Blake had accused. In fact she'd imagined . . . yes, she could say the words in her head, she'd thought of going down on Mr. Sloan. In his office. So there.

"Well, forget the little bastard."

She didn't think her boss would turn out to be little in any sense of the word. Oh! Kirby was still talking about Blake.

"He was too short for you anyway. And balding. You were way too good for him." Image was all-important to Kirby. "You've just let that whole business beat you down."

"He didn't beat me down," Kristin protested.

He'd merely caught on to something she'd known since her first time during college. She wasn't good at sex. She hadn't given him complete satisfaction. She certainly hadn't found it for herself. Still, in her fantasies, Kristin *was* like her sister. She did all sorts of toe-tingling sexual things. With her boss. Those thoughts actually made her hot, wet even, and she didn't have any trouble melting into orgasm.

Kirby studied her. "Have it your way. Blake didn't beat you down. But did he ever make you orgasm? Even once?"

"Kirby." There'd been a few, but none particularly memorable.

Nothing like the remarkably memorable ones she'd had fantasizing about Mr. Sloan, no vibrator necessary.

"Kristin," her sister mimicked her tone. "Which means he didn't, right?"

She and Kirby had never really discussed her sexual relationship with Blake. Kirby would have had all sorts of great advice, the first being that the lack of sparks under the covers wasn't all Kristin's fault, and Kirby would have been right. Kristin knew that intellectually, but get her heart to believe it? Not an easy accomplishment. Especially when her insecurity problems started with comparing herself to her sexy, hot, over-the-top, confident sister in the first place.

"Could we please talk about something else?"

Kirby spread her hands. "You know what they say. When a horse dumps you, you have to get right back in the saddle and ride again. You *need* to start dating."

The old adage that time healed all wounds, as bad a cliché as Kirby's, was also completely wrong. The longer

Kristin waited to hop back into the dating arena, the worse the fear of failing once again became.

When Kristin didn't comment, Kirby rolled onto her back and crossed her legs at the ankles, not indicating an ounce of embarrassment with her nudity.

"Kristin, we've got to break out of the rut we're in."

Thank God for the change of topic. "We? What is it you want to change?"

"My wardrobe."

"Your wardrobe?" Kristin echoed, suddenly confused.

"Yes. I'm going to throw out that little red dress. You know, the one you salivated over at Neiman Marcus last New Year's."

"I didn't salivate." She had.

"You said it cost too much—"

It did.

"—but you know you just thought it was too sexy for you. Which is ridiculous."

"If I'd worn it, I'd have looked ridiculous. It was too red, too glitzy, too . . . not me." Still, she had adored the sequined bodice and the full, flirty skirt.

She'd wanted that dress badly; only she hadn't bought it, because she'd been comparing herself unfavorably to Kirby. Again.

"Well, you can have it if you want it. Otherwise, I'm sending it to the consignment store."

Now, that was a lie. Kirby was using reverse psychology here.

"But if you take it, you have to wear it to our birthday party Friday night."

Ah, the punchline. It was really Kirby's birthday party, she was throwing it herself. But she'd added Kristin's name to the invitation. Kristin had chosen the half-day celebration she and Kirby were having right now. The morning off work. A lovely brunch. A good facial. A steam bath. And no need for a stunning red dress.

"I couldn't wear it." Could she?

She took in a deep breath of eucalyptus. If push came to shove, maybe. She *needed* a push. And a shove.

"There's going to be tons of gorgeous men there. You can practice your seduction techniques."

"I don't have any techniques."

She could, however, use the stuff of her fantasies. If she found a man who reminded her of Mr. Sloan.

Kirby grimaced. "You'll learn quickly enough. If you've got any balls when it comes to men, that is."

Kristin would have laughed if Kirby's words hadn't been so on target. "I have tons of . . . *cajones.*"

Liar, liar, pants on fire. She was turning thirty, and she didn't even have the courage to put on a sexy dress. Pitiful.

"Chicken," Kirby couldn't seem to resist adding.

How long could she go on being afraid of a little red dress? A year? Ten years? Fifty years living with nothing but fantasies, her body aging, gravity taking over, biological clock in overdrive? Oh. No. The thought was more debilitating than the idea of seducing a room full of Kirby's gorgeous men. She wouldn't be just an old maid, she'd be a shriveled husk. God forbid.

Could she get back on the horse? Actually, the question was, what would her life become if she *didn't*?

"All right, I'll wear the dress." She'd find the *cajones* somewhere. "And I want to borrow the shoes that go with it, too."

Maybe someday she'd even have the courage to wear something equally provocative to work to see if Ross Sloan finally noticed her. Maybe, just maybe, his eyes would pop out and he'd ask what her first name was.

"Here's the R and A analysis you asked for, Mr. Sloan."

"Thank you, Miss Prescott."

Besides being the best damn secretary Ross Sloan had ever had, Kristin Prescott had the most amazing set of calves; he'd been staring at them for the entire six months she'd worked for him. Of course, she'd never caught him at it. In today's politically correct environment—and because he respected a woman's right not to be ogled if she didn't want to be—he'd kept his behavior exemplary. When she was looking.

She wasn't looking now. Sitting back in his big leather chair, he watched her glide. Tall, elegant, even in low-heeled, sensible pumps. A rump that wiggled instead of jiggled. He'd have loved a glimpse of the rest of her legs, but her skirts never rose above her knees. He'd fantasized about them instead.

"Ah, Miss Prescott, one more thing."

He'd let her get all the way to the door before calling her back, feeling a bit like a teenage boy rather than a thirty-six-year-old CFO. There was something . . . exhilarating about his watching, about her, something that excited him in a way he hadn't been for a long while.

"Yes, Mr. Sloan?"

He glanced down at the spreadsheet she'd left on his desk. "Any thoughts on Cooper's work here?"

She returned to the side of his desk, leaning over and bracing herself with one hand. He angled the report toward her.

"Well . . ."

She tucked a stray lock back into her otherwise tidy bun. Masses of rich copper-colored hair. He'd never actually seen it down, but he'd sure as hell imagined it falling all over his lap.

"Go ahead," he encouraged, breathing in the fresh fruity scent of her hand lotion.

She had beautiful hands, long slender fingers, and today, a fresh manicure.

She pointed a polished fingernail to one particular number. "Cooper thinks we're overreserved on this one, but he seems to have forgotten introducing the QX at the beginning of the quarter. I don't think we've seen the fallout of new product returns yet."

Damn, she was good. She'd have made one fine accountant. Her quick head with numbers allowed him to give her assignments far beyond the capabilities of some secretaries.

Which was why she was far too important for him to lose over a brief fling. He'd certainly thought about it, but however enticing the idea of her long fingers clasped around his cock in the middle of the night might be—

His watch beeped loudly. Miss Prescott gave a little start, almost as if she'd walked in on his thoughts.

Damn. His appointment. Or rather, his date with Samantha Johnson.

"Have to run, Miss Prescott. Can you e-mail me the soft copy of the analysis?

"I already did, and I forwarded you Cooper's e-mail, too."

Everything, she took care of absolutely everything for him. Almost.

Too bad she couldn't take care of his little problem with Samantha.

Ross Sloan walked out the door, waving a negligent hand. He didn't turn, didn't say good night, didn't look at her. Just that meaningless wave.

She'd bet a year's paycheck he'd have done more than wave at her if she'd been wearing that slinky red dress.

The sexy little thing Kirby had given her, complete with sequined purse and heavenly spike-heeled shoes, sat in a box on the floor by her chair. She hadn't lost her bravado in the time it took to get from the steam room to Kirby's to work right after lunch. She might not feel totally natural in the short, red, sequined dress, but she'd give it her best try at Friday's birthday party. If she didn't lose her nerve in the next two days.

Oops, negative thought. She squashed it immediately and straightened the folders on Mr. Sloan's desk. That done, she had no other business being in his office. Except for those fantasies of hers.

How many times had she imagined Mr. Sloan making love to her on that big mahogany desk? Or in that cushy leather chair? Against the door?

Goodness, maybe she did need to buy a vibrator.

Or a pair of red thong panties to go with that red outfit.

The phone suddenly chirped, making her jump. She snapped up the receiver. "Mr. Sloan's office. Miss Prescott speaking."

"Is he there?" A woman's voice, with a definite edge.

"Mr. Sloan's left for the day."

"Damn. I need to get hold of him ASAP."

"You could try his cell phone."

"Fine. What's the number?"

"I'm sorry, I can't give that out." One of Mr. Sloan's dictates. Upon pain of death, don't give out the cell number.

"I already have it, just not with me at the moment. This is Samantha Johnson. You must know who I am."

Of course she did, but perversely Kristin answered, "No, I'm sorry, I don't."

"This is ridiculous. Are you his secretary?"

She imagined Ms. Johnson with too much dark hair above her upper lip. The image fit perfectly with the woman's demanding tone. Kristin pursed her lips. "I'm his administrative aide."

"Whatever." Kristin could almost see the heedless flip of the woman's hand.

"We had a date tonight," Ms. Johnson went on, "but I'm stuck in a meeting that's going to last at least another two hours."

"I'm sorry. But I still can't give you his number."

A puff of irritated breath. "He's going to hear about this. In the meantime, *you* can find him to tell him I can't make it."

Kristin narrowed her eyes, but kept her voice polite, like any good little *secretary*. "I can certainly try to do that for you, Miss Johnson. When and where were you supposed to meet him?"

"The bar at the Ambassador Hotel at six."

"I'll call him on his cell." Kristin liked the parting shot.

"Fine." Click. Extra-hard click.

So now she was his social secretary, too. She had half a mind to let him wait in the Ambassador's bar.

Okay, so that was a bit bitchy.

The truth was that Mr. Sloan used her that way only in emergencies. He was actually a good boss, treating her with respect, saying please and thank you, complimenting her work. A patient mentor.

She punched the speaker phone and started dialing his cell.

Then she saw his cell phone on his desk. He'd forgotten it. Which wasn't like him at all. Must have been the fact that he thought he'd be late. For Samantha. Yuck. How could he drink champagne with a woman who had a mustache, even if the lip hair was only in Kristin's imagination?

She glanced down at her watch: 5:55. The Ambassador was only across the street. She could drop by before catching her bus and save him the embarrassment of being stood up.

She snapped off his desk light, left the office in darkness. Yanking her purse from her bottom drawer, she was almost out the door before she remembered Kirby's "present." Darn, she couldn't traipse through the Ambassador hauling the huge box. To keep it safe, how about her locker down in the gym on the fifth floor?

Or she could wear it to the hotel and give her boss the shock of his life. The brilliant idea stopped her dead. Practice for Friday night. No, Friday was practice, this was the real thing. Ross might think she had a hot date. He might even think she was a hot babe like Kirby. Though he knew Kristin was a twin, he had yet to meet her sister.

Maybe he'd think she *was* Kirby.

She held her breath until she felt dizzy. What a concept. Kristin suddenly knew exactly what she wanted for her birthday.

Mr. Ross Sloan. Even if it meant pretending to be Kirby.

*   *   *

Ross saw her the minute she entered the hotel bar.
Miss Prescott. His Miss Prescott. In an exceptionally short
red dress with an unbelievably gorgeous pair of thighs to
match those calves, better even than he'd imagined. Jesus.
Reality certainly surpassed fantasy. Damn. That red
dress . . .

It didn't matter. In the morning she'd still be his secretary. And he needed her.

She turned, her gaze traveled over the cluster of tables
flanking the small dance floor. The bar was by no means
full, and if she'd been looking, she couldn't have missed
him sitting at the far end of the counter.

She never even looked.

Just as well, it allowed him to observe every curve revealed by the brevity of her skirt. Her hair cascaded over
shoulders covered only by the thin red straps of her dress.
Oh, yeah, her hair was exactly the stuff of his fantasies,
full, rich shades of reds and browns, curling softly over the
tops of her breasts. Speaking of breasts, if he'd seen her
like this in his office, he'd never have been able to keep his
hands off her.

His heart stopped as she touched the red and black
beaded choker at her throat. Just a brief caress. His eyes
tracked the brush of her fingers down the slender line of
her throat, leading his gaze to the soft swell of a plump
breast. Magnificent. His smart, efficient secretary was sexy
as all get-out.

His temperature rose by degrees as she moved to the bar
and slid onto a free stool, crossing her legs. Endless legs.
The red dress rode up her thigh. She signaled the bartender, and the man jumped to attention as if she'd handed
him twenty bucks. Ross understood the feeling, he'd
jumped to attention himself.

She ordered and, when her wine came, lifted the glass
to her delicious red lips. She raised a finger and slid it

across her bottom lip, trapping a droplet. He barely suppressed a groan, closing his eyes briefly, just to find his sanity.

This couldn't be *his* Miss Prescott. He opened his eyes.

Oh, but it was. Beneath the chatter of voices, the laughter, and the thrum of elevator music, the soft chink of her nails against the glass floated down the length of the bar. His groin tightened. God, there was something about that sound. It sent him into orbit.

He forgot his boredom of late. His Miss Prescott was a breath of fresh air from the stuffy executive offices he'd been inhabiting, both professionally and personally. He forgot Samantha was over half an hour late before leaving a message with the bartender.

Samantha was intelligent, witty, and a good conversationalist with a slightly ribald sense of humor. He continued to admire her business acumen, but her need to dominate the boardroom carried straight through into the bedroom. He enjoyed the woman-on-top position, but lately, Samantha was incapable of doing it in any other way. The lack of variety and her increasingly brittle manner had begun to chafe. The end for them was near. Which would explain why he hadn't gone out to the lobby to call her when he realized he'd left his cell phone on his desk. He'd actually preferred people-watching. Then Miss Prescott walked in.

The tap-tap of her long, lightly painted nails beat deep inside. A pale shade of polish, he'd noticed her fresh manicure this afternoon. Suddenly parched, he took a swig of his scotch and soda. She had long, slender fingers. He imagined them on him, scratching his back, kneading his shoulders. All over him. Ah, God. He stood, then picked up his drink.

Limits, political correctness, and the employee handbook be damned. He wanted her. Always had. He sure as hell wasn't going to let the date she was obviously dressed to kill for get to her first.

"Miss Prescott, I almost didn't recognize you," he lied smoothly as he took the seat next to hers. Not a chance he'd have missed her.

His knee brushed hers, then came to rest against her thigh. She didn't move away, simply stared at him with those big green eyes.

"Mr. . . . uh . . ." Her fingers continued tapping, his blood pulsed in time.

"Don't tell me you've forgotten my name in the space of"—he flipped his wrist to look at his watch—"an hour?"

Something flickered in her eyes, an unreadable flash. She bit her bottom lip. A deep breath lifted her breasts.

"I do believe you've mistaken me for my sister."

Shit. He knew she had a twin, but it couldn't be. He didn't want it to be. "Your sister?"

She smiled, just a slight curve of her mouth. "You must think I'm Kristin."

"But you're . . ."

Damn, he couldn't even remember the sister's name. Christ.

"Kirby."

"Ah yes, sorry, I'd forgotten." He lifted his drink, took a swallow, and moved his knee away from her thigh.

"Well, that's not very gallant."

What? Moving his leg or forgetting her name? He didn't feel gallant, in either case. He felt gutted.

"Don't you think you ought to introduce yourself?"

"My apologies," he managed, then stuck out his hand. "Ross Sloan. I'm your sister's boss."

She grasped his hand lightly, her fingers cool and moist after caressing her wineglass. A little zing snapped to the tip of his cock, and he held on longer than necessary. A pulse beat at her throat. Then she dropped her gaze and pulled free with a laugh and a bright smile. Her eyes shone with a wattage higher than his secretary's. Higher and oddly false.

"I'd almost think you were disappointed I'm not Kristin, Mr. Sloan."

Flirty, teasing, she didn't sound like his Miss Prescott, but something about her made him wonder.

She finished the last sip of her wine, set the glass down, and her fingers immediately began tapping the stem. Nerves?

He stared at her nails. He was positive that was the same shade Kristin wore today. Peach or coral or some such color. Women seemed to have a name for each infinitesimally different shade. Come to think of it, she even smelled the same. A fruity, citrus scent. Every day he knew the exact moment Miss Prescott freshened her hand lotion, the aroma drifting into his office, breaking his concentration, making him think of other places he'd smooth the cream into her skin. They were twins, but down to the same nail polish and hand lotion?

She crossed her legs the other way, moving her thigh even farther from his, then looked around the bar. "I'm afraid I must have missed my friends. I was running a tad late."

He swallowed the dark liquid in his glass. A subtle pickup line stating her availability? Or nervous chatter? He couldn't be sure. She licked her lips and didn't quite meet his gaze. Primitive instinct told him she was exactly who he wanted her to be, but with a few more minutes and a bit more discourse, he'd be sure.

"Then I suppose it's also my good fortune that my date has stood me up."

Her eyes widened, first surprise, then a flash of something else. Guilt?

Finally, she said in a mocking tone, her voice artificially deep and her eyes on her wineglass, "A man admitting he's been stood up. That's a first."

"May I buy you a fresh one?" He indicated her empty glass and added a distinct, "Kirby?"

She hesitated, then said, "Thank you."

He crooked a finger at the bartender, ordering the same for her and another for himself. "Would you join me at a table?"

A table, where there'd be time enough to confirm her true identity. He'd wager the woman with her tasty thigh two scant inches from his was *his* Kristin. Not her sister Kirby.

TWO

Glasses in hand, Ross followed the magnificent, red-clad view as Kristin threaded her way through the tables to one in the back, a quiet corner. Dark. A single candle flickered on the black top.

"Good choice," he approved.

She smiled. A soft, shy, yet full-of-promise smile. He knew that smile, experienced the same visceral punch he had every morning upon first seeing her. Kristin's smile, no one else's—even if they were identical twins.

But if this gorgeous lady was Kristin, why pretend to be her sister? The question intrigued him. Embarrassment that her boss had discovered her more seductive side? Could it be she was cruising the bar? No. Definitely not. Not his Kristin. Before the night was through, he fully intended to discover the reason for her disguise.

He held out the chair for her, allowing his fingers to skim her bare arm as he seated her. He felt her shiver in his groin.

"Thanks," she murmured as he took the seat next to her.

A hint of a blush bloomed on her cheeks. He catalogued

the reaction, which was inconsistent with a casual perhaps accidental touch in a bar. Very consistent, however, if a six-month history lay between them. He pushed Kristin's wine closer, then leaned in. Wanting a clear head, he didn't touch his own drink as she took a sip of hers.

"So, your date stood you up," she said again, almost searching for something to say. Nervous. Tense.

"I've already gotten over it. Do you want to call your . . . friend?"

"Friends," she corrected quickly. "Girlfriends. And they'll be on their way to the club by now."

"You could catch up with them there." Though he had no intention of that happening.

Another tinge of red colored her cheeks. She hesitated, then pressed her lips together. "I don't think so."

He inhaled her intoxicating scent, as he did daily whenever she was near. He moved his chair closer to her side so that once again his leg rested against hers. Her heat seeped through his suit pants. Jesus, he wanted her. The intensity could only be for Kristin. The music, the joking, laughter, voices, everything around them faded. He had to tear his eyes from the choker at her throat before he lost it completely.

He needed some way to trip her up, prove her to be Kristin. The twin angle was his best weapon. "So, tell me why your sister isn't more like you?"

She jerked at the impact of his question. Her gaze darted over his shoulder, down to her wine, the tabletop.

"I mean, being twins, you're pretty different." He glanced at her lovely shoulders, then to the amount of cleavage at the scoop of her dress. He leaned a tad forward, breathing her in, teasing himself.

"I . . . we're . . ." She raised her glass for another sip of pale wine. "We're not really so different."

He'd bet they were. The short skirt revealing plenty of leg, the naked curve of her shoulders, the deep neckline; he'd bet his last dime the woman who always wore knee-length dresses to work wouldn't bare that much thigh even in the evening. "I've never seen your sister wear something like that. She seems to prefer longer skirts that provide more coverage."

He flicked a finger along the dress strap, then pulled back, but not before he felt her slight shudder.

She laughed, a little forced, not her usual sweet note, and her gaze darted once more to inanimate objects close at hand. "Well, she wouldn't wear it at the office."

As she dipped her head, a lock of hair fell across her cheek. He brushed it back, his finger sliding along the shell of her ear. Her breath caught, and her pupils widened. He wanted to go on touching her but let his hand drop back to the table to rest near hers.

"So she's got plenty of sexy little red dresses in her closet?"

She took another sip of wine, licked her lips, then straightened. "You don't really know her at all, Mr. Sloan."

He couldn't gauge the expression on her face. The smile vanished, the false laughter quenched. Her jaw rippled as if she'd clamped down. He was playing his hand too aggressively, perhaps even giving the impression that he didn't like Kristin just as she was every day at the office. He wouldn't go so far as to reveal she'd entered his fantasies at the oddest times, especially late at night, but she needed to hear he believed she had plenty of positive attributes.

"Don't get me wrong. I have immense admiration for Kristin."

"Oh?" She looked at him then, her interest piqued, head tipped, a sudden spark deepening the green of her eyes.

"Hell, she practically runs my life for me. I'd miss all my meetings if it weren't for her."

"Oh." Her voice softer, a little deflated, she dropped her eyes and fingered a small defect in the lacquered table.

He knew in his gut what his cock had already reacted to. Only Kristin would care what he thought of her. Only Kristin would want to hear about more than her efficiency. And only if she'd allowed herself some of the same thoughts about him, thoughts that belonged in the bed-room, not the office.

He took a leap into the deep end. "You're done with your wine, Miss Prescott. I could ask you back to my apart-ment for a fresh glass. But that's not why I want you there."

"I've already had two," she murmured, ignoring his last statement, her gaze still on the empty glass. "I don't think I should have another."

"No wine then. Just come home with me." He reached out, thumbed the choker at her throat, barely touching her flesh, but feeling the heat all the way to his nuts.

A flush crept over her skin. Her breath caught, she bit her lip. Then she raised those exquisite eyes to his. "Why do you want me to come home with you?"

His finger slid down her neck, along her collarbone, to the strap at her shoulder. He slipped it over the edge. "I want to touch you. I want you to touch me."

Her pupils dilated as her breath quickened. "Only touching?" she whispered.

Ah, God. "I want to taste you." The image, the desire, had plagued his fantasies for damn near six months.

He leaned close to press a kiss to her shoulder, then let his finger follow a path to the swell of her breast. "I want to make love to you." Her hair caressed his cheek as he raised his head. "What do you want?"

She pulled her full lower lip between her teeth, then let go. Her mouth begged him to kiss her. Her gaze flashed from his eyes to his lips, as if memorizing his features. Or making a decision. "I want to go home with you."

He barely heard the words, couldn't be sure she'd said them aloud. No. Dammit. She'd said yes. He didn't wait. Throwing a tip on the table, he pulled her to her feet and out the door. Impatience had never been his style, but he'd waited too damn long for Miss Kristin Prescott. He'd be lucky if he could wait the time it'd take to reach his apartment. He sure as hell wouldn't wait for her to change her mind.

* * *

The San Francisco night was cool. The fog rolled in, blanketing the streets and adding to the intimate moment. He pulled his jacket off and laid it across her shoulders, then took her hand.

Dear God, what was she doing? He thought she was Kirby. He was reacting to the dress. This wasn't about her. Everything had happened so quickly. Kristin couldn't catch her breath, couldn't believe she was heading towards his car. He'd commented on her attire so he had noticed her at the office, though granted, he'd only praised her time management skills instead of something more personal. Still, there was something about the urgency lacing his voice when he'd asked her back to his apartment, as if he'd been thinking about it for months instead of minutes. She'd reacted to that more than anything else. She wanted to be the woman *he* wanted desperately. Kirby hadn't been in that bar. Kristin had. She was the one he'd asked to his apartment. He didn't even know Kirby.

Kristin let her hand rest in his, relishing the warmth of it. The strength. The safety. He set her on fire. She'd had no choice but to say yes. Her fantasy was about to come true, and she wouldn't let her insecurities stand in the way.

Outside the Ambassador Hotel, they waited for the light to change. He raised her hand to his lips and kissed her fingers, his smoky gaze meeting hers.

Enjoy the moment, she told herself. Don't think about Kirby. Don't think about tomorrow. She'd worry about work later.

The light changed, and they were across, heading toward the parking garage. She didn't know what to say to him. Didn't know what to do. She wasn't inexperienced, but . . . she was with him. Everything was new and different, the possibilities limitless. A few steps, a short elevator ride, and there was his car, a long, sleek, black luxury model. He unlocked the door and opened it for her. The perfect gentleman.

He terrified her. Those limitless possibilities included his disappointment when he found out she was only dressed like Kirby but couldn't perform with her sister's finesse and sexy confidence.

Just as Blake had said.

What was she thinking when she'd started this? Moreover, how on earth had she found the courage to walk into that drugstore on the way to the Ambassador and buy a packet of condoms? She imagined they glowed even through the small purse. A beacon shouting a warning. She'd felt eyes, pairs and pairs of eyes on her back as she'd left the store.

She turned, her hand on the door, ready to tell him she'd changed her mind. So sorry. Such an idiot. Can't do this.

He was so close, his scent enveloped her, a mixture of spicy aftershave and hot desire.

"Jesus, I can't wait." The husky whisper went straight to her starving heart. Then his arms were around her and his lips on hers, and she couldn't remember who she was.

He tasted of whiskey and hot male. What a mouth! What a kiss! Better than any of her bedroom fantasies.

She opened her lips to his tongue and slid her arms around his neck. His jacket slipped from her shoulders to the garage floor, and his hands branded her waist. Hot, hot, hot. She just might burst into flames in his arms. She pressed her breasts to his chest, felt the hard ridge of his penis against her belly, and she wanted more. A tiny moan escaped into his mouth.

The sound seemed to set him off. His hands slipped from her waist to her hips to her bottom. The soft jersey of her dress slid like silk as he bunched it in his fingers. Ooh, the kiss went on and on until she thought she'd faint. Then his hands were on the bare skin of her thighs, kneading her flesh.

She'd allow him anything, allow him to take her right there on the passenger seat. She'd waited so long and wanted him so badly. She'd even ignore the click of high heels on the concrete garage floor. She didn't care who saw them.

He found the sense to break the kiss, resting his forehead against hers. His breath came in hard gasps. He let her dress slide back into place.

"Why, Miss Prescott," he murmured. "I do believe I was about to lose control."

She laughed into his shirtfront, the sound strangely sultry, seductive. Not like her. Not at all. Just like Kirby. "I do believe I wanted you to lose it, Mr. Sloan." She started to tremble with reaction. What if everything went wrong?

He tightened his arms. She felt warm and wanted. And hot, so hot.

"Perhaps we should get to my apartment before I do lose it."

She laughed again despite the butterflies in her stomach and raised her face to look at him. His gaze was dark, mirroring her flushed skin. He wanted her. He'd liked her kiss. Even if he thought he was kissing Kirby, it was her mouth he'd ravaged. Keeping one hand on her arm, he bent for his jacket.

"I'm sorry, I forgot about it."

He placed it around her shoulders, his heady male scent surrounding her. He held out a hand, indicating the seat. She slid into the car and marveled that she was actually going to do this. With him. The man who'd haunted her every fantasy for six months.

He closed the door and sealed her in before she could chicken out.

She wasn't quite sure how long the drive to his apartment would take. When he started the engine, then put his hand on her bare thigh, she prayed not long. A tiny part of her feared he'd change his mind given time to think about it.

"Are you all right?" he asked, as he maneuvered out into the street, then reached across the console once more.

No, not at all, with his fingers stroking her thigh, raising her dress. She had the almost uncontrollable desire to guide his hand closer, higher, inside her panties. . . .

"I'm fine, thanks."

"So polite, Miss Prescott. I like that about you."

Did he really? Her face flushed with embarrassment, but he stared forward, watching the traffic.

"You're making me crazy, you know."

She smiled and hugged herself. She wanted to be a woman that drove men crazy. Drove *him* crazy. This was her fantasy.

"I thought men never admitted things like that."

"Only when it's obvious."

His hand was driving *her* crazy.

There were too many cars, too many pedestrians, too many red lights. What were all these people doing in the city anyway? Didn't they know she had terribly naughty things she wanted to do with this man? Right now. She felt almost giddy with newfound power.

He gently parted her legs. Kristin held her breath. He looked at her, and she couldn't help another flush of color. His questing fingers brushed her panties, the material rubbing the hardened nub of her clitoris. She bit her tongue to hold back a moan.

I can't believe I'm doing this. What if someone sees us?

"Do you like that?"

"Mmmm," was all she was capable of.

"Christ," he exhaled.

Then his hand was gone as he hit a remote and pulled into a parking garage. She didn't know exactly where she was, but she did know he lived somewhere along Lombard Street. A secretary had to know these things. The garage gate clanged behind them. He deftly pulled into a spot and jerked to a stop. Nerves taking over again, she licked her lips in the tense silence.

He groaned. "Don't make me do it right here, Miss Prescott."

He wanted her right now. In the car. The knowledge fed something starving inside her.

"At least let me get you inside."

She let her lips curve slightly, praying they wouldn't quiver. "Yes, please."

He actually fumbled with the door handle trying to get out. She loved it. He wanted her. *Her.* Kristin.

She wasn't quite sure how she managed it, but her legs slid out sleekly, seductively, as he held the door open. The elevator took forever. He stood against the opposite wall watching her, undressing her with his glowing eyes. She wanted to preen. She wanted to come. This man found her sexy.

In the next moment, her stomach tumbled. What if she didn't do things properly?

Outside his door, his keys seemed to appear in his hand. She almost shouted at the weak voice in her head. She would not spoil this moment. Then they were inside. Through a full wall of windows, the city gleamed, winking lights on the wharf, beyond that the dark of the bay, lights blazing on Alcatraz.

She closed the door behind her and leaned against it to steady herself.

"I promised you wine," he said in the darkness.

"I'm not thirsty." Not for wine. For him, yes. For his touch. She'd been living in a desert far too long.

He moved to the wall next to her, leaning against it. She put a hand over his on the switch. "No lights—yet."

She willed him to make the first move because she knew she couldn't. He tugged at the lapels of his jacket still around her shoulders, and she stepped willingly into his arms. His tongue invaded her mouth as he aligned her body with his. On tiptoe she wrapped her arms around his neck, sinking into him, and his jacket fell to the floor. Her breasts rubbed his chest. He was hard, so hard.

He whispered against her mouth. "You kiss like a wet dream."

She'd never been anybody's wet dream. His praise melted her fear like an ice cube, and this time she took his mouth. Parting her lips beneath his, she let him stroke her tongue. The dark gave her courage, and she opened wider for him. Her fingers tunneled through the hair at his nape and anchored him to her. His lips and tongue alternately teased and consumed. She gave a little purring moan in her throat.

He pulled her arm from his neck, guiding her hand to the front of his trousers. She didn't wait for instructions, stroking his length. When he groaned, she squeezed. When his body jerked involuntarily, she slid her hand down to cup his testicles through the material. His breath hitched. He devoured her with his mouth. Desire. Need. The power went to her head. She didn't need words to know that her touch on him was just right. His hands were already pulling her dress up to her hips.

The sweet caress down the center of her panties threatened to push her over the edge. Passion. She was spilling over with passion. He shoved his hand inside the cotton, slid a finger along her outer lips, then penetrated her cleft.

"Christ, you're wet."

Make me wetter. She longed to whisper it aloud, to free herself, but she could do nothing more than moan into the mouth that consumed her.

Her panties slipped down her legs. Darn, she wished she stopped to buy something sexier than plain white cotton. Then she kicked them aside so she wouldn't trip at a crucial moment. His knee between her legs forced her to widen her stance. He slipped inside to circle her clitoris.

Oh. My. God. She felt all slippery and warm and delicious, his cheek against hers wonderfully rough and manly. She was going to come even before he entered her. His lips dropped to her neck, nipped at her sensitive flesh, then stroked her beaded choker.

She wanted so badly to touch his bare flesh, to hold him in her hand, stroke him as he stroked her. Do it, do it. Her fingers trembled as she unbuckled his belt. His zipper rasped in the quiet, only slightly louder than his breath against her ear. Her heart stuttered, but before she put her hands on him, he slipped two fingers deep inside her and pumped, his thumb circling the nub of her clitoris.

"Wait. Oh God, not yet." She wanted him inside her when she came.

"Tell me what you need." He nipped her earlobe, while still driving her mad with his fingers.

She needed to feel him. In her hand. In her mouth. Inside her body. No one had ever asked her what she needed. "I'd like to touch you, Mr. Sloan." The formal slipped out, making her feel illicit and hot all at the same time. But if he called her Kirby now, she'd die.

"I'd like that very much, Miss Prescott." He slipped his fingers from between her legs, taking her hand in his. Together they delved into the front of his slacks. Crowding her back against the door, he rubbed her palm with hot, hard flesh. Then he let her go. His eyes glittered in reflected light, holding her gaze. She wrapped her hand around him one finger at a time. She squeezed. His nostrils widened slightly as he drew in a long breath, and his eyelids half-closed.

"Is that good?" *Is that the right way?*

"Fucking perfect," he answered on a long, slow out-breath.

Something blossomed inside her, heated her from the inside out. She boldly slid her thumb across his crown, finding a warm, slick bead of moisture. When his eyes drifted shut with what could only be pleasure, she slid her hand to his base, tightened, then relished the slow glide of his flesh all the way up.

He pressed hard to her belly, murmuring against her ear. "I haven't been this close to coming from a hand job in years." He traced the shell of her ear with his tongue. "But let's not waste it."

Her heart beat in time with his. His approval swept over her on a tide of heat, to her fingers, her toes, and deep inside her body. The words burst out of her. "I want you inside me, Mr. Sloan."

He pulled her hand away. "Then we need a—"

She cut him off, knowing what he wanted. Her face burned in the darkness, but she'd come too far to back down now. Ross wanted her. Badly. It was all that mattered. "In my purse."

Finding it buried beneath his jacket, she pulled out a condom package. He took it, stepped back, and ripped the foil. She'd never watched a man put on a condom, those things had always been done in the dark while she'd stared at the ceiling, embarrassed. Yet there was nothing embarrassing in the practiced movements of his hand on . . . oh my God, he was huge.

Then he was fully sheathed.

Pushing her up against the door, he lifted her skirt and pulled one leg up to his hip. She did the rest, raising her legs to wrap them around his waist. Her arms linked around his neck. With one powerful thrust, he drove into her. So easy, so smooth, and so big. She was *so* wet for him.

She cried out when he began to move inside her. She hadn't been with a man in such a long time, and never a man like Ross. The sensations. The heat building. His breath at her ear. It was all so much, too much.

The explosion started inside and spread through her like wildfire. She screamed, almost frantic as he pumped. Then he cried out, too. Not Kirby, something unintelligible, something that sounded like Kristin.

Finally she tumbled into oblivion.

THREE

It seemed like hours, though it couldn't have been more than minutes. They'd crumpled to the floor together, and he still throbbed lightly inside her. She wanted to keep him there forever, but . . . they were done. It was over.

Time for him to throw her out. Isn't that what men did after they were finished with their own satisfaction?

That sounded a little bitter. She wasn't, really she wasn't. She now had something very special to remember her thirtieth birthday by. She would have liked a little more, though, not a whole night, mind you, just . . . a tiny bit more.

She resisted the urge to wrap her arms around him, hug him close, even if only for a moment. Men didn't like that kind of demonstration, not from one-night stands. Not that she had any experience in one-night stands. Two lovers before Blake, she'd dated them for weeks before agreeing to sleep with them.

She pulled her head away from Ross's shoulder and rested against the door.

"Mmm, thank you," she whispered in her best Kirby-imitation of sultry, then wriggled away from him.

After disengaging her arms and legs, she got on her knees and sought her cotton panties—darn it, darn it, why not silk?—and her purse. Then she stood and stepped into the underwear.

Ross came to life, stood, and watched her. "What are you doing . . . um, Kirby?"

"I'm getting dressed." Though there wasn't much *to* getting dressed.

"Why?"

She slipped the panties into place, suddenly embarrassed beneath his steady gaze. She searched for her shoes that had somehow fallen off, probably while her legs had been up around his waist.

Oh God. What should she say? Kirby would know just how to handle the situation.

The words just started rushing out. "Well, it was wonderful and all." But way too fast.

She added, "It's late." Not that late.

Ross just looked at her.

"And it's a week night." How would she be able to look at him in the office tomorrow?

"So, thanks and all."

Kristin stopped. Kirby would never sound like this. She'd have pulled her man close, given him a sizzling kiss to keep him thinking of her, then said something like, "I'll call you." Or she'd have disappeared into the night without a word, just a smile.

During her rambling thoughts, he'd moved closer. Running his hand down her arm, he leaned in to kiss her neck and whispered, "You aren't thinking of leaving, are you?"

Yes, desperately, even while she desperately wanted to stay, mortification be damned. She managed to nod her head.

"But we haven't even started yet."

They'd written the beginning, middle, and end. Hadn't they? And men . . .

"Don't you have to wait . . . a while . . . or something?"

Jeez, how gauche. She was ignorant, unworldly, and not at all like Kirby.

She clutched her bag to her chest. Indecision and embarrassment colored her face.

She stared at a button on his shirt and looked so damn kissable with her hair in disarray, tumbling around her face and shoulders. Though not a virgin, she was still curiously shy and untried, so invitingly different from the Samanthas of the world. Just what he needed.

Oh no, he wasn't letting her go so easily. There were many things to show her. He'd only just whet his appetite.

As he nipped her earlobe, he put a hand at her waist and pulled her closer.

"Well now, I've got a few things in mind while I'm . . . recharging."

Not that he'd need much time. Things were already stirring, but he wanted to get rid of the damn condom.

He left the lights off as he led her through the living room to his bedroom. She didn't seem ready for lights yet. She was nervous like a kitten, a very sexy kitten. He watched her eyes widen as she took in the dominating force in his bedroom. He knew she was wondering how many women he'd had in that king-size bed.

Nowhere near the number she was probably thinking.

Instead, her next words surprised him. "Kristin's going to kill me for sleeping with her boss."

He debated his answer, then decided in favor of knowledge. Anything he could glean about the workings of her mind would help him woo her.

"Why?" he asked.

"Complications."

He ran his thumb down the inside of her palm, enjoying her involuntary shiver. "Does she have to know?"

He waited, trying not to hold his breath and not really knowing why her answer was so important.

"She'll know just by looking at me. We never could keep secrets from each other."

He dropped his voice. "What exactly do you think she's going to do about it?"

She was silent a moment. He hoped, wanted, needed her to tell him the truth. Though, for the life of him, he couldn't have said why it mattered so much.

She swallowed and closed her eyes. When she re-opened them, the irises had darkened from pale green to deep forest.

"I don't know what she'll do." She wet her lips. "Proba-bly feel uncomfortable."

He wanted her to feel anything but comfortable, wanted her to moan and writhe beneath him. He wanted her to come with his mouth on her. His cock throbbed, reminding him he hadn't removed the condom. He wondered if she'd still be in his bedroom when he came out of the bathroom. He couldn't risk leaving her alone.

"Come here."

He led her into the bathroom, flipped on the light so that he could see the rosy glow of his lovemaking on her skin. Her pupils disappeared to pinpoints against the brightness of the spot lighting. She turned, looking everywhere but at their reflection in the mirror.

Her embarrassment was still in full force. He couldn't let it get in the way. He had to do something about it.

His belt hung open. His pants, though buttoned, were unzipped. He tugged her hand, and her eyes fell to watch him. He undid the button, holding her gaze as he removed the condom, as he touched himself intimately. It was all so erotic. She pulled her lower lip between her teeth, then sucked in a breath.

Christ, he was a goner.

"Are you going to tell Kristin about watching me?"

She swallowed, shook her head slightly, but didn't shift her eyes. She stared at his cock, and it responded to her look.

"You're hard again," she whispered.

The way she looked at him, as if she wanted to gobble him up, would make any man hard.

"Are you going to tell your sister you took me in your mouth?"

Her shocked gaze shot to his. "I didn't."

"You will."

Her pupils dilated with her obvious arousal, but she didn't say anything.

"Are you to going tell her how you screamed when I went down on you on the bathroom counter?"

"But you didn't, and I didn't," she whispered, her cheeks turning that lovely shade of rosy embarrassment. Her tight nipples gave her desires away.

"Oh, but I will, and you will." He threw the condom in the trash and reached for her. "Which do you want first?"

Her breath came in fast little pants. "I . . ."

"Tell me what you want."

"I want to . . ." She rolled her lips together, took a deep breath, then started again. "I want to taste you, Mr. Sloan."

He'd swear she'd never said even that much before. The fact that she did so now, for him, pushed his excitement to unparalleled heights. "I like it when you talk dirty." Though he wanted her to get far more explicit. "So by all means, taste as much as you want."

He held her hand as she slowly went to her knees in front of him. His heart seemed to stop when she looked up at him. Her lips were wet and red and lush. Her cheeks glowed now with the flush of desire. Her eyes were incredibly green, incredibly innocent despite the fact that his cock twitched only inches from her luscious lips. Everything about her focused on him, on wanting him, on tasting him.

She opened her mouth and took him inside. He resisted closing his eyes in sheer, unbelievable ecstasy. He couldn't, wouldn't miss a moment of the sight of his cock in Miss Kristin Prescott's mouth.

She tested him, as if the taste of a man was new, as if the feel of a man in her mouth was something untried. He could have told her to suck harder, to take him deeper, faster, but with her unpracticed touch, she almost had him coming. He wanted to raise his face to the ceiling and howl. Instead, he took her head in his hands and held her right where he wanted her as he fed his cock into her mouth.

"Ah, God, don't stop, Kristin."

She stopped and sat back on her heels. Shit. What had he said? Christ, her name.

"I'm sorry."

"You called me Kristin." Her eyes were wide and stark.

"You look like her. I'm sorry."

She put a hand to the tile floor and pushed herself to her feet. "My name is Kirby."

"I know that." Now, tell her to confess now.

Real fear shone in her eyes, where a moment before had been desire. She backed up a step, stopped by the toilet seat.

Her glance fell to the mirror. She quickly averted her eyes. Her pulse fluttered at her throat. "Kristin wouldn't do anything like this, you know. She really wouldn't."

Oh yes, she would, but why the hell couldn't she admit it?

"Maybe she won't, but you will, won't you?"

She swallowed, licked her lips. He took her by the arms and pulled her to the counter, then lifted her to the white tile.

She exhaled sharply.

"You do want it, don't you?"

He almost shook her, needing her to admit how badly she wanted him. To admit she'd do all the things Miss Kristin Prescott had never done, but had wanted to. That she'd fantasized about doing them with him.

He slid his hands beneath her skirt, tested the elastic on her panties, then stopped.

"Take them off for me," he muttered, his mouth against her throat and that damnably erotic choker.

"I can't."

The huskiness of her voice said she would with a touch of encouragement.

He took both her hands in his and let her follow the line of her thigh, let her feel the heat of her own skin. She made a small sound, almost a whimper.

"Take them off for me," he said, this time looking straight in her wide green eyes.

Raising her hips, she slipped the scrap of white down her legs and let it fall to the floor.

"Do you want me to taste you?"

Her chin lifted as if she wanted to nod yes, but couldn't.

"Say it. Say, I want you to make me come with your mouth, Ross. Say my name."

Her breasts rose and fell. He placed his hand on her inner thigh, then let his fingers slip just inside her, touching her clitoris, teasing her.

"Say it," he urged. In a few seconds he'd be begging her to say it.

He spread her legs, moved between them, his finger still on her little button.

"Say it."

She leaned back on her hands, adjusting to give him better access.

"I want you to . . . Ross."

Then she moaned.

God, it was enough. He dropped to his knees and put his tongue to her sweet spot. She cried out his name as he sucked and licked and teased. He slipped two fingers inside her, moving them rhythmically in time with his tongue. She shifted and buried her fingers in his hair, then flooded his mouth with her sweetness, coming endlessly.

Moments later her shudders subsided. They both caught their breaths. Finally Kristin sat up and looked down at him, still crouched between her legs.

"That was . . . um, nice." She licked her lips, her eyes wide and innocent. "Now it's my turn to taste you again."

He knew he'd died and gone to heaven.

* * *

God. She was sitting on a cool tile counter with her legs spread and her dress hiked up to her waist. With the lights on.

And a man between her legs.

"Maybe we should go into the bedroom." So the tile floor didn't bruise her knees when she . . . did it.

Ross put his hands on her thighs and rose. "Works for me."

Placing both hands along the sides of her breasts, he helped her hop down. "The sooner, the better."

Her ankles wobbled as she touched the floor. She grabbed his arm for support. He was so . . . built. His firm muscles beneath her fingertips made her throb anew.

He took her hand, led her to the door, then switched on the bedroom lights.

"Why don't we leave the lights off?" She paused. "It's more romantic." And easier for her.

One corner of his mouth lifted in a smile. "I can't see you with the lights off."

She nuzzled his shoulder to hide her embarrassment. "Yes. But you'll still be able to feel . . . my mouth."

He turned, took her face in his hands, and held her so that she couldn't look away. "I want to watch my cock between your lips. I want you to look up at me while you're sucking me. I want to see you swallow every last drop of come."

Oh God. A rush of moisture coated her thighs. She'd been wet when he took her with his mouth. Now, his words drenched her. She swallowed her nervousness. She could do this. With the lights on. She wanted to.

She wanted to remember Ross's face as he watched her. She needed to know he liked it.

He shucked his trousers and briefs, then loosened his tie.

She stayed his hand. "Leave it on. It's sort of sexy, doing it with your tie still in place and your shirt buttoned."

"Miss Prescott, I do believe there's a wanton woman beneath that little red dress. I like it."

Kristin was beginning to believe she liked it, too. She'd done this before, taken a man in her mouth, though Blake made sure she realized she still hadn't done things right. With Ross, it was different. Everything felt new and special. Intimate and heavenly.

He sat on the bed, dragging her between his knees. His penis bobbed invitingly an inch from her lips.

"Wait."

She sprang to her feet. Ross made a grab for her but missed. She teetered on her heels, then crossed the bedroom carpet to her purse on the counter in the bathroom.

"I'm dying out here with you in there."

"Just a minute."

She uncapped her lipstick. A deep luscious red. Kirby's color. She applied the color heavily, hoping it would drive Ross crazy when her lips encircled his penis. She wanted to be perfect for him.

"Okay, I'm ready." She stopped with a hand on the doorjamb.

"Christ," he swore, his gaze riveted to the deep crimson of her lips.

His hand stroked his hardened shaft. Her mouth went dry. He was impossibly large, impossibly hard.

She wanted him in her mouth.

She crossed the carpet and sank to her knees between his legs. He held his massive tool out to her. Her lips closed around the tip.

"Put your tongue in it."

She'd do anything to please him. She grazed the small slit at the top of his penis as he directed, then closed her lips over the taut skin to suck just that small bit.

"Oh God, yes, just like that."

She reveled in his words. A tiny drop of semen seeped out. She lapped at it, then puckered and slid her lips completely over the head. Ross groaned. He pulled one of her hands from his thigh and wrapped her fingers around the base of his shaft.

"Squeeze it," he ordered in a harsh rasp.

She did.

"Yeah. Perfect." His hands fisted in her hair and urged her head down.

He touched the back of her throat. Her eyes watered, but she didn't stop. His groans pushed her on. Sliding up again, she followed with a stroke of her hand, tightening her fingers as she went.

His touch urged her to a faster pace. He pushed the hair back from her face, held it out of the way. She looked up to find his gaze on her red lips. On her between his legs. On his penis vanishing into her mouth. His lids were heavy, his brown eyes almost black.

"God, you look beautiful when you're doing that."

She felt beautiful. Not sordid. Not common. But sexy. Beautiful. Perfect.

She eased back and nipped the head of his penis, then slid down once more, using her teeth. Lightly grazing.

"Put a finger right there," he gasped, directing her to a spot just on the underside of his testicles.

She pressed. He jumped. Twining her hair around his fingers, he guided, lifting his hips to meet her. His shaft turned to steel. He uttered one guttural moan, then his semen gushed into her mouth.

She swallowed the salty fluid, still lightly stroking him with her lips and squeezing his penis with her fist. She tongued the small crevice at the tip because she knew he liked it. His body jerked.

"Jesus Christ."

He pulled her mouth away, then hauled her onto his lap, and fell back across the bed with her.

"Was it good?" Kirby would never have asked, but Kristin had to know. Had to hear him say she was perfect and banish the specter of Blake's criticisms forever.

"I can safely say I've never felt better in my life."

She smiled, snuggled against his side. This was wonderful.

He rolled on top of her, insinuating his leg between

hers. One hand skimmed her length down to her hemline.

"Now, let's take off that dress, Miss Prescott."

He eased a hand up her inner thigh to her curls, stroked her outer lips with a fingertip. Then he trailed his tongue around her ear. His breath whispered against her hair. Tingles spread through her belly.

"Because in a very short while, I'm going to fuck the hell out of you. Again." He laved her throat. "And again."

She shivered with his use of that dirty word, which was suddenly not so dirty but completely erotic.

"Promises, promises," she murmured, feeling bold and yes, very sexy.

"You should know, I always keep my promises."

Then he tugged her dress to her waist.

FOUR

Beneath the harsh fluorescent lights, Kristin stared at herself in the ladies' room mirror. She still couldn't believe the things she'd done with her boss last night.

The things she'd let him do, begged him to do. The things he made her scream for.

She'd never screamed with Blake. Then again, Blake hadn't told her over and over how exquisitely she used her mouth on him or how delicious she tasted on his tongue or how ideally her body fit his. She tried to count the number of times Ross had said she was perfect. With each word of praise, her fears diminished and her desire flew out of control. She'd hold it close to her heart that for one night Ross thought she was perfect.

Her cheeks were suddenly rosy red. If anyone came in here, they'd know for sure what she'd been doing last night. Because the glow on her face wasn't just mortification, it was razor burn, delicious, sensitive whisker burn from Ross Sloan's five o'clock shadow.

She had the same razor burn on her inner thighs. And elsewhere. She put her hands to her cheeks, trying to stop

the heat from spreading. How could she face him in—she
glanced at her watch—fifteen minutes?

She added extra foundation, hoping and praying it covered the evidence. Her very thoughts would give her away
if she wasn't careful.

"Kristin Prescott," she whispered to the reflection in the
mirror. "You're thirty years old. Get a grip. He thought you
were Kirby."

The moment he'd called her Kristin, she'd almost run.
But it was a mistake. He'd never have taken her to his
home if he'd known the truth.

Now, though, her one shining night was over. She'd
awakened in his bed at one in the morning and left him
sound asleep. The doorman had called her a cab, and she'd
hustled home. Once safely locked behind her door, she'd
wadded the panties and shoes inside the red dress and
stuffed them at the back of her closet.

In his bedroom she'd been the perfect lover. Now she'd
go back to being the perfect secretary. He'd never know the
difference.

She straightened her tailored jacket, adjusted her calf-
length skirt, pushed a few stray strands of hair back from
her face and went to face the lion.

He wasn't in yet. Her outer office door had still been
locked, his inner sanctum empty. Except for a hint of his
aftershave. Or was the scent just in her head? On her
clothes? On her body?

She became aware of phones beginning to ring outside
in the cubicle area, of voices, fingers on keyboards, and the
aroma of a fresh pot of coffee. They were mere background noise to the lingering smell of him and the images
it evoked in her mind.

Ross didn't appear until she'd already typed three letters into the computer, opened all the mail, sorted it, tossed
the trash, left him a stack on his desk, and relived every
single touch he'd gifted her with last night.

"Good morning, Mr. Sloan," she said in her usual
placid tone.

Her eyes met his as he strolled through her office to his. She'd never noticed how deliciously brown his eyes were, how penetrating, or the softness of his hair, a shade lighter than his eyes. She'd run her fingers through it last night, over and over, lost in the sensation.

"Good morning, Miss Prescott."

He stood in the open doorway a moment longer than usual, looking at her as if he suspected the images running through her brain.

"I trust you had a good evening."

She bid her cheeks not to flame. They didn't listen. "It was fine, thank you."

She didn't ask about his. She already knew.

After a slight hesitation, he disappeared into his office, closing the door behind him. A first. He always left it open so that he could call out to her for anything he needed.

Her breasts ached with the thought of the things she could do for him.

She turned back to her computer, but couldn't remember a thing she was supposed to do. She hadn't lost that file, had she?

Then she remembered his date. Picking up the phone, she punched his intercom.

"Yes, Miss Prescott?" The deep tone made her lightheaded.

"I forgot to tell you . . ." Her voice trailed off, realizing she never forgot to give him his messages. Stoically she went on. "Samantha Johnson called after you left last night. She had to cancel your . . . appointment with her. When I realized you'd left your cell phone behind, I left you a message at the . . ." Bar, hotel, what?

"Restaurant?" he prompted.

"Yes. I do hope you got it before waiting too long."

Silence, except for the rustle of papers, then she detected a faint drumming sound. Finally he said, "I got the message, Miss Prescott. Thank you for being so . . . diligent."

Had she imagined that slight delay? Yes, of course. No hidden meanings there, only her guilty conscience.

"You're welcome, Mr. Sloan."

She disconnected, thinking how odd it was to call him Mr. Sloan when she'd screamed his first name several times last night.

But she'd been Kirby then.

Her face heated again. She faced her computer just as his office door opened.

Looking up, she found him staring at her once more. Goose bumps rose on her arms despite the heat that suddenly seemed to invade her body.

"Miss Prescott, would you mind if I asked for your sister Kirby's phone number?"

He wanted to know Kirby's number!

Sometimes, she really thought there was something wrong with her. She wasn't smart enough. She wasn't beautiful enough. She wasn't sexy enough. She wasn't a skilled lover.

When Ross Sloan stood there on the other side of her desk, tall, commanding, utterly delectable in his crisp white shirt, blue suit and striped tie, and asked for her sister's number, Kristin *knew*, with absolute certainty, that there was something terribly wrong with her. She should have been jealous; she should have been angry. She most assuredly should have been hurt.

Instead, she saw him standing naked right in front of her, his penis long and hard, and she pictured herself on her knees, taking him into her mouth as she watched him through her lashes. She could even taste his saltiness and smell the soap still clinging to him.

"Miss Prescott, are you all right?"

He'd leaned down and peered into her face. That was why she'd smelled the soap, he was so close.

She blinked. "Yes, yes, I'm fine. My sister's number. That's a very odd request, Mr. Sloan." She spoke too quickly, but she couldn't stop. "But I won't ask. It's really none of my business."

"I met her last night—"

She held up a hand, cutting him off, shaking her head.

"No, no, I said I don't want to know when or how you met her. I mean, I know my sister . . . really, I don't need an explanation. I mean, *really,* I don't want to know."

He was still naked. She couldn't seem to see him with his clothes on. What on earth was wrong with her?

She rushed on. "I can't give you her number. I can, however, call her and tell her to call you. Will that work?"

She stopped, finally out of breath and out of words.

Ross looked as if he'd been run over by a freight train, a dazed look on his face. His eyes slightly unfocused.

"Mr. Sloan?"

He started. "Uh, yes, that would be fine. You call her."

He gave her one last searching look, then he succumbed to his beckoning office door, closing it a touch too loudly.

Kristin let out the breath she'd been holding.

He wanted to see *her* again.

She had no intention of calling her sister. Of course not. She had every intention of dressing like Kirby. She simply couldn't help herself, she was a woman obsessed. She'd show up in Ross's office . . . for lunch. No, that wouldn't work. There'd be too many people in the halls or the cubicles outside her office door. Besides, she wouldn't have time to run home for the change of personalities. After work. Yes, after work, that was better. Seven o'clock. Most of the office would be empty by then.

What was she thinking? Less than an hour ago she'd been standing in front of the bathroom mirror telling herself it was over. Seeing him again was impossible. It was stupid. What if he left early? It was absolutely, positively . . . inevitable. Nothing in this world or the next could have stopped her.

Last night Ross Sloan said she was perfect. She'd do anything to hear it again. Even pretend to be her sister for the second night in a row.

Okay, how to plan it all out. First, she would call time and temperature and pretend she was leaving a message for Kirby. In case he was listening. Goodness, how high-schoolish. Like saving your boyfriend's message on the recorder and listening to it over and over again. She wasn't thirty—she was regressing. But then, living in Kirby's shadow, she'd missed much of that boyfriend stuff in high school.

Half an hour later she braved Ross's office to tell him she had a dentist appointment that afternoon and would have to leave work early. Yes, she'd forgotten all about it, so sorry. He didn't look like he believed her because she never forgot anything.

Well, well, well. Wasn't that all very interesting. Kristin would have her "sister" call him. She had a dentist appointment she'd forgotten. She was quitting early yet she'd rushed out of the office at noon, cell phone in her hand. Kristin always worked through lunch if she had a doctor, dentist, or any other kind of appointment that took her away from her work. She was an exemplary employee. Even down to calling her boss at the hotel bar to tell him his date had canceled.

His little Miss Prescott had known exactly where he'd be last evening. Meeting her "sister" was absolutely no coincidence. She'd dressed for him. She'd come to the bar for him.

Ross rubbed his hands together, anticipating whatever plan was running through her efficient brain right now.

The street was crowded and noisy, and Kristin couldn't hear a thing. She crossed the road and entered the lobby of the Ambassador Hotel. Scene of the crime. She felt . . . odd, shivery, and excited.

Hiding behind a tall, leafy potted plant, Kristin plunked down in a lobby chair and punched her boss's number into her cell phone.

He should be out to lunch. She'd just leave him a sweet little Kirby-type message.

"Ross Sloan here."

Uh-oh. "Hi."

"Miss Prescott?"

She found her Kirby voice. "Miss Kristin Prescott or Miss Kirby Prescott?"

A slight exhalation. A hesitation. "Ah, Kirby. So glad you decided to call."

She could almost see him in his chair. His voice sounded huskier than normal. Was he thinking about . . . sex?

Mmmm, just thinking about their night together made her . . . squishy.

"As I recollect, Ross, you issued the distress call." There was such power in being on the other end of a phone. She could say *anything* without a single consequence. It was liberating.

"Distress?" He paused, letting the word hang in the air between them. "I was more than distressed this morning when I woke to find you gone."

She closed her eyes, hoped nobody would hear her, and let Kirby take over completely. It was so easy without having to look Ross in the eye. "I like to wake up in my own bed."

"What time did you leave?"

She crossed her legs and relaxed into the cushy chair. "Early enough to get a nice rest after I got home." She stretched out a leg, pointed the toe of her shoe. "And I slept so well after . . ."

"After fucking me all night?"

The word shot heat down between her legs. Dirty words. A few days ago the crudeness of it might have offended her. Today . . . well, goodness, today, she wanted to use it herself, test it, feel it on her tongue. Hear the effect it would have on him.

"Are you trying to shock me, Ross?"

"No. Just reminding you how good it was."

A little shiver ran down her arms. Her fingers tingled. The hotel lobby was now crowded with lunch-goers hitting the restaurant.

She lowered her voice. "Are you looking for validation of your sexual prowess?"

He laughed softly. "I got my validation every time you screamed as you came. Want me to tell you how many times that was?"

Oh my. A flush rose on her face. She might burn up at this rate.

"I remember exactly how many times it was, Ross. Which is why I thought I needed my rest." She paused. "I also thought you might need your rest." Time to take control of the conversation. "Why'd you ask Kristin to have me call you?"

"I want to see you again."

She fiddled with the material at her throat, a ridiculous Peter Pan collar like a little girl or a schoolmarm. The top button slipped loose beneath her fingers.

"See me? You mean for dinner. Or . . . for more?"

"Dinner. *And* more." His voice was lower, throaty.

She imagined him leaning on his desk, the receiver close to his sexy lips. She imagined those lips on her.

Another button slipped its mooring beneath her restless fingers. "Perhaps you could be a little more . . . specific."

"Ah, so you like phone sex."

She'd never had phone sex. So many things she'd been afraid to try. She suddenly needed to try everything. Courage came with the fact that he couldn't see her. She spoke before she lost the nerve. "Have phone sex with me."

He sucked in a breath. "Where are you right now?"

Should she tell him? What would he think? "In a hotel lobby."

He didn't even ask for an explanation. "Are there a lot of people around?"

A few milling about, none terribly close, no one sitting or standing right by. "I can talk without being overheard."

"Oh, my sweet Miss Prescott, I know you can talk. I can hear. I just want to know if you'll be able to touch yourself."

Her hand froze, and she realized her fingers had been

absently stroking the tender skin of her throat, sliding down between the unbuttoned lapels of her blouse. "Touch myself?"

"That's what phone sex is all about, Miss Prescott. I tell you where I want to touch you, and you pretend your hand is mine."

Oh, oh, oh, goodness gracious. She couldn't catch a breath. "You mean . . ."

"Yes, I mean I tell you how I want to take your nipple in my mouth and suck until you moan, and—"

"And I'm supposed to put my hand right there?" Her voice rose a note, though, thank goodness, she managed not to squeak.

She was in a crowded hotel lobby. Anyone could see. Still, there was nothing wrong with just talking about it.

"Then I tell you how I'm sliding your panties down your legs. Are you wearing panties?"

Oh, she couldn't breathe at all. There was a terrible rush of wet warmth between her legs. She squeezed them together, but the sensation only increased. She was so hot, flushed. A man over by the elevator was staring at her.

"No," she uttered the lie, "no panties." She hoped that leering man couldn't read lips.

Ross groaned. "You really do drive me crazy."

Ditto. Crazy enough to actually voice what she was thinking. "So, what are you going to do since I'm not wearing panties?"

Heavens. She was really getting into this new little game. She wanted to know, had to know. Would die if she didn't know. Right. This. Minute.

FIVE

He'd created a monster. A beautiful, sexy, desirable monster.

Or maybe she'd created him.

Ross had always been highly sexed, yet somehow Kristin's innocence pushed him to another level. Talking dirty had never really been part of his repertoire, but the excitement in her breath, the anticipation in her voice, her wonder of new things heightened his own intensity. No other woman made him hard with just the thought of her sitting in a hotel lobby without her panties on. He didn't even care that she most likely wasn't telling the truth.

Talking dirty with his Miss Prescott made his cock rock hard.

The phone rang again. He jerked, hoping, praying it was her, even though she'd only just hung up. He'd love to hear her beg right about now. Waiting until tonight just might kill him.

"Ross Sloan here."

"Ross, it's me."

Me? Not the "me" he was waiting for.

He paused too long.

The disgruntled feminine voice continued. "Samantha."

Samantha who? Yeah, yeah, he knew.

"Oh, hi."

"I'm sorry about last night. I hope you got my message." She purred like a cat, something that once had intrigued him.

"Not to worry. I got it." Oh, he got it all right. Thank God she'd canceled at the last minute.

"You didn't wait long?"

"No. Miss Prescott is very efficient. She didn't keep me waiting long." Nope, only until he'd gotten her inside the door of his apartment.

"Good. Can I make it up to you tonight?"

"Sorry, not tonight."

"How about tomorrow then?"

Friday night. No, he had plans, big plans.

"Sorry, that won't work either. I'm afraid I'm busy."

Busy tonight, tomorrow night, busy for the rest of his friggin' life.

Christ. The rest of his life? Where the hell had that come from?

"Ross, do we need to talk?"

"About what?"

"Our relationship."

Relationship? He enjoyed her company, and he'd enjoyed sex with her. What they had between them was friendship and a mutual respect. Perhaps the subtle change in her attitude was the essence of his recent discontent. She talked a good line, agreed sex was sex, that was all she wanted, *et cetera, et cetera*. Yet, with a word here, a look there, an unnecessary touch at an inappropriate moment . . . it was becoming obvious she wanted far more than she'd let on.

"Samantha, I think it's time—"

She cut him off. "I have to admit, Ross, that I'm not sensing the enthusiasm I'm looking for."

"You're right, Samantha." She'd said she was an up-front woman. Beating around the bush, so to speak, wasn't a requirement with her. Time to put those words to the test. "I had time to think about it last night, and I do believe we both need to find more . . . enthusiasm elsewhere. With other people. Don't you agree?"

"It's that little secretary, isn't it?"

Too late, he realized his error in talking about "other people."

"Secretary?"

"The little twit who wouldn't give me your cell number last night."

"Oh." The lovely Miss Prescott, the delectable Miss Prescott. He wondered when he'd become such a bastard, thinking about the new while he was offing the old with so little emotion. "There isn't anyone else, Samantha. I'm just . . ."

Tired. Of hard-edged women like Samantha. He wanted soft curves like Kristin.

"You're a real prick, you know."

"I didn't realize we'd progressed to the point where I could make you feel that way."

He'd ignored her hints. If that made him a prick, then he was definitely a prick. He should have nipped it in the bud.

"You're fucking her, aren't you? That's why she wouldn't give me your number."

"Hey, hold on a minute. Do not talk like that. She has explicit instructions not to give out the number."

"I didn't have it with me."

"And she doesn't know you from Adam."

He closed his eyes the moment the words were out. Another big mistake.

"You bastard. You fuck. I don't need you anyway. I can find a CEO, you know."

The phone went dead. He held the receiver out, staring at it, the dial tone excruciatingly loud in the quiet office.

She was right. He was a stupid bastard. For believing her when she said she only wanted sex, no commitment, just good, hot sex when they both needed it. And for hurting her in the process. How could a woman like Samantha Johnson not know the score? Especially when *she'd* written the rules.

What about Kristin? Beautiful and delectable, but a shy innocent who just might be in over her head in the sex game. What the hell was he doing playing with Kristin Prescott at all?

Okay, so he was a bastard. Ross knew the minute he saw Kristin that he simply wasn't capable of turning back the clock twenty-four hours.

Actually, he'd known it subconsciously that morning, when he'd awakened to an empty bed with an uncomfortably empty feeling in his gut that no amount of food or coffee seemed to fill.

He stood to one side of his desk and stared out his open door as she came in from lunch. She didn't see him, merely went to her desk, and stuck her purse in the drawer. Her hair, long and luscious, was pulled back in the usual binding, a pretty gold clip that fastened everything away from her face, revealing her kissable neck and delicious earlobes. Her beige skirt covered her knees. Her full blouse, buttoned to the throat and covered with a blazer, hid her breasts. Her lips shimmered with the lightest shade of pink, and her cheeks glowed with a dusting of blush. She wasn't overdone, but any man could see there wasn't a plain thing about her.

He had to have her.

On the phone, she'd asked when "Kristin" usually left for the day. When he'd told her, "Kirby" said she'd come by his office at seven, a good hour or so after Kristin's quitting time.

Of course, now there was the dentist appointment Kristin had.

She had some sort of plan. For him. He had no choice but to find out what it was. He'd go freaking mad if he didn't. His thoughts smacked of obsession, but he didn't care.

She was the best damn . . . what? Not lay, she wasn't that. Definitely not a fuck. God, no.

She was so much more. What they had done was so much more. Not sex, not fooling around. None of those flip terms he could apply to what he'd done with Samantha. He simply couldn't categorize it. Except that he knew he wanted more of it, more of *her*.

What the hell would the employee handbook say about his increasingly obsessive thoughts? The way his hands, mind, and body kept wandering back to her no matter what he was doing?

Kristin sat down at her desk and flicked on the monitor. Over the top of it, she noticed him watching her, just a brief meeting of the eyes. A flush of color swept over her cheeks, and he knew she was thinking about the things he'd said to her over the phone not fifteen minutes ago, the things she'd said to him.

Most definitely, she was thinking about the way he'd touched her last night. Oh yes, she *was* thinking about that.

"Did you have a good lunch, Miss Prescott?" he called out, moving to the door of his office.

"Very good, thank you, Mr. Sloan."

He'd never noticed the way her voice seemed to strike a chord deep inside him.

He cleared his throat. "The lease agreement for the new servers has to be signed today. Did Calhoun do the ROI?"

"It's all on your desk."

"I can't find it."

"It's in the blue folder marked Signatures Required."

"Are you sure? Maybe you need to show me exactly where you put it, because I don't see it."

She pursed her pretty lips and rose. Her cheeks flooded with even more color. She didn't meet his eyes, and he didn't move from the doorway, merely turned to the side.

As she passed by him, her arm brushed his chest, her perfume drifted around him, and her nipples turned to hard little points. He ached to touch them. Instead, he followed her to the desk where she leaned over, shuffling folders and papers around. She had an extremely nice backside. And those calves. He stood back to watch the play of her bottom beneath the material of her skirt.

She turned, blue folder in her hand, and caught him staring at her tight little ass.

He'd never been caught before.

His gaze rose slowly to her face, easing over her breasts, her throat, and everything unmentionable along the way.

Kristin was hot, oh so hot. Her skin felt as if it was on fire. Was he thinking how much she looked like Kirby? Was he thinking about Kirby's panties, or rather, the lack of them? She was well aware that by looking at her, he could imagine Kirby.

She had a folder in her hand, a blue folder, and she honestly couldn't remember why.

"Oh. Contracts. Signatures. They're all in here."

Three steps closed the distance between them. With a murmured thank you, he took the folder, but stayed so close she was sure she couldn't take a breath without her nipples rubbing his chest.

Ohmygod, he was going to kiss her. He was thinking Kirby and was about to kiss *her*.

I'm not my sister, I'm not my sister, went the refrain in her mind, even as she leaned into him and her eyelids drifted down.

"I know you're not your sister."

Darn. She must have voiced the thought aloud. She covered her confusion with a stern voice. "You're standing too close."

She placed her hand on the folder he held against his chest and pushed. Only to end up pinning herself against the desk when he moved forward instead of back. She was trapped. Also breathless and incredibly warm and wet between her legs. She shouldn't have touched him.

"What did she tell you about me, Kristin?"

Thank the Lord for small things. He was on a fishing expedition, that was all. A mixture of relief, and unaccountable disappointment, weakened her knees.

Then she realized he'd called her Kristin. Mr. Sloan never called her Kristin. He *always* called her Miss Prescott. What exactly did he want?

Embarrassment threatened to sear her face. So did need. She wanted him to touch her so badly, her fingers trembled against the folder still plastered to his chest.

"She didn't tell me anything," she whispered. "I didn't ask. It isn't my business."

"Does it make you feel uncomfortable?"

She swallowed. Yes, she was intensely uncomfortable. Mostly because she wanted to throw herself at him right here and now. Forget tonight. She wanted him *now*.

"What's wrong, Kristin? Your face is flushed and your pupils are dilated."

Add that she was all hot and bothered, wet between the legs, and her nipples were hard and aching against her blouse, he would have summed up how she felt. God, if he stopped looking at her face, he'd surely notice her other reactions.

She snatched the folder and held it to her own chest, covering the evidence. "Mr. Sloan—"

She got no further before he cut her off. "Don't you like me dating your sister?"

Dating? They weren't dating. They were . . . having sex. And she didn't want to talk about Kirby. She didn't want to have to come to work and pretend like this. She wanted what happened between them outside the office to remain that way, completely outside the secretary-boss relationship. Completely safe.

But, God forbid, she also wanted him to know exactly who he was making love to.

How could she control this feeling, whatever on earth it was, if he kept talking about it and making her all mixed up and crazy?

Kristin blew out a deliberately delicate breath of air,

then pursed her lips. "Actually, Mr. Sloan, it does make me uncomfortable. This is a business situation, and I feel distinctly uncomfortable bringing anything personal into it. So, if you want to know what my sister thinks about . . ."

The size of his penis. The level of his skill. The duration of his stamina. How good it felt to fall asleep in his bed, in his arms. To wake up to the soft rhythm of his breathing.

"Whatever it is you want to know," she said, gritting her teeth against the desire to beg him to make love to her right there on the desk, "you'll have to ask her."

End of discussion.

She dropped the folder on his desk, and this time the immovable object moved when she shoved. She beat a hasty retreat to her desk and kept one eye on the clock, counting the hours, minutes, and seconds until she could leave for her bogus dentist appointment. Then she'd have hours to practice. Hours to turn herself physically and mentally in a hot, sexy, confident woman Ross couldn't resist.

Dammit, he should have kissed her, should have backed her right up against his desk and kissed her for all he was worth.

He'd practically out-and-out told her he knew she wasn't her sister, but she'd chosen to misinterpret. Why hadn't he pushed?

Because he wanted to get laid tonight?

Or because he wanted Kristin to trust him with the truth?

The wayward thought struck him in his mid-section. What the hell did it matter anyway whether she made love to him as Kirby or Kristin? She'd come to life in his arms. She was doing the discovery thing. Women did it at all different stages of their life. Kristin Prescott just happened to pick now, and, thank God, happened to pick him. So what the hell did it matter?

The truth hit. He winced. The longer the game continued, the harder it would be for him to pretend he was the only man who could teach her what she wanted to learn. The thought of another man being the one to teach her anything drove him crazy.

She'd stuck her head in to say goodbye almost three hours ago. He'd been sitting in his chair ever since.

People had popped in and out of his office with questions, comments, bullshit, and he couldn't remember if any of it had been of importance.

It was almost seven now. The main office had quieted. Though if he listened carefully, he could still hear the telltale click of a few keyboards. He wondered if Kristin was afraid of being caught in her sister costume. Or perhaps that was part of the excitement.

There was a light tap on his doorjamb, and he realized he'd been so lost in thought he hadn't seen, or heard, her approach.

Christ. His heartbeat accelerated. She provided a vision that literally punched him in the solar plexus.

She wore a long olive-colored dress with a high Chinese collar. It should have been circumspect, but she'd left the lower buttons undone. All the lower buttons, from her calves right up to her crotch. When she moved, the lacy edge of her panties peaked out.

"Hello, Ross."

She'd changed her walk. It was a soft, sexy sway that drew his gaze to her hips, then back again to the glimpse of white panty.

He couldn't say a thing. It was as if his tongue were glued to the roof of his mouth.

"Aren't you going to say hello?" She almost purred.

No, he was going to throw her on the desk and do what he'd thought about doing all afternoon.

"Come here."

Ah yes, he could manage that much dialogue.

A smile crossed her face. A sexy, sure smile. She glided across the carpet, then ran a finger along the edge of his desk. This was the woman who asked him to have phone sex with her in a crowded hotel lobby. Pretending to be her sister somehow allowed her to do things she'd probably only dreamed of. Last night she'd been hesitant. Tonight she'd ratcheted up the confidence level.

He wanted her exactly like this.

The couch. He wanted her on that hot leather. No, he wanted her on her knees on the carpet in front of him, sucking him off.

A raging hard-on pressed against his zipper.

"Now, what's that, Ross?"

He caught her staring at the obvious bulge. Her seductive little smile crooked at the corner.

"Is that Mr. Happy happy to see me?"

He almost laughed, but he didn't want to scare away her control over the situation with a single wrong gesture.

"Mr. Happy is very happy to see you. Why don't you come here and take him out to play?"

She laughed and took a step closer.

"You're a very funny man, you know that?"

"I'm a very horny man. Wanna do something about it?" He somehow managed to act nonchalantly.

Then, she did the unthinkable. She hitched her skirt and climbed aboard his lap. His brain shut down all rational thought and reverted to instinct. He put his hands on her hips and pulled her down, grinding his cock against her. The on-top position suited her so damn well.

"He's getting happier all the time, isn't he?" She put her hands on his shoulders and let him guide.

"You're making me insane."

He closed his eyes, sliding his hands through the slit in her skirt, kneading her thighs.

She leaned down, rubbed her lips against his. "Ross, don't you want to know if I locked the door?"

"I don't give a damn if you did or you didn't." Closed was good enough.

He tugged at her panties. Her shoes dropped to the floor. Thank God, she didn't believe in nylons. At least not for tonight. He might go up in smoke before he ever got inside her.

She wriggled this way, then that, and the white confection masquerading as a pair of panties drifted to the carpet. He delved his fingers inside her. She was wet, hot.

"God, you're so ready."

Her eyes, the color deepened to a forest green, were dilated to the max. "I'm always ready."

Her hand pressed intimately against his cock and massaged him through the material of his pants. Then she tugged at his zipper and pulled him out, her palm wrapping around him.

"Do you want to do me, Mr. Sloan?"

"God, yes."

She raised her other hand. In it was a condom packet which now fell onto his lap. She'd thought of everything. He looked up, met her soft green gaze. Then she swallowed, rubbed her lips together, and smiled softly. Despite her seductive actions, her confidence was fragile. He could crush her with one wrong word or negative action.

"Put me out of my misery," he whispered.

She squeezed. His balls ached. She scooted back to sit on his knees, her cute butt resting against his desk.

"Put it on," she cooed.

He didn't have to be asked a second time. He ripped the package with his teeth and had the rubber on in two seconds flat. Grabbing her hips, he hauled her forward. She pulled her dress out of the way.

He was so hard, he couldn't think, only act. He nudged at her opening. She spread her legs wider over his lap, holding herself just out of his reach, her knees hitting the arms of the chair.

"Am I perfect, Ross?"

"Christ, yes."

Hot, slippery, exciting, and a goddamn tease. He wanted her badly, but even worse, he wanted to play her game through to the end.

Sighing, she took him in a fraction of an inch at a time. Not enough, nowhere near enough, but he refrained from taking control.

"Does that feel good, Ross?"

"You know damn well it does."

He took a deep breath, trying to clear his head, trying to keep the pending orgasm in check. She gave him another inch of her wetness.

"Have you ever wanted a woman so badly you did her right in your office?"

"No. This is a first."

The first woman he'd ever given the upper hand to. He closed his eyes, relished her heat. She was more than worth it. In that moment, he'd admit to anything she wanted. Kristin Prescott on top was a thing of beauty he'd never tire of.

Finally she took him fully and then stopped, resting with her hands on his shoulders. He pulsed inside her. If she moved, he'd come, he was sure.

"Now what?" she sighed.

"Don't you know?"

He'd barely gotten the words out when she squirmed in his lap, not stroking him, but turning him into a raging lunatic just the same.

She drew a finger down the center of his chest. "Why don't *you* tell *me*."

"Touch yourself for me."

Her green eyes widened. He'd caught her off guard, turned the tables on her. He didn't want to grind her down, he simply wanted more of her. All of her.

"Touch myself where?"

He flicked a thumb across her clitoris. She gasped and arched, her eyes closing briefly.

"Here. Just like you said you did over the phone."

She drew in a breath, blinked, then let it out slowly. "Don't you want to do it for me?" She tried to seduce him with a sultry little hum.

"I want to watch you."

He wanted to watch her walls tumble down, her Kirby disguise fall away. He didn't think his Miss Prescott could pleasure herself for him, not yet. His balls ached with the idea of it while his head throbbed with the need to hear the truth.

She moved, rose a scant few inches, then clenched around him. He squeezed his eyes shut to keep from coming.

"*You* touch *me*," she breathed.

His hands went to her hips trying to still her, but instead they set a rhythm designed to drive them both over the edge.

"Tell me what you really want, Ross. Right now, right this minute."

He stopped fighting, just went with a male's instinct and put his thumb to her hot little button as he buried himself inside her.

"Fuck me, Miss Prescott."

That's exactly what she did. Throwing her head back and using his shoulders for leverage, she fucked him faster, harder, better than any woman he'd ever known. He feasted on the long column of her throat, letting her set the pace, create the rhythm, and drive him higher, then finally over the ever-loving, goddamn precipice.

As he came, his lips against her throat, he felt the scream she didn't give voice to.

He wanted the seductress she was now, but he wanted the prim, proper, efficient Miss Prescott just as badly, so badly it scared him.

He wanted both.

The most frightening thought of all was that what they'd done was not just fucking.

Christ, it might actually be making love.

SIX

After depositing his suit jacket over the back of a dining room chair, Ross led the way into his bedroom. He flipped on the light, then crossed to his king-size bed and sat down.

Kristin stood paralyzed halfway between the door and that massive bed, very much aware of the mirrored closet doors.

She felt as if she couldn't hide from him in this room.

Ross leaned forward, a hand dropping to the edge of the bed on either side.

"What's the matter?" he asked.

"Nothing." Everything.

She was suddenly impossibly shy. Which seemed impossibly stupid after what she'd done with him in his office. What she'd enjoyed doing to him. She'd been the seducer, and she'd relished the power. She couldn't say where on earth that level of confidence had come from. All that practice in her apartment while she was getting dressed? Whatever, the moment she'd entered his office, she'd given her Kirby role all she had. On the drive over, no, before, when he'd asked her to touch herself, her insecurities popped up their ugly little heads. Some men liked to watch. The idea even excited her, but some unexplainable *thing* inside her balked. She was going to ruin everything if she didn't stop giving in to these bouts of doubt.

So stop.

She repeated, more for her own benefit than his, "Absolutely nothing's wrong. Ross."

He reached down to unlace his shoes and remove them, then he stretched out on the thick wine-colored bedspread, propping himself on his elbows.

"Then take off your clothes for me."

"What?" Her breath froze in her lungs.

He smiled wolfishly. "Do a striptease. For me."

Get naked while he watched? Heat rose to her cheeks.

"Please, Kirby."

He wouldn't have had to beg Kirby. She would have done it without asking, with just a look from him. Kristin's stomach flip-flopped. "What about you?"

"Ladies first."

She didn't know how to do a striptease. And she didn't have much to strip off anyway, just the dress, bra, and panties. Kirby would know how to remove her clothes in just the right way to make him wild.

Kristin put her fingers to the first button of her dress.

How would Kirby do it?

Forget the button. Looking straight at him, she smoothed her hands over her breasts, plumped them for him. She continued the slow descent over her abdomen, then bent slightly to reach the inside of her knee. Trailing her fingers up her thigh, through the slit of her dress, she gently pushed aside the placket, exposing herself inch by inch.

Ross shifted on the bed. His gaze seemed dark and unfathomable, tracking the leisurely progress of her hand as she neared her mound.

"That's good, Miss Prescott. Makes me hot." He palmed his crotch. "And so fucking hard."

Oh. Ooh. That word. She was doing things right.

Turning just enough to hide a complete view, she reached inside the slit of her dress. Lace tickled the tips of her fingers.

He loosened his tie.

Bracing a hand on her thigh, keeping one side of the dress closed, she slipped a finger beneath the elastic and pulled. The panty gave, inching down one cheek, then freed itself from the other. A scrap of white appeared against her thigh.

She shimmied, and her panties fell to her high heels. Without allowing Ross even a glimpse of the curls at her apex.

"Christ," he hissed, "you are a perfect little tease."

Perfect. She did so love that word. Stepping out of the lace confection, she bent to retrieve them in a dainty dip.

Ross made a sound. There was nothing unfathomable about his expression now. His nostrils flared, his breath quickened, and his gaze turned hot.

An answering heat burgeoned between her thighs.

"Give them to me."

He held out a hand, she tossed, and he caught the white lace in his big fist. He took them to his nose and inhaled.

"More." His eyes blazed.

She returned to the buttons of her high collar, loosening three, to just below the center clasp of her bra.

Ross sat up, her panties clenched in his hand.

Moisture pooled between her legs, a single drop slid down her thigh. Goodness, it was hard to breathe.

She parted her lapels to reveal sheer lace cupping her breasts, her pink aureoles plainly visible. Unsnapping the clasp, she pushed the lace edges aside until her fingers touched her aching nipples.

The peaks hardened.

Ross's throat worked to swallow. "Miss Prescott, you truly amaze me." He reached down to adjust his bulge, then kept his hand there.

She traced a nipple, glided across the tip, then pinched lightly. Fire shot to her clitoris.

She teased herself as well as Ross.

Her fingers trailed down to the next button. It fell open almost on its own.

Another, then another, until only two buttons held her dress together, one below and one above her mound.

She liked the idea of peekaboo. Ross seemed to like it, too, his slacks a veritable tent over his erection. Her performance had riveted and rendered him speechless.

She turned on her heel, thinking to delay and tantalize by giving him her back.

She'd forgotten the mirror. Kristin almost stumbled on her too-high heels.

God. She came face-to-face with herself in the mirror. Her cheeks flushed. Pink-tinged skin visible through the open dress. Her nipples flirted with the lace bra. Her lips plumped, and her eyes darkened to a deep green. Mussed hair crowned her head. She looked wanton.

She looked sexy.

"Don't stop now." Ross's voice cracked on the last word.

She stepped to the right so that she could see him. So that he could see her, both from the front and the back.

Oh my God, she wanted him to take her now, just like this. Wanted him to lift her dress and enter her from behind. With her hands braced against the mirror, reflected lips an inch from her real lips.

What on earth was happening to her? His eyes on her made her *feel* sexy. Powerful. She'd never felt like this in her life. Gorgeous and sexy enough to bring a powerful man to his knees with desire for her.

Ross made a sound, his face distorted.

"Take it off," he rasped.

Parting her feet to gain a steady stance, she watched her own hands flick first one button, then the last. Her fingers scraped the material from her shoulders, pulling the bra with it.

The dress slipped down her body to land at her feet.

"Christ, you're beautiful."

In that moment, she believed him.

Before she knew it, his hands were on her hips and his mouth on the flushed skin of her neck. He pulled her back against his hips, then lifted his gaze to study her in the mirror. His hot glance caressed her body.

She pushed her bottom against his erection. Rotated. So hard, so hot. Another drop of moisture breached her nether lips, creamed her inner thigh. New emotions blossomed inside her. The desire for power. The heady sensation of being wanted.

"I want you now, just like this. I want you to watch while I fuck you."

Watch?

Oh my God. That was just a fantasy. It didn't, however, have to remain so.

She tugged her lip between her teeth, bit down hard. She was vulnerable without her clothes. His trousers and shirt chafed against her back and bottom.

She wanted him inside her so badly she didn't care. She wanted to expose herself to him. To the mirror. To herself. This may be her only chance. For this one glorious moment, she wanted to be all the sexy things she'd dreamed of. She wanted to put herself out there. Explore. Act. Be bold. Step off the cliff and soar like a bird. No regrets.

He put his hand between her legs, and she thought her knees would buckle.

She gave herself up to him and to her desires. For tonight, she'd do anything he asked.

She was naked, her legs spread. His hand nestled between her pussy lips. Her juices gushed against his fingers. He wrapped an arm around her, just below her breasts.

He wondered if she'd struggle. She didn't.

"You're so wet, baby."

Her limbs trembled as his touch glided over her clitoris. She lay her head back against his shoulder and sighed. He tongued her ear, holding her fast against him as she squirmed. So wet and creamy, her clit burgeoning, begging for a firm stroke.

"You like that?"

Her answer was a raised arm trapping his lips against her neck. Her breast lifted with the action. Her nipple danced.

He'd never seen a more beautiful sight in his life. Her russet-colored hair against his white shirt. His dark hand against her reddish curls. Her pretty pink lips making love to his fingers as his touch made love to her.

"Put your finger where mine is," he growled against her ear.

"I like yours better."

"Please."

She rubbed her tush against his aching cock.

"Harder," she commanded. "Faster."

But she didn't gratify him with the touch of her fingers pleasuring herself.

He'd make do with what he could get. He stroked her. Harder. Faster. The way she wanted. Then he slipped a finger inside. Her body clamped around it. Her soft breathy moan gripped something vital inside him.

He had to have her. Now. It didn't matter that he'd had her only an hour ago. He needed her again.

They were only steps from his bureau. He moved her, placed her hands, molded her fingers to the wooden edge. He didn't remove his pants, just unfastened the belt and the zipper. He sheathed his cock in a condom.

The height of her heels required him to bend only a couple of inches. He parted her legs, then pushed at the small of her back.

She opened to him. God, if he didn't get inside her right now.

He plunged into her tight embrace. She threw her head back and cried out. Her hair tumbled down her back. Incessant moans escaped her lips.

He looked toward the mirror, savoring the sight of his hips forged to her backside.

He eased out until only the tip of his cock remained inside her, then slowly pulled her hips once more to his. He slid into her delicate folds.

The sight of his cock penetrating her turned him inside out. He'd staked his claim, marked her his. Reaching around to imprison a breast, he flicked her nipple.

She gasped, but her eyes remained closed.

He withdrew once more, then reached and grasped her chin.

"Watch us."

"I—" She stopped, and if anything, squeezed her eyes even more tightly shut.

He wanted them open. He wanted her to know exactly who was inside her. He wanted to relish her expression, watch her come apart. He wanted to call her Kristin.

He tugged her chin back to meet him, ravished her lips with his tongue. He thrust his cock deep inside her, using his other hand to finger her clit. She writhed against him and took him deeper still.

"Look at us," he rasped urgently.

He needed her to acknowledge what they were doing.

He pulled out, testing his strength when all he wanted was to ram himself home.

She opened her eyes. Her mirrored gaze dropped to the sight of his cock an inch from her opening, then back up to his face. "Why did you stop?"

He couldn't explain. "Reach back and put me inside you."

She hesitated, facing the wall over the bureau after a glance at their reflection.

He swiped a finger across her clitoris. A shudder worked its way through her body.

"Take me," he murmured into her hair, resting his cheek against the back of her head.

She braced herself with one hand and reached between her legs with the other to place his cock at her center. She looked at their reflection.

"Put it inside."

Holding him, she eased back. His crown breached her. He gritted his teeth and controlled the urge to explode from the mere touch of her hand on his fully roused cock.

"God, you feel sweet," he groaned.

Watching in the mirror, he wrapped his fist around hers at the base of his cock, then slid in deeper. Her eyes, also fixed on the sight, widened. She'd been wet before, but something seemed to let loose inside her, and even more sweet cream enveloped him.

"Does that feel good?" he whispered as he nibbled her spine.

"Oh, please."

She jerked, then suddenly slammed back against him. Both hands once again clenched the dresser as she found her rhythm. She came apart within the shelter of his arms. She slammed against him, her moans keeping pace with her frenetic movements.

Her wildness undid him. When she screamed her completion, he tumbled after her, pumping frantically until the last of his spunk filled and threatened to overflow the condom.

He wrapped his arms around her tightly, one hand reaching up to caress her chin. At some point she'd closed her eyes, lost to the bliss.

His body hunched over hers. Her skin was the color of a rose-filled sunset. Breath whooshed through her parted lips, while her lids, now at half mast, regarded their reflection.

"That was incredible," he murmured as his gaze caught hers in the mirror.

"I've never done anything like that before."

It was a dazed admission from the real woman inside her.

"Did you like it?"

She tugged her bottom lip between her teeth, working it to a rosy red plumpness, then let it loose. "I liked it."

He slid his fingertips up a sensitive inner arm. She shivered. "What exactly did you like?"

She moaned and arched her neck, then returned her gaze to the mirror. "I liked watching. Myself. You."

He pushed for more. "My cock moving inside you?"

He couldn't pinpoint exactly what he wanted to hear. Perhaps more of that *ownership* of their act. He wanted her words.

"Yes."

"Say it."

She swallowed, ducked her head. Then, with a quick movement, she raised her eyes to his once more. The words he wanted suddenly rushed out.

"I loved watching your co . . . um, penis slide into me."

She couldn't seem to say *cock,* proving she was still his Kristin.

"Tell me more."

She licked her lips and gave in. "I loved stripping my panties off for you. I loved watching your hand between my legs. I loved watching *us*. It made me come so hard I thought I'd never stop."

She clasped her hand over his as he tweaked her nipple, forcing his fingers to pinch harder than he'd intended.

"I want to do it all again."

Christ.

Maybe, if he kept pushing her to greater and greater sexual heights, she'd finally admit to being Kristin.

SEVEN

"Kirby?"

"Kristin?" The voice on the phone was sleepy. "What time is it?"

Kristin pulled the blanket closer around her shoulders, holding it together at her throat against the night air on Ross's balcony. "Two o'clock."

"In the afternoon?"

"Morning."

Sleep leached from Kirby's voice. "What's wrong?"

"Nothing. I just needed to talk to you."

Her fingers, molded to the cell phone, were cold. Cold from the chilly night air? Or just plain old cold-feet cold?

"Kristin, you're scaring me. You should have been asleep four and a half hours ago."

She closed her eyes, tired but not drowsy. "I did a bad thing."

Feigned shock laced Kirby's voice. "You?"

"I had sex with my boss."

It was out. Her terrible secret. Well, half her secret. The other half being that she'd introduced herself as her sister.

Kirby laughed. "Is this April Fool's or something?"

"No. I slept with him."

"Are you having a nervous breakdown?"

She could almost see Kirby sitting up, switching the light on as if that would help her hear better.

"No."

"Then I must be having the breakdown."

"You said I should go for it."

"I didn't know *it* was Ross Sloan."

"Neither did I. Until I did it."

"Do you want me to come over?"

"I'm not at home."

"What?" It was almost a screech.

"He's sleeping."

"You're spending the night with him?"

"Why do I feel like I'm repeating things?"

"You're not, you're just clarifying." Kirby huffed a breath over the line. "Why are you calling me, Kristin? Why aren't you in bed letting him keep you warm?"

"You didn't say congratulations, Kirby. You told me to get some . . . *cajones*. And I did."

Kirby was quiet a long moment.

Ross should have woken up when she got out of bed—that's what they did in the romance novels, going at it a second and third time. Okay, it would have been the fourth. She'd only brought a three-pack of condoms. They would have had to use his.

"Kirby? Are you still there?"

"Kristin, I didn't mean you were supposed to jump in bed with the first guy available. And not your boss. My God, that's your *job*. You know what happens to girls who sleep with their bosses?"

"Yes, I know." Despondency crept into her tone.

Kirby gasped. "Oh God, don't tell me you think you're in love with him."

Kirby believed in mutually satisfying relationships that enhanced her image as a confident, savvy, and sexy businesswoman. She prescribed to the theory that a good-looking man on her arm, and in her bed, was good for business, especially in the cut-throat world of cosmetics. Love never entered the equation.

Loving Ross wasn't something Kristin even wanted to contemplate. "Of course I'm not in love with him."

It wouldn't do any good if she was. In the months she'd worked for Ross, he hadn't given her a single sexual glance. Not until she became Kirby. What had he said that first night? Something about immense admiration and making sure he didn't miss all his meetings. How debilitating to be described as if she were a well-oiled machine.

The blanket slipped off one shoulder. She yanked it back up. "He doesn't know he's sleeping with me."

"Huh?" A very unKirby-like sound.

"I wore the red dress you gave me. To a bar. He was there." The whole story came out a little hesitantly, but Kirby didn't utter a word to interrupt. "And now I'm at his house. I think he wants me to wake up with him in the morning.".

No sneaking out, he'd said right before he fell asleep. What did that mean? That he cared? Not knowing was killing her.

"Why didn't you correct him as soon as he made the mistake?"

Kristin bit the inside of her cheek. "He didn't make a mistake. I *told* him I was you."

Silence. Dead silence. Very uncomfortable silence. Then, "You pretended to be me? For two nights, you've been pretending you're me?"

There was an edge to Kirby's voice that only a twin would recognize.

"We've pretended before." Lame, very lame, Kristin knew.

"We were eight years old, Kristin. That was fun and games."

"So was this."

At first. Okay, not even at first. She'd had feelings for Ross Sloan almost since the day she'd started to work for him. Partly because Blake had recently dumped her, but mostly because her boss was . . . irresistible.

"It was an experiment," she amended. "I wanted to prove I had some . . . *cajones*."

Kirby ground her teeth, something she did only in extreme cases involving strong emotion. "Pretending to be me doesn't give you balls. Being yourself and seducing him, now that would have shown you had balls, Kristin."

Kirby was right, but now she was trapped in the lie.

"How do I tell him the truth?"

"Find your balls, that's what you do. I cannot believe this. You whine that you can't find a man who interests you. Then when you find one, you don't even have the guts to—" She cut herself off. "I'm disgusted with you."

Kristin had been hoping for sympathy. She'd been hoping to tell Kirby how free she'd felt in Ross's office. How she'd teased him and talked dirty. How he'd practically dragged her back to his place, making love to her, feeding her cheese and fruit, then making love to her all over again. Three times in one night. She'd had at least six orgasms. Six. It was a miracle.

Orgasms with Blake had taken profound concentration.

But Kirby had hit her with the truth—right between the eyes. Kristin couldn't have done all that. Only Kristin pretending to be Kirby could have done it. How could she tell Ross now? What would he say, do?

"Are you still there, Kristin?"

"Yes." Meek. Pathetic.

"You make me so mad. This isn't what I meant, not at all."

"I'm sorry I pretended to be you."

"Why? Because I'm mad? You're missing the point here."

She hadn't missed the point at all. The point was that she was still Kristin the perfect secretary. She'd sneak out of Ross's house before dawn, change into her secretary clothes, then type up his letters as if she'd never watched him bury his penis deep inside her body. She'd never breathe a word of how she really felt about him.

She'd just go on pining for a man who actually wanted another woman because she was afraid he'd reject her.

She was afraid he'd ask why she couldn't be as hot and sexy as Kirby.

"Shall I tell you what you're going to do, Kristin?"

"Yes."

It was, after all, the reason she'd called.

"You're going to invite him to our birthday party tomorrow night."

Kirby's birthday party. She'd forgotten. "I don't think that's such a good idea."

"You're going to invite him, and we'll tell him together."

The thought struck terror into Kristin's pumping heart. "No."

"Then I'll tell him the truth before the next date *Kirby* has with him."

The sliding glass door opened behind her. Kristin started. "I have to go."

"He just walked in on you, didn't he?"

"I'll call you tomorrow."

She hung up on her sister's choice and definitely unrepeatable words.

"What are you doing out here?"

"Talking to my sister." Well, at least it wasn't a lie.

She laid the cell phone on the table beside her, her heart still pounding, her veins filled with adrenaline. Kirby wouldn't tell, she just couldn't.

Ross, wearing a pair of soft faded sweatpants, hunkered by her chair.

"What were you telling her?"

"That I had six orgasms."

He laughed softly as he brushed his forehead along her arm. "Did she freak?"

Oh boy, did she ever. "Yep."

He tugged at the edge of the blanket. The cool night air caressed her breasts and tightened her nipples.

"Maybe we ought to make it seven."

She should have been exhausted from the workout he'd given her, but heat pooled between her legs.

There were still so many things she hadn't done. With him. So how could she tell him the truth now?

His hand slipped beneath the blanket's folds. "You're naked."

"I didn't feel like putting my dress back on."

He rubbed a finger against her nipple. Impossibly it got harder. She shifted, her legs parting beneath the cover. His questing hand roamed over her abdomen to the top of her curls.

Truth. Tell him the truth. Find some of those *cajones*.

"Ross?" She could barely breathe and all that came out was his name.

"Yeah?"

Truth. "I want you to touch me."

Well, it *was* the truth, and it did take courage to ask. She held her breath, waiting.

His fingers slid between her legs, parting her, but he moved only against the outer lips, massaging, making her wet, but not giving her what she needed.

"Is this how you want me to touch you?"

"No. Yes. I mean . . ." She licked dry lips. "I want you to touch me . . . on my clitoris."

He slipped his fingers into the moist center, gathering her juices, spreading them, then sliding up to her clitoris. He rubbed, and she moaned. All feeling, all thought centered on that one spot on her body.

"What else do you want? Tell me, and I'll do it. Anything."

Oh, there were so many things, but right now all she wanted was his mouth right where his finger was.

"Lick me, Ross, use your tongue. Please."

She wasn't embarrassed as she begged. After everything they'd done together, she'd gotten past embarrassment.

He moved in front of her, going down on his knees and pushing the blanket aside.

"It would be my pleasure," he murmured, as he spread her legs, then put his tongue on her.

Oh my. She pulled her knees up, and her head fell back. Her hands tangled in his hair. Such soft hair.

"That feels so good."

He didn't stop to answer, thank goodness. She curled her legs around his shoulders. No man had ever touched her quite like Ross. Almost with reverence, certainly with total enjoyment.

For now, she didn't want to miss a moment of it. The sight of his head between her legs, the incredible feel of his tongue on her, even the soft moans she made. Everything.

She began to build, to burn, to feel every bit of her soul being sucked down to where he lapped at her. This was courage, wasn't it? Letting him make her come out here in the open. Asking for it. *Begging* for it.

Her legs anchored him. She couldn't keep her eyes open, her head still, or her mouth shut even though they were outside. She was so close.

He stopped.

She opened her eyes to find moonlight reflected in his as he looked up at her.

"Why?" was all she could manage, her voice strangled with longing.

He reached for her hand, pulled it down between her legs until her fingers rested just above her clitoris.

"Touch yourself for me. I want to watch."

She wondered if a man could honestly understand the exposure in that small request. A lifetime of inhibitions and fears thrown aside. This was so much more than what he'd done to her in front of the mirror. He couldn't possibly understand what he was asking.

But then he wasn't asking it of *her,* he wanted it from Kirby.

Kristin would do anything he asked just so the moment never ended. It wasn't *cajones,* it was desperation.

Her fingers slid through her tight curls, almost as if they didn't belong to her. The edges of her vision melted away, everything became unreal except for him.

He watched her eyes, not her hand. His quickened breath demonstrated he knew she'd succumbed. She closed her eyes and laid her head against the back of the chair.

"No, look at me." His voice was low, urgent.

Her eyes flew open at his demand. Flames danced in his eyes.

His gaze captured hers even as he put his hand on top of her shaking fingers and guided them between her folds. She bit her lip at the first contact, all slippery and warm. His touch rough, hers soft. She reveled in the difference. He nudged her down to her opening, where their fingers, acting almost as a single unit, gathered moisture and slid deliciously back up.

"How does that feel," he whispered as he moved up her body to bring his lips to her cheek.

"Good." Terrible. Wonderful. Momentous.

"How good?"

Her hips moved under their combined ministrations. Heat soared through her belly, then down her thighs. The muscles of her throat worked, but words simply wouldn't come.

"Do you like how hard it's making me to watch you touch yourself? I want you to come on our hands."

She was so close to doing exactly what he wanted. "Oh, please."

Fire shot down to her center, where their fingers moved.

Everything she was, everything she wanted to be for him, lay beneath that pulsing touch and their fingers.

Oh God!

She screamed. He cut the sound off with his lips, his hand still working in tandem with hers. Her body bucked, the orgasm going on and on into the night.

EIGHT

Goodness, it was agony, complete and total agony. Kristin thought she could handle seeing Ross at the office, but after the things they'd done last night, the things she'd done to herself at his request, her emotions were colossally more tumultuous than the day before. If that were possible.

God, who was she becoming? She wasn't fully Kristin—Kristin could never have performed any of those acts with the abandon she'd experienced—but she wasn't Kirby either.

She'd insisted on taking a cab home as the sun came up. Ross had watched her dress, thrown on those faded sweats, kissed her at the door, then walked her down to the waiting cab where he'd kissed her again.

Even though she was tired, so tired, Ross's proximity gave her strength—and fed her guilt. She had to tell him the truth. After what they'd done last night, she couldn't possibly keep on claiming she was Kirby.

"Do you have that Richardson agreement ready, Miss Prescott? I want to get it to the lawyer today for review."

"Yes, Mr. Sloan."

She'd just finished the spellcheck on it. The number of errors she'd made was atrocious, a side effect, she suspected, of her guilty conscience and lack of sleep.

She handed him the freshly printed pages, staring at his long beautiful fingers, fingers that brought such pleasure, fingers that asked for so much from her.

Did she imagine it? Or was he looking at her differently? It was as if he could see through her clothes straight into her heart. Everything was there for him to read.

His gaze focused, then fell back to the document. All business once more, he studied the pages.

"E-mail it to Harrison for his review," he said as he handed the papers back. "Tell him I need it back tomorrow. Good work, Miss Prescott."

He'd always been a boss that complimented, appreciated, and mentored. He was like that as a lover, also.

The office was suddenly suffocating, even though he was on the other side of the desk, separated by the expanse of wood, folders, computer monitor, and her clothes.

"Do you want some coffee, Mr. Sloan?"

She'd never hovered over him, but if she got coffee for herself, she brought one for him. Maybe, this way, he'd go back into his office and quit crowding hers. She simply couldn't concentrate on anything.

"That would be fine, thanks."

She felt his eyes on her as she walked out the door. It unnerved her further. Was he making comparisons to her alter ego when he watched her walk?

In the coffee room the pot was empty. She dumped the old grinds, put a new filter in, a bag and a half of coffee, then dumped that into the trash as well.

"Darn it."

She looked around to make sure no one had seen the silly maneuver, then started over. Where on earth was her head?

Okay, Kristin, don't answer that.

She finally got it right. Then her shattered nerves got the better of her once more, and she stuck her cup directly under the drip just to speed things up. And burned herself. Boiling coffee streamed over her hand, down the front of her skirt, and splashed her blouse. Her thumb throbbed with the slight burn.

"Darn it, darn it."

She'd lost control over her life, even the routine day-to-day acts she swore she could have done in her sleep. She didn't know what to do about it.

Kirby had said it all last night. Tell him the truth. Tell him she'd been pretending to be her sister. The worst he could do was fire her.

Her stomach clenched.

The *worst* he could do was tell her he didn't want her if she wasn't her sister.

She dabbed at the coffee stains on her clothes to no avail. Then she managed to make her coffee too sweet and his too milky.

Of course, she could always just quit.

She could hear Kirby whispering "chicken, baach, baach, baach, chicken."

Okay, okay, she'd tell him the truth. Soon. After lunch, maybe.

Carrying the coffee back to her office, she set hers on her desk, then eased into his office, placed the cup on the edge of his desk, and rushed back out with a hurried explanation.

"Have to run home to change my clothes. Spilled coffee. Terrible mess. Be back soon."

Mr. Sloan called her name. His voice kept coming closer and closer, but she made it out the door, purse in hand, before he darkened his office door.

She dug in her purse for her cell phone as she hailed a cab. There wasn't time to wait for the bus. Kirby didn't answer her emergency call. Leaving a message, Kristin babbled something about her bad day, having to rush home to change her clothes, and begged her sister to call her back ASAP.

The problem was she knew Kirby's advice would be the

same as it had been last night. It was long past time to tell Ross the truth.

Kristin didn't know where those *cajones* were going to come from.

Ross glanced up as the outer office door closed. Kristin was back, and closing the door as if she had something very special planned for lunch. He waited for the tell-tale snick of the lock, but heard nothing more than her footsteps across the carpet.

The woman was always taking him by surprise these days. She'd rushed out an hour ago with a few frantic, jumbled sentences and a monstrous coffee stain marring her skirt and the pristine white of her blouse.

She made him demented. Just as the question on his mind had all morning. Why had she done everything he'd asked last night? He'd thought she'd refuse, end the charade, and confess her identity. Instead, she'd given him something he'd never meant to take.

Her trust.

She lowered a barrier that had nothing to do with her disguise and gave him a piece of the real Kristin Prescott, no matter what name she chose to call herself in the dark of the night.

More important, as she'd come, her fingers entangled with his and their eyes locked, he'd felt her orgasm almost as if it had come from within himself. In that moment, everything ceased to be a game, a challenge. It had become something much more powerful.

It was something he didn't think he could go on without now that he'd tasted it.

He shoved his keyboard away and sat back in his chair. He felt another of her plans formulating around him, and he welcomed it with mixed feelings. He wanted her, but he wanted her as Kristin, out in the open, pure and simple.

The woman in his doorway tucked a slim purse beneath

her arm. Her silvery silk blouse, the top two buttons open, revealed an excessive amount of cleavage. A slit up the side of her short, red leather skirt exposed her leg to mid-thigh.

He knew her immediately, and though she bore an uncanny resemblance to his secretary, she wasn't his Kristin.

The height of her spiked heels required extreme dexterity to cross his office carpet without a major accident. She dropped her purse on his desk and raised one perfectly plucked eyebrow. "So, let's get something straight. I'm Kirby Prescott. And the woman you're taking to bed is my sister." She paused, obviously hoping for a reaction.

He felt the sand in his hourglass draining away. Damn. He and Kristin needed more time to work this out. Without interference.

"It's not your fault," she went on. "You didn't know. But it's got to stop before Kristin gets hurt."

He rolled his mechanical pencil between his fingers. He had to admire the way she looked out for her sister. Even if it was sticking her nose where it didn't belong. He also had to admit his own culpability. For Kristin's sake. "It is my fault."

She smiled then. "I like that. A man taking blame."

Blame wasn't the issue. "I take full responsibility for my actions."

"Fine. You take responsibility." She tossed her hair over her shoulder. "But why do I get the feeling you're not surprised by my little revelation about your lover's true identity?"

He tossed the pencil onto the desk and rose, looked her over with a completely unemotional gaze, and said, "I never thought she was you."

"So it was Kristin you were after all along?"

"Yes."

Kirby pinched the bridge of her nose, then glared at him. "You're diddling your secretary, for God's sake."

"I know." Though he didn't like the terminology. It cheapened everything he'd done with Kristin.

"We're talking about her *job* here. Nothing good ever

comes out of an affair with the boss. Men in authority and all that."

He sensed a bit of personal experience in her tone. "I'm not going to fire her, if that's what you're thinking. I have no intention of hurting her in any way."

"You already have." Her mouth dropped open in a huff. "You bastard."

He had the notion to squash Kirby's overblown antics right now, especially since she didn't have a clue as to his reasons for allowing her sister's charade to go on. But he wouldn't do anything to make this worse on Kristin, especially not a knock-out fight with her twin. "I deserve that," he agreed.

"Yes, you do. I can't believe you'd stoop this low. There must be tons of women out there who'd give you what you need. Why'd you have to pick on Kristin?"

"She's who I wanted." The sister might as well know that, too. He wasn't letting Kristin walk away from this.

She whirled around, then turned back, her arm bangles jangling as she jammed her fists on her hips. "Well, I'm not going to let you screw with her life. She's my sister. I'm going to tell her about your rotten little game."

He did have to give the woman credit for her concern. Worry lines creased her forehead and battle fire sparked in her eye. "You don't have to." He'd wanted Kristin to admit the truth, but things had gone beyond that now. "I intend to tell her myself. As soon as she gets back."

"What, and then you'll throw her out on her butt?"

"No. I already told you—"

"I know what you said. You won't fire her. But once she knows you know, she won't have any choice but to leave." She cocked her head, eyeing him. The battle light raged into a conflagration. "Unless you think you can get her to service your professional needs during the day, then pop over to your house and service your other needs at night without anyone being the wiser."

He reminded himself once more that this was Kristin's sister. Letting his anger get the better of him, as much as this woman was really starting to piss him off, would only make the situation worse, much worse. "That's not my aim."

"Then what is, Mr. Sloan?"

He would explain once, and only once, then all bets were off. "I fully intend to tell her I knew she wasn't you from the beginning. Then I'll tell her we won't be going on like this anymore, that it's against all the rules in the employee handbook. And finally—"

A gasp from the doorway hit him in the gut. Kirby Prescott turned, almost in slow motion.

Her identical twin stood framed in the office door.

I knew she wasn't you.

Kristin wanted to curl up on the floor and die. Even Blake's final cutting remarks hadn't sliced through her the way Ross's drawled words carved straight to her heart.

It should have meant something that he'd known who she was all along, but he'd never noticed her until she donned Kirby's persona. When she'd dangled temptation in front of him, he'd gobbled up the lure. As long as neither acknowledged the truth, it was okay. But now . . .

She couldn't blame him for wanting to end it now that the truth was out in the open, her trickery exposed.

Ross shifted behind his desk. Kirby looked at her with . . . goodness, was that pity?

Kristin held up a hand. "You don't have to say anything."

"Kristin—"

She cut him off. "Really. I heard enough." *We won't be going on like this. It's against all the rules in the employee handbook.* She was a rule he'd broken. God, what had she been thinking when she dressed in Kirby's castoffs? One night, that's what she'd been thinking. She should have stopped there. This was so embarrassing and humiliating. "You don't need to add anything else."

Kirby stepped back as if to give them room.

"As it happens, I've got quite a lot to add, Kristin."

Goodness, he looked so beautiful standing there. He

was everything she'd ever wanted, ever dreamed about. So much more than Blake, so much more than any man. She'd given him a piece of her soul last night. Only he didn't want it. What happened wasn't his fault. He hadn't asked for that big a piece of her. She'd been the one to give it without telling him exactly how much her actions meant. The floor wasn't good enough to curl up on. She needed a rock to crawl under. A cliff to jump off.

"We'll talk about it as soon as your sister leaves." He looked pointedly at Kirby.

"Please, let's just forget it." Kristin would never forget a moment she'd had with him. "I'm really sorry about everything, Mr. Sloan."

He slammed his fist on the table. "Godammit, call me Ross. I'm sick of being Mr. Sloan to you."

She deserved his anger. It didn't matter that he hadn't been fooled: she'd still lied to him.

Kristin chanced a quick glance at Kirby. Her sister stared at her with an all too familiar set look to her face. Oh yes, Kristin knew exactly what that look meant. Find some *cajones,* Kristin.

At this moment Kristin didn't even know the meaning. She just needed to get out. O-U-T.

"I think it's better if I quit."

He stepped back as if she'd belted him. "Quit?"

"I'll send you a formal e-mail for the record." Then, before she did the unthinkable, like burst into tears, she scurried out of the office without even gathering a single personal item.

Her heart splintered into a million pieces before she made it through the outer office door.

Ross stared after her, panic constricting his chest. He'd let her go, let her walk out the door and out of his life. And she was going to send him a damn e-mail resignation.

Kirby Prescott still faced the now empty doorway. "Well, that wasn't exactly the outcome I had in mind."

He glared at Kirby, the only one left to take his feelings out on. "That's what you said you expected," he growled.

She returned his angry gaze with a mild one. "I didn't expect her to walk in on us in the first place." She glanced at her thin gold watch. "I thought we'd have a little more time for our discussion. Maybe you should go after her."

"Don't offer me advice." He lashed out with the only thing he had, words.

"You're right. I shouldn't tell you what to do. I've already fucked things up royally."

He almost smiled. Kristin's untimely appearance had obviously quelled her sister's earlier anger. And Kirby's comment was an apt description of what they'd accomplished with their argument. *Fuck* would never have fallen from Kristin's lips, yet Kirby had said it with a total lack of impact. How could Kristin ever have thought she could fool him?

"At the risk of making things worse," Kirby drawled. "I will say this, Ross. Kristin's young. She still believes in love. However you decide to handle the situation, don't hurt her."

They were, of course, the same age, but Kirby Prescott seemed years older than her sister, in both experience and cynicism.

He waited for a threat to follow up her statement. None came. "So, do you still want me to leave her alone?"

She cocked her head. "Depends on whether your intentions are honorable."

"Like, do I care about her as more than my secretary? Do I want a relationship with her? Am I in love with her?"

The words, even the thoughts, didn't scare him half as much as they would have a week ago.

"Any of the above will do."

This time he did smile. "And if the answer is yes to any of them, I have your permission to go after her?"

"Of course."

She gave him a half smile that would have felled another man, one who wasn't already in love with her sister. He was immune.

"The answer is all of the above. Any clues where she might have gone?"

"Not a one." The half smile blossomed into a full one. "But I do know exactly where she'll be tonight."

NINE

Kristin stood amid the lacy undergarments Victoria's Secret was so famous for. She wasn't a girl who went shopping when the chips were down. She was a girl who wallowed in the things that would make her feel the worst, such as sexy underwear she'd only feel comfortable in while pretending to be her sister.

Pathetic.

Ross Sloan had only noticed her as a woman once she'd wrapped herself up in her Kirby costume. When the truth was laid out on the desk between them, she'd run out in humiliation. She didn't even have the *cajones* to face the consequences.

Now, here she was, surrounded by sexy black lace, a reminder of everything she wasn't.

She fingered the underwire of a pushup bra. She'd bared her breasts for Ross last night. When he'd asked her to touch herself, when he'd laced his fingers with hers and kissed her as she came, she'd laid bare every insecurity, every fear, every emotion.

Last night had been her one true moment in thirty

years—when she'd thrown caution completely and totally to the winds. And soared.

Ross had taken less than twenty-four hours to clip her wings.

"May I help you, ma'am?"

The salesgirl was young, pert, and cute, her lithe body wrapped in a tight bodysuit, a gold buckle barely holding the lapels together over her décolletage.

"I'm just looking, thank you." *I'm just dying here, so let me do it in peace.*

The girl refused to take a hint.

"You look like you've just had a fight with your boyfriend."

Kristin almost laughed. So far from the truth. Ross wasn't her boyfriend; he wasn't even her lover. He was simply a man she'd had sex with.

While pretending to be someone else.

Tossing her long black hair over her shoulder, the young woman pointed to a small rack frothing over with colorful accoutrements. "I bet we could find something over here that would make everything better."

"I don't think lace and crotchless panties are going to do it."

The girl took Kristin's arm and guided her to the rack. "It isn't the lace. It's how you feel when you're wearing it."

How true, in so many ways. It wasn't the act of touching herself, it was how beautiful she'd felt doing it for him. Once she'd gotten over the fear and shock. She'd offered him something she'd never had the courage to give anyone else. Her complete breakdown of all inhibition. For some odd reason, that eased the turmoil roiling inside her.

She'd had the *cajones* to put herself out there.

Tapping her lips, the sales clerk smiled. "Now here's something guaranteed to make him forget all about that little argument."

She held up a peach bra with matching thong panties.

"It wasn't a *little* argument."

Last night, she'd thought she'd succumbed to Ross out

of desperation. She didn't want him to lose interest. In the brightly lit store overwhelmed by sex, sex, sex, she saw her actions for what they were. A gift of trust.

He'd asked, she'd given.

Only a woman in love would have trusted so completely.

Kristin tipped her head. Was he accepting the gift from a Kirby look-alike? Or from Kristin herself?

Last night, he'd known who she was. He'd . . . known.

"His fault or yours?" the youngster asked, as she took back the lace confection and pulled out another set, oblivious to her customer's sudden revelation.

"Both," Kristin whispered, almost in wonder, her mind working. They'd both been too busy keeping their own secrets to understand the subtle meanings behind their respective actions.

The salesgirl beamed, all white teeth and red lips. "Honey, you've got it bad if you're taking partial blame."

Out of the mouths of babes. She did have it bad, so bad that overhearing Ross's conversation with Kirby had literally crushed her. She'd immediately seen a big neon sign flashing "rejection" and run without even asking if that's what he'd meant.

She looked over the next lacy offering the young woman held out, then slowly shook her head. "That isn't going to fix it."

The girl tipped her head. "Then, honey, you'd better do whatever it is you have to do."

This twenty-something, petite slip of a girl had life figured out far better than Kristin had managed to do in thirty years.

Whatever she had to do. This wasn't just about Ross. It was about the woman she chose to be.

She perused the stock of pretty underthings with a more calculating eye. She wanted to be a woman who wore black lace, who took risks. A confident, sexy, powerful woman. Not a shriveled up, unloved husk.

Whatever she had to do all of a sudden became terribly clear.

She had to find the courage to tell Ross Sloan that she loved him and wanted him in her life forever.

Kristin smoothed the musky, Kirby-like lotion into her calves. Well, after all, it was Kirby's bathroom and not a Kristin-like scent in sight.

She got ready with Ross in mind. If she knew her sister at all, and she did know her oh-so-darn well, Kirby would have invited Ross to the birthday party. Kristin had worried herself sick about that on the way over to Kirby's. Now, after mucho angst in the shower, Kristin realized it was actually the best way.

Not that she'd let on to Kirby about her suspicion. Not yet anyway.

Kirby watched her in the bathroom mirror. "You're mad that I went to see him."

Kristin met her sister's gaze in the glass, as she adjusted the strapless black bra into place for the tenth time. The matching thong looked pretty hot, if she did say so herself. She'd made the salesgirl's day, too. She felt powerful, not with the purchase or the feel of expensive, sexy lingerie against her skin, but with courage. No matter what Ross's answer might be.

"I'm not mad, Kirby."

"Yes, you are. You think I should have minded my own business."

"Well, it did make it seem like you had a lack of faith in me." Not that she'd instilled any faith.

Kirby snorted. "You damn well know you wouldn't have told him the truth unless I pushed."

"Yes, well, he already knew the truth."

Kristin selected a bottle of Kirby's perfume, no clue as to brand or scent, nor did she care. She trailed a dab on the tip of her finger from her throat down between her breasts.

Goodness, how sensual. Skin on skin. The sultry fragrance carried on the air with the last of the steam from her shower.

"Kristin, what's wrong with you? You're not yourself. You don't even seem to care that you just quit your job."

She stood before the sink, clad only in a thong, bra, and high-heeled shoes. She wasn't embarrassed. Not in the least.

Kirby was right, she wasn't herself—her old self. This was the new Kristin. She reached across to the dress hanging on the back of the door and stepped into it. "Zip me, · would you?"

Kirby did, then patted the back into place. "You're not answering me."

Kristin smoothed the silky material over her abdomen. "I care. And I've given a lot of thought to what I'm going to do about it."

"And that would be?"

"First, I'm going to enjoy myself at *our* birthday party." She stressed the pronoun for Kirby's benefit. Before, it had always been Kirby's party. Now she wanted to claim it for herself as well. She wanted to enjoy life instead of avoiding it. "I promised I'd wear the dress tonight. I even paid a pretty penny to get it dry-cleaned this afternoon." She finished applying a rich shade of red to her lips, smacked them, then caught Kirby's shocked expression in the mirror. "Remember? I promised to try my seductive wiles on a gorgeous man."

"I remember. But that was before."

She tinted her cheeks. "Before what?"

Kirby pressed her lips together and narrowed her eyes at Kristin's reflection. "Before you boffed your boss pretending you were me. And don't tell me he doesn't mean anything to you. I know you've got feelings for him."

Cocking her head, she met Kirby's gaze in the mirror. "I have feelings, but this time I need to handle them in my own way."

"Right, and that would be by sending him your resignation through e-mail."

"No." Kristin leaned into the mirror, adding her eye-liner. "That would be by telling him what they are. To his face."

Kirby smacked her lightly on the rear. "That's my twin. Grab the bull by the horns."

"I thought it was riding the horse again."

"Whatever."

Holding out her hand, Kristin said, "Can I borrow your mascara, too?"

Kirby slapped it onto her palm. "I decided to give you a little help, too."

"Help?" She stopped mid-wand swish.

"I invited Ross to the party tonight."

Kristin didn't even try to hide her smile as she put the finishing touch to her lashes. "Like I didn't have a clue that's what you'd do?"

Kirby raised one eyebrow. "This is a pleasant surprise. You're not even mad about this either."

She swept a blusher brush across her cheeks. "I was actually counting on it, and sister dear, you didn't let me down."

The question was whether Ross would accept the invitation. Not that it mattered. She knew where he lived and where he worked. She'd give him her little speech wherever she found him. Doing it tonight, however, would be so much easier.

Kirby tapped Kristin's shoulder to gain her focus. "You really do seem different, but I can't put my finger on it. You're not gonna pull an Uzi on us or anything, are you?"

"It's called *cajones*. I've got them in spades." All right, so there was a little tremble in her fingers, but she would not back down. "Now you better get dressed before they all start banging on your front door."

"Let them wait." Kirby didn't make a move. "You know, I might give you a ton of shit all the time, but I do love you."

"I don't expect you to change any time soon. And I love you, too."

"Then let's get this show on the road."

*   *   *

Two hours later Kristin stood surrounded by a gaggle of the hot-looking men Kirby always bragged about. Ross still hadn't shown.

Kirby appeared out of nowhere, brushing Kristin's shoulder as she walked by, and whispered, "Don't worry, he'll be here."

Kristin wasn't worried. She hadn't changed her mind. She wouldn't, not now. Even if she had to confront him at work on Monday. Or at his apartment tonight.

The music—loud, just like Kirby liked it—vibrated off her chest. Expensive champagne titillated her pallet. The men, for some reason, fawned over her.

It was the dress. Or the shoes. Or maybe the fact that they'd all had just a bit too much of the bubbly.

No, she realized with a sort of wonder, it was *her*.

"Kristin, you're a woman," a nameless hunk said as he maneuvered a rival for her attention out of the way.

Yes, she was, definitely.

"We want your opinion." That was Gary something-or-other, cute face but far too much cologne.

"Tell us what you think of dating coworkers," said yet another prime piece of masculinity. What was his name? Ah yes, Chet, from the computer department at Kirby's cosmetics firm.

Right now, though he spoke to Kristin, Chet's gaze lay suspiciously on Kirby as she flitted at the other end of the room. Kirby was not just his coworker, but his boss. Kristin had met Blake at work, and that had turned out badly. She'd also met Ross, and though she was keeping her hopes high that would turn out exactly the way she wanted it to, she wasn't about to get poor Chet's hopes up over Kirby.

"Dating a coworker is fine. Just make sure it's not the boss."

Chet slumped. Gary slapped him on the back. Nameless Guy snickered.

"So. No dating the boss. Have I got that right, Miss Prescott?"

The three men shuffled a bit and stared over her shoulder at the newcomer. The skin on the back of her neck tingled. Warmth pooled low in her stomach and regions south.

She turned to meet him head-on.

The three hunks surrounding her paled in comparison to Ross. Goodness, he was gorgeous in that white polo shirt and black jeans. Something sparkled in his eyes, though she couldn't be sure whether he teased or tested her with his comment.

"Actually, it would depend on the boss's intentions, Mr. Sloan. If my boss intimated he'd fire me if I didn't date him, well, that would be bad."

"What if he told you he wanted to sleep with you, no pink slip, no strings attached?"

Her heart leapt into her throat. No strings?

No guts, no glory.

She took one deep breath for glory. "Well, if my boss asked for sex with no strings, I'd have to tell him I wanted strings."

Ross shifted, widening his stance. "What kind of strings?"

Now was the time to try out her freshly acquired *cajones*. Looking him straight in the eye, she said, "I want a relationship."

His eyes deepened to a mesmerizing dark chocolate. "You don't sound hypothetical when you say that, Miss Prescott."

"That's because I'm not being hypothetical, Mr. Sloan." She was so faint she saw spots before her eyes, but she refused to stop now. "I'm telling you flat out that I'm in love with you."

Kristin held her breath. Someone—it could only be Kirby—clapped their hands once.

A smile started to grow on Ross's handsome face. "Well, then let me say—"

She held up a hand. "I'm not done yet."

"By all means, go on, Miss Prescott. I'm dying to hear everything you have to say."

She needed to get it out. That was the guts part. That's what she should have given him this morning. "I played at being Kirby because I couldn't tell you how I felt. And I shouldn't have run out today. That was stupid and childish. *I've* been stupid and childish for the last couple of days."

"So you want a relationship with me?" His voice was low and filled with an emotion she couldn't put a name to.

She suddenly realized the room was quiet, as if it and everyone in it held their breath. God, they had witnesses. Yet even a room full of people couldn't phase her now.

She stiffened her spine and went for it. "Yes, I want a relationship. With you." She stopped, tipped her head, and said a silent prayer. "What do *you* want?"

He crossed his arms over his beautifully sculpted chest. "Well, first, I need to recall what the employee handbook says about sexual harassment."

Chet leaned over her shoulder and grunted, "Huh?"

That something sparkled again in Ross's eyes, and Kristin knew they'd gone from testing to teasing. Her heart felt close to bursting in her chest. "Yes, Mr. Sloan, as my friend here so eloquently said, huh?"

"What I'm driving at is, there are rules on relationships in the direct chain of command. I just can't remember what it says about consensual relationships."

Kristin was sure he'd never even looked it up.

Gary stepped forward and stuck a finger in Ross's chest. "Look, just tell the lady whether you're in love with her or not."

Ross frowned at him, then gazed at Kristin with eyes that had begun to smolder. "You don't understand. She's my secretary. I might have to fire her before I can have a relationship with her."

No-name Dude turned to Kristin. "What's more important? Him or the job?"

She looked straight at Ross. "Him. Besides, I've already quit."

Kirby appeared at Ross's left. "Well, then there's no problem, Mr. Sloan. You can tell her if you want a relationship."

His gaze never wavered from Kristin's. "Yeah."

Kirby poked him. "Just yeah? What the hell does that mean?"

"I want a relationship. I'm in love with you. I shouldn't have let you leave the office this morning without telling you. And I think, maybe, you can still be my secretary—if I marry you."

"What does the handbook say?" That might have been Gary, but Kristin couldn't quite be sure over the roaring in her ears.

"I happened to look that up, and it doesn't put any restrictions on married couples." Ross winked at her.

"Then she accepts," Chet said as he poked *her* in the ribs. "Right, Miss Prescott?"

Ross loved her. Goodness. He'd even mentioned marriage. "Shouldn't we date first? We haven't done that yet."

A smile spread across Ross's lips. "There's lots of things we haven't done yet, Miss Prescott. But I'm more than willing to give you whatever your heart desires."

Oh goodness gracious. Guts *and* glory. She leapt into his arms.

He held her close, pulling back only enough to touch noses with her. "I love you, *Kristin* Prescott." He dropped his voice for her ears only. "I should have told you how much I loved you last night when I had you exactly where I want to keep you for the rest of your life." He kissed the side of her neck, sending a shiver straight to her toes. "Forgive me?"

The clapping, cheering, and ribald comments drowned out the reply she whispered against his lips. "Yes. I do. And I love you, too, Mr. Sloan."

He kissed the tip of her nose. "Then don't you think you should start calling me Ross now?"

SKIN DEEP

Jasmine Haynes

ONE

"Dinner on Saturday sounds great, but don't invite one of Ross's friends this time." Tucking the phone receiver between her shoulder and her ear, Kirby Prescott kicked off her shoes, then propped her bare feet on her desk. Her wraparound skirt fell open to her thighs.

Her sister Kristin sighed. "I thought you liked Steve."

"He was short." And completely without a sense of humor. He hadn't even cracked a smile during dinner. He'd also eyed her high heels with disdain, and she was sure on a first date, he'd have insisted she wear flats. A woman simply wasn't dressed without a gorgeous pair of spiked heels.

Kristin *tssked* primly. "What about Mark?"

"I'm afraid bald is out, too." Especially when a man tried to hide the fact beneath a tacky comb-over. It indicated a lack of self-confidence. "If God doesn't crown a guy with abundant hair, he should accept it gracefully."

"All right. What if I find someone proud of his shiny pate?"

Was there such a creature? Besides, for a woman in Kirby's chosen profession, image was everything, and that went for the men she dated, too. Cosmetics was a cutthroat industry. She'd managed to introduce her custom line into many of San Francisco's exclusive salons. She wouldn't let anything stand in the way of future expansion.

"Short or bald is out, Kristin."

Kristin huffed out an exasperated breath. "As much as I love you, I sometimes worry that you're shallow."

For just a second that stopped Kirby. Was she shallow for putting image above everything? No, her *business* was first on her list. "My, my, you really have found your balls, haven't you, little sister?"

They were twins, but Kirby had exploded into the world first. Kristin would always be her little sister, in more ways than one.

"I'm not trying to hurt your feelings, but—"

"I know exactly what I am, so you can't hurt my feelings."

It wasn't as if the men she dated wondered why she went out with them. She was eye candy as much as they were. Sure, she welcomed the flirting, the entertaining conversation, and yes, even a man's unique and tantalizing scent or the soft caress of a slightly roughened finger along her arm. Still, the goal on both their parts was ultimately the same. Contact. Networking. She'd made connections aplenty at those dinners, parties, and various other engagements she'd attended.

"There's more to life than just business," Kristin said. "What about marriage? And kids?"

"God forbid. I want variety. I'd die if some man tried to tie me down." She thoroughly enjoyed a man's company; she didn't, however, need to wake up beside him in the morning.

Kristin's voice faltered. "You make it sound like a death sentence."

"I didn't mean that. It's fine for the right person. For you. Not for me." Her priority was her business, her career.

"If I found the right man for you—"

"Do not, and I repeat, do not matchmake for me." Enough was enough. Her twin had become disgustingly monogamy-minded since catching Ross. Then again, maybe it was all those wedding plans and baby-name books warping her brain. Kristin was the mother type. Kirby couldn't pull that off and didn't want to.

"Spoilsport."

"I like being single." Kirby liked having choices. She liked making her own decisions. She liked being her own boss and controlling her own destiny.

"I just want you to be happy."

"What makes you think I'm not happy?" Kirby leaned her head back against her leather chair. The sun streaming through the window of her high-rise office warmed the top of her head, but Kristin's statement set her nerves on edge. She had her own flourishing business. She had delicious male companions to drape on her arm. She had freedom. Why wouldn't she be happy?

"You rarely smile."

"Let's drop the subject, shall we? Dinner Saturday sounds great. What do you want me to bring?"

"Just yourself, sweetie."

Which was a good thing. She wasn't particularly domestic. Her best cooking came out of a gourmet take-out box from Petrici's. "I found a great new chardonnay from a winery down in Templeton. I'll bring a bottle of that."

"Wonderful. Five o'clock?"

"Sure." They'd hustle her out by ten so they could spend the rest of the evening in bed, getting all starry-eyed. Which was fine. She'd still be able to make it for a drink or two at one of her favorite nightspots. Maybe even find a little company.

Except that after being around Kristin and Ross, sometimes she didn't have the energy for company. Sometimes, all she wanted was a hot bath, lots of scented bubbles, and her vibrator, Mr. Perfect.

"Love you. Gotta go. I have another call coming in."

She didn't, but she cut the connection anyway. What was wrong with her these days? It wasn't her biological clock ticking, the way Kristin seemed to think. Still, something *was* missing.

She wasn't envious of her sister having a man like Ross. She wasn't even envious of the way he looked at Kristin with that adoring gaze, like she was the queen of his world and he'd do anything, absolutely anything, for her.

That kind of look would petrify Kirby.

No, it wasn't envy of what those two had together. It was . . . the intensity with which they felt it. Kirby had known that feeling, and not so long ago. She'd felt the same thing as she watched her business grow, spending fourteen to sixteen hours a day making it all happen. She'd been alive, focused, obsessed. Rebuilding her business after almost losing it all—thanks to a *man*—had been the most important thing in her life.

She'd done it, but now she'd hit some sort of plateau. Nothing seemed to excite her. Not even sex. Oh, that was still fine, but sometimes she actually preferred Mr. Perfect to the real thing. In fact, she'd starting thinking of Mr. Perfect *as* the real thing. Take him out of his box, elicit five or six quite respectable orgasms, then put him away again. Out of sight. Out of mind.

She *had* become shallow, but not the way Kristin meant. Maybe it was having turned thirty a couple of months ago. Maybe it was Kristin's upcoming life change. Who knew? Somewhere along the way, Kirby had stopped experiencing life with . . . passion.

There was only one thing that still managed to excite her, and she could certainly do with a little pick-me-up after that conversation.

Yes, what she needed right now was a Jack Taylor fix.

After telling Cindy, her secretary, to hold all her calls, Kirby locked her office door.

Seated once more behind the desk, she snapped her ear-piece in place. She liked her hands free when she phoned Jack. Propping her feet on the wood edge, she undid the third and fourth buttons of her blouse.

During the day, while at work, she limited herself to a sedate two open buttons. With the locked door discouraging visitors, she indulged herself.

Let's see, it was four o'clock back East. Perfect. Jack liked a little pick-me-up to get him through the late afternoon.

She dialed his direct line.

"Jack Taylor's office."

Damn. His secretary. That meant he was in a meeting.

"This is Kirby Prescott. Is he in?"

"I'm sorry, he's got someone with him right now. Would you like his voicemail?"

"Thanks."

She left the message, unplugged her earpiece, then prowled her office in bare feet. After a very long five minutes, the phone rang. Jack's number came up on the digital readout.

She jammed the plug for her earpiece back into its socket. "Jack, that latest shipment of glycolic is crap. It separates. I can't use the stuff."

He was silent a moment. "Are you wearing panties?"

She smiled, her muscles relaxing. She flopped back into her chair and tucked her feet beneath her. "No."

He groaned, barely more than a rush of air across the phone line. "All right. Send the whole lot back UPS Red. I'll get a replacement shipment out tomorrow morning. Too late to do it today."

"You're a doll, Jack." He was way more than that. He was an animal.

"Are you wearing a bra?"

"Yes."

A rustle, the sound of metal chinking, then the rasp of a zipper came through the earpiece like an electric zap. Then his delicious voice. Even when he was all business, his voice could almost make her come. "Was it the new formula that got screwed up?"

"No, this was the old stuff. I haven't even received a sample of the new."

"All right, I'll look into what happened. You should have had it on Tuesday."

"Thanks, Jack."

"Take off your bra."

"Don't you want my new order first?"

"After you describe your nipples to me. Are they hard?"

Squeezing her legs together to intensify the pleasant throb between them, she massaged the stiff peaks through her silk blouse. "Very."

"God. I want to touch them. Your blouse, your bra, I want them off now."

"You are so demanding."

"Yeah. And you love it. Now take them off."

He was right, she did love it. His command made her stomach flutter. Normally, Kirby didn't take orders, she issued them. Jack Taylor was her secret indulgence and submission to him her secret vice. It wasn't like this was real life, after all. It was fantasy.

She unbuttoned her blouse and scraped the bra across her nipples, moaning loudly for his benefit.

"You like that, don't you?" he said.

"The lace of my bra is scratchy. It makes my breasts tingle."

"I thought I told you to take it off."

"I'm working on it." She unsnapped the front clasp, the lace slithering across her nipples as the cups popped free. "Oh, Jack, will you look at that? My nipples just got all hard." She circled one with a finger. "Do you wish you could touch them?"

"God, you're a tease."

"I aim to please."

"You please me, all right. Now, pinch those tight nipples for me."

She did, electric shock streaking down between her legs. "That feels so nice."

"Imagine that I've got your nipple in my mouth. I'm thinking you taste like honey."

"Bite it."

"Sure, baby."

She pinched harder, then clamped her legs together at the burst of heat.

"Jesus, I want to fuck you right now. I want my hand in your pussy. Do it for me."

"Do what?" She liked specifics, liked hearing them said in that deep growl that indicated he was turned on.

"Spread your legs and put two fingers in your pussy."

Twisting to prop her feet on the desk, she slid her skirt up her thighs and parted her folds with her fingers.

"Jack, you make me so wet. Feel how wet I am."

Her fingers slid in her juices.

"Touch your clit. Massage it. Pretend it's my tongue. You do want my tongue on you, don't you?"

"Oh God, yes, Jack." She closed her eyes and let her head rest on the back of her chair. "I want you to suck my clit until I scream."

She withdrew her fingers and rubbed the wet tips across the aching points of her breasts. "Have you got your cock out?"

"In my hand, baby. And it's hard as a rock."

This was so freaking kinky, and she loved it. Sex in the afternoon, in her office, over the phone with a man she'd never met. It couldn't get any better.

"Rub the tip against your clit."

With her eyes closed, the sun beating on her head, she imagined clasping her hand tightly around that hard cock and rubbing herself to orgasm. Her hips rotated, picking up the rhythm of her fingers.

"You want me to eat you, baby?"

"Not yet. I want to suck you."

She'd been known to have five orgasms in one phone conversation. This time she felt like slowing it down, like concentrating on him, on his voice, his groans, his orgasm. "Imagine me taking just the crown between my lips and licking that little drop of come out of the center."

He made a soft guttural sound she felt way up inside. "Go on."

"Now I'm sliding down, swirling my tongue all the way, until I'm taking all of you." She worked herself gently as she talked, keeping close to the edge, but still in control. "I'm sucking hard on the way back up. I've got your balls in my hand and I'm squeezing. Do you like that?"

"Jesus, you're going to make me come."

"That's what I want, Jack. I want your come filling my mouth. I want to swallow every last drop."

His breath sawed in her ear. "You make me wild and crazy. I want to fuck you so bad."

"Stick it in me then. God, Jack, I want it. Hard and fast. Make me scream."

"I'm ramming you against the desk, baby, and God, are you ever gonna scream."

She shoved two fingers inside, but it simply couldn't fill her the way she knew he would if he ever got close enough. Instead, she attacked her clitoris, slipping, sliding, stroking. Her hips bucked against the assault.

"Come, Kirby, do it now, while I'm fucking the hell out of you."

She came when he told her to, came hard, doubling over with it. "Oh God, Jack. Oh God. Please, oh please."

The orgasm seemed to last forever, her muscles spasming around her fingers. She wanted to scream, but Cindy would hear. Not that she cared, she just didn't want to share this time with Jack.

His gulp of air and deep groan signaled his own release. For a space of time there was nothing but the harsh play of his breath across the phone line and her own soft sighs as she floated back to earth.

God, it had been intense, just what she'd craved.

He let out a long breath, then said, "Jesus, that was good."

Damn right. Jack was the best. "Thank you."

"Always my pleasure to pleasure a lady." His breathing hadn't returned to normal. She liked that she could do that to him.

She wondered how he cleaned up afterwards. The thought should have had a dampening quality to the whole interlude, but instead it made her want to touch herself again. He'd have to take himself in hand to do the cleanup.

Damn, she could have another go at him. She could spend the entire afternoon living out her fantasies. It was getting sort of crazy. "Jack, we have to stop doing this."

"Yeah, right." He laughed. "You're addicted. You can't stop."

He was right. She was addicted to the kinkiness of it, to the potential exposure, and to the fact that she could imagine him to be anything she wanted him to be. He was on the East Coast, she on the West. They'd been supplier-customer for two years, phone sex lovers for a year. She'd never asked to meet him; he'd never suggested it either.

The really strange thing was, they talked, too. About everything. Sometimes, she actually unloaded on him. Kirby didn't unload on anyone, because that might give away too much. It was sort of absurd the way she trusted him with her secrets, and even ludicrous how damn good talking with him felt. After all, he could have been some scummy creep who'd suddenly show up on the West Coast, trying to blackmail her. Though being her supplier and working for a large corporate group, he had more to lose than she did. Still, even without that safety net, she felt, well, safe with him.

Safe. Long distance. Their relationship was almost a fantasy. He didn't live close enough to screw over her life or her business.

The best thing was, all she had to do to get rid of him was hang up.

TWO

Jack Taylor threw the soiled napkin in the waste basket, zipped his pants, and buckled his belt. In some sane part of his mind, he knew that locking his office door and whacking off in the middle of the afternoon was not a good idea. Idiotic, yet he couldn't get enough of Kirby Prescott, and he wanted far more than what he already had with her.

"So, tell me what's wrong?" he spoke into the phone.

"Nothing's wrong."

"Kirby, my sweet, I can hear it in your voice."

"I'm not your sweet."

Oh yes, she was. She just didn't know it yet. "Did you have a fight with your sister about whether you'd wear daisy yellow in the wedding?"

"Daisy yellow is insipid. She wouldn't even suggest it."

"You did have a fight with her, didn't you?"

"It wasn't a fight."

"What was it, then?"

"You're scary. How did you know I even talked to her?"

"You always come harder after you've had a fight with her."

"It wasn't a fight, Jack. It was a discussion."

"What did you discuss?"

He knew he'd get it out of her eventually. He knew a helluva lot about Kirby Prescott. She didn't have many female confidants, and certainly no male ones, except for him. She kept everything inside, tied up with a nice, neat little bow. Until he got her talking. After sex. Almost like pillow talk. It was then she told him about the best parts of herself, though she'd never characterize it that way. That's when she revealed her goals, her aspirations, her dreams. Her fears. Her desires.

He could almost hear the little wheels of her mind working. How much to reveal? How much to keep to herself? Inevitably, she'd tell him everything.

"I get the sense that she thinks I'm envious that she's getting married."

"Aren't you?"

She gave a quick, definitive answer. "No. I've got my business. What more do I need?"

He knew just how much more she needed. It was there between the lines of everything she'd said to him over the last two years. She needed to feel and feel strongly. She needed to give everything she had, to let it all go, and just . . . feel. She'd never admit that she wanted to fall in love. She probably didn't even know it on a conscious level. But he knew. Loving was the only way to experience the fires of emotion she thought she'd lost.

He would show her the fire.

Kirby broke the silence first. "Okay, sometimes, I wonder what it would be like to, you know, be with someone full time. But then he'd probably tell me I couldn't work long hours or I had to be home to cook him dinner or, God forbid, he'd want me to quit work to stay home with kids." She stopped, then dropped her voice to that seductive pitch that had him hardening again. "And most assuredly, Jack, I'd have to give you up."

No, she wouldn't. He'd save that surprise for later, though. "Ah well, we can't have that. How would I survive my afternoon meetings?"

"I knew you'd understand."

He did, perfectly. Kirby's biological clock was ticking. The finalization of his plan wouldn't come a moment too soon. He wasn't about to let some West Coast bozo answer the call of the wild before he got there.

"Got a hot date this weekend?" he ventured.

"Yes, as a matter of fact. Dinner with my sister and her fiancé on Saturday."

He smiled, pleased that she wouldn't be with another man. The sister's fiancé didn't count. He glanced at the airline ticket on his desk, the one he'd booked over two weeks ago.

"I'm flying out tomorrow morning. Let's do dinner Friday." Though waiting the extra day to see her might just kill him.

The stunned silence was palpable, followed by her long exhalation of breath. "You're coming out here?"

"Yeah. Business. I'm staying the weekend." He was coming for *her*, but he wouldn't tell her that. He wasn't sure she was ready to hear it, yet, but he'd make sure she was by the time he left Sunday afternoon.

"You've never had to fly out here before."

The slight note of trepidation in her voice rumbled through his gut. "There's always a first time."

A first time to meet. A first time to fuck. A first time to bury his tongue snugly against her and drink her in as she came. A first time to feel it all, not just hear it or imagine it.

"Umm," she murmured. The sound vibrated through him.

He could almost hear her mind working. If they met face-to-face, their relationship would change. The stakes would be raised. They'd become more to each other than just voices on the phone.

If things didn't go well, they might have to give up their afternoon phone trysts.

He wouldn't let her doubts stop him. After all, he hadn't let his own doubts get in the way. "I'll pick you up at seven. What's your home address?"

She gave it to him. Almost by rote, it seemed, without thinking. Because he told her to. So, there was hope. As long as he kept a firm hand on things. As long as he didn't let her think too much, didn't let her natural tendency to retain control rear its head.

"And Kirby, don't wear any panties."

He cut the connection, then buzzed his secretary. "Put all my calls into voicemail for the rest of the afternoon."

If she called back to cancel, she'd find him unavailable.

He *would* see her. He *would* have her. No question about it. Of course, he'd have to lead her to the inevitable conclusion. After the weekend he'd planned for her, a lot of loving, a lot of fire, saying no to him would never enter her mind.

He'd been a product manager when it started, Kirby his best customer, even if her orders were peanuts, comparatively. First, there'd been a little personal inquiry, getting to know the woman behind the voice. Then, suggestive flirting. When he'd become VP of Sales, he refused to give her up, hadn't even told her about the promotion. Because he'd feared losing her. The flirting had turned to discussions about their tastes in the bedroom. That day, *the* day . . . all he could remember now was sitting at his desk with a painful boner that required immediate relief. He'd told Kirby about it, complained there was no way he could leave his office to attend his meeting with that thing standing at attention. She'd offered to talk him through release.

They'd been doing the phone thing a couple of times a week ever since.

He was obsessed. He couldn't stop doing it. He admitted that fact, and he didn't care.

Intelligent, confident, driven, with just a hint of vulnerability, Kirby was all the things he most admired in a woman. She sizzled with sensuality. He wanted her in his life, not twice a week over the phone, but *in* his life, a part of it. So, over the last six months, he'd painstakingly set in motion his plan to have her. Permanently. Career women freaked out at the idea that a male wanted to "have" them, as if it were a stamp of ownership that curtailed their right to vote or otherwise impaired their decision-making ability. So he hadn't told her about the new sales office he was opening in San Francisco or that he intended spending at least half his time there, maybe far more. Nor that he'd done it all for her. A woman like Kirby would think he expected her to give up something in return.

This weekend, he planned to demonstrate that she wouldn't have to give up anything except her vibrator.

No, not even that. He was sure they could make good use of it together.

She'd never nervously anticipated a date before. Not even in high school when Bucky Williams, captain of the football team, had asked her to the prom when she was a sophomore.

At sweet sixteen, in the back seat of Bucky's dad's Oldsmobile, he had managed to give her her first orgasm.

What the hell was she thinking about old Bucky for?

Because she was freaking nervous, petrified even, of meeting Jack.

What's up with that?

She liked their phone sex just the way it was. She loved the mystery of an unknown face. She craved the sound of his voice, felt it clear up inside her, like a hard cock or a stiff finger. Those two delightful things were all she'd been thinking about when she'd agreed.

If you could call it thinking.

Once said, though, she wouldn't go back on it. That smacked of fear, and she wasn't afraid. She simply preferred the status quo.

So she'd taken Friday afternoon off. She'd shopped, ordered dinner from Petrici's on the way home—because she wouldn't waste a minute getting him into bed—then

soaked in a steaming tub with fragrant bubbles. Legs
smoothed with a twice-over shave and skin softened with
an erotic concoction she'd formulated herself, she rose
from her bath. The light scent of the oil lingered. She sold
it with the guarantee that it tantalized male senses. The
barely-there makeup she applied softened her nose, added
a sultry pout to her lips, and augmented the almond shape
of her eyes. Moussed hair, soft not sticky, fell past her
shoulders in glorious waves.

Thigh-high stockings clung to the tops of her legs.
She'd done without the garter and, of course, without the
panties per Jack's request. She'd chosen a halter dress that
caressed her breasts within its sensuous folds. When she
leaned forward, Jack would catch a glimpse of breast. The
indecently short green skirt swished around her thighs. Her
matching heels caressed her feet. She couldn't understand
why so many women said they were uncomfortable. The
key was not to walk around in them for very long. She
didn't plan on doing much walking tonight.

She was gorgeous. One look would enslave the man.
He'd be panting like a dog.

So why was she having trouble catching her breath?
She'd stopped five times in the middle of her makeup to remind herself to breathe. Her stomach fluttered. Her heart
seemed to cease in her chest. She hadn't even bothered to
pour herself a glass of wine, she was already too damn
light-headed.

Get a grip. It's only Jack. What's there to be afraid of?

Men didn't make her quake with fright. She made *them*
quake. He was just a salesman, for God's sake. She was the
CEO of her own corporation. Okay, so the business was
small in the grand scheme of things, but it was hers. She
could hold her own with Jack. She wasn't the gullible
young woman she'd been when she'd first started out in
business. She allowed no one to take advantage of her or to
gain the upper, controlling hand, not in her career or her
life. She'd let that happen once, five years ago, but never
again.

So why did it seem that her self-confidence had deserted her?

What if Jack was dogmeat to look at? She could always close her eyes while he was doing her. What if he smelled bad or had atrocious breath? She'd wear a nose pin. What if, God forbid, he had a small dick? No way around that one.

"Jesus," she muttered at the reflection in her mirror. "Jack is the hottest thing since someone invented battery-operated vibrators. And most important, he's got a round-trip ticket."

She straightened her shoulders, fluffed her hair, then stroked her hands over her bodice. For just a moment she imagined the fingers caressing her breasts were Jack's. Her nipples hardened against her palms. "I'm gonna get laid tonight," she whispered. "Boy, am I gonna get laid."

The doorbell rang.

Her stomach flew up into her throat. Racing out of the bathroom, she almost tripped on her high heels—something she'd never done before in her life. She managed to slow down in the hallway, smoothing first her skirt, then her hair. She'd look calm when she let him in, even if she didn't feel exactly calm.

With one more quick check in the front hall mirror, she opened the door.

Then she saw him.

Oh shit.

THREE

Christ, she was more beautiful than he'd ever imagined, even in his wildest fantasies. Her hair, the color of garnets in sunlight, curled softly past her shoulders. Her lips shone like rubies, and her eyes took on the hue of her emerald dress. Said dress draped her body, baring creamy kissable shoulders, accentuated her splendid breasts, and swirled around her thighs, calling attention to a delectable pair of legs he could worship with his hands and mouth. Her exotic perfume drifted in the air around him, intoxicating him as much as the sight of her.

She could have been fat, buck-toothed, and horse-faced, and it wouldn't have made a damn bit of difference. He'd want her anyway. He wanted that voice. He wanted the woman who'd unabashedly shared her dreams, her desires, her sexuality.

The package she came in was a bonus.

All Jack wanted to do was get inside, inside her apartment and inside her. The graphic vision of himself buried between her legs shot blood to his groin and stiffened his dick.

When he finally raised his gaze to her incredibly green eyes, he found them riveted on the massive boner tenting his trousers. Her luscious lips parted in an unconscious invitation.

Jesus H. Christ, he'd intended to wine and dine her first, not screw the hell out of her before they'd exchanged a word. Not that it was a bad idea.

"Are you wearing panties, Kirby?"

She started. Her eyes widened. "Jack?"

That voice. Just the sound of his name on her lips sent his libido a notch higher. But hell, she didn't even realize who he was.

"Expecting someone else?"

Her gaze traveled the length of him. She swallowed, licked her lips. "I ordered dinner. I was waiting for . . ." She trailed off.

He hoped she hadn't expected the take-out guy to ask if she was wearing panties. "Do I look like a pizza delivery boy?"

"Umm, no."

The Kirby he knew on the phone oozed confidence. That woman would have grabbed him by his tie, yanked him inside, and ripped open his pants. This Kirby, as gorgeous as she was, seemed . . . unsettled.

He could work with that. In fact, he liked the hint of anxiety. "Let's start over. You close the door, I'll ring the bell, and we'll see how the next one goes."

She didn't say anything, didn't smile, just stared at the top of his head.

It hit him then. She was staring at his head. His almost bald head. And she stared *down* at him, since her high-heeled fuck-me shoes made her just about three inches taller than him.

Jack Taylor hadn't been self-conscious about his stature since high school. He hadn't worried about his lack of hair since he'd started losing it in his twenties. In fact, he'd found the combination an advantage. People tended to underestimate him, as if his height and haircount somehow diminished his intelligence. He supposed it was akin to being a buxom blonde with a high IQ. All people saw was the exterior. Then you had them where you wanted them, advantage to the intelligent, big-breasted blonde . . . or the short, bald guy.

Kirby Prescott, on the other hand, looked at him as if he were a rodent.

He was up to the challenge. In fact, he looked forward to it, as much as he looked forward to sliding his hands beneath her dress.

Down the hall, the elevator dinged and a snappy, white-jacketed courier flounced off, carrying two black-and-white-striped bags declaring themselves products of Petrici's. Italian seasonings scented the air.

The take-out.

Kirby didn't do things by half measures. No Kentucky-fried or pizza for her.

Finally she smiled. He'd been waiting for that smile, and his heart actually flipped over as it transformed her face. Maybe he was wrong about the rodent thing.

"Dinner. I thought we'd eat in instead of trying to find a restaurant where we'd have to wait hours for a table." She puffed out a little breath of air. "Actually, that's a lie. I decided right away that we wouldn't go out. I hope that's okay."

Kirby knew she was talking too fast. She also knew she'd stared at his head way too long. She could see the bald top of it. From above. God, she had to get out of these heels—and fast. He might be an inch or so taller than her if she wasn't trapped in these damn shoes.

She grabbed the bags from her favorite Petrici's boy, smiled, and hoped he'd just disappear. He didn't. She blushed. She actually freaking blushed, and she never blushed. Just like she was never nervous. Ha!

What was the kid waiting for anyway? He stared at Jack, then glanced at her. *Go away, you little nimrod.*

Then she remembered. The kid wanted his tip. She'd already paid for the food by credit card, but she always tipped generously to ensure good service the next time. Even as she wondered where her purse was, Jack reached into his hip pocket for his wallet.

"Don't worry, I'll get it," she said, her voice coming out unnaturally high and, God forbid, shrill. Because when Jack shifted, his pants stretched tight across his front again. He might be on the short, bald side, but the one thing she knew she didn't have to worry about was the size issue. The man was impressive below the waist.

"I've already got it," he said, waving her aside.

He palmed the boy some bills, who politely shoved them in his pocket without looking.

Alone again, as the kid disappeared inside the elevator, she had no choice but to invite Jack in. "I hope you like Italian."

"I'll eat anything," he answered.

Her stomach jumped at the sexual reference. Oh yeah, she knew what he'd like to eat. She wasn't handling this well. She felt as unsure as Kristin. It was just that bald head. It was distracting. It wasn't even a sexy complete-bald like the Commish after he started doing *The Shield*. Jack had hair on the sides and back, just above the collar of his white shirt. The fact that he was shorter than her in heels didn't help her composure, either.

God, she really *was* shallow.

She hurried to the kitchen, her steps awkward, the bags suddenly heavy. The front door snicked behind them. Shutting her in with Jack.

She was afraid all that stuff about retaining control because of the distance crumbled to dust when he stood inside her apartment.

She dumped the bags on the counter. Her timing sucked. She should have had the dinner here and already set out. Lace, silver, and candles adorned the dining room table. The wine chilled in the refrigerator.

A glass of wine, damn, that's what she needed.

First, the shoes. Putting one hand on the counter, she leaned down to push off a heel.

"Leave them on."

Despite his height, he sure managed to fill the doorway. He had a stirring breadth to his shoulders and chest. Quite a nice bod, in fact. There was something about a well-dressed businessman that got her juices flowing. He was actually pretty damn good-looking, too. Straight nose, firm jaw, longish eyelashes over a smoky pair of gray eyes.

But . . .

"I like the shoes. They make me hot. Leave them on."

The way he was looking at them made *her* hot, and unbearably moist. Plus, she couldn't very well say she was taking them off so she wouldn't be taller than him. That would be just plain rude.

"I should have told you."

Her heart started to pound. She really didn't want to discuss this. Some things were better left unsaid. Like at the end of the night when you'd had the worst possible date of your life, you didn't say *I'd rather slit my wrists than see you again*. You gave a polite no thanks. No need to get mean about it.

"Told me what?" She put her foot, still ensnared inside the shoe, back on the tile floor.

He smiled. "You're shocked because you expected six-foot-two and a mane like a lion."

"I—"

With several steps into the room, he crowded her against the counter without actually touching her. Suddenly he didn't seem so short. Or maybe she was just shrinking against the tile counter.

"Don't deny it, Kirby."

"I wasn't going to."

He put a hand under her chin, his thumb caressing her jaw, his fingers circling her throat. "Good. Because before the night's over, you're not going to give a damn how tall I am. You're going to crave the feel of my scalp beneath your fingers when I tongue you to the best orgasm you've ever had in your life."

Oh my God. A fresh bud of moisture blossomed between her legs. Suddenly this was Jack, her Jack, her afternoon delight. What did it matter how short he was? In bed, they'd be equals.

Except when she wanted to be on top.

He reached behind her. A bag rustled. His chest brushed her breasts. Her nipples tightened. He smiled, knowing exactly what he did to her. A plastic container hit the counter. With his lips only centimeters from her ear, he said, "First, we should eat. To keep your strength up. You're going to need it."

She pushed against his chest with her fingertips and rose to her full high-heeled height. "I think you're the one who'll need to keep up his strength."

His chest was firm beneath her touch. She let her hand rest there, his heart beating against her palm, his body heat reaching out to her. She didn't have to look *that* far down. Besides, this wasn't a life commitment, it was just a night. Filled with the promise of hot, delicious sex. Then he'd go back to the East Coast. Maybe they'd talk on the phone again, maybe they wouldn't. It didn't matter.

All that mattered right now was tonight.

Returning from the kitchen, Kirby placed the frothy confection on the table between them, then stood back to survey the treat. Parfait stripes, strawberries, and loads of whipped cream.

Jack's mind went into overload with possibilities.

"You didn't answer me about the panties, Kirby. I told you not to wear any."

"I don't do well taking orders, Jack."

Her dress was short, her legs endless, and the creamy column of her throat begged for his kiss. Hands resting at her waist, she looked down at him, her lips parted with a woman-on-top smile.

She took orders well on the phone and enjoyed every moment. He'd have to show her it was no different in person.

During dinner, they'd done the mating dance. They talked, but about what, he couldn't remember. He watched her lips as she spoke, her tongue as she licked away the cream sauce. Her nipples captured his attention with every breath she took. Her fingers seemed to constantly caress her skin, skimming her collar bone, dipping down to the swell of her breast. He didn't taste the linguini or savor the clams. He savored her.

She was a goddamn tease, and that made him hornier than hell. The sparkle in her eyes said she loved what she was doing to him. If he'd had no sense of restraint, he'd have shoved his chair back from the table, freed his raging hard on, and taken her right there, plate of linguini unfinished and . . .

He had shown restraint, however, and while she'd teased him, he'd known, evidenced by the thrust of her nipples against her dress, that she teased herself as well.

Dinner and the dance were over. They'd now moved on to the battle. He intended to win.

She stood only an arm's length away. Still seated, he could have reeled her in, pulled her between his thighs, could have tested for the panty line through the silkiness of her dress. Or buried his face at her juncture. Instead, he rescued a blob of whipped cream that threatened to topple off her parfait. Looking up at her, he sucked the sweet cream from his finger.

Kirby pulled her lower lip between her teeth. Her pupils dilated.

"I think we should eat dessert on the couch, don't you?" He pushed away from the table, grabbed two spoons and the dessert, and headed for the comfort of the living room.

She didn't say a word, but the soft swish of her skirt told him she followed.

She was a leather-and-chrome lady, the sofa, chair, and ottoman made of an artfully worn-looking beige leather, the coffee and end tables, glass and chrome. Not a single fingerprint marred the surfaces. The matching artwork was tasteful and expensive, but standoffish, black-and-white photos of burgeoning, long-stemmed flowers. The delicate blossoms reminded him of a woman's vulva, which was probably what Kirby had intended. The room did not look lived in, as if she didn't spend much time at home. No *TV Guide*, no heel prints in the ottoman, no thumbed magazines, no well-read paperback romance novels. But then, Kirby would never have opened the pages of a romance. She was a woman who turned her own fantasies into reality.

Tonight, he'd do it for her.

The tops of the strawberries had been trimmed and dusted with sugar, a sprinkling of it powdered the glass as he set the bowl on the coffee table. He enjoyed the image, as if he'd placed his stamp on the impersonal room. On her. He plucked out a piece of fruit, sucked the sugar off, and popped it in his mouth. Then he smiled and picked out another. "Good. You want one?"

She eyed the berry in his hand.

"You have to come here to get it."

She stopped on the other side of the coffee table. "What makes you think I want it at all?"

She wanted it all right, that telltale pulse at her throat gave her away. She just didn't want to give in. On the phone, she was a slave to his voice. Face-to-face, she hung on to her control like a shield. He knew the chink in her armor. Kirby loved to come. She was dying to know if what they shared on the phone would be magnified tenfold in person.

"Come here, and I'll feed it to you." He dipped the strawberry in whipped cream and held it out.

"I can feed myself, thank you very much." Still, she licked her lips with anticipation. He knew if he got his hands between her legs, he'd find her body hot and wet for him.

Without saying a word, he flicked the strawberry with the tip of his tongue. She swallowed, and, as if he were the Pied Piper, stepped toward him, seemingly entranced by the berry so close to his mouth. And his tongue.

He slipped the fruit between her lips when she got close enough for him to smell her subtle, yet erotic perfume. Then he eased down onto the sofa and patted the leather.

"Sit. Then you can feed me one."

She sat on the couch beside him, one leg crooked beneath her, the dress coming to rest near the tops of her thighs. The lace of thigh-high stockings peeked from beneath the hem. Leaning forward, she freed a strawberry, capturing a good dose of whipped cream on the tip.

"So," she said, smiling, "is this supposed to be sexy? You feed me, I feed you. Sounds like some hokey movie on the Romance Channel."

God, she was tough. A lesser man might have paled beneath her sarcasm. Since the moment she pulled away from the kitchen counter, straightened her shoulders, and stared down her nose, she'd been challenging him. Every movement she made, every nonchalant flip of her hair, every stroke of her fingers against her skin, all were designed to bring him to his knees.

What Kirby didn't realize was that on his knees was exactly where he wanted to be. On his knees, with her legs draped over his shoulders, while he tasted the sweetness between them.

"Hokey, maybe. But I'm going to enjoy eating out of . . . your hand."

Melting whipped cream dripped onto her finger. He leaned forward to lick it off. She made a honeyed little sound that wrapped around his cock. He closed in, plucking the strawberry from her fingers with his teeth and putting his body right where it wanted to be. Between her thighs.

With his chest, he forced her back against the arm of the sofa.

"What are you doing?"

"Checking for panties."

He slid his hands up both thighs, stroking the silk thigh-highs with his thumbs until he found his mark. He caressed her with his fingers.

"It was my choice not to wear them," she said, ever the woman in control. A slight hitch in her voice gave her away.

He moved her more fully beneath him, tugging one leg up along the sofa back.

"Wait. My shoe. The heel will damage the leather."

He pushed her leg higher, resting her calf along his arm, the shoe now dangling. "See, no damage."

"This is awkward, Jack."

Still challenging. He reached to the side for another strawberry. This time he pushed her skirt higher, revealing her beautiful snatch.

"Jesus, you're pretty down there."

She made a noise in her throat. "You're crazy."

"That's exactly what you do to me, baby." Then he parted the lips of her delectable pussy and brushed her clit with the strawberry and cream.

Kirby gasped. "That's cold."

"It won't be for long."

Kirby bit back a moan. He was right. Already the whipped cream dribbled down between her pussy lips. He moved the berry against her. Oh, that felt incredible. Nubby, scratchy, delicious.

She clutched Jack's shoulders, dug her nails into the soft cotton of his shirt.

"You're going to come all over this sweet little strawberry."

All through dinner, she'd wanted to jump him. She'd flirted and teased outrageously. He hadn't risen to the bait. Now . . . he just might succeed in making her scream.

She'd never had a problem screaming before. It wasn't a sign of being out of control. It *was* control and meant that *she* was in control of her own orgasm.

Somehow, everything was different with Jack. He'd told

her not to wear panties. So she hadn't. He told her to sit and eat fruit from his fingers. She did. Now, he was telling her to come and she would.

If she didn't stop him first.

"I'm not ready to come yet, Jack." She bit her lip, hoping the light pain would keep orgasm at bay.

He slid the strawberry down her flesh, then into her slick channel. All the while watching her with those amazing gray eyes. "You can come as many times as you like. Starting right now."

The nubby skin caressed her inner walls as he slowly pumped the berry. She stopped breathing, caught herself, and dragged in air. The burst of oxygen made her dizzy.

He was willing her to come, forcing her. With those eyes and those fingers and that damn piece of fruit.

She'd been so willing to do anything for him when he was three thousand miles away. Now . . . it felt like giving up a part of herself.

Kirby pushed at his shoulders.

Jack slid back, and down, his face suddenly inches from her clitoris. Then he was on her. His tongue lapped her engorged button, then his lips plucked the strawberry from inside her.

"Jesus, that tastes good. All sweet and tart. You're so hot, and you smell so damn good—I want you to come."

He went for her clitoris with gusto and replaced the strawberry with his fingers. First one, then two. He alternately licked, then sucked, all the while working her insides with those remarkably dexterous fingers.

Kirby couldn't help herself. She arched against the arm of the sofa, grinding herself against his face. Her hands went to his head of their own volition. No hair to tangle in, just enticingly smooth scalp. He clutched her butt, held her close and ate her like she was the parfait.

So good. Don't come. Yes, please. No. Yes.

She exploded from the inside out, her body bucking against his mouth, her head hanging off the sofa. Eyes closed, stars bursting behind the lids, she screamed. Not because she wanted to, but because she had to.

Round one went to Jack Taylor.

Boy, did it ever.

But she had all night to turn the tables on him.

FOUR

Kirby stood and straightened her dress. "Very good. You didn't even get a drop of whipped cream on the material."

Jack smiled and backed off, relaxing against the leather. "That's because I licked you clean before any of it got on your clothes. Didn't want to waste a lick." He smoothed a hand down his torso. "Look, I didn't even mess up my tie either." He winked. "You enjoyed that orgasm. Don't worry, it won't be the last one tonight. I promise." He looked forward to the next. Immensely.

She fought a smile, the corner of her mouth twitching. "You know, I don't remember you being this cocky on the phone."

He raised one brow. Cocky? Him?

God, she was hot, her face flushed with orgasmic aftermath, her lips full and red where she'd bitten them just before she gave into that cry. The sound of it still vibrated in his gut. He was going to relish making her scream over and over, until finally she couldn't help but scream *his* name. Oh yeah, things were happening right on schedule. Before the weekend was out, she'd know exactly to whom she belonged. To whom she *wanted* to belong.

"Just stating the facts, ma'am."

She huffed. He smiled. It earned him a narrowed glare.

"I'm going to wash the dishes. The dishwasher's on the fritz, so we'll have to do them by hand. Up to helping me?" She grabbed the bowl, whipped cream now soggy, parfait untouched. Despite her casual tone, her hands trembled.

He was up for more than dishwashing. "I wouldn't do otherwise."

He followed her sweetly swaying ass into the dining room, picking up the two plates of congealed linguini. In the kitchen he placed them on the counter. "You want to save any of this stuff?"

She gave him a look, head lowered, eyes raised to meet his. "Do I look like I'm into leftovers?"

Nope. Kirby wouldn't take anybody's leftovers. Another thing he liked about her.

She flipped open the trash can and scraped the remains into the plastic liner, then put the plates in the sink.

"You want to wash or shall I?"

"You dry." She tossed the towel at him. He'd known she would test him. There was that age-old thing about men not drying the dishes.

Pouring soap on the mess, she filled the sink with water. Suds rose up her arms. He envisioned her in a steaming bath, her nipples flirting with bubbles, teasing him until he had to lick them bare. His cock twitched. He wanted her, God, how he wanted her, but he had so many pleasures to give her before he got his own.

She sponged and rinsed, letting the water drain off the china, then handed the plate to him. He dried and stacked.

"I love watching a woman being domestic," he said, just to get a rise out of her.

She eyed him. "And I adore a domesticated man."

He laughed. "A domesticated male would bore you."

She pursed her lips, but didn't answer. He knew he was right. Her breasts jiggled as she scrubbed at a dried bit. He took a step back to admire the curve of her ass and the toned calves as she worked. The high heels did him in. He tossed the towel on the counter and moved behind her, placing his hands on her hips to steady her as he rubbed his cock between her butt cheeks.

She elbowed him, splashing suds and water. "Don't you think we should wait until the dishes are done?"

"No." He raised her dress and squeezed her firm globes, then slid a finger forward to her pussy. "You're still wet."

"What do you expect? My hands are in dishwater." But her backside dipped into his crotch.

"I'd like to do you right here, with your arms sunk in hot, sudsy water."

He touched her clitoris. She shuddered.

"Not yet. Besides, the condoms are in the bedroom."

A subtle reminder that she didn't trust him enough to let him do her without protection. He wouldn't have considered it anyway, so the dig didn't make a difference. He massaged her clit. Her legs trembled slightly. "I've got one in my back pocket."

After a beat of silence, she said, "Jack, you're being a bad boy. You need to wait until you're asked."

Ah, so she still wanted to call the shots. She hadn't liked having an orgasm she didn't request and didn't orchestrate. He could work with that. What she hadn't figured out yet was that her feigned indifference only made the battle more enticing.

Jack probed her entrance with his finger, gathered more of her delicious cream and headed back to her clit. She parted her legs to give him greater access. With his other hand, he unzipped his pants and pulled out his cock. Using her own juices, he coated the tip, then rubbed between her cheeks. A puff of air sighed out of her. Feeling like a lion, he nipped at the soft skin of her shoulder.

"I can whip that little package out of my pocket right now. Just say the word."

She braced her hands on the edge of the sink, her fingers whitened despite the heat of the water she'd had them in. Her body pushed back and rotated against his cock.

"You know you want it," he whispered against her over-heated flesh. He also knew she'd fight him all the way. He relished the pleasure of pushing her over the edge, could wait for it, because when she did succumb, she'd blow them both away with the explosion.

She did want it, so badly that if he put his cock at the opening of her vagina, she would push back and ram it home. She just wanted to feel him all the way up to her throat, which, based on his length against her backside, was quite possible.

Stupid, stupid. Worse, her thoughts were out of control.

God, she wanted to turn, to see him, to put her hands on him, maybe even to fall to her knees and take that massive tool in her mouth. Damn, wouldn't he love that—her in thrall?

Forget it. Been there, done that, and the emotions weren't ones she cared to repeat.

"Not right now, thank you." She managed to sound quite prim, successfully hiding the emotions rumbling inside.

She used the edge of the sink to push herself upright, drawing away from the hardness of his cock and the tip of his finger against her clitoris. Sensation rippled through her body. She barely managed to keep yet another orgasm in check.

She thought she felt him chuckle against her back.

"Later," he said, amidst the sound of a rasping zipper, then he reached around her for the towel he'd abandoned.

She handed him the last of the utensils to dry, then let the water gurgle down the drain. Using the spray, she washed the remains down the garbage disposal.

Her legs were still shaky, and her head swam. Damn, she just needed to get out of these shoes, to feel steady on her feet again.

She reached out for the towel to dry her hands. Instead,

Jack captured them, drying them with exquisite gentleness. Her skin tingled despite the fact that not a speck of male flesh touched her through the terrycloth.

She raised her gaze to his. He had incredibly lush lashes for a man. Men didn't deserve sexy lashes like that. A cocky, assured smile creased his mouth, and his gray eyes seemed to sparkle with mirth.

Bastard. He thought he was winning.

Just when did this become a battle?

Kirby knew. The war started on the couch when he made her come against his mouth even though she'd said she wasn't ready. Her body still quivered with need. That word didn't exist in her sexual lexicon, at least not applied to herself.

The man had gone down on her before he'd even kissed her. She'd let him and loved it. So far, he was controlling all their play.

"I can see you thinking again, Kirby. That's not a good thing."

"You haven't kissed me yet, Jack." She puckered her lips and smacked them for him.

"I gave you a much more intimate kiss."

He had an answer for everything. Had he been that way on the phone? Hmm, maybe. Definitely. She hadn't minded his demands then, not with a disconnected voice thousands of miles away. Now, well, she had a few demands of her own.

"I want a real kiss. On the mouth. And it better be good." She liked kissing, especially with a man who knew how to use his mouth as well as Jack did.

His smile grew. "I like a woman who knows what she wants and isn't afraid to ask for it."

At some point tonight, she'd figure out how to get the upper hand. Something had to work. "Shut up and kiss me." She'd always wanted to say that.

His lips were suddenly only a breath away. "My pleasure."

He captured her face in his hands and pulled her to meet

his mouth. His lips touched hers, tasting faintly of wine and her own essence. His tongue stroked her lower lip. She parted her own to let him slip inside. He certainly didn't slobber. He simply sucked a moan out of her before his hands even slipped down her back to pull her against him. His cock hit just right, somehow finding its way to her cleft.

Kirby wrapped her arms around his neck and angled her head. God, he tasted so . . . male. Their height difference actually seemed an advantage. She could take more of him, feel more of him. He held her steady as she parted her legs, pushing against him. He skimmed firm hands over her, slipping inside the opening of her halter dress to flick her nipples with his thumbs.

His kiss tantalized, rather than overpowered. Kept her on the edge, wanting more of him, but giving her only a taste, a gentle suction, then darting away. She followed where he led. When he cupped her butt and pulled her against his hard cock, she matched his rhythm, rocking against him, pleasuring herself.

"More?" he whispered against her mouth.

Yes, yes, more of everything. She barely managed to keep the whispered words from leaving her lips. With a mere touch, he brought her too close to begging.

She pulled back, mentally as well as physically, and shrugged. "That was very nice."

He leaned in for another quick taste of her lips. "Yeah."

"I think we need another glass of wine." She needed to occupy her hands and lips with something other than Jack. He disturbed her equilibrium, and worse, she liked the phenomenon. Breezing around him, she opened the fridge, the frosty air relieving the heat of her body. She pulled out the wine and returned to the dining room. The glasses filled, she set the bottle on the table. Picking up the crystal, she allowed herself a deep swallow.

Jack moved in behind her, reaching for his own glass. His arm brushed hers, his body heating her through the

thin material of her dress. Just like that, he stole her breath
and set her nerves tingling again.

"I think it's your turn now, Jack, don't you?"

Warm breath caressed her nape. "My turn for what?"

"Well, you've seen to my immediate relief. We should
deal with yours now, don't you think?" Attempting to stay
the trembling of her fingers, she held the stem of her glass
too tightly.

"Your wish is my command."

Oh yes, she would command. In a very short while, he'd
be the one close to begging. Anticipation flowed through
her veins, as potent and heady as the wine. She'd make him
scream. She'd make him beg. She'd make him lose control.
God, how she wanted that.

She turned then and smiled. "Follow me."

He looked forward to whatever she'd planned. Hints of
imagined triumph glinted in her green eyes, visions of
bringing him to his knees flashed. Oh baby, he'd follow her
anywhere. And he did, through the living room, down a
short hall lined with black-and-white prints of a half-naked
woman. The sleek lines in the pictures were Kirby's. Beyond that, the photographer had captured the essence of
womanhood. A carefully arched back, the hint of plump
breast, the lush curve of a perfectly rounded ass. Artful yet
seductive, the photographs were designed to mesmerize the
viewer. Jack would have been mesmerized if the real item
hadn't been leading him down the proverbial garden path.

An alluring scent grew stronger as they neared a doorway. From within, soft candlelight flickered. She turned,
crooked her finger, then disappeared inside. He had the
sense that forbidden pleasures or exquisite pain awaited
him, whichever Kirby desired to bestow.

The woman would make him pay for almost making her
come with just a kiss. She'd been close. He'd known it, yet
he'd stopped it with a word. A challenge. One she'd ac-

cepted. A good strategy always included advance and retreat. Give and take.

He stopped in the doorway to her inner sanctum. After
the leather, glass, and chrome of the living room, he didn't
expect the sheer femininity he found inside her bedroom.
The high brass bedstead frothed with frilly pillows and a
lacy spread. An almond-colored vanity gilded with gold
filled one corner, the surface covered with atomizers of all
colors and shapes. Candles flickered, providing the only
illumination.

Kirby had set her wineglass down on the bedside table
and now stood before a long cheval mirror. She held her
hair aloft, breasts thrust forward, and she stared at him
from the depths of the mirror. Then she leaned in and
freshened the deep red lipstick on her luscious lips. Most
had worn off during dinner, the rest she'd sucked from her
lips when he'd made her come on her couch.

He wanted to throw her on that high bed, kiss all her lipstick right back off, then fuck the hell out of her amidst the
array of fluffy pillows.

He'd wait, though. Until *she* couldn't wait a second
longer.

"Take off your clothes, Jack."

He stepped into the ultra-feminine room, set his glass
on the bureau, then loosened his tie and tugged his shirt
from his trousers. He undid the first four buttons, then
yanked the whole thing over his head and threw it on a
rocker sitting next to the bureau.

He met her gaze in the mirror. Her eyes widened
slightly as she took in the sight. He didn't work out in a
gym, but he did enjoy fixing up the old farmhouse he'd
bought two years ago. He'd ripped out the rotting porch,
replaced it, hauled away the rocks protruding from the
hard earth surrounding it, and planted new trees and flow-
ering shrubs.

Kirby would look perfect in the swing on the new front
porch, the scent of honeysuckle on the breeze. He could

take her on that swing, rocking her gently until she was mindless. Until they were both mindless.

"Like what you see?"

She shrugged. "You must work out. Now strip out of those pants."

"Yes, ma'am."

He did it slowly, watching her every reaction as he undid his belt buckle and inched down the zipper. Her nostrils flared like a magnificent racehorse, her breath quickened. Then she put her hands on her hips, nonchalantly, as if she felt nothing. Or maybe to hide the sudden shakiness of her fingers.

Jack saw everything. He knew she wanted as much as he.

Zipper undone, the white of his briefs showing through the open slacks, he halted the strip tease to toe off his shoes and kick them aside. Finally he shoved the pants and briefs over his hips, down his legs, and removed every last stitch of clothing, including his socks.

His cock stood at attention. He wrapped his fist around it, pumped twice until a drop of pre-cum pearled at the tip. He watched her reflection as she licked her lips.

"Touch me, Kirby," he murmured.

"How bad do you want it?"

He turned the key to her desire. "Real bad. I can't wait another second."

She came close enough to trail her hands down his chest. She combed through the smattering of hair, then followed the line of it down his abdomen. His dick jumped in his fist.

Nails dragging across his skin, she passed over his pulsing cock, then cupped his balls in one hand. And squeezed lightly. He closed his eyes, hissed in a breath.

"Touch me, baby." He unwrapped his hand and let his dick fall into her outstretched palm.

She rubbed the underside of his shaft, then slid a finger along the slit, spreading the tiny droplet of come around the tip. Closing her fingers around him, she moved her hand up and down, though she didn't give him the pressure he craved.

"Harder," he urged.

She looked into his eyes and smiled. "When I'm ready."

She was going to make him pay. Hell, it would be worth the torture in the long run. He wasn't ready to come for her yet. Not that he couldn't. Just that he wouldn't. The longer he held out, the better it would be. For both of them.

He'd waited so goddamn long for this first time, he wouldn't let it be over just for lack of a little self-control.

He captured her lips with his mouth, sucked at her, then slipped his tongue inside. Her fingers tightened around him as his tongue pumped her mouth, forcing a groan to well up from deep inside him.

"Ooh, Jack, I think you're getting harder."

Clearly, she enjoyed having the upper hand. He looked down, and the contrast of her red nails encasing his straining flesh ratcheted up the tension in his gut.

Control was needing it so bad you thought you'd die if you didn't get it, but still holding out. With her mouth on him, it would take every ounce of willpower he had not to burst.

Jack liked a challenge.

"Suck it, Kirby. Do it now."

"Don't rush me."

"Don't tease me."

He could have pushed her to her knees, but triumph was in getting her to do it all on her own.

She stroked him. "Poor Jack. Maybe I should put you out of your misery."

She dropped to her knees, meeting him eye-to-eye, so to speak.

He almost came when she closed those gorgeous red lips of hers over his crown. Her tongue probed. He sucked in a breath and tightened every muscle in his body.

Then she swallowed him whole.

FIVE

God, he was huge. She'd seen the bulge in his pants, felt him rub against her. To actually hold him, and finally to take him into her mouth . . . it was an indescribable pleasure.

Kirby loved sex. She loved orgasms. She loved the feel of a man inside her or his tongue on her clit. She also loved a big, hard cock in her mouth. Jack was bigger and better than any she'd ever had.

He touched the back of her throat. Her own juices flooded her thighs. He groaned and wrapped her hair around his hands, massaging her scalp as she worked him. She held him to her, the muscles of his butt bunched in her hands.

She pulled back, sucking hard, dragging her teeth along the hard ridge. Finally she swirled her tongue around the tip and went back for more. Despite his grip on her head, he didn't push or shove. He let her control.

With one hand, she reached under and squeezed his balls gently. He bucked against her, quivering in her mouth. She looked up. His head thrown back, neck corded. He was beautiful. From this position, he was a tall, muscled warrior towering over her.

She sucked and licked and reveled in the sounds he made. She longed, also, to put her hand between her legs. That was the thing about blow jobs. They made her as hot and as close to orgasm as they did the male recipient.

Suddenly he heaved out a great exhalation of air. "Shit, I gotta sit down before I fall."

Pulling out of her mouth, he slumped back on the bed, his butt just at the edge. Kirby stood and stepped between his spread legs, the urge to climb on top of him and take him into her trembling body nearly impossible to ignore.

But ignore it she would. She *would* make him come first.

He opened his eyes to mere slits. "For God's sake, don't stop now."

As if stopping ever entered her mind. Falling to her knees once more, she put her hands on his hard thighs and took that magnificent cock in her mouth again. He scraped her hair back from her face, and she angled to give him a better view.

This was the real Jack. She hadn't realized until this moment how much better it was with his hands on her, his eyes on her, watching her devour him. All those phone orgasms were nothing compared to this.

She wanted his come in her mouth. She wanted to swallow, to take everything he had to give. She craved it. She wanted to hear him cry out her name the way he did on the phone. The sound of that would be better than her own orgasm.

She raised herself long enough to demand, "Come now."

"Oh, Christ." He raised his hips and pushed back inside. "You're too good." He tugged on her hair. "But when I come, I'll come inside you."

He would not. He'd come now. She sucked harder, pumped faster, and rubbed his balls. He writhed against her, groaned, and arched once more.

"I'm going to be inside you the first time, Kirby."

She took him in as far as she could. A moan escaped him, and his belly rippled beneath her fingers.

"Inside you," he repeated, the tone clipped, as if he could barely manage to get the words out. This time he tangled his fingers in her hair and pulled to the point of pain.

He slipped from her mouth, rock hard, the tip engorged.

"I want you to come in my mouth."

"I'm coming inside *you.*"

She stared at him, her body screaming, her mind railing. The condoms were on the bedside table. Did it really matter whether he lost control in her mouth or her body? No. Just as long as he lost control.

She did so want that beautiful tool inside her. She wanted to ride it, wanted to come with it buried deep.

"Fine." Reaching for the first packet, she ripped it open with her teeth, the way a man would, then rolled the latex down his shaft, hoping it would be big enough. It left almost two inches of naked flesh at the base.

She hiked her skirt and climbed on top of him, ready to impale herself. She was more than wet enough to accommodate him.

His hands on her hips held her away from her goal. "Take off your dress. I want to touch your breasts."

She fumbled at the small gold belt around her waist, then undid the back zipper. Grabbing her dress by the hem, she jerked it over her head and threw it on the carpet.

Instead of her breasts, he went straight for her clit. That touch hit her like a zap of electricity. In one swift move he put two fingers inside her, using his thumb to massage her tight button. As if it no longer belonged to her, her body rocked against him, dying for his cock, but bending to the will of his fingers.

"Is that good, baby?"

She closed her eyes. Her head fell back. "Sweet Jesus, yes, but I want you inside me. You said that's what you wanted."

"I want to make sure you're wet enough. I don't want to hurt you."

"You're not going to hurt me."

He grabbed her, both hands at her waist, and propelled her to the side until she was flat on the bed, pillows plumping all around her, and Jack towering over her.

"I just want to make sure you're ready, baby."

"I *am* ready, dammit."

"But it'll be better."

He pushed between her thighs, parted her folds and found her clitoris. Magic fingers. Oh God, oh God, how was she supposed to resist when he touched her like that?

"Don't resist. Let it go."

She hadn't spoken aloud, she knew she hadn't. Jack just seemed to know.

"Let me make you feel good," Jack murmured.

"I don't want to feel good. I want to come."

He buried his face in her throat, his finger against that overly sensitive spot, and he shook. He was laughing at her. Oh dammit, he could make her body sing, make it weep.

He started to slide down her length, and she grabbed his ears. "You are not going down on me. You are getting inside me."

"Yes, ma'am. Whatever you say, ma'am."

She spread her legs. He grabbed her butt and plunged home.

Jesus. Home. Buried so deep inside her, he could die with a smile on his face.

"I do realize you conned me out of the on-top position."

He moved inside her, slowly. Excruciatingly slow, her soft flesh surrounding him, welcoming him. "Kirby—"

Digging her nails into his butt cheeks, she ground against him. "I *was* wet enough."

He gave her a deep thrust. "Shut up and let me fuck you."

"*Let* being the operative word." She bit her lip, stifling a sweet little moan.

"You love it. Admit it." Before the weekend was out, he'd have her admission that she couldn't live without it.

He grabbed her leg and raised it to his shoulder, allowing him deeper thrusts.

She moaned then and shoved her head back into the mountain of pillows. "Oh. That feels . . ."

"Perfect."

"Okay is how I'd describe it." She strained against him, pushing and pulling at the same time. Arching her body to allow him maximum depth.

"Liar." Short, sharp thrusts brought him closer to the edge. "You're almost ready to come."

"I am not." Her rapid breaths put the lie to that.

He reached between them and flicked her hot button. She sank her fingernails into his forearms.

"Come with me, baby," he coaxed.

Her muscles clenched around him. He kept his finger on her clitoris, swirling it in rhythm with each plunge. She bucked against him. He abandoned her clit, bracing both arms beneath her legs. They bounced against his biceps as he pounded hard, the new angle giving him the deepest penetration. She closed her eyes and panted.

"Make me come, Jack. Please make me come. Oh God! Oh yes! Please." She went over the top, chanting his name. Her walls milked him as she came hard.

Then he was falling with her, overcome by the most powerful, incredible orgasm he'd ever known.

Jack sprawled on top of her as if he were boneless. Or dead.

God. Yes, God. She'd seen the big man himself. Isn't that what people said? *I saw God.* When what they really meant was they'd just experienced the ultimate pleasure they wished would never end.

"You're squishing me," she said, pushing against his shoulders, the words dispelling the far too pleasant afterglow.

He rolled off her. "You know, I don't remember you fighting me this much on the phone. In fact, I distinctly remember you begging."

"I never begged." She had. Of course. If she really mulled over the last few minutes, she'd begged again.

A bit demeaning, yet utterly satisfying. She was weightless, floating, satiated.

Jack rolled over and propped his head on his hand to look down at her. "Were you always such an argumentative pain in the ass?"

"Were you always a dictatorial asshole?" She uttered the phrase lightly, but she'd known her share, one in particular who'd tried to control her life. She didn't truly believe Jack compared in any way.

He smiled. "Touché." Leaning down to nuzzle her ear, he murmured, "Don't tell me you didn't like that. It was good, and you know it."

She shrugged. "It was adequate." Not to mention stupendous.

"You're pissed because I didn't come in your mouth."

Oh yeah. That had been on her mind. "I did want that."

He ran his tongue along the outer shell. "There'll be another chance. I swear."

She pulled away from his distracting play. She couldn't think when he was doing that. "Jack darling, you need to learn how to take a little direction instead of always giving orders."

"You liked it well enough on the phone."

"That was on the phone."

"And in the flesh, it's different?"

Yes, it was different. She couldn't hang up on him. Then again, why was she fighting him anyway? It was only for the night, and he was so very, very good.

When she didn't answer immediately, he flopped back on the bed, throwing his arms wide. "All right, baby. I'm sorry. Blow me. Suck me. Swallow me. I'm all yours."

His cock, amazingly enough, stood straight up.

"You can't be ready yet."

He stroked himself. "I'm always ready. Now suck me."

"Jesus. You're still wearing the condom."

"I'll get rid of it."

"I'm exhausted. I need a rest." But she did so want him in her mouth again.

"I thought you said it was just *adequate.* How can you be exhausted after an *adequate* orgasm?"

"Jack. You're directing again."

"I was just trying to ascertain the facts. Sorry." Clearly, by the glint in his eye, he wasn't sorry at all.

The man was definitely getting to her. Two amazing orgasms, a far more than adequate fucking, and he could kiss the panties right off a nun. She wanted more, more, more. That was exactly where the problem lay.

With Jack, she wasn't top dog. No, she was the one being led around on a leash. She hadn't even asked what he'd planned for the rest of the night, as if she was leaving the decision completely up to him.

"Are you spending the night, Jack?"

"Yeah."

She raised one brow.

"I mean, if you'd like that."

She didn't know what she wanted. Certainly another orgasm. Or two or three. But the whole night? Though she preferred going to a man's apartment, where the time they parted was up to her, she occasionally invited a date home. Though not to stay the entire night. That was the crux of the matter. Jack made her want to say yes to an entire night. "You make me indecisive."

"And you hate that."

"Yeah."

"I have a hotel room. It's your choice, sweetheart. You wanna kick me out?" It didn't appear that he'd mind what she chose. His body was loose, relaxed, his hands stacked behind his head. Well, everything except his cock was relaxed. That still stood at attention, waiting for her.

She bit her lip. Jesus, she wasn't usually a lip biter either. *What's up with that? Make up your friggin' mind.*

Tell him to go or stay or whatever the hell, but be done with it.

He reached out a hand to stroke her face. "I want to be with you. I want to make you come again. And again. I want to wake up in the morning with you in my arms. I want to spend the whole weekend with you."

The *weekend*? In his arms? Oh my God. An infinitesimal yet detestable part of her actually yearned for it. She hadn't experienced a morning after since . . . well, not in a long, long time.

"It's up to you, Kirby. But you do have to ask for it if you want it."

Her heart pounded. She suddenly wanted to feel what it was like to wake up with this man's arms around her. Yet she was terrified of it, too. In case she liked it way too much. She'd been conned before.

This was Jack. He was different. Wasn't he?

Would she kick herself for not testing it out? It was only a weekend, after all.

Thinking, thinking, thinking.

"You're dangerous when you think that hard, sweetheart."

Done thinking. "Stay."

Oh God. She was committed.

SIX

"It's early still. Let's go out for a drink at one of your favorite spots."

He was extraordinarily pleased with himself. It had been touch-and-go there for a minute, but she'd succumbed. His, for the weekend. After that, a lifetime. He'd break that part of it to her gently. Kirby spooked easily. Tonight was too early to reveal the true nature of his campaign. By Sunday she'd be spouting the idea herself.

"You have *got* to be kidding." She rolled, her back to him, her luscious backside inviting his touch. He skimmed a finger down the cleft of her buttocks.

"I want to show you off. Every man will know you've been well fucked. By me."

"You're a conceited pig."

He smiled. "Yeah."

He leaned over to bite her neck. That's when he noticed her grip on the edge of the bed. Tense, white-knuckled. She wanted him again, but had a tight hold on her need. "Don't worry, baby," he whispered. "The night's young. There'll be plenty more orgasms, I promise."

She made a disgusted sound into the mountain of pillows, and Jack rolled off the bed. The damn condom was beginning to constrict. "Let's take a shower. I'll let you blow me before we head out."

He was rewarded with the pelt of a pillow on his ass as he crossed to the bathroom. He laughed. Damn, he felt good.

Soon, he'd feel even better. Kirby craved excitement. He had something planned for her that would take her to new heights.

Kirby waited until the shower stopped running. Jack was the most cocksure jackass—no pun intended—she'd ever had the pleasure of bedding.

That said it all. He was good, good on the phone and even better in her bed. She didn't want to go out, she wanted to keep him all to herself. She was greedy.

She also didn't feel like being paraded through a downtown bar like a trophy.

Closing her eyes, she clutched the side of the bed harder, thinking of a night long ago. Her twenty-fourth birthday. Stares from a crowd, who'd considered her nothing more than a trophy on a powerful man's arm. A little nobody. She'd had big dreams, though.

She'd almost let that man squash them.

Damn Jack for making her think about Ian. If she really thought about it, she'd been making comparisons all night.

Ian was long gone—thank God for that. They'd been lovers for three years. At one time she'd even considered spending her life with him. But Ian had also made the loan for her first business venture. There'd been strings attached, in the form of his "advice," which meant he'd questioned her every decision. When bad had slipped into worse, when she was actually beginning to believe she was a failure, he'd suggested marrying her and taking over *her* business to get it back in the black. Instead, she'd liquidated everything to avoid the stigma of looming bankruptcy. And to get Ian out of her life. She'd started fresh.

As difficult as it had been in the beginning, she'd re-claimed what she'd lost, both in terms of her confidence and her career. She'd found the perspective to realize that compromising her original decisions to satisfy Ian had been equally responsible for her faltering bottom line. She'd vowed never to jeopardize her decision-making ca-pabilities again.

She'd vowed never to give a man that much control over her career or her love life.

Kirby climbed resolutely from the bed. No past shadow would dictate her current actions. She would meet Jack's little test head-on. Oh yes, she was well aware he was test-ing her. He'd seen right through her hesitation at the front door. He'd apologized later in the kitchen for not warning her about his appearance, yet he'd issued a subtle chal-lenge on his way to the bathroom. Was she woman enough to care nothing for what other people thought?

Hell, yes, she was woman enough to handle anything he could dish out. After which, she'd drag him back to bed, fuck his brains out, then wave a fond farewell as he boarded his plane.

Fresh from her brief shower, Kirby flicked through her clothing. What to wear? What to wow her audience with? What to wow Jack with?

He came to stand at her back, the heat of his bare chest searing her skin, though he didn't actually touch her. Reaching past her, he tugged out a flowing wraparound skirt of burnt orange, deep brown, striking red, shot through with gold.

"This," he said. "Then I'll make you stand over one of those vents like Marilyn Monroe and watch your skirt fly up."

"Then I better not wear panties."

"Around me, you're never to wear panties. I want you at the ready."

She huffed. The truth was, Jack always made her ready,

on the phone, his voice husky and needy in her ear, at the dinner table, on the couch. In front of the kitchen sink with her hands in dishwater.

She hadn't blown him in the shower, despite the fact that he'd waved his deliciously hard cock at her continuously. She'd batted it away. He'd laughed and called her feisty. Nothing bothered him.

She longed to discover just what would make him react to her refusal with something besides laughter. She wanted him to beg.

The sight of her skirt flying up, flashing every man on the street, just might do it.

"Fine. Whatever," she answered casually, taking the skirt from his hand and wondering if it needed pressing. Glancing at her watch, she decided not. Close to ten-thirty, she wouldn't waste the time. "Do you want to drop by your hotel room for a change?"

"I put on fresh underwear and shirt before I came over. Cleanliness is next to godliness." He grabbed his shirt from the rocker, shook out the wrinkles, undid the rest of the buttons, and pulled it on. "With tie or without?"

He'd look too damn good either way, his broad chest disappearing beneath fine white linen. Her fingers itched to rip the shirt back off. Maybe she should make him wear sackcloth. "Tie."

Avoiding the sight of him donning the rest of his clothes, she rummaged through her lingerie drawer. The matching camisole, a gold tone that enhanced the golden threads in the skirt, lay beneath her melange of dainty panties and thongs. The spaghetti straps precluded the use of a bra. Now for the shoes . . .

She hunkered at the bottom of her closet, searching for the strappy flat sandals, the ones with the suede ties that laced up her calves.

"No way," he said, surveying her choice as he sat on her boudoir stool tying his shoes.

"They're perfect."

"You've got gorgeous legs. You need to show them off with a pair of high heels."

"I am not walking around San Francisco in high heels. I'll break one of my ankles."

"I'll hold your arm." Shoes tied, he joined her at the bottom of her closet. Pawing through the impressive selection, he finally pulled out a pair of platforms. "Here. No spikes. It won't be so easy to break an ankle."

"They'll look ridiculous with this skirt."

He looked at her. "They make me hot."

She rolled her eyes. "That's supposed to be my inducement?"

No. Inducement was the heat in his gaze as it drifted from her lips to her breasts to her aureoles almost bared by the deep cut of her camisole. God, the man knew how to make a girl's toes curl with just a look.

Taking the platform sandals, she crossed to sit on the edge of the rumpled bed. She hadn't bothered fixing it after their roll in the hay. There was plenty more rolling to be done before the bed required making.

Retro-eighties, the platforms had a rise of at least five inches and a leather strap that buckled snugly just above her ankle. Jack admired the view as she stood.

"I've changed my mind. I want to do you right now with those shoes on."

The words were excellent, but laughter and challenge sparkled in his gray eyes.

It wasn't time yet, he needed to be on his knees and begging before she gave him what he wanted. "You promised me a night out and a drink first."

She blew out the candles, then checked her outfit one last time in the mirror. She started. The platforms did add a few inches to her own height. Then again, the height difference between them was mitigated by his ideally proportioned and quite magnificent body.

She sucked in a breath and turned.

Folding his arms over his chest, Jack raked her with a

glance. Touched by its heat, her nipples pebbled. Charcoal slacks, white shirt, muted olive tie, and biceps worthy of Mr. Universe, her mouth dried up. Wasn't that new hunk movie star kind of short and definitely bald? Well, she certainly wouldn't kick *him* out of bed for eating crackers. Not with those muscles.

The same and a bit more went for Jack.

The lady was primed, pupils dilated, breath quickened, nipples taut and begging to be sucked. Hand at her elbow, Jack guided her from his plush rental car. The new leather scent combined with her unique perfume intoxicated him.

Maybe a touch, here in the parking garage before they went into the bar. Just a quick slip-slide between her delicate pussy lips, so that her scent would linger on his hand.

Christ, he wanted to fuck her. His lust had built from the moment during their last call when she'd agreed to this sojourn. It hadn't peaked yet, hadn't abated, despite his monumental orgasm. Jack liked riding this particular knife-edge. The pressure in his balls might be strong, but his willpower was stronger.

What he'd planned for her was worth the wait. His dick hardened, lengthened at the mere thought. He reached down to adjust his trousers, but his briefs still cramped him.

She'd chosen a bar just off Union Square. Being a Friday night, parking spaces were scarce. They ended up on the top floor of the garage. The elevators were slow and jam-packed. With his hands on her hips, he moved her in front of him, then eased her back, demonstrating how damn hard she made him.

She pushed her bottom against him. Holding her still, he braced himself against the wall of the elevator and pumped gently, imperceptible to anyone but her. Her sigh was a mere exhale of air. Her shudder could be written off as a shiver from cool air. Except that the crowded elevator was hot and stuffy. He straightened, then made sure at least two inches separated them. He regretted now that he hadn't stuck his hand up her skirt while they were still in the car. She would have been wet, and he'd bet she was wetter now.

He wondered how long he could keep her on the edge.

Street level greeted them with the choke of exhaust fumes, the babble of laughter and voices, and the splash of color from bright clothing to flashing neon. He loved the city, any city. He loved the way the sidewalks undulated with streaming crowds and the noise, so loud that horns, hawkers, drums, guitars, human voices, and the beat of six million feet became indistinguishable. Where the only way to be heard was to pull Kirby close, put his lips to her ear, and breathe his words against her hair.

Of course, he still would have done that even if they were a million miles from nowhere.

She took his hand. He liked it. "Come on, it's this way."

He had to read her lips.

Bodies threatened to separate them. Kirby disappeared through gaps in the throng, forcing him to follow her trail with only their hands linking them. He never let go. Wouldn't *ever* let go.

Finally she stopped in front of a neon sign advertising one of his favorite beer brands. A crowd shuffled by the double front doors, waiting to get in. The windows shuddered with the beat of the music. Rock. Maybe. Hard to tell through the loudness.

"It won't take long to get in," she said.

Her tempting lips were easy to read, but he tapped his ear and leaned closer to her mouth. Dragging in the scent of her, the subtle perfume, the hint of womanly perspiration from the fast walk, he ached to lick the saltiness of it from between her breasts.

"I said, it won't take long. The place doesn't really fill up until midnight."

Her warm breath fanned his ear. The tip of her tongue grazed the outside, then she tugged his lobe into her mouth, bit gently with her teeth.

Tease. Under cover of the swarm of barflies, he palmed her breast, then pinched the nipple. She slipped her hand between them and squeezed his dick.

So, she wanted to play.

He parted the folds of her wraparound skirt and caressed the silky skin of her thigh. She reached down to cup his balls, hefting their weight in her hand. He wanted to come in her fist.

In retaliation, he slipped a finger between her pussy lips. Ah yes, that's what he needed, to feel her heat, her juice, her body's tremble. She groaned and rocked her pelvis so that his finger rubbed her clit. Then she froze.

Less than a second later, she tugged his hand from his intimate foray. "Naughty, naughty," she murmured.

Cupping her butt, he looked up into her sparking eyes. She was the perfect height for a little neck biting, lip nibbling, and most especially, clit teasing. "You started it," he said.

"You are a dirty man."

He grinned. "You ain't seen nothing yet."

She flounced, giving him her back. Kirby had mastered the feminine flounce—was that the right word?—the toss of the head, the fling of the hair, the purse of the lips, which was supposed to be aloof, but only made him want to kiss her senseless. She'd been too damn wet to be aloof.

They were up next, which is what had stopped her. Jack took care of the cover charge even as he pushed her through the doors. Inside, it was standing room only. With his hands on her hips, he angled her toward a waist-high countertop that ran along the edge of the dance floor, managing to squeeze them in at the middle.

He didn't know how the hell he was supposed to show her off in here. That was probably her intention. Luckily, *his* intention was something far different than he'd told her, and this dive provided all manner of opportunity.

Over a hundred pairs of shoes pummeled the wooden floor as the music battered mercilessly against his eardrums. The noise, the crowd, the unrelenting crush of overheated bodies made his blood pulse faster through his veins until his heart pounded with the beat.

He leaned into her, his chest brushing her breasts, and shouted, "What do you want to drink?" Fat chance there was a waitress in this multitude. He'd have to wade through the crowd to the bar on the left.

She shook her head, tipping it in question. He mimed a glass to his lips. She pointed to the beer sign in the window. Pushing through the crush, he slapped down cash for two cold ones, and forged a path back to her.

The strobe lights, the absolutely deafening pitch of the so-called music, and the overpowering stench of sweat offended him, but back at her side, he could breathe again.

That's what Kirby did to him, sucked the breath out of him when he was away from her. Breathed it back in when she was near. He wondered if she had a clue about the effect she had.

His gaze followed the decisive line of her jaw, the clean slope of her nose, and the high aristocratic forehead. Her lips tugged on the beer bottle, a trickle of condensation dropping to her chin, rolling down her throat, finally disappearing beneath the low cut of her flimsy shirt. God, she was more than he'd ever hoped for, wished for. When he'd flown out early Thursday, he'd known only that she was what he wanted, her sensuality, her intelligence, and her strength. What the hell else could any guy ask for? He wouldn't have asked for another thing. Yet, here she was, in all her brilliance.

She'd never let him walk all over her. She'd give him shit every moment they were together. She'd constantly battle for control of their relationship and snarl and growl whenever she didn't come out on top. She'd never take a cent from him, and she wouldn't give him a dime of hers. She'd ask his advice, and then she wouldn't take it. She'd slam him down, then she'd apologize with kisses.

He couldn't imagine a better way of spending the rest of his life. Living on the edge. With her.

Someone bumped his ass, an elbow jabbed his rib. Jack

pressed closer to Kirby. He placed a hand on her hip and nestled her against his crotch. She fit flawlessly. Instead of pulling away, she looked him in the eye, put the bottle to her lips once more, and chugged.

His cock turned to rock against her. He cupped her butt, sliding a finger down the cleft, her skirt gossamer-thin beneath his touch. Someone bumped his arm, splaying his fingers against her firm cheeks. He squeezed. The flash of a strobe light swept across her face and revealed her dilated pupils.

He wanted to push her to the limit. She'd let him. Afterward she'd tell him what an egotistical bastard he was.

Kirby Prescott was a fighter. He wouldn't have loved her if she was any other way.

SEVEN

Jack set his beer bottle down. Using his other hand, he reached between the bar table and her abdomen and anchored her solidly against his cock. Then he rotated against her.

Kirby watched the heaving mass of humanity on the dance floor. The man affected her, without a doubt. She'd gotten a bit carried away out there, stopping him only when she felt the urge to beg again.

How did he do that?

Dammit, he was doing it to her again! With just a glance, a touch . . . his magnetism.

His cock gently seduced her hip as he lowered his hand from her belly to the juncture of her thighs. He didn't probe, simply rubbed, until her body reacted with a rush of moisture and a matching rhythm.

Her head ached from the ruthless beat of the music. Her legs wobbled. She spread them to steady herself. Jack pressed deeper.

He was a bold one, but she didn't push him away. The

chaos, the crush of bodies, and the pulsing strobe isolated
them. She wanted his hands on her.

He delved into the opening of her skirt. Hot air rising
from the dance floor caressed her in tandem with him.
Parting her lips, she closed her eyes and tipped her head
back. Her nipples pearled against the soft camisole. Being
an exhibitionist wasn't one of her faults, but the unceasing
thrum of the bass guitar inside her chest seemed to take her
out of herself. Like a drug. A hypnotic trance. She wanted
Jack to touch her with an intensity that bordered on the uncontrollable. She gripped the edges of the counter.

He parted her pussy lips with callused fingers, a fleeting
reminder of the nubby skin of the strawberry he'd teased
her with. She quivered when he found her clit, then bit
down on her bottom lip to keep from crying out.

Jack whispered against her ear, his breath hot on her
flesh. "I want you to come, Kirby, right here. I want your
cream all over my hand. I want you to scream."

So many wants he had. At this moment she had exactly
the same want, and she wanted to come with his hands on
her more than she'd ever wanted anything. She'd think
about how damn scary that was later.

Grasping her hip and pulling her hard against his cock,
he stroked her clit. Nearly boneless, she put her arm
around his shoulder and let her head fall to the side of his.
He swayed with her, as if they were moving to the music
instead of the insistent caress of his fingers.

He dipped his middle finger low and shoved it up inside
her, keeping his thumb on the bud of her clit. When he
drew it out again, he was slick and smooth, coated with her
flow. Had she ever been this wet? Or this delirious?

If he wished, he could hoist her up on the bar and fuck
her right there. She'd have let him.

The music rose to a crescendo. Her hips bucked in time,
to it and to Jack's remorseless massage.

He moved his head and whispered once more, "Come
for me, baby."

She put her hand on top of his, controlling the pace, the rhythm. Heat built, then exploded between her thighs. She clamped her legs together, afraid she'd fall with the force of the orgasm, but Jack held her up. The press of her thighs only increased the tension and kept the waves rolling through her longer, more intensely.

Jesus! It was the best damn orgasm she'd ever had. Even better than on the couch, when he had his mouth on her. Better than Mr. Perfect.

Yet, she still didn't scream for him. She had enough control for that.

When the last wave faded away, and strength returned to her lower extremities, she brushed nonexistent wrinkles from her skirt. "Bastard." It came out much less aggressively than she hoped. Probably because she was feeling positively mellow.

Jack smiled. The pass of the strobe high-lighted his Cheshire Cat grin. The man was too pleased with himself, and with her reaction. He needed a little set down to show him who was in control.

Her legs shook as she pushed away from the bar. She turned, gliding past him, through the herd, elbows first. Jack wasn't far behind. She burst from the overheated bar onto the street and gulped air. Jack placed a soothing hand on her back. She'd have liked nothing more than to sink into his touch. For effect, she shook him off.

The platform shoes hindered her usual long-legged stride. Her skirt swirled around her calves and caught between her thighs. She sidestepped an entangled couple, raised her arm to pass cleanly over a wheelchair-bound veteran, and swung into the street to avoid a slow-moving gaggle of teenage girls. A car honked. Jack grabbed her arm and pulled her back to the sidewalk.

"Are you trying to get yourself killed?"

Her ears still hummed from the music and her elevated blood pressure, but his lips formed the words precisely enough for her to understand. "I was well aware of every car." Still in an orgasmic daze, she hadn't paid attention to the proximity of the street traffic. "I'm heading back to the garage. You've had enough fun for one night."

He yanked her to a stop. "You had fun, too."

She raised one brow. "What do you think?" What she'd felt was a little too intense to be called something as simple as fun.

"You pissed?"

She cocked her head. His smoky gray eyes moved over her face. She suddenly realized he wanted her to be mad. He wanted to feel like he'd gotten her to do something against her will.

It made him feel like he was the one in control.

"No, Jack, I'm not mad. Not at all." She stepped closer. "In fact, I liked it so much that I've got a little surprise for you."

His mouth quirked. "Payback time?"

"You're going to like the payback, I swear."

For the longest time, she'd wanted to feel something, anything. She'd wanted intensity. With Jack, she just might have gotten more than she bargained for. An intense experience was one thing, but losing control of a situation was quite another. She'd done that with Ian. She'd learned one should maintain the on-top position, in both the professional and sexual arenas.

She knew just the maneuver to show Jack who was in charge.

She grabbed him by the tie, turned, and started walking. Her shoulder purse swung with the brisk stride.

He chuckled. Most men would be horrified to be dragged along the street by a woman. Not Jack.

How was she going to wipe that smug smile off his face?

A glimmer of a plan formed in her mind.

Shit, the woman could make him come in his pants. The commanding grip she had on his tie, the straight, sleek lines of her back, and the fluid movement of her hips were as potent as her flawless nipples and beautifully sculpted snatch.

At their approach, the beefeater-garbed doorman of the St. Francis doubled over with a belly laugh. A young couple pointed at his predicament, not the boner in his trousers, but the tie wrapped around Kirby's fist. Passersby halted, entertained, even mesmerized, by the spectacle.

Jack merely shrugged, grinning idiotically, and held up his hands in surrender to his audience. "Who *wouldn't* let her lead him around by his . . . tie?"

Everyone got the joke; everyone laughed, everyone except Kirby, who stopped so abruptly that he slammed into her. She backed off, turned, and leveled him with a glare that could flay flesh. Then she jerked on the tie and plastered her lips to his. No open-mouthed sizzler, this kiss was an Amazon-Queen, you-better-shut-the-hell-up kiss. Oh yeah. He couldn't wait for her next move.

She placed the flat of her hand on his chest and pushed, giving herself breathing space, then turned and started dragging him again.

Jack raised an eyebrow for their audience and let her haul him away. He'd really touched a nerve back there in the bar, and not just the one in her clit. This was a good thing. Tonight, she'd fight him like a cat. By Saturday she'd try to retreat and withdraw. On Sunday she'd be lapping cream out of his palm.

In the empty elevator she slammed him back against the wall, murder in her eye. Though truth be told, he couldn't tell if her ire was real or feigned. It didn't matter either way. Any display of emotion told the story.

He tried really hard not to smile.

"Don't you dare laugh."

"I wouldn't dream of it." Jesus, his lips were aching with the effort it took not to stretch into a full spectrum, all-out, shit-eating grin.

"You're playing with fire here, mister."

Hell, he knew that. Did playing it safe ever get anyone what they most desired?

Her hand trembled and her chest heaved with short, sharp breaths. She stood close enough to brush him with those delectable nipples.

She devil-eyed him again. "You are going to be so sorry."

"I already am." Far from it. She was wild, exotic, uncontrollable, and irresistible.

The elevator dinged as it stopped abruptly, causing her to stumble against him. The hard ridge of his cock brushed against the joining of her thigh and hip. She narrowed her gorgeous green eyes.

"You *will* pay," she warned once more.

He had no doubt that he would, and he'd probably die from the pleasure of it.

She jerked on his tie. He followed.

The top floor of the garage was open to the night air. A strong breeze blew across the parking deck. Kirby's skirt billowed. Muted city sounds rose to the eighth floor.

At the rear of his rented Beemer, Kirby finally let go of the tie, the silk mangled by her tight grip. He did his best to smooth it down, but the damage appeared to be permanent.

She half-leaned, half-sat on the trunk lid, bracing herself with flat palms. "You thought what you did was hot, didn't you?"

This time he allowed himself a grin. "No, baby, *you* were hot."

"You don't know the half of it." She widened her stance, leveling her platforms on the concrete. The breeze picked up the edge of her skirt and fluttered it aside, unveiling a smooth expanse of leg clear up to her thigh.

"How do you want me to pay up?" he said, lust in his voice.

She smiled. Her luscious red lips almost sealed his doom as he thought of them tightly capturing his cock.

"I want you to fuck me, Jack."

"Oh, baby, I'm going to, you can be sure of that."

"I mean right now and right here. On the trunk of your

car." She slid a finger into the gap of her skirt and pushed the material aside to reveal her succulent pussy.

His mouth went dry.

She combed her red-lacquered fingers through the springy curls at her apex. Her middle finger found the folds of her pussy, its tip disappearing for one eye-catching moment.

"I don't have a condom."

"I have one." She snapped the catch on her slim shoulder purse, delved inside, coming out with the package. Instead of ripping it open, she held it out to him.

The proverbial gauntlet.

She licked her lower lip, caught it gently between her teeth, and watched him through her lashes. "Come on, there's no one around. Do me. You know you want to."

Christ, that was an understatement. He could barely drag in a breath of misty midnight air. His flexed fingers itching to rip every stitch of clothing from her body. Then he would ram himself home and keep on going until her screams split the night.

He wanted to scream with her. The little witch knew it.

Payback's a bitch.

"Are you chicken, Jack?"

"You win," he murmured.

She batted her eyelashes and let the condom fall to the concrete. "And that means?"

"That you know I'm not going to fuck you out here where anyone could walk out of the elevator and call the cops about your lewd behavior."

She put a hand to her chest in mock horror. "*My* lewd behavior? What about your behavior in the bar?"

The wind teased her skirt, but didn't manage to blow it across her sweet, inviting pussy.

"That was different. Way too much noise and too big a crowd for anyone to notice. I bet we weren't the only ones sneaking a little feel."

She rose, smoothed her skirt back in place. She straightened his tie, fixed the knot, then ran a finger down the center of it.

"Just remember to ask first, Jack. That's all it takes."

Losers asked and risked rejection; winners found a way to make the other party think it was their idea all along.

He took her chin in his hand, held her when she tried to shrug away. "Tell me, would you have said no in the bar?"

The lie she wanted to utter parted her lips. He could see it hovering there. The words never materialized. Kirby loved playing the game, she loved nuance and subtext, but she wasn't a flat-out liar. "I wouldn't have said no," she admitted.

"We've known each other long enough to render the question unnecessary."

She managed to pull free of his grip this time. "We only met tonight."

"Face-to-face, yeah. But we've *known* each other far longer."

He'd hit a nerve with that one. She backed up until her legs hit the car. "On the phone. People can say anything on the phone."

"You felt comfortable enough to say *everything*. I learned all I ever wanted to know about you."

Her body stiffened. She crossed her arms beneath her chest, her nails biting into the flesh of her arms. "We don't really know each other."

"I knew you wanted me to finger-fuck you in that bar. You knew I wouldn't jeopardize your life and your career by fucking you up here where anyone could catch us."

"I'd say you were probably more worried about your own career. After all, they fire salesmen for being caught in *flagrante delicto* while they're on business trips."

"You aren't a business trip."

"What am I, Jack?"

Her eyes widened as she sucked in a breath. He was sure she hadn't meant for that question to pop out. If this had been Sunday instead of their first day, he'd have told her exactly what she was, what she meant to him.

Gut instinct told him she'd run like hell if he told her now.

"You are the most seductive woman I know, and you make me lose my head." It was the utter truth, but totally noncommittal—therefore unthreatening.

Some of her tension drained away, and her fingernails eased off the half-moons she'd made in her arms. "I do want you to fuck me. At my apartment."

"Now, that sounds like a wonderful, mutually acceptable idea. Are you sure? I mean, if you want to say no, or you change your mind, you just tell me."

She slugged him lightly on the arm, a ghost of a smile curving her lips. "Shut up and get in the car."

"Yes, ma'am. Whatever you say." He fished the keys out of his pocket, the task made difficult by the painful erection filling his pants.

An erection which she would soon alleviate in the most delightful of ways.

EIGHT

Kirby couldn't tell whether she'd won that round. Jack hadn't done her right there on the car, but she'd expected he wouldn't. Okay, she'd hoped to break him with the sight of her pussy, her hand stroking and inviting. Barring that, she'd counted on at least making him admit defeat. Yeah, right. She couldn't be sure, but he might actually have turned the tables on her.

Jack Taylor did *not* know her. Her body, yes, but that was all. Okay, well, sure, he knew some of her minor secrets, like being slightly envious of Kristin's newfound happiness. She'd also discussed certain aspects of her business with him. He'd always offered good advice. Knowing those things didn't mean he *knew* her. For God's sake, they'd only met for the first time tonight.

Dammit, the man mixed her up. She loved sex. She loved orgasms. She loved men in general. Still, when it came time for them to leave, she could always close the door without a qualm.

Not with Jack. He was oh-so-good in bed. And out. On a couch or in a bar.

After unlocking her front door, Kirby bumped it open with her hip and breezed through, catching it with the tips of her fingers before it slammed on Jack. In the kitchen, she fished the second, already uncorked wine bottle out of the fridge. Yes, he was good, and he was hers for the weekend. Why not enjoy the moment? She led the way down the hall to her bedroom, swishing her hips to tempt him. Dumping the contents of their half-full glasses from earlier in the evening into the bathroom sink, she refilled.

When she came back into the room, Jack sat on her vanity stool next to the bed. Still fully clothed, he hadn't even loosened his tie. She handed him a glass and tapped the edge of hers to his. "It *was* good, Jack."

He saluted her with his own glass. "What? The couch? The bed? Or the bar?"

His mind worked along exactly the same lines as hers. "All three. But I think we're setting our sights too low."

He raised a brow. "Regarding position, location, or quantity?"

She lifted one corner of her mouth. "All three."

He reached for her. She stepped back. "Are you as good at taking direction as you are at other things?"

"Yes, ma'am, absolutely." His hand disappeared mysteriously behind his back. The vanity mirror reflected his crossed fingers. Jack did love his games.

She, however, was a very good player herself. They were both in for an interesting ride. "Good boy, Jack. Now I want you to watch while I undress."

His gray eyes smoldered with anticipation. "It would be my greatest pleasure." She could tell he hid a smile with a sip of his wine.

Setting her glass on the vanity, she put her left foot on the stool right between his legs. His erection was evident. He had, in fact, stayed hard all the way back to her apartment. She'd wanted to touch it, maybe suck it, just a little. She'd also been thinking about ways to bend him to her will.

Jack was a tough nut to crack, so to speak. A little tease might do the trick.

She undid the strap of her platform and slipped it off, then repeated the task with her other foot. She couldn't resist running her toes up his hard length. He captured her ankle and guided her foot lightly up and down.

"Trusting, aren't you? I could squash it."

"You could." He eased his hand up her calf. "But you won't."

"Why? Because I wouldn't want to damage the goods before I've used it up?"

"Because you're far too sweet and lovable for that."

She laughed outright. "I'm positive no man has *ever* called me sweet and lovable."

He glanced down, continuing to masturbate his cock with her foot. "I can't imagine why not."

"Because I'm not lovable," she said sweetly. "In fact, I'm very nasty."

"I know that, too. And I like it." He smiled, then flipped the hem of her skirt. "Are you going to take this off?"

She tugged her foot from his grasp and stepped back. Putting her palms to her camisole, she cupped her breasts and flicked her nipples with her thumbs. They sprang to life.

Jack licked his lips, then took an extra swallow of wine.

What would it take to drive this man crazy? He'd come in her, yes, and she'd known it had been good for him. He loved her mouth on him. He licked his lips and breathed hard at the appropriate times. His almost constant state of arousal was self-evident. Yet . . . she couldn't seem to drive him to an act of desperation. Not the way he did her.

If he'd lost enough control to do her on the garage rooftop, she'd have let him. In fact, she'd have reveled in her ability to get him to do it.

But he'd said no so easily. Maybe that's what drove her the hardest. He could say no, but she never even tried to stop him doing whatever he wanted, wherever he wanted to do it.

Except on the phone. On the phone she'd believed he was as involved as she. Believed? No, she'd been certain she'd pushed him over the top. Maybe he needed a little reminder of how good the phone sex was.

She skimmed her fingers beneath the silk of her camisole, cupping her breasts once more, then rolled her nipples between thumb and forefinger. "You make me want to touch myself, Jack."

"Then take off your top and let me watch." His voice dropped a note, his breath quickened, deepening to a rasp. She'd heard that very same sound in her ear so often that all she had to do was close her eyes and imagine she wore her earpiece and Jack was three thousand miles away.

Dispensing with the camisole, she flung it across the room where it landed on the top of the cheval mirror.

"God, your nipples are so sweet, like Bing cherries."

"Touch yourself through your slacks."

He wrapped his fist around it, as much as his slacks allowed. "Take off your skirt."

Ignoring his instructions, she hiked it up to her waist, turned and climbed onto the bed, giving him her backside.

"Jesus, I want to be inside that sweet ass."

She looked over her shoulder. Oh God, he looked a little wild. His eyes were hooded like a bird of prey, his muscles, stretched across his face, and his mouth, open, jerking in a sharp breath. This was what she wanted. This was what she'd envisioned as she listened to him on the phone.

She rolled and flopped back on the pillows, angling herself toward him. "I want you to watch me come. From over there." She sucked her middle finger into her mouth, wetting it thoroughly. Jack watched, the look on his face one of entrancement. His hand stroked his cock.

"I want you to unzip your pants and come when I do." Just like on the phone.

He didn't say a word. The clink of his belt buckle and the rasp of his zipper said it all. He took that massive tool in his hand, the head purple, pulsating. He groaned. "Do you know how many times I've imagined watching you get yourself off? A hundred, a thousand. Baby, please, put me out of my misery."

She didn't remove her skirt, merely ran her hands down her thighs and shifted her legs in anticipation.

"Jesus, Kirby, I think I'm going to die here before you actually put your hand between your legs."

"That's the point." Her pussy wept for her touch and for his eyes to be on her as she did it. "Tell me what you want me to do, and I'll do it. Anything." Just as he always demanded on the phone.

He pulled in a deep breath and slowed the furious pace of his hand. Holding off orgasm, she knew, all the better to enjoy the show.

"Hold out your breasts for me."

She slid her hands up and down her torso. She held her breasts, plumping them for his pleasure. Sucking a finger into her mouth once more, she wet it. Circling first one nipple, then the other, the buds hardened into points.

Jack massaged the crown of his cock, and his gaze ate up her every movement. "Pinch them."

Pleasure-pain rippled through her body as she tweaked them hard. She didn't hold back her moan, didn't want to. Jack loved her little noises across the phone wires. She knew they drove him wild. She closed her eyes and savored his labored breathing.

"What do you want me to do now?"

"Spread your legs. I want to see that gorgeous pussy."

She trailed her fingers down her abdomen, tugging aside the material of her skirt to expose the crisp hair between her legs. She pressed her flesh with her fingertips, then drew her feet up and let her legs fall apart to reveal the object of his desire.

"Oh Jesus, you are so beautiful. Now, slide your fingers inside."

She pulled the folds aside to give him a better view, then slipped an index finger across her clitoris. Her body jerked, the bud ultra-sensitive to the slightest touch. She bit her lip, pushing off the impending orgasm. She wanted him to be insane by the time she exploded.

"God, you're wet. I can see it from here. Two fingers. Inside. Now." His command came out as little more than a desperate rasp.

The fit was exquisite. The hot gleam in his eyes even more so. Her clit wanted attention, and she wasn't as dexterous as he, unable to manage both activities at once.

She teased her clit with a light caress, then used the slick fluid of her desire to stroke her flesh to an unbearably hard nub. Heat shot from the spot to her thighs, to her abdomen, then up into her womb itself. His gaze made her own touch almost intolerable. With one finger, she circled the little button, then stroked, circle, stroke, circle, until she was almost mindless.

Reaching back to grab one of the brass rails of her bed, she arched, lifting her pelvis off the bed and opening herself fully to his fervent gaze.

"Is this how you imagined it all those times on the phone?" She had to know, needed his confirmation.

"Jesus, you can't begin to know how much better it is right now. I want to touch you so bad, but I want to watch you even more." He sat forward on the stool, using two hands now, one cupping and squeezing his balls, the other hammering his cock like a piston.

She held her hand still and rocked against her finger. Short, quick movements centered on her clit. Orgasm was so close, the electricity building. Her body, a live wire. She jammed her heels into the bed, moaned, gasped, then whispered fuck-words—every hot, dirty epithet she'd ever heard.

"Oh God, Jack, I'm going to come. I want your cum on me when I do."

"I've got a better idea." She hadn't sensed his movement, but he hovered over her now, one hand on the bed beside her, the other on his cock with a steady even stroke.

"You've gotta be kidding."

"This'll be better for the wait, baby, I swear." He cocked his head. "You know, building the tension and all."

"Couldn't you just have let me finished, then started all over again?"

Jack frowned. "Where's your sense of adventure?"

Kirby growled. "Right about now, throwing you alive into a pack of hungry hyenas would be a great adventure."

"They only eat dead meat."

"Dead meat is exactly what you're going to be if you don't find a really good way to make it up to me."

"Oh, baby, I do love a challenge." Then he tore off his clothes.

NINE

"I shouldn't have told you I was about to come. I've completely lost my orgasm now." The tight bud of her clit ached, her impending explosion dulled, a need not yet ready to be realized.

"You're going to find it again, and it'll be even more fucking unbelievable. Trust me."

Kirby had her doubts when men said that. Invariably they proved completely untrustworthy. "I wanna come."

Her vision blurred. Her lips pouted. The savage excitement in Jack's voice as he tossed his clothes across the room got to her. An avid gleam sparked in his eye as he kept a close watch on her continued activity—she still fondled her sex, gently keeping herself close. He was right, it could be better. It could be cataclysmic, out of this world.

"Where's Mr. Perfect, your vibrator?"

"My vibrator?"

"Yeah." An enticing gleam shone in his eyes.

"I never told you it had a name."

"Yes, you did."

"No, I didn't."

"Then how would I know?"

Maybe she had told him, she'd never been ashamed of Mr. Perfect. She rolled onto her stomach, propped herself on her elbows, and pointed to the bedside table. "In the drawer."

Jack searched the contents of the side table. "Look what I found." A condom packet. He set it within easy reach, then turned back to the drawer. Finally he held the vibrator up like a trophy. "Got it." Then he held it out. "It's pink."

"Girls like pink."

"It's not very manly."

"It's eight inches long and five inches in circumference. That's more manly than most men I've known."

He widened his eyes and pointed at his chest. She smirked. "If I was talking about you, I certainly wouldn't tell you at this crucial moment."

He snorted. "So you measured this thing?"

"I read it on the package."

"I like an informed shopper. What's this?" He indicated Mr. Perfect's three-and-a-half-inch protrusion just above the battery pack.

"It's a swan." She wrinkled her brow. "No, maybe it's a rabbit." She shrugged. "I can't remember anymore. It vibrates. In just the right spot."

"I thought the whole thing vibrates."

She rolled her eyes. "You just aren't up on the latest sex toy technology. The penis sort of twirls. And when it's all the way inside, the rabbit ears vibrate against—"

"Your clit."

She smiled. "Yeah."

He perused the instrument with newfound admiration. "Jesus. It's fucking ingenious. Is that where 'sit on it and twirl' came from?"

She laughed, then hid her face in her arms. "This is serious business. Don't make me laugh."

He climbed on the bed beside her, leaned down to kiss, then lick her forearm. "Sex isn't supposed to be serious. It's supposed to make you want to laugh because it's so

much damn fun and want to die because it feels so goddamn good. Otherwise, what's the use?"

Kirby turned her head to the side to look at him. "I
never thought of it that way."

Jack grinned at the look on her face. "That's because
you've never done it with me before."

"We've done a lot just on the phone."

"Baby steps. This is the real thing, sweetheart." If she
chose to look deep enough, she'd have seen his heart in
his eyes.

Instead, she buried her face in her arms again and
laughed. Or shuddered.

Enough truth for one sexual session. Jack slapped her
butt. "Get up on all fours."

She did, after tossing aside her skirt, though he'd been a
little worried she might run for the hills.

"No, face away from me."

She turned. Her ass cheeks were warm and slippery
with her cream. She squirmed and wiggled her butt at him.
He rewarded her with a caress straight down the crease and
almost into her slick pussy. She put her hand between her
legs and met his fingers in the middle.

Jesus. The unspoken intimacy in that. He was sure she
didn't see the symbolism.

"Spread your legs and play with yourself."

She braced herself with her left hand and used her right
to rub her clit, her fingertips touching his. Then she looked
back at him over her shoulder.

"Face the headboard. I want this to be a surprise."

"I already know you're going to stick the vibrator in me.
How can it be a surprise?"

"It's different when you can't see. Now do what I tell
you."

He shifted, his cock bumping her side. He rolled against
her flank, creating his own friction, while spreading her
outer lips.

Could he actually hold his own orgasm long enough to
do her with the vibrator? He'd almost come when she put

her hand between her legs. He'd experienced all manner of sexual delights, but nothing like this. Nothing had ever felt so good as it did with Kirby.

"Are you wet enough?" he whispered. Hurting her wasn't in the plan.

She rubbed her fingers all over his. Her moisture was incredible. "What do you think, big boy? Now get on with it." She wriggled her ass impatiently.

He positioned the vibrator at her pussy. "Do you know how fucking hard you're going to come?"

"I can hardly wait." She eased back, taking the tip inside. "Don't turn it on yet, wait until it's all the way in."

He pushed gently, her body gave, then practically sucked the damn thing in. She sighed, a long, slow, satisfied breath of air.

"There's more, baby, you can take all eight inches."

"I know," she quipped.

He slapped her fanny again. "Don't try making me jealous."

She was silent a moment as he fed her more of the silicon giant, then she turned once again to look at him. "Do you like this, Jack?"

He grabbed her other butt cheek and rubbed himself against her. "Feel how much I love it. Now spread your legs more and get down on your elbows."

She stuck her ass in the air and gave him better access. The vibrator sank almost to the base. Jesus, she had to feel filled to capacity. "Make sure you've got your rabbit ears tuned to the right frequency."

She stifled a laugh and reached between her legs. "Good to go."

He flipped the switch, and she groaned. Mr. Perfect hummed and bucked in his hand as her hip rocked against his cock. She started to pant, going up on her hands, then back down. He pumped the vibrator gently, her own body's reactions doing the rest.

Beneath her breath, Kirby chanted, "Oh God, oh God."

He held her fast against his cock, bumping and grinding

in time with her rhythm. A small spurt of pre-come coated her flesh.

Then she chanted his name. "Jack. Jack. Jack!" He almost came, knew he was a goner if he didn't hang on to his last ounce of control.

"Baby, Jesus, baby. I wanna try something else." He gritted his teeth, actually bit his tongue.

"Don't stop." She gulped air. "Don't. You. Dare. Stop."

"This'll be better." He clicked the switch to the Off position.

She wailed, yet stilled her frantic movements, willing to follow his lead. He couldn't have asked for more, and he'd give her something she'd never forget. Something she would never know with another man. Not ever.

"What?" she demanded, her voice harsh, belligerent from her frustration.

"Squat like you're riding me."

"You're such a bastard." Keeping the vibrator tucked inside her, she lowered her hips, then shuffled forward until she supported herself on the brass headboard. "Now what?"

"I want you to fuck it like it was my cock."

She raised her arms, raked her hands through her hair, and arched her back. She settled down once more, hands back on the headboard. "You better make this good, buddy."

That sinewy stretch told him just how good it already was. "Fuck it, baby. Please."

"Say pretty please." She twitched her butt.

"Pretty please with sugar on top."

"All right. Just this once."

He laid on his side, braced himself with an elbow, gripped the vibrator firmly, and flipped the On switch. Its low hum filled the room. Then Kirby began to move. It was all he could do not to squirt all over her ass.

The sensuous slide of the pink monstrosity, in and out, in and out, was an erotic peepshow. Still humping, she let go of the headboard, straightened, and pulled her hair on top of her head with one hand.

"Is it good, Kirby?" He didn't even recognize his own voice, thick, slurred, hoarse.

"It is *so* good."

She groaned, a super-sexy sound, driving him crazy. Her hand cupped her breast, then moved across her belly in search of her clit. God, he wanted to watch her finger working her clit to orgasm, but even more, he needed to watch that huge fake cock filling her. She spread herself wider and took more of the thing inside. Moaning, tossing her head, her hips moved faster, and even faster.

"How good is it, baby? Does it feel so fucking extreme that it hurts?" That's where he wanted her. So out of control for him.

She threw her head back, her hair cascading over her shoulders and down her back. "Make me laugh, Jack. Make me die!"

He would have come then, knowing that she was his. With a monumental effort worthy of David fighting Goliath or Moses parting the Red Sea, he held himself back.

Her juices smeared the hand clutching the vibrator. Gathering her moisture, he coated his painfully pulsing cock. Then, tightly gripping the device in both hands, he rose to his knees behind her. His dick found a home between her butt cheeks. He ground against her.

"Harder, baby," he panted in her ear. "Faster." *Want me. Need me. Give it to me.*

She rode that goddamn vibrator like it was a bucking bronco. He loosened one hand, and wrapped his arm around her waist to hold her more firmly against his cock. With the delirious rise and fall of her body, her gasps for air, and the tautness of her muscles, he spun out of control. The top of his cock blew off. When she screamed her orgasm, he screamed just as loudly, then shot his load all over her ass.

It was only with his last ounce of willpower that he managed not to say he loved her.

TEN

"Did you just scream?" Kirby muttered, too over-come to open her eyes or lift her head from the pillows.

"I gave a very manly shout. *You* screamed. I sure as hell hope your neighbors didn't call the cops." Jack wrapped his arm beneath her breasts and pulled her closer.

The movement shifted pillows, toppling one down over her nose. She batted it away. "My neighbors wouldn't dare. And you definitely screamed."

Her thighs were sticky, her muscles had liquefied, and her lashes seemed gummed together. She couldn't have opened her eyes even if she'd had the urge.

"Was it good for you?" he whispered, stirring the fine hairs at her nape.

Stupendous. Fantastic. It was as incredibly unbelievable as he'd said it would be. "It was okay."

He chuckled. "You are one tough lady, ya know."

"Yeah, I know." But he was tougher. Because he wasn't afraid to ask if she'd thought he was good. He'd even laughed when she didn't give him the expected answer.

He gave her a squeeze, then moved away. "I'll be back in a minute."

Footsteps padded across the carpet, then the bathroom light beat against her closed eyelids, followed by the sounds of running water. She hadn't moved by the time he came back. Sitting on the bed, he placed a warm washcloth against her lower back.

She jerked. "What are you doing?"

"I'm washing you."

Oh my God. The man was washing away his cum. He prodded her legs apart, then cleaned between her thighs. The bed gave as he rose, went to the bathroom again, and returned. This time the cloth was steaming. And soothing.

"Does that feel good?"

Everything Jack did felt good. Too good. No man had ever washed her after sex. She would have laughed if one had tried.

Jack's ministrations only made her want to cry.

He tossed the pillows aside, pulled the coverlet easily from beneath her, then covered her. Moments later, after disposing of the washcloth—and her washed-up Mr. Perfect, she hoped—he crawled in beside her, fitting his body snugly to hers.

"Go to sleep, sweetheart," he murmured, stroking hair back from her face and tucking it behind her ear.

She didn't say a thing, just burrowed deeper into the bedclothes, nestling against him.

She was utterly terrified at what might come out of her mouth if she allowed a single word to pass her lips.

Jack woke to a room filled with the light of early morning, sun pouring through the mini-blinds. He stretched, feeling for her, but knew she wouldn't be beside him. Last night he'd pushed her limits, today she'd retreat. Still, he felt damn good despite the emptiness of the bed. Making love with Kirby was both a powerful stimulant and a deep, relaxing tranquilizer. He'd slept more restfully than he had

in months, despite the fact that he hadn't had more than
five hours of sleep. Now he was energized, rip-roaring
ready to do battle.

He had no doubt the day ahead promised war. Heavy
artillery. He decided the best approach was a full-frontal
attack.

Climbing from the bed, he grabbed their used wineglasses and headed down the hall.

Kirby, seated at the dining room table, munched a piece
of toast. A mug of coffee steamed at her fingertips as she
read the morning paper. She glanced up, her eyes widened,
then her gaze quickly shifted back to the paper.

"You're naked."

He looked down as if he'd only just noticed. "And
hard, too."

She snorted. "Not right now, Tiger. I'm sore."

Little liar. Her nipples had peaked beneath her silk robe.
Absolutely gorgeous without a trace of makeup, she was in
fine ice-queen form and ready to reassert control. But
Kirby Prescott was running scared. She knew how phe-
nomenal last night had been. How rare. She ran from how
much better it might get, so exceptional that she'd find she
couldn't live without it. He'd let her run today. In the end,
he might not even have to convince her. When she really
examined what had happened between them, there was
every possibility she'd figure it out on her own.

"We can stop at the store and get some lube. You can
soak in the tub. That'll help." He could wash her again,
with lots of bubbles, splashing water, moaning, groaning,
and turgid nipples finding their way into his mouth. Not
necessarily in that order.

She smiled honey, melt-in-your-mouth sweet. "Haven't
you heard that no means *no?*"

He strode purposefully forward, brushed kisses in her
hair, on her ear. She held him away with the flat of her
hand on his chest. He ignored her hesitance, which was
nothing more than he'd expected. Withdraw and retreat.
Then tonight—or tomorrow—acceptance. Before he left

on Sunday, he'd tell her about the new sales office, which would segue into his moving out permanently after a few months. His ultimate goal was to help her grow her business into everything she'd always wanted it to be. He could help her do that, give her her heart's desire. They'd be a team, in and out of bed. For the rest of their lives.

He'd show her how damn good it could be.

Proceeding to the kitchen, he set the wineglasses in the sink, then opened and closed cupboard doors until he found the mugs. Pouring himself a cup of the aromatic coffee, he returned to his lady love and flopped down in the chair beside her. Crossing one leg, his foot atop his opposite knee, he settled into the chair, cradling the mug in his hands just above his abdomen. His dick stood tall.

She glanced sideways, eyeing it, then quickly averted her gaze. She used the coffee as an excuse to lick her lips. Those nipples surging against the flowered robe told the true story.

She wanted him again, but she wasn't about to admit it. He smiled broadly. "Let's drop by my hotel so I can pick up a change of clothes, then we'll go for a drive."

She arched a brow. "A drive? I've never considered myself as a fifties housewife who enjoys a Sunday drive with the hubby and kiddies."

Hardly a hausfrau. She looked like a beauty queen, pampered, adored, spoiled, and very well-satisfied, if that glow on her skin meant anything. "We could always stay here." He tapped his cock for good measure, setting it waving. "And fuck like . . . rabbits."

"We've already discussed that issue." She gave him a narrowed-eyed look, which, he supposed, should have been menacing. If he worked for her, that look might have made him quake.

As it was, he knew he'd gotten in a well-aimed round that reminded her about last night. "Get dressed. It's a long drive."

She flipped a page of her paper, one he was sure she hadn't even read. "Where?"

"Santa Cruz."

She looked up. "Santa Cruz? That's two hours."

"So we should get a move on before the traffic gets bad. They're doing Civil War reenactments at the old steam train park."

"Civil? War? Reenactments?" Three separate questions. Three reasons to say no.

He wouldn't give her a chance. "Yeah. I love that stuff."

She shot him a typical Kirby you've-got-to-be-kidding arch of her brow. "I'm afraid I've got paperwork to do."

"No way. You promised me the weekend."

"I only said you could spend the night."

"That's not the way I remember it."

He stood, set his coffee cup down deliberately, then took her chin in his hand. "You gave me the weekend, Kirby. I'm not letting you renege."

She shrugged off his touch, then her gaze dropped to his bobbing cock. She licked her lips. He could have sworn she didn't even realize she did it. "I never said the whole weekend," she whispered.

"I said it, you agreed."

"I can't think when you're naked."

"You don't have to think."

She put out a hand, gently rubbed his shaft, up, down, then slid a finger along the crease at the tip. He wanted her to suck him, but he wouldn't ask.

She held him with a light touch and licked a tiny drop of cum that had oozed out. He could shoot his load in her mouth in two seconds flat if she circled him with her lips. He tangled his fingers in her hair, but applied no pressure.

She looked up, her eyes a dazzling green, her lips plump, wet, and tempting though unadorned by lipstick.

"Your choice, sweetheart. Blow me or get dressed and drive out to Santa Cruz with me."

She flashed a glance from his face to his cock and back up again to his face. He dropped his hand from her silky hair. Then she shrugged, let go of his aching appendage and pushed back from the table.

"Santa Cruz," she said, rising and moving past him down the hall.

Jack smiled, even though she wasn't there to see it, maybe *especially* because she wasn't there.

In those few seconds, with his cock in her hand, she'd debated which was the winning and the losing proposition. She'd deemed the blow job to be the more dangerous of the two choices.

Both choices were winners as far as he was concerned. Now all he had to get was get *her* to face that fact.

ELEVEN

Civil war games? The man was demented. She'd only chosen to ride along because otherwise they'd have spent the day in bed. She needed a rest, not just physically, but mentally. Jack confused her. Strike that. She confused herself.

Last night had been incredible. She'd never experienced sex like that before. But sex was just sex. Enjoyable, fun, satisfying. And Jack was Jack, her phone buddy.

Except that last night had seemed like . . . more. Sure, she'd done some kinky things in the past, but nothing on the scale of what she and Jack had done last night. Sex at a bar, almost-sex on the trunk lid of a car, and then, that whole thing with her vibrator. She'd been ready to climb the walls. She *had* climbed the walls.

Jack had screamed. He'd been equally out of control.

Then he'd washed her. Tenderly. As if he cared. God, why did she have to keep thinking about that? Why was that so friggin' special? Why had the memory of it woken her at a little before five? His arm had been around her waist, his nose in her hair. He hadn't snored. He hadn't even moved. Yet he was so . . . there.

She hadn't wanted to get up. She'd wanted to snuggle. Was that bizarre or what? She wasn't a snuggler. She was a get-up-and-go woman.

She'd almost finished the pot of coffee by the time he awoke, but she hadn't been any closer to getting her feelings in order. She'd wanted to put on a pleasant, hope-you-slept-well, thanks-for-the-great-fuck smile. Instead, the first sentence out of her mouth had been a bit bitchy and designed to keep him at bay.

During the long drive, she'd repeated to herself, *I am not going to be a bitch, I am not going to be a bitch.* The hot sun, the dusty park, the million screaming children, the whistle of the steam train, the boom of cannon fire, and the constant pop of the fake guns were not helping the situation.

Now Jack was trying to feed her hot dogs, for Christ's sake.

"I don't eat hot dogs. They're made out of guts. It's disgusting."

"But the mustard's good." He demonstrated with a big bite, licking the yellow goo from the corner of his mouth, moaning, groaning, and rolling his eyes with delight.

He sounded like he was having sex.

"You don't know what you're missing."

She remained petulant and silent.

He put his arm around her. "Here, just try a bite."

Jack wagged the hot dog in her face. Her stomach rumbled. She'd only had a piece of toast, but that was hours ago.

"Come on. Try it. I promise you won't gain five pounds from one bite."

"I'm not worried about my weight."

He stroked her hip, high enough to be innocuous in present company. "Come on, baby. You'll like it, I promise."

Why did she get the feeling he was talking about a helluva lot more than the hot dog? She leaned forward, closed her eyes, opened her mouth, and let him feed her a bite.

The tang of the mustard in her mouth, the slightly sweet, juicy meat, the lingering smoky aroma of barbecue . . . God, it was almost orgasmic.

Jack licked a bit of mustard from her lower lip. "Good?"

She wanted to say it was okay. Or adequate. Or something. It was better than good, and all she could do was stare at him. She'd never seen a more arresting pair of eyes, shadowed by such thick lashes. If she wasn't careful, she'd lose herself in them.

Lose herself?

That was the problem with Jack. He inspired a woman to give up her independence. Her control. Her freedom to come and go as she pleased and enjoy a man when he took her fancy.

"The hot dog was good, Jack, but I don't want the whole thing. One bite was enough." One night, one weekend.

The ever-present grin left his mouth. "You want something else?"

"A bottle of water." Just enough to sustain her in the heat. "Thanks."

He backed away, his head cocked to the side, and he looked at her, as if he knew there was a subliminal message he couldn't figure out. Then he joined the line at the concession stand.

Kirby drew in a deep breath and turned to watch the steam train, packed with families, pull away from the old wooden depot. Adults and kids alike waved at the passengers. The shrill whistle blasted, followed by the hiss of the steam engine, the rattle of iron wheels along the track, and the excited shouting of children aboard.

Jack had gotten her on the train earlier in the day. They'd chugged slowly up through the redwoods, in and out of sunlight, the air cooler and easier to breathe, the higher they'd climbed. Kids had raced up and down the car, bouncing like rubber balls. Jack was just as bad, talking, laughing, joking with everyone. The guy was just a big kid on a daylong outing.

Something warm and wet bumped her leg. She glanced

down to find a little dog nosing her calf, its owner, a little gnome of a woman, exerting a death grip on her Flexi Lead.

"He's a freak. He likes the smell of suntan lotion. But he won't bite."

Jack had stopped at a store just outside the park, purchased a tube, and insisted they liberally apply it to arms, legs, and necks. He'd also slathered it over the top of his head, then forced her to rub it in while he made exaggerated murmurs of enjoyment. She smiled against her will. He was damn good at getting her to smile. He'd done it time and again on the steam train.

The dog licked Kirby's leg.

"Stop that, Gort."

Gort? What kind of name was that? "He's cute." Kirby let the ugly little thing lap at her skin.

"He likes the ladies. Sort of like my old man in that way."

Kirby smiled. "Sort of like most men."

"He's a horn dog, Gort is."

Kirby laughed out loud. "He's not going to start . . . you know."

"Humping your leg?" The old lady scratched the side of her nose. "Just kick him if he does."

"She wouldn't kick a poor little dog." Jack returned, holding out her bottle of water, already uncapped.

"Oh yes, I would, if he started humping my leg."

The woman cackled, her sun bonnet flapping with her movements, but she didn't pull the little miscreant dog away.

Jack bent down, holding out his fingers for the dog to sniff. "What's his name?"

"Gort," Kirby supplied.

"From the movie?" He squinted up at the gnome lady.

"You're not old enough to know that movie."

"It's a classic. Everyone knows *The Day the Earth Stood Still*," he answered, straight-faced.

Kirby didn't.

"My, my, you've got yourself a real live one there, dollface. Ain't many these days can appreciate classic sci-fi. Hang on to him."

Dollface?

The dog sniffed Jack's soda cup. "I think he's thirsty. Kirby, give me your water."

"You can't let him drink out of her bottle."

Hugging the bottle to her chest, Kirby wanted to second the woman's declaration.

Jack took a big gulp of his soda, poured the rest out in the dirt, then held his hand up for Kirby's bottle. She handed it to him.

He filled the cup and held it out to the dog. For a minute Kirby heard only the peals of laughter, high-pitched voices, the train whistle in the distance, and the sound of that dog lapping at the water.

When Gort was done, the old woman beamed at Jack, tugged on the leash, and waved at them as she walked away.

"I'll get you another one."

"I'm fine." She still had over half the bottle. "Do you want some?" It was the least she could do since he'd dumped his cup for a little dog.

He took the offering, slugged down two swallows, then handed it back. "You okay, Kirby?"

Her? Okay? "Of course."

He still looked at her, almost as if he were trying to read her mind. Then he took her hand. Her fingers felt strangely cold in his warm grip.

"Come on. Let's go watch the games. I want to see who wins."

"The North won, Jack."

"Jesus, don't spoil the end for me."

Deck chairs, blankets, towels, and a sea of human bodies filled the lawn across from the "battlefield." A third of the women dressed in era clothing, bonnets, lace hankies, and long, belled skirts. When they sat, the hoops collapsed, surrounding them like satellite dishes. Of the men, the blue guys were definitely the better dressed of the bunch. More starch in their uniforms. The gray-clad guys looked as if their wives had made their wardrobe out of sacks. Maybe that was the stuff called "homespun."

Jack pulled her to the end of a row of standing ob-
servers. Her feet hurt from too much walking on gravel-
covered roads. Too much sun and the cannons made her
head ache. She'd forgotten her sunglasses, too.

"Daddy! Daddy! I can't see. I can't see."

Children could be very repetitive. Kirby tried to ignore
the little boy hopping from one foot to the other as he stood
beside his father.

"Let Eric have his turn. Then we'll switch. I only have
one pair of shoulders."

Jack turned. "I'll put him on mine, if you'd like."

The dad eyed Jack, searching for the child-molester
mien, then said, "Looks like you've got a ride, Donny."

Jack bent down and the little guy climbed aboard, holding onto Jack's ears as he rose into the air.

Kirby felt faint. She wasn't comfortable with kids. She
didn't want to have any of her own. She didn't even want to
get married unless it was to a man as dedicated to his own
career as she was to hers. Jack, however, looked so
adorable with that blond-haired, blue-eyed cherub up on
his shoulders, his hands massive against the little shins he
held in place.

Jesus, he looked like . . . a father. Like he'd make a
good father. Oh my God.

"Jack, we have to go."

"This is the best part. They're going to do a charge
across the open field. And look at all those Union guys hidden in the tree line. It'll be a massacre. We can't miss that."
His eyes bore the same glow as the child clinging to the top
of his head. Kirby couldn't see anyone in the tree line, and
she was sure Jack was making it up for the sake of the
boy's excitement.

Bloodthirsty.

"I don't feel well. It's sunstroke or something. We have
to go."

"But I only just got to see," Donny wailed, and looked
down at her with beseeching little-kid eyes.

She didn't like kids that looked at her with puppy-dog

eyes. She didn't like dogs, for that matter. Jack loved them, dogs and kids. He probably loved cats, too. She'd never seen him angry. She'd never seen him mean. The thing he seemed to know how to do best was laugh. And make her come like a volcano.

Ian would never have poured water for a thirsty animal. Ian would never have let a kid ride his shoulders. Ian had never made her feel the way Jack did. Nobody ever had.

Her eyeballs throbbed. Her stomach started to rise to her throat.

First comes love, then comes marriage, then comes Kirby with a baby carriage.

She was going to throw up, right here, right now. She dropped the bottle, put her hand to her stomach, and ran to the portable toilets. Damn, they were so far away. Jack called her name. All she could think about was that she'd have to throw up in a Porta Potti.

How humiliating.

TWELVE

"I'm sorry. I didn't know you were really sick."

"You thought I was just being a bitch again."

He'd grabbed a few napkins from a vendor, poured the bottled water over them, and now held them to her pale, overheated face. She'd lost her lipstick, and perspiration dotted her forehead.

"I don't think you're a bitch, Kirby. I wouldn't have come all the way out here to see you if I did. Now let's go sit in the shade until you stop shaking."

"I should have brought a hat and my sunglasses."

"I should have prepared you better. I'll get another bottle of water for the drive home."

The line was too long, and without him, Kirby looked like a lost waif. Better not tell her that. Kirby would hate being called a waif. Jesus, he was an ass for not paying attention. She lived in San Francisco, for God's sake, where there was always a breeze and the fog rolled in to cool things off. He was from the East, where eighty-five was considered mild. He shuddered to think how she'd react to humidity. She was like a delicate seaside flower: Take her out in the burning desert, and she withered from excessive heat.

Another cannon thundered, and she gripped the side of the bench she sat on. He plunked down the ridiculous sum the vendor asked and rushed back with two precious bottles of springwater.

Her lips had regained a little color, and the feverish gleam in her eye seemed to have eased. He uncapped a bottle and held it out. "Drink."

She did, swilling water in her mouth, delicately spitting it into the trashcan next to her, then downing almost half the bottle before finally taking a breath.

"Better?"

"I'm fine now. But those toilets stink." She wrinkled her nose. "I almost threw up from the stench alone."

He put the back of his hand to her cheek and found her skin still a little clammy to the touch. "Let's go home."

Home. Home was wherever Kirby was. He'd been a selfish prick to force her out, especially since he'd known she hadn't slept well. He was even a worse prick, because he'd hoped it would cause her to drop her guard. He hadn't even made sure she ate properly.

"We can stop for a sandwich on the way home. I'm sure they've got something with just bean sprouts and eggplant."

"I hate eggplant, and bean sprouts taste like grass. I want steak."

He leaned back and surveyed her. "You're scaring me here, Kirby."

She glanced toward a group of teenagers tossing water balloons at each other. A girl shrieked as one of the guys, presumably her boyfriend, pulled off a magnificently executed throw that hit her dead center in her rather impressive chest. Water exploded, up into her face, down the front of her minuscule T-shirt, and of course, drenched her breasts. Still screeching, she held the shirt away from her body, but not before all the boys saw her nipples. Poor kid.

Sixteen and severely traumatized. It would take her another ten years to grow out of the ordeal.

"How old are you, Jack?"

"Hey, I wasn't looking."

A ghost of a smile curved her lips. "Liar. You wouldn't
be a man if you didn't look." She stopped, looking once
more, almost thoughtfully, at the laughing teenagers. "So,
how old *are* you?"

"Thirty-six." He was sure he'd told her somewhere
along the way. Then again, his strategy had concerned figuring *her* out. What he revealed about himself hadn't been
so important.

"I'm thirty."

"Yeah. I know."

"I like my life the way it is."

A chill started in the center of his chest. "Yeah."

"I love my business."

He fiddled with the cap from the water bottle, hoping
she wouldn't notice. He struggled to exhale the breath he'd
been holding. "And?" There had to be more.

She cocked her head, stared at him, then sighed. "And I
think you're right, I should have a little something to eat."

Damn. She'd been on the verge of something. He'd seen
that gleam in her eye, the one that said she was thinking
overtime. Oddly, he'd had the feeling whatever she was
thinking would turn out to be good for him.

Then she'd shut down.

Jack smiled. He never let himself get down for long.
He'd get her to tell him whatever was on her mind when he
was buried deep inside her delicious body.

She'd decided on barbecued beef, and they split the
sandwich since Jack claimed he wasn't all that hungry after
the hot dog. With the air-conditioning on low, she leaned
back against the headrest and closed her eyes. The movement of the car lulled her.

With water and food, her stomach settled. The overwhelming heat flushing her body had dimmed, all except the sexual glow that just being around Jack seemed to generate. That, however, was a good thing. Especially for the rest of the weekend.

She'd known how old Jack was, had sought only confirmation. The man's biological clock was ticking. Soon, he'd be manic to start a family. There'd be no room for her, nor for their phone calls, and no weekend trysts on quick business trips. He'd be a married man. She probably only had a matter of months left to enjoy him. Sitting in the sun, his thigh next to hers, she'd realized there was so much more to enjoy.

He was a highly sexed male animal. Not all men were, no matter that they pretended otherwise. He was her perfect match in that regard. Kirby knew the sex wasn't over. She didn't want it be over yet. It was just too damn good. Almost addicting. Jack made her *feel*. She wanted more of it. A lot more of it. In a variety of ways. So many exciting, even kinky things to try with Jack. The distance between their domiciles was icing on the cake. It would be like leading a double life. She'd enjoy every moment of it until the instinct to settle down took him over.

"Jack."

"Yeah?"

She kept her eyes closed, enjoying the warmth through the windshield and the soft, lazy drone of the car's engine. "I've been thinking that I need to start doing a little business traveling."

"Really?" Skepticism flavored his tone.

She opened her eyes to glance at him, putting her hand on his thigh. "I should at least fly out to get a tour of your facility."

A brow raised, he studied her a moment, then turned back to the road. The corner of his mouth lifted with a smile. "Sounds like an excellent plan."

She was about to ask him to elaborate on how excellent he could make it when her cell phone chirped inside her purse. Dammit. Fishing it out, she punched a button.

"Where are you? I was getting worried."

"Kristin." Shit. She'd completely forgotten about dinner. Kirby glanced at her watch to find it was already a quarter after five. "I'm late."

Kristin's "duh," though unspoken, came through clearly in her deliberate pause. "You're never late."

"To tell you the truth, I forgot." She glanced at Jack, his brow raised in a question.

"You never forget anything either," Kristin said.

She had, the minute Jack told her he was flying out. She'd forgotten everything. "Well, a friend from out of town dropped by unexpectedly for a visit and I—"

"A male friend?"

"Yes."

"You don't have male friends."

"Of course I do." She just couldn't think of any at the moment. She couldn't refer to the men she dated as friends.

"He's a sex friend, isn't he? Why didn't you ever tell me about him?"

"Because."

"Because why?" Kristin's voice rose with suspicion.

"Later, okay?"

"Is he with you?"

"Yes."

"Bring him along then."

"Why don't we just make it next week? I promise not to forget again."

"You don't want me to meet him. That means he's somebody important."

"No." He was just . . . her "sex friend." She glanced at Jack. One hand nonchalantly guiding the wheel, his other crept to her thigh to play with the hem of her shorts. A question still glowed in his eye.

"Yes, he is, yes, he is." Her sister's chanting reminded her of little Donny's repetitive voice.

"Kristin—"

Jack tugged on her shorts. When she looked at him, he mouthed, "I don't mind going."

Not "You go, I'll entertain myself," not even "It's our last night, I want to be alone with you."

That irked her. He was pushing again, in a sneaky way, because he knew her sister's name was Kristin. He was finagling a meet with her family, using that easygoing manner of his. As if her suggestion that she fly out for a little hot nookie invited him to intrude on other parts of her life. Give the man an inch, and he tried to take a mile.

She'd never intended for him to meet her family. He was hers. Her secret, she mentally amended.

"Are you still there, Kirby?"

"I'm here."

"We've got plenty. Bring him. I want to meet him. Ross is nodding yes."

She was being ganged up on from all sides. Damn Jack, too, he was grinning again, as if he could hear Kristin.

"All right, fine. We'll be there in an hour." She'd show them that Jack was nothing important. She'd show *him*.

This might turn out to be a good idea.

Because if, God forbid, she started creating some weird, romantic illusion that Jack was Mr. Right, Ross would make the perfect foil. Jack's five-foot-something and bald head up against Ross the hunk. The image should be enough to squash anyone's romantic illusion.

Happily ever after was just a fairy tale with the potential to undermine a woman's independence.

THIRTEEN

Kirby had that battle gleam in her eye as she knocked on the apartment door.

In the car on the way home from the reenactment, Jack had silently crowed to himself. The withdraw-and-retreat phase had gone much faster than he'd figured. Fancy that, she wanted to make a few business trips out to see him. Things seemed to be moving along at very nice pace.

Then her sister called, and they entered a phase he hadn't even known existed. Kirby was certainly a quick-change artist, and that referred to her mood swings rather than her attire. One moment she was offering him the world, the next, she'd cut him off.

In the end they didn't make it to her sister's until seven. Kirby'd spent an inordinate amount of time cloistered in her bedroom. She'd insisted he was dressed okay in black jeans and a black button-down shirt he'd picked up at his hotel. When she finally emerged from her room, he recognized that the battle lines had been clearly drawn.

She'd donned a delicious little black dress with straps that looked thin enough to fall apart at first tug. He'd enjoy a little tug-of-war later. Her heels were maximum fuck-me height, at least an inch over the green pair she'd worn Friday, the ones that had almost made him shoot his wad the moment he first saw her. He was in for a rock-hard night. He could only hope the sister didn't blush as easily as Kirby claimed she did.

She'd brushed her auburn hair to a lustrous shine and lined her lips with a dark burgundy that somehow made her green eyes deepen to the color of the ocean just before a fierce storm. Arched brows and a coppery shadow gave her the Cleopatra look, one designed to bring him to his knees.

She'd outdressed him, and she wanted him to know it.

Turned out, she'd outdressed the sister and the fiancé, too, but Kirby didn't care. She entered the apartment, head high, back straight, and tits out.

Ross, the fiancé, seemed dazed, as if he'd never borne witness to Kirby's power before. Kristin, while of equal beauty, lacked the glamour. Not that she needed it. After the initial bombshell of Kirby's appearance, Ross had slipped his arm around Kristin and kissed the top of her head. A sweet, simple gesture that Jack envied.

Kirby envied it, too, he could tell. Her chin, if possible, rose another notch. In a moment, she'd likely topple backward with the weight of her haughtiness. God, ya had to love the woman.

A large room served as both living and dining room. A table of dark wood and four chairs took up a corner next to an archway that presumably led to the kitchen. The plain but expensive furniture filled but didn't overwhelm the living area. A large southwestern-style print hung over the couch, and an entertainment center sporting the latest technology occupied the opposite wall. The room had masculine written all over it. Kristin Prescott obviously hadn't put her stamp on it yet.

When Kirby failed to perform the introductions, Kristin stuck out her hand. "Hi, I'm Kristin." She gave his a gentle shake.

"Jack Taylor."

Even though they were twins, neither could be mistaken for the other. Same silky auburn hair, same sparkling green eyes, but Kirby was somehow . . . more. Kristin was a bright smile, Kirby, a sultry pout. Kristin was loose-fitting jeans and embroidered blouses, Kirby, sexy, solid black. Kristin was sex with the lights off underneath the covers, Kirby, in an overcrowded, rowdy bar.

Though he realized he'd chosen the harder path, Jack wouldn't have traded places with Kristin's fiancé for even a small piece of Bill Gates's fortune. He was well aware that the man had been checking him out. His arm around Kristin's shoulders anchored her to his side, and his keen gaze passed from Jack to Kirby and back again. Finally the man put out his hand. "Ross Sloan."

Firm grip. More pressure than necessary. A slightly narrowed gaze. Jack appreciated the warning. He suspected Kirby didn't often invite her "dates" to Saturday dinner at her sister's, and Sloan, being the new "man of the house," had assumed the role of protector for both women.

"I forgot the wine," Kirby said.

Kristin cocked her head. Her gaze followed the same ping-pong path that Sloan's had. The woman was dying to ask a million questions. "That's okay," she said. "I've got some in the fridge. How did you two meet?"

"Jack's my sales guy from back East," Kirby answered for him.

He'd have his hands full with her tonight, in more ways than one. By the tilt of her chin and the spark in her eye, she meant the flat statement to show him his place. Kristin guessed it, too. Acting as the mediator, she said, "Well. That's nice. Ross, why don't you and Jack attend to the grill, while Kirby helps me with the salad?"

The little peacemaker pulled her sister through the archway into the kitchen.

"Pissed her off earlier?" Sloan asked as he led the way across the main living area to a set of sliding-glass doors, beyond which was a magnificent view of the Bay.

Jack didn't appreciate Sloan's knowing tone, as if the man had Kirby summed up and found her less than ideal. "She's not open for discussion."

Hand on the door, Sloan gave him a considering look. "No disrespect intended."

Jack nodded, apology noted and accepted. The scent of sizzling steaks permeated the balcony, drifting through into the living room. Jack wasn't hungry, at least not for anything other than Kirby's delectable body.

"You want a beer?" Sloan offered. "They're in the cooler over there."

"Thanks." Jack pulled one out for himself. "You already set?"

Sloan glanced over his shoulder, back through the open archway where their women could be seen, but not heard. His eyes fastened on Kristin. "Yeah, I'm set. Perfectly."

Well, there was no accounting for tastes.

"He's gorgeous," Kristin said as she rummaged in the refrigerator.

"He's short and bald."

"He's cute. And those eyes. Smoking. How long's he staying?"

"He's leaving tomorrow."

"Are you sad?"

Kirby snorted. "Give me a break. He's just my salesman."

Kristin straightened, the unopened bottle of wine in her hand. "Why do you keep saying that?"

"Why does it matter?"

"Because you forgot our dinner date, and you forgot the wine. And you said I couldn't set you up with a short or bald guy, and then you show up with someone who's both."

"I'm not sure that made a single bit of sense." Which was, she knew, an avoidance tactic. Jack's height and hair follicle count had ceased to be an issue except when she was trying to find reasons to make sure he got back on that plane tomorrow.

"How long have you been seeing him?"

"We've just talked on the phone. This is his first trip out here."

"Hmm," Kristin murmured. "Is he good in bed?"

"What makes you think I've been to bed with him?"

"Because of the way he looks at you."

"And how's that?" A chill traveled up her spine. She didn't want anyone knowing her secret passion.

"His eyes touch every part of you whenever he looks at you. Like he's touched every bit of flesh under that dress."

"Kristin. I'm shocked." Her sister's statement, so accurate, made her tingle.

Kristin lifted one shoulder and gave her a sly wink. "So, how is he?"

"Let's not talk about it. What drawer is the bottle opener in?"

"That one."

The drawer was neat and orderly, just like Ross. Kirby wondered what Jack's kitchen drawers would be like. Pulling out the opener, she took the bottle and went to work on the cork.

"You like this guy a lot, don't you?"

The coldness of the bottle slid up her arms. Instead of the denial she wanted to make, she found herself asking, "What makes you say that?"

"You've never cared enough about any of the others to get mad."

"I'm not mad." The cork popped with a small whoosh and a fruity aroma rose to her nostrils.

"Maybe *threatened* is a better word."

"Threatened?" She didn't like the way the word came out, just short of shrill. "Where are the wineglasses?"

"Above the fridge. And yeah, threatened. It's in the way you say *salesman* and keep harping on the fact that he's not so tall and doesn't have tons of hair." Kristin leaned back into the refrigerator and came out with a fully prepared salad and a couple of bottles of dressing. "And those shoes."

Kirby looked down at the black suede heels. "What's wrong with these shoes? I love them."

"But they're so high. Like you're trying to emphasize your height."

"For your information, Jack says the shoes make him hot."

Kristin's brows shot up. "Ooh. So, you're wearing them for him? Thought he was just your *sales guy*?"

"Bite me, sister dear."

"And you're being bitchy, too."

"I *am* a bitch, Kristin. Just ask Ross."

"He doesn't think you're a bitch."

He did. She hadn't tried terribly hard to be nice. Because he had certain traits that reminded her of Ian. Suddenly that bothered her. She didn't want to have to be a bitch around any man that had more than the average guy's testosterone. It also bothered her that she *had* intended some weird sort of slam against Jack with all that salesman stuff. "I think I'm hormonal."

"Or in love."

"Absolutely not." Her belly clenched.

"Gee, that was a definitive no."

"It wasn't something I had to think really hard about." Nor would she mention the sudden lump in her throat.

"But you like him a lot, don't you?"

Denial leaped to her tongue, but didn't make it past her lips. She thought about Jack and the kid, Jack and the dog, Jack soothing her with the washcloth. She didn't think about the sex or how good it was. No, she thought about how she craved the sound of his voice, not just whispering dirty words in her ear, but something as mundane and silly as asking how her day was going or telling her a funny story about a meeting he'd just had.

"Yeah, I like him."

Kristin clapped her hands and bounced in her tennies. "I knew it. I knew it."

"Don't start making it into more than it is. He lives in New York. I live here. And neither one of us is going to move."

FOURTEEN

"So, you're in sales, what kind?" Guy talk. They'd politely exchanged business cards, neither paying much attention to the print, then talked shop. If you had nothing in common except the women you slept with, the safest topic was professional.

"Cosmetics. Kirby's company is a niche market for us, custom blends for small boutiques."

Sloan made a gesture with his barbecue fork. "Doesn't sound like there's much profit in it."

"Actually, it's the opposite. Very high margin. Surprising what women will pay for something they think no one else has."

"Smart business move on her part, then."

"Very smart. When she brought the idea to us, I was intrigued."

Especially with Kirby.

Sloan checked his watch, lifted the barbecue lid, and flipped three enormous steaks. "So, you have other customers you're visiting on this trip?"

Not a very subtle way of asking whether Kirby was his

only business in town, but a typical almost-brother-in-law query as to Jack's intentions. "We're opening a sales office in San Francisco. Finalized it this week."

"Honey," Kristin called from the kitchen. "Don't burn the outside of the steaks, okay?"

"Yes, dear," Ross called back before lifting the lid and staring. "Do you think she'll notice?"

"Nah," Jack said. "That's not burned, just heavily grilled."

"Yeah, that's what I thought." Sloan quirked a brow. "So you're moving out here?"

"After a time. I'm hiring an East Coast VP of sales. If he works out the way I'm expecting, then I'll make the move out here and split my time between New York and San Francisco."

"*You're* hiring the VP?"

"Yeah, since he'd be reporting to me."

"I thought you were just—"

Jack saved him the embarrassment of having to repeat Kirby's words. "We had an opening for a senior sales and marketing VP last year." Jack swigged down a slug of beer. A smooth brew. His host liked the good stuff. "The company gave me a shot at it, and so far, they're satisfied."

"Sounds like it was a good opportunity."

"It was. I'll be hiring a customer service manager out here. I did a round of interviews yesterday, but I've got to come back out at the end of the week for another set."

Sloan smiled. "And is that the only reason you're coming back out?"

Jack looked through the door toward the kitchen. "I've another reason, too."

"When are you going to tell Kirby all of this?"

"What makes you think she doesn't know?"

Ross glanced once more toward the kitchen. "Instinct." Then, with a noncommittal grunt, he flipped the steaks.

It occurred to Jack there was a distinct possibility that Sloan might spill the beans over dinner. The prospect didn't worry him. Coming with dinner conversation might actually make the idea of the San Francisco office less threatening to Kirby. She'd see it as just another business venture in which he was involved.

He'd have to tell her the full ramifications soon. Before he left tomorrow. Because when he came back, he was coming back for her.

Kirby could do no more than pick at her steak. At least Ross had the forethought to cook only one hunk of meat for both Kristin and her.

Speaking of hunks, Jack held his own with her sister's tall, dark, and handsome fiancé. The two of them laughed and joked like old friends. Just what had they talked about on the balcony that suddenly made them so chummy?

Not sex. Jack wouldn't do that.

If not that, then what?

"When's the wedding?" Jack asked, obviously trying to include the females in the conversation.

He sawed off a chunk of meat. Considering that they'd eaten only three hours ago, he was doing quite a job on the massive filet Ross had grilled him.

"The middle of September," Kristin answered. "Will you be out here then, do you think?"

Kirby kicked her under the table.

"If that's an invitation, I wouldn't miss it," he said.

Kristin smiled guilelessly, the witch. "It's definitely an invitation."

Ross put down his knife and fork and raised his wineglass in a toast. "Well then, Jack, here's to the success of your San Francisco sales office and a permanent move out here by September."

Kirby felt a hitch in her chest. "What sales office?"

Jack hesitated a moment before answering, "We're opening an office here in San Francisco. Friday, I signed the final papers on the lease, the bank accounts, PG and E, etcetera. Maybe you know of a good receptionist that's available."

He hadn't told her about any sales office, but then she hadn't asked. Yet, he'd mentioned it to Ross as if it were nothing more than casual male discussion. "You're moving out here? Permanently?"

"I'll still personally handle your account, Kirby," he said, as if that made up for the fact that he hadn't even hinted about the real reason for his trip.

He'd blindsided her. Or maybe he hadn't thought it would make a difference to her one way or the other. Or maybe . . . or maybe she didn't know what the hell it meant—to her specifically. Somehow, she'd just assumed he'd flown all the way here to see her. "Well. That's very nice. Does this mean a promotion?"

"He's already senior VP of Marketing and Sales, Kirby. Where else is there to go except CEO?"

Ross's comment slammed into her chest. Jack was a VP? A *senior* VP?

Jack looked at her, his next words sounding as if he'd read her mind. "I got the promotion last year."

"Oh." He hadn't told her. What else had he been keeping from her? A wife and kids back in Yonkers or something?

A flush rose to her cheeks when she realized everyone was staring at her. The silence was a dull roar in her ears. She had to fill it, however inadequately. "Well, I'm sorry I didn't offer congratulations at the time."

"At the time it wouldn't have been appropriate to boast to a customer."

She wasn't just a customer. She hadn't been since the first time he'd asked her to undo her blouse.

Jack had been keeping secrets. Or worse, maybe they weren't even secrets, maybe he just hadn't considered her worthy of sharing his triumphs.

Ross held up the bottle. "More wine, Kirby?"

"Thank you." She let him fill up her glass.

"Is the meat too rare? They were thick pieces. I can throw it back on for a few more minutes."

Since when had Ross Sloan been so solicitous? Especially to her? Was her sudden turmoil reflected on her face?

"Actually, the outside's a little on the burned—"

Jack cut her off. "I have to admit we stopped for sand-wiches just before you called. Kirby's probably not all that hungry."

Don't talk for me. She wanted to shout at him, but she didn't trust herself not to go all hysterical.

Hysterical? Of course she wasn't. She held on to her shredding emotions. "I should have told you, Kristin. Sorry. I really did forget about dinner."

"That's okay. Whatever you don't eat, I can use to make a steak salad for dinner tomorrow. Ross loves steak salad, don't you, sweetie? Even if the outside's a little . . . crispy."

How domestic. How terrifying.

Suddenly she just had to get out of there. She didn't care how bad her explanation sounded. "We went over to Santa Cruz, and I think I got sunstroke or something. I haven't fully recovered. My headache's come back."

"Maybe we should get you home to bed."

At Jack's words, Ross's lips formed a full-blown smirk. He knew Jack didn't mean home to bed to sleep, but home to bed to . . . fuck.

She folded her napkin. Slowly. Deliberately. And placed it beside her barely touched meal. "Thanks for having us."

"Call me tomorrow so I know you're okay," Kristin said with sisterly concern. The twinkle in her eyes contradicted her words. Even her sister thought they were going home to do it.

"Sure," Kirby said. But things wouldn't be okay. Things were getting out of hand. So much emotion over Jack's failure to tell her his business plans was over the top. Defi-nitely not a good sign.

She only hoped it wasn't too late to regain control.

FIFTEEN

"No. I am not pissed," she said.

"Yes. You are. You were silent all the way home."

Jack led the way into the bedroom. She should have been leading him. Instead, he took the liberty of flinging himself down on the bed, scattering pillows all over.

"If you're pissed that I didn't tell you, then let's get it out in the open and discuss it."

"It doesn't make any difference to me." She studiously avoided swear words. Swear words indicated passion. And lack of control.

"I thought, coming from Sloan, you wouldn't see it as such a threat. I was wrong."

There was that word again, first from Kristin, now from him. "I do not see it as a *threat*. It doesn't mean anything other than the fact that you'll be able to fuck me on a more regular basis."

"That's a little cold."

She *felt* cold. Or worse. Scared. Because it did matter. It mattered that he'd lied to her. It mattered that he hadn't told her himself. It mattered that she didn't know where he thought all this was going. It mattered most that she even gave a thought to where their relationship might go. She hadn't truly cared what a man thought, said, or did since Ian had said he'd marry her and fix all her little business problems, as if she were a child.

She slipped out of her high heels and crossed to the closet. "Jack, let's be honest. Until yesterday, we hadn't even met each other. We were just phone-sex buddies." He was a goddamn VP. Why, they were almost equals. They *were* equals. He probably made a helluva lot more money than she did, too. VPs were as dictatorial as CFOs, like Ross. Or silent partners, like Ian.

"We've always been more than phone-sex buddies."

She didn't have a good comeback for that, so she ignored it. "Now I find out you're opening a sales office in San Francisco, and you might be living out here by September. I liked things the way they were."

"Because they were safe."

"Because there were no demands."

"Because you didn't have to make any changes in your life."

"That's right, I'm *not* changing my life." For a moment it was hard to suck air past the gigantic lump in her throat. Two breaths later, though, it seemed to get a little easier. "Now, would you please get off the bed? I'd like to lie down. I wasn't lying about not feeling well."

He rose and started prowling the room, touching the atomizers on her vanity, picking up her hairbrush, then putting it down. "I didn't lie."

Okay, so her emphasis on the word was as telling as actually having interjected a few cuss words. She'd let the cat out of the bag, might as well deal with it. "I suppose you're going to say that omission isn't lying."

"It is. I'm sorry."

She knew damn well he wasn't. He'd manipulated her. Just like Ian, who'd been so damn good at it. Sometimes she hadn't even realized he'd slammed her abilities until hours later, sometimes even days. She undid her zipper, tugged the straps off her shoulders, and let the dress fall to the carpet.

Silence. Jack watched. And wanted. She didn't acknowledge his desires. Instead, she bent at the waist, giving him a clear view of her panty-less ass, picked up the dress, and hung it on a hanger.

"I think you should sleep at your hotel," she said, going into the bathroom. She needed time to screw her head on straight, time to put everything in perspective. So *what* if he was a VP and hadn't told her, or that he'd be out in the Bay Area more often? It wasn't a crisis. He was very good in bed. Now, *that* was a proper perspective. She just needed a little time to assimilate it. She brushed her teeth, removed her makeup, and cleansed her face, spending only half her usual time.

Jack still stood by the vanity when she flipped off the bathroom light.

"No," he said distinctly.

"No what?"

"I'm not going back to my hotel. We need to talk."

She tossed the extra pillows into the corner and climbed into bed. "Call me on Monday. We can talk then."

"We'll talk now."

"I don't like your tone of voice, Jack. I think you'd better leave."

"No."

"If you don't, I will. And I don't care if it's my apartment."

He started prowling again, opening and closing the drawers of her bureau. "I realize I made a big mistake."

He stopped, shuffled through one drawer in particular.

"What are you doing?" Dammit. "Stay out of my stuff."

"I'm sorry about the whole thing." He closed the drawer.

Kirby closed her eyes and pretended she could go to sleep.

He continued, his voice husky and inviting, like on the phone. "I shouldn't have lied."

He shouldn't have, but it also shouldn't matter to her this much. God, she needed to be alone, to sort it all out rationally. "I mean it. You go or I will. We can talk about this on Monday." When she wasn't so mixed up. When she could think clearly. When she wasn't lying in a bed steeped with his scent and fragrant with last night's sex.

God, she'd never be able to get between these sheets without smelling him. She wouldn't be able to wash him out. She'd have to throw the bedclothes out.

The bed dipped. She didn't dare open her eyes. He'd see her dilated pupils. He'd guess that beneath the covers her nipples were hard and her body was wet. All in all, it was a very debilitating situation.

"Go away," she repeated, contempt oozing from each syllable.

The air rushed out of her lungs as he climbed on top of her, using his weight to hold her down.

"Get off me," she managed to squeak even though she could barely breathe.

Jack didn't obey. Instead, he gathered both her wrists in one hand and pulled her arms over her head. "I am not leaving. You are not leaving. We're going to talk."

Then he tied her hands to the rails of her brass bed.

Now, that *really* pissed her off.

SIXTEEN

"Goddamn it, Jack."

Gasping for breath, she bucked and rolled beneath him. Jack pulled back, giving her room to breathe. She attempted to kick him, but the covers kept her legs pinned.

"Untie me."

He yanked the spread back, throwing it over the end of the bed, and grabbed an ankle. She kicked and flailed, but he hung on, and finally secured her left leg to the bottom of the bed. He went for the other ankle and was rewarded with one helluva good jab, her big toe to the underside of his chin. Then he had her right leg cinched as well.

"That hurts. They're too tight."

"Quit struggling, and they won't dig into your skin."

"This isn't funny. What did you tie me up with?"

"Your scarves. I'm not feeling in very good humor."

"Well, you were in damn good humor at Ross's. At my expense."

"Is that what this is all about? Because you think I humiliated you in front of your sister and her fiancé?"

She didn't say anything. Probably because she'd figured she'd said too much already. Goddamn it, he hated the silent treatment. It had driven him damn near psychotic in the car on the way home. It was a woman's greatest weapon, and it made him feel impotent and helpless. Which was why they employed it. There must be a secret tome somewhere to which only women were privy, and the first commandment was: When you're losing an argument, just stop talking.

"All right. You were humiliated. It wasn't my intention."

She stopped struggling, but squirmed down into the mattress and the pillow. As if she weren't listening and didn't care.

"I'm sorry." How did women do that? Get you to apologize when you hadn't done anything to apologize for?

She refused to acknowledge him.

He couldn't take his eyes off the dusky rose color of her aureoles, her tight little nipples. Succulent sweets he'd pulled into his mouth less than twelve hours ago. He could still taste her, the essence of Kirby, mixed with strawberries and whipped cream.

"I am not leaving until you answer me."

She drew in a deep breath. It came out as a sigh. Her body relaxed, the muscles of her legs and arms went lax against the restraints. He'd spread her legs to tie her down. Now her knees turned out, and her bush opened to him. A hint of pink. Moist, hot pink. His goddamn jeans suddenly threatened to cut off the blood supply to his dick.

He flexed his fingers, then fisted them. "Refusing to talk to me is childish."

She let out a throaty little hum, as if she were getting ready to sleep. He felt the intimate sound in his balls, the tip of his penis, his chest, his heart.

He held control of the situation by little more than a thread. It started to unravel with each silent moment beating against his eardrums.

"I'm spending the night. If you won't talk to me, we'll talk in the morning."

He expected that declaration to garner something, at least for her to say he wasn't sleeping in her damn bed.

She didn't open her mouth or her eyes. No movement at all except for the gentle rise and fall of her chest, drawing his attention once more to her pert nipples.

He ripped his shirt over his head, forgetting it wasn't a T-shirt. Buttons popped and flew across the room. He jerked off his jeans, almost castrating himself on the goddamn zipper. Another evil device invented by women.

Payback for the chastity belt.

Maybe they were taught how to tease and emasculate starting in the cradle.

Pants, briefs, and shoes sailed across the room and hit the wall with a thud. She didn't even blink. He climbed on, straddling her. His cock bobbed and waved. Jack stared at her lips, bare of lipstick, but no less luscious.

Suddenly he wanted her mouth on him. Her lips, her tongue, hell yes, even her teeth. He moved forward until he reached her armpits. Then he sat back, not hard, not enough to squash her again, but just so he could feel her skin against the underside of his balls. Her nipples jutted like diamond points against the inside of his thighs.

"Suck me, Kirby." He stroked himself, touching the tip to the corner of her mouth.

She didn't say anything.

He reached behind and put his hand on her hot mound. Her moisture creamed his palm. He rubbed, then slipped a finger between her folds. He circled the hard nub of her clitoris. She was hot, aroused. She was also goddamn silent.

She had to know she was driving him mad. He could work her over, make her come, and, he'd bet, she still wouldn't make a peep.

He was going to try anyway.

He entered her with his middle finger, the spread of her legs making access easy, and used the heel of his hand to keep the pressure on her clitoris. She lay beneath him, maintaining perfect control over her body. He slid back

out, dragging his wet finger across her clit, across her belly.
He rubbed each nipple with her juice, then stuck his finger
in his mouth.

"You taste good, Kirby. Want me to go down on you?"

She had to be aching for it, dying for it. He was. The
whole time his finger had been buried in her, he'd stroked
himself until the crown of his penis had purpled with the
impending explosion. Who said men couldn't multitask?
He wanted to come in her mouth. He wanted her to swallow. He wanted to lose his load against the back of her
throat.

He did the only thing a man barely holding onto his sanity could do. He closed her nose with his thumb and forefinger and turned her head toward him.

Kirby's mouth flew open, and she shrieked. He put his
cock just inside her plump, rosy lips. The caress didn't
come close to easing the ache in his balls. He needed her to
accept him willingly.

"Jesus, God, Kirby, please suck it. Suck it or I'll die."

She opened her eyes. Then, thank the Lord, she swirled
her tongue around his tip. For the first time, he was glad
she wasn't talking to him. He eased into the depths of her
mouth. She took him, her tongue on the underside of his
shaft, then sucked hard. He pulled back. She rose to meet
him, keeping him inside, rocking him in and out. He put a
hand to the back of her head, supporting her, spreading his
fingers through her hair. She moaned deep in her throat.
The vibration slid up his cock.

"So good." He fought to keep his eyes open. He wanted
to see it all. Her mouth encircling him. Her cheeks sucking. The bright snap of her eyes.

She quickened her pace, taking control. He didn't give a
damn. All he wanted was to come.

"Jesus. Harder. Fuck. You do that so fucking good."

His balls tightened to the point of pain. His cock hardened to steel, and the pressure built low in his gut. Intense.
Heart-stopping. Each breath was a sharp ache in his chest,

his throat. He let go of her head, grabbed the brass rails he'd tied her to, and let her have her way with him.

His insides exploded into shards of white light. He shouted out her name, then he lost himself in her mouth. She worked to contain him, draining every last drop, swallowing it, her mouth sucking him dry.

He pulled out, collapsed back on his haunches, his belly against her lips. She licked at the perspiration gathered on his skin.

Every orgasm she gave him was infinitely more incredible than the last.

Rising above her, he took her chin in his hand. "Thank you."

She didn't say a word. He didn't care.

"I promised you multiple orgasms." He slid down her body, first tweaking her nipples with his fingers, then drawing one into his mouth. She moaned and rose to plaster herself against him.

He moved on from that delicacy to the delights of her beautiful bush. Droplets of moisture gleamed on her curls like dew. He lapped them up.

He started his seduction with his fingers, stroking her clit with the same rhythm he'd watched her use on herself. Kirby didn't need his fingers inside. She was a button woman all the way. He put his hand under her butt to steady her and went to work with soft wet slides and strokes, then little circles. He went to her channel only to maintain the slickness of his fingers. Before long, her hips danced to the rhythm of his touch. He knew she was close when she started to pant, then moan.

She came undone against his fingers, but before she had the chance to lose the high, he put his mouth to her, then his tongue. He used the same gentle pressure, stopping only to suck her clit into his mouth. Her hips bucked, and she gave voice to her desire, her mouth opened in a sweet low wail. She came again, he drank her in.

He didn't let her go. He kept her on the edge, forcing her over, then pulling her back for more until he heard tears in her moans. Until he thought she was going to hy-perventilate.

Until she finally screamed his name when she came for the sixth time.

SEVENTEEN

He'd tied her down, forced his cock down her throat, shot off in her mouth, and made her come countless times.

It had been pretty spectacular, at least as far as the orgasms went. He'd gone too far, though. He'd withheld important facts from her, something which she'd come to realize he'd done purposefully. Then he'd shackled her. She couldn't lose sight of all of that despite the orgasms.

"Satisfied, Jack?"

He crawled up from between her legs, then flopped against her side. "Hell, yes."

"Then maybe you could untie me now."

"Shit, I'm sorry." He tugged the scarves loose from her wrists, clambered to the end of the bed, undid those restraints, then returned to collapse beside her. His hand curved under her breast.

"Thank you."

She rubbed at her wrists. They didn't hurt, but he'd noted the action.

"Oh, baby, I'm sorry." He kissed the inside of one wrist, sending a fresh tingle along her nerve endings.

"Do you remember last night when I asked you to come in my mouth?"

"Hmm," was his answer as he stroked her arm.

"You said no."

"I didn't know what I was missing."

Which was not in line with what *she* thought. "You wouldn't, because you were controlling events."

"I just wanted to come inside you that first time."

"You've been controlling everything since the moment you walked in my front door." Orgasmic delight had not clouded her brain. Her body had become a battle zone, and he'd used her love of sex to gain the upper hand. She'd done her share, admittedly, but primarily in reaction to his underhanded tactics.

Something, her steady tone, her less than malleable body, something, penetrated his afterglow. He abandoned his slow caress to prop himself on his elbow. "I've been making love to you."

She laughed. It was the most ridiculous thing she'd ever heard. "You just came in my mouth because you thought you could manipulate me. It's the oldest trick in the book. You withheld it earlier, but now you gave it because it suited your purpose."

"And what was my purpose?"

"To control me." She'd enjoyed his demands on the phone. Face-to-face, though, the tone of their skirmishes had changed.

"I just wanted you to talk to me."

She raised her brows. "With your cock in my mouth?"

"I only thought of that afterward." He bent to flick his tongue across her nipple. It immediately peaked. "But then your gorgeous breasts called out to me, and your snatch begged for my attention. I couldn't resist."

"You tied me down, Jack. Without my permission."

He stilled. The laughter in his eyes died. "I didn't think you'd listen to me any other way."

"I don't think there's anything to listen to. We had a very nice time. You fly back tomorrow. I think we should end it with that."

He sat up, throwing his legs over the edge of the bed. "Don't start this again."

"I'm not starting it. I'm ending it."

He put a hand to the top of his head, scrubbed at his scalp with blunt fingers. "You don't really mean that."

She reached down to pull the covers to her waist. The room seemed suddenly cold. "I do mean it. I've enjoyed our phone talk. But I knew on Wednesday that taking it any further was a mistake. We ruined the fantasy."

"We lived the fantasy."

"Maybe you did."

He rose, stood by the side of the bed and stared down at her. "We both did. You know it can't get any better than that."

"Which is another good reason we should end it here and now."

He didn't say anything, just let those smoky gray eyes of his roam her face. His gaze touched her eyes, her lips, her hair, as if he were memorizing her.

Finally he spoke. "You're right. I did lie. I deliberately did not tell you about the promotion because I thought you'd want to work with one of the other salesmen, thinking I'd be too busy to give you good service." He stopped a beat, letting his double entendre sink in. "I didn't tell you about the sales office, because I thought you'd run. I didn't tell you that I've been working on setting up this office for months. I broached the subject to the executive committee, and I suggested the site."

He'd made plans behind her back. His conniving was worse than she'd thought.

"I didn't tell you that I loved you, because I didn't think you'd be ready to hear it until after you let me make love to you."

The declaration slammed into her like a wrecking ball. She nearly curled into a fetal position, but she didn't. She couldn't let Jack see that. He'd find a way to use it against her. In the wrong man's hand, a woman's emotions could become weapons. She hadn't truly believed Jack would sink to that level.

She hadn't believed he was capable of employing Ian's tactics, but Jack was indeed dictatorial, autocratic, and arrogant.

"I planned to tell you before I left. Tomorrow. Time to absorb it before I called you on Monday. But then I'd probably have broken down and called you Sunday night."

Was this his version of baring his soul? Telling her exactly how he'd planned to manipulate her?

"I do have plans for us, Kirby. I won't deny that. We'd make a perfect team. I've got all the contacts you need to help grow your business."

Her heart shriveled to the size of walnut. "My business?"

"It would be the logical conclusion. After we're married, we can run it together."

She sat up, stuffed a couple of pillows behind her, and scooted back against the brass bedstead. "This was all about my business?"

He stopped, looked at her as if, for the first time, he'd figured out how his plan would come across to her. "The business was secondary." He put out a hand. "No. I mean . . . I thought of the business as a way we could share the rest of our lives."

"You want ownership in my company."

Anger reddened his cheekbones. "Screw your company. It was never about that. It was about *you*. I want *you*."

"I thought you *loved* me." Which wasn't the same thing as wanting, not at all.

"I do."

Icy tendrils crept down her neck, her chest, her arms. Her blood slowed to the movement of sludge. Poor Jack. He hadn't executed his plan well. She'd figured it out before he'd managed to put everything in his name, take control of the bank accounts, and undermine her with her clients. She hadn't let Ian get that far either. Instead, she'd liquidated and gotten out.

"Kirby."

"Been there, done that, Jack. No one will get their hands on my company. No one will have a say but me."

She didn't know what to do with her hands. They trembled. It was bad enough keeping her voice steady, she couldn't control her hands, too. She stuffed them beneath the covers.

"I think you should get dressed and go."

"A man tried to take it all away from you once, didn't he?"

She smiled, a brittle grimace that felt as if it would crack the muscles of her face. "Worse, Jack."

Ian had wanted her to think everything was her fault. He hadn't wanted her business as much as he'd wanted to crush her self-confidence. Why, she'd never quite understood, and she'd long since stopped trying to figure it out.

"I'm sorry."

"You can see why I'm hesitant to put myself into the same situation again."

He backed up a step, then another. "You really think that's what I want? To gain control of your company?"

"Isn't it?" Ian had wanted her self-esteem. Jack wanted to control.

He put a hand to his chest, rubbed the muscle just above his heart. "If you honestly believe that, then you've been right all along, Kirby. We *don't* know each other."

He gathered his scattered clothes and left the bedroom. Five minutes later the front door closed.

Kirby laid down in her bed and cried for the first time in almost five years.

EIGHTEEN

Christ, he was a fucking idiot. He should have known there was a helluva lot more to her than just an ardent feminist whose watchword was *equality*. He'd even sensed that hint of vulnerability. He hadn't put it all together.

Until it was too freaking late.

She hadn't called his hotel Saturday night, nor Sunday, before he left. His bag packed and ready, he'd waited until the last possible moment, almost missing his flight in the process.

She never called. Fuck. It hurt, a dull ache in his chest that only worsened once the plane reached cruising altitude, as if the cabin pressure constricted his breathing.

He'd thought he knew her inside and out. He'd assumed she was a self-made woman. Oh yeah, she'd been born with more testosterone than your average female, but he'd never considered that she'd also had a few painful experiences along the way that helped make her the woman she was. His whole campaign had been destined to fail. Simply because he'd developed a campaign instead of just telling her flat out that he'd give up his job, his career, anything, everything, to be with her. He'd carry her mail, pour her coffee, rub her feet after a long day, and bury his tongue against her clit every single goddamn time she wanted it. Wherever, whenever, and however she wanted it. Okay, maybe he wasn't capable of the coffee and the mail thing, but he should have come clean from the start instead of trying to force her to see she couldn't live without him.

Because Kirby could live without him. Even if she loved him, she would be just fine without him. Truthfully, he wouldn't have wanted her any other way. That was one of the things he loved about her, her self-reliance. He'd just never guessed at the reasons for it.

His life had always been about planning the next battle. And winning. It never occurred to him to do it any other way, not even with Kirby. He couldn't count the number of times this weekend that he'd asked her to trust him. He was, in fact, the one who didn't know how to trust. He'd connived instead of offered. He'd withheld instead of letting loose. He'd studied her like she was the enemy and plotted ways to ensnare her.

It was too late to undo the damage of his ill-advised campaign. He had only one choice.

Let her think about what he'd said and make her own decision. No phone calls. No pushing. No plan of attack.

Simply sitting back and waiting to see what she decided would be the hardest battle Jack Taylor had ever fought.

Damn, she was tired and dragging by the time she stepped into her office on Monday morning.

Kirby hadn't slept well. She kept smelling Jack all over the apartment. She'd washed the sheets, disinfected the bathroom, and vacuumed. Yet she could still smell him. Was it aftershave? She hadn't remembered him wearing a scent. Maybe it was the soap he used. Or his toothpaste. Or just the male musk of his body. Whatever, it lingered. It kept her awake. It entered her subconscious in the middle of the night after she'd finally fallen asleep only to wake in the midst of one of those orgasms Jack was so good at. A dream she'd failed to fall back into.

"You look like crap," Cindy, her secretary, commented.

"On that cheerful note, hold all my calls."

"I put the package you were expecting on your desk," Cindy said before she closed the door. "It came after you left Friday."

"Thanks." She shut the door and shut out the world. Maybe she should have stayed at home. She threw her purse on the small conference table in the corner, closed her eyes, and put her fingertips to her temples. Exhaustion fogged her brain. God, she even smelled Jack here, in her office.

The package sat in the middle of her desk, on top of her daily scheduler. As usual, he'd sent it directly to her rather than having it go through her Receiving department. Halfway across the room, she could make out the logo. Jack's logo. It was undoubtedly the replacement order. She'd forgotten all about it after his call. Or it could have been the new formula. He'd said he was going to check into it, but he hadn't mentioned anything when he arrived.

She hadn't given a damn about anything other than getting in his pants.

Shit. She didn't need the visual reminder of him now. She already had all the memories, and this weird phantom scent haunting her.

Rounding the desk, she opened the middle drawer for her box cutter and slit the tape across the top. Foam popcorn spilled out, and she dug her hands in to pull out one of the twelve replacement bottles he'd sent. Unscrewing the lid, she dabbed her finger in the cream. At least it hadn't separated like the last lot. She rolled a daub between her thumb and forefinger, then smoothed it over the back of her hand. Good consistency. Light scent. Perfect.

She reached automatically for the phone to call Jack, to let him know she'd gotten it.

Jesus, she couldn't call him. He'd lied to her and manipulated her.

Still, it would be rude if she didn't at least let him know. Bad business practice.

Dammit. So easy to call. She had him on speed dial. Her temples ached over the decision. A strange tightness took hold of her chest, making it difficult to breathe. She sat down, her bottom hit the chair wrong, and sent it scooting out behind her. She almost fell. Hanging on to the edge of her desk, she started to laugh. She laughed until her sides ached as badly as her head and tears spilled down her cheeks.

Her phone beeped, then Cindy's voice came over the intercom. "Are you all right in there, Kirby?"

"I'm fine." Which was so untrue.

"Well . . . call me if you need something."

What she needed was to call Jack. But she couldn't. He'd walked out—no, she'd kicked him out—and there was no going back to the way it had been.

The worst was that she felt it in a purely personal sense when her first concern should have been for how the debacle would affect the business.

Monday night provided no better rest than Kirby had had the night before. Tuesday, which she'd hoped would dawn as a brighter day, started with a spilled mocha, stains on her linen skirt, and a run in her hose.

She couldn't remember if she'd felt this bad when everything ended with Ian. Time had a way of dulling the pain, and she could only hope it would dull this ache permeating her entire body.

"Do not say I look like crap," she told Cindy as she passed through to her office.

Cindy trailed her, making it impossible to sequester herself. "I wondered if we could use a little help around here. My sister-in-law just got laid off, and I thought maybe we could have her in to do some filing. She's good with computers, too."

Kirby hung her purse and jacket on the coatrack. "You'd know better than I do about what kind of help you need."

Cindy bit her lip. "Well . . . I . . ."

"You don't really need any help, do you?"

"No. But they've got a couple of kids, and this is really going to hurt them."

Kirby rolled her head, her neck popping. "I'm sorry. I'll do a little checking around." Then she remembered Jack's sales office, and her heart started to pound. Was it serendipity? Or bad luck? "Can she handle phones?"

"Sure. She was a receptionist at her previous job."

"Well, I did hear about something over the weekend. Let me make a call, and I'll get back to you." Her palms got sticky just thinking about the excuse to call Jack.

Excuse? She didn't need an excuse.

"Thanks, boss."

"Close the door on your way out."

In the now all-too-quiet office, Kirby carefully rolled her chair out and sat down. No falling this time. She reached out to hit Jack's speed dial. And stopped. Her hand shook. Her face felt flushed. She was breathing hard, and her temples throbbed. Her whole body ached. She was sure this was how junkies felt when they needed a fix badly. God, she was like an addict, and Jack was her drug of choice.

She didn't have any choice about how badly she wanted him. She didn't have a speck of control. When she closed her eyes, she felt him inside her. Even now her body juiced up just imagining his voice on the phone. It hadn't been like this before. Sure, she'd looked forward to those calls, but she hadn't *needed* them, not the way she did now.

She put her hands in her lap, clasped them together to stop their trembling.

The phone rang.

Oh God, it was him. She leaped at the phone, knocking over her pencil holder. It exploded across the floor in front of the desk, spewing its contents on the carpet, but she got to the receiver before it chirped again.

"Hello."

"Kirby?"

She sat back down with a lurch, and her vision blurred. "Kristin. What's up?"

She tried to calm herself with a deep breath, but disappointment beat against the backs of her eyes.

"What's wrong?"

"Nothing." She knew she sounded . . . unnatural. "I was just in the middle of some paperwork." God, she couldn't even think about paperwork. Or seeing clients.

"Well, I'll make it quick. Ross and I want you and Jack to come to that new Fusion restaurant with us."

She almost hiccuped. "Jack?"

"He told Ross he was coming out at the end of the week. And don't tell me he's not spending the weekend with you. I know you better than that."

He'd told Ross he was coming out? And he hadn't told *her*? Maybe if she hadn't kicked him out . . . No, this was just more of Jack's duplicity. The bastard. For the first time in three days, Kirby's head cleared. "He's not spending the weekend with me. I'm not seeing him."

"You're not seeing him? What does that mean?"

"I mean, last weekend was enough." Last weekend was the cure. She didn't need Jack. She didn't need his phone calls. She didn't need his hands on her. She didn't need his tongue on her clit or his cock in her mouth. Or those multiple orgasms or . . . well, maybe it was better not to think about that stuff. Better to remind herself that she still had Mr. Perfect. Then she thought of what Jack had done to her with Mr. Perfect. God, that wasn't a good thing to think about either.

"But, Kirby, he was so nice. I really liked him."

"You don't know him. We didn't even spend the whole evening at your place."

"Because you had to get home to jump his bones."

"That's not why I left. I was tired. Too much sun."

"Too much sex. Or not enough. You're an idiot if you let that man go."

"He's short and bald." The words seemed to have become a chant to ward off Kristin's persistence. Or her own inexplicable emotions. *Short* and *bald* didn't have meaning anymore. Jack wasn't too short where it counted. She liked his shiny head between her legs. She liked the unique sensation of smooth scalp beneath her fingertips. "This conversation is going nowhere."

"I'm glad you noticed that. I hope you come to your senses. Let me know when you do."

Kristin hung up without saying goodbye. Her sister actually hung up on her. Kirby stared at the phone in disbelief. Jack had come between them.

Kristin didn't even know him and hadn't figured out he was an arrogant, dictatorial asshole. He'd been after Kirby's business, as she'd discovered just in time. He was Ian all over again.

Wasn't he?

The answer had been so clear-cut on Saturday night.

Kirby started to ache all over again. Because she didn't know any more. The memory of Jack's parting accusation hung in the stuffy, overly warm office.

What if she was the one who didn't really know him?

What if she had been wrong?

NINETEEN

Kirby felt like a ghost haunting the lobby of the Ambassador Hotel. This was ridiculous. She didn't know why she was here, and even worse, why she was skulking behind a huge vase of flowers.

Her palms had started itching and sweating yesterday, Wednesday. Though she'd told herself she was a jerk, she'd still driven down to the Ambassador. Maybe Jack wasn't even staying here again. If he was and she saw him, she didn't have a clue what she'd do.

She just wanted to see him.

Damn Kristin for telling her he was coming back.

"Fancy meeting you here."

She jumped, dropped her purse, and almost knocked the damn vase over. "Don't sneak up on me like that."

"I wasn't sneaking," Ross said, picking up her purse and handing it to her. "I called your name, but you didn't hear me."

No, she'd been concentrating on shorter men without any hair. There'd been plenty of them milling about in the Ambassador's plush lobby. None of them had been Jack.

Wasn't this just about the most humiliating moment of her life? Busted by her sister's fiancé. "I'm waiting for a client. She's late." She lied smoothly, glancing down at her watch. "An hour late." She put her purse strap over her shoulder. "Well, I guess she's not coming. I'll see you later."

He stopped her with a hand on her arm. "I have a dinner meeting in half an hour. Why don't we have a drink first?"

"Sure. I'd love a drink." It would make Kristin happy. Ross really wasn't all that bad. And a drink was a good excuse. If Jack did happen by, he wouldn't think she was there because of him.

Ross made a courtly gesture toward the bar, then followed her. Happy hour had filled most of the tables, but they found a nook over by the front windows. The waitress was quick to take their orders, eyeing Ross with an eat-him-up look.

"So, you dumped him."

Damn that Kristin and her big mouth. "Who?"

"Don't play stupid with me, Kirby."

"We hadn't advanced to the relationship stage, so it can't be called dumping him. And this really isn't any of your business."

"I know. But I'm tired of dragging all my friends out to dinner so you can put your nose in the air."

"I don't do that."

The waitress set their drinks down and ogled Ross as he leaned to one side for his wallet. He put some bills on her tray, smiled, and turned back before she'd even walked away. Did he notice the way women drooled over him? No. He had Kristin, and if nothing else, Kirby was sure the man adored her sister. It was his saving grace. She sighed. Damn. She was being totally bitchy, if only in her mind. This week was really wearing on her.

"Is it just because they're my friends, and you don't like me?"

"I don't dislike you. I'm glad you're marrying my sister. But I don't need you or Kristin to find dates for me."

"She wants you to settle down and be happy."

Last week when Kristin said virtually the same thing, Kirby had snorted. Be happy. Settle down. B.J.—Before Jack—the thought hadn't seriously crossed her mind. Somehow, in little more than twenty-four hours, Jack had turned her world upside down and inside out.

Which was probably the only reason she opened her mouth and confessed what she did, knowing Ross would understand. "He's just not right for me. I'm headstrong."

"A ballbuster."

She didn't take offense. "Why, thank you, Ross."

"That's why you need someone like Jack. He'll squash you down when you're getting uppity."

Her? Uppity? "You know this about him after half an hour over a hot barbecue?"

"We bonded."

She snorted. "Yeah, two dictatorial assholes" slipped out before she thought better of it.

He raked a hand through his hair, then laughed. "And thank you. You know what your problem is?"

"No. But I'm sure you're going to tell me."

"You don't know the difference between a good dictatorial asshole and a bad one."

"I wasn't aware there was a difference."

"Sure there is." He sipped on his scotch and soda. "A good dictatorial asshole does everything in his power to protect the woman he loves, to take care of his family. He might forget to compromise and he might issue a few commands, but he'll never do anything to hurt the ones he loves. He'll cherish them until the day he dies." He spread his arms. "On the other hand, a bad dictatorial asshole doesn't even know how to love."

She simply stared at him, speechless. For the first time she had an inkling of the qualities with which Kristin had fallen in love. Okay, she'd had plenty of clues as to his true nature, but she'd chosen to ignore them, concentrating instead on his arrogance. Beyond that, she had to admit that he was smart, funny, strong, loyal, and adored her sister to distraction. More than just a pretty face and a sexy body, he was goddamn profound.

No wonder he and Jack had "bonded" in less than half an hour. One good dictatorial asshole acknowledging another, one man earning the respect of the other.

Neither of them would have respected a man like Ian. They would have seen through his façade in minutes.

Oh my God, what have I done?

"I've gotta go," she said, grabbing her purse and pushing back her chair.

He looked up at her. "Was it something I said?"

She smiled. The first genuine smile she'd ever given him. "Yeah. It was. And thanks."

TWENTY

Not calling Kirby was killing him. Jack had hoped and prayed she'd make the move, and he couldn't count the number of times he'd been *that* close to picking up the phone. Kirby wasn't a woman who could be pressured. He didn't have a chance in hell if he tried that trick.

Jesus Christ, what if she never called?

He damn well wouldn't think like that. She was a smart woman. She'd figure out in the end that he wasn't like the bastard who had turned on her. If she didn't, then they didn't have a chance in hell anyway.

He set his briefcase on the desk and threw his bag on the hotel bed. God, he was tired. It had been a long day, a long wait at the airport, and an even longer flight. By New York time, it was almost midnight. He had five interviews scheduled tomorrow, a meeting with his banker, and an appointment with a potential receptionist.

The woman had called him in New York, saying she'd gotten his number from Kirby. That call had been his only ray of hope. If Kirby really thought he was such a dick, she wouldn't have sent him her secretary's sister-in-law.

He held on to that conclusion like a talisman. By now, Sloan would have told Kristin he was flying back into town, and Kristin would have passed it on to Kirby.

He sat heavily on the bed, took his shoes off his aching dogs, and put his head in his hands, grinding his palms against his tired eyes. He was letting the happy couple do his dirty work. He should have been ashamed, but with Kirby, he needed all the help he could get.

A knock on the door snapped him out of his thoughts. He'd ordered dinner and a bottle of beer. One to ease the growling in his stomach—airline food stank—and the other to help him sleep. Drowning his sorrows.

When he opened the door, he was sure he'd actually fallen asleep and the vision standing before him was a dream. God, she was more beautiful than he remembered. Decked out in a short skirt and heels that screamed fuck me, Kirby smelled like cinnamon and spice, hot and sweet. He wanted to bury his face in her hair and hang on until the real knock on the door woke him.

"May I come in, Jack?"

He held the door open, drinking in the sight of her, the delicious huskiness of her voice, and the waft of her perfume as she passed him. He prayed he wouldn't wake up until he'd at least gotten her clothes off. Or maybe, until he'd reached the part where she wrapped those long sexy legs around his waist. He wouldn't let her remove the shoes. . . .

"Jack, are you okay?"

No, he'd died and gone to heaven. Though it was beginning to dawn on him that this was no dream. "I'm fine. You look good." *Why are you here?*

"Thank you." She twisted the strap of her purse, and if he didn't know better, he'd think she was nervous. "Okay, I have something to say, so don't interrupt—"

"How'd you find out my room number?"

"I bribed the bellboy. He looked it up." She wouldn't have had to pay much. One look from her would bring most men to their knees. "You should find another hotel. Anyone could have—"

"How'd you know I was here?"

She rolled her eyes and pursed her lips. God, he loved it when she did that. "I can't say what I came to say if you keep interrupting me. So shut up."

"Yes, ma'am." His heart hammered so hard, he wasn't sure he could take in what she said.

"Okay. Now, as I was saying, I have something to say." Her mouth opened and closed twice, but Kirby had seemingly lost her train of thought.

"You already said that."

"Dammit, Jack."

Her eyes darkened, and Jesus, was that a trace of moisture at the corners?

"I'm sorry. I won't say anything else until you're done." The waiting just might kill him.

She took a deep breath, her breasts plumping against her blouse. "All right. I just wanted to say that you were right. We didn't really know each other."

A fist closed around his heart. She was going to offer him a freaking apology, then be on her merry little way.

"I was wrong. You're not like . . . you're wouldn't do the things I accused you of. I'm sorry I said that. I didn't mean it."

And? *And?* He put his hands behind his back so she wouldn't see them clenching.

"I want to start over, forget Saturday night ever happened."

God. He saw spots, felt dizzy, and his knees threatened to give out. "That sounds fine."

"Just fine?"

More than fine. He wanted to reach out, hug her to him, touch her face, her lips, her hair. Then rip her clothes off and fuck the hell out of her. "Okay, let's forget about Saturday night and start over."

"Thank you, Jack."

"You're welcome." Since when had they become so frigging polite?

"I have something I want to ask you to do."

Jesus, anything. "All right."

"I want you to take off all your clothes and lie down on the bed."

Was this a good or a bad thing? It didn't matter. "Sure. I can do that."

He slid the knot down on his tie, unbuttoned his shirt, removed it, and hung it over the back of a chair. Kirby reached for her purse on the desk. Unbuckling his belt, his fingers trembled, and he fumbled a moment with the zipper, then he shoved his pants off his hips and down his legs. He folded them and put them on the chair with his shirt. His cock was so damn hot and hard, it almost burst above the elastic of his briefs.

She stared. Her nipples strained against her blouse. Then she pointed and said, "You can take those off, too."

Not a problem. They were binding as hell. He jumped to her command, then lay down on the bed, his cock sticking up like a flagpole.

Kirby busied herself, pulling wads of colored cloth from her purse. Jesus, what did the woman have planned for him? He didn't care what it was as long as he got to touch her, to be inside her, to fill her, and shout that he loved her while he did it.

She climbed onto the bed beside him, her hands over-flowing with soft, patterned silk. He remembered. Her scarves. She was going to administer a test just as he'd done to her.

"Trust me," she whispered, the timber of her voice clutching at his balls.

"I do."

She sat back on her haunches, her legs curled beneath her, her thighs slightly spread. Her excited, musky scent drove him wild. His cock twitched.

"There's no headboard. Where am I going to tie these?" She held out the froth of color.

"Try the bed legs."

She smiled. He'd kill for that smile.

She leaned over the side of the bed, her pert ass in the

air. It was all he could do not to take one lovely cheek in each hand. She muttered a few times, her ass wriggling. She sat up again.

"Hold out your arm."

He did. Willingly. She tied the silk around his wrist, making sure there wasn't much give. Then she crawled over him, her skirt bunching high up her legs. His cock brushed her thigh. Her bush grazed his stomach. He almost came. She repeated the procedure on the other side. His hand rested briefly between her legs, and his fingers ached to reach beneath the short little skirt. He didn't. This was her show. He wanted her to have it. All of it.

This time she didn't have to ask him to hold out his arm. He put it in the noose himself. Afterward, she sat back to admire her handiwork.

"Aren't you going to do my legs?"

"Are you going to kick me?"

"No."

"Then I think we're okay the way we are."

They weren't, not really. He wanted so much more from her. He could, he *would*, wait.

She rose to her knees and inched up that little skirt. His breath came faster. His pulse pounded. His cock grew at least an inch, well, at least it felt that way. A tantalizing glimpse of her sweet snatch came into view. His arms jerked involuntarily, he wanted to touch her so badly. Pulling her skirt to her hips, she spread her legs to straddle him and sank down on his hips, trapping his cock close to her moist heat.

She stroked the tip, gently sliding her finger into the slit. Cum oozed. She smoothed it over the head. "You have the most beautiful cock I've ever seen."

"Thanks," he said, his voice little more than a guttural moan.

"Now, I've tied you up because I still have something to say, and I wanted your complete attention."

"Sweetheart, you definitely have my complete attention."

"Shut up, I'm talking here."

"Yes, ma'am."

"As I was saying, I've got something to say. But first, I have to make sure you're securely fastened." She lifted her hips. His cock followed like a homing device. Wrapping her fingers around him, she squeezed—God, he would die, he really fucking would because she felt so damn good—and slid him into the opening of her pussy.

He'd had her with a condom, he'd had her with his tongue, but he'd never felt anything like the warm, silky feel of her vagina. "What about a condom?" he croaked.

"I'm on the pill. So I don't need one. Do you?"

Jesus H. Christ. "No." No protection meant trust. On both sides.

She guided him, stroking from the base up, taking him inside her. His hips bucked once, burying him high. He closed his eyes, shoved his head back into the pillow, and groaned. She settled on top of him, wiggling, twisting, until she finally found just the right position.

Then she stopped moving altogether.

He wanted to dig his heels into the bed and ram up inside her as far as he could go. He had waited so fucking long, not just tonight, not just the few days since the weekend. No, he'd waited a lifetime for her.

"Don't stop, Kirby, please. I'm begging you." He let his gaze roam her face, his eyes searching hers.

"You see, that's the problem."

Christ, here it came. The slam. Payback time. He could take it. He would take it. Then he'd convince her to stay with him no matter what. His cock throbbed inside her. Her pussy milked him. "What's the problem?"

"I wanted you to beg."

"I am begging. I'll beg all you want."

"I changed my mind."

He closed his eyes, swallowed, opened his mouth to drag in a great fistful of air, then looked at her once more. Jesus, could she possibly know how incredible she looked sitting there? Above him. Her hair wild. Her lips plump. Her eyes the deep exotic color of a rain-soaked jungle.

"Please don't change your mind, Kirby. I want you."

"I mean I changed my mind about needing you to beg."

She leaned forward, spreading her hands on his chest. Catching his nipples between her fingers, she pressed. His hips bucked once more, his body no longer in his control.

"Only a dictatorial asshole wants to make her partner beg. It's all part of the control, of needing to be on top all the time."

"I don't mind if you want to be on top." Anything, as long as she fucked him, as long as he stayed right where he was for the rest of his life.

"I don't want to be like that with you. I don't want to be a dictatorial asshole. I am, you know. I can admit it now."

She was telling him something, but his brain resided between his legs right now, and hell if he could figure it out. "What do you want to be like?"

She smoothed her hands down his chest, his abdomen, almost to their joining. "Do you know the difference between a good dictatorial asshole and a bad dictatorial asshole?"

"Huh?" She'd lost him. Completely. He hoped to God that didn't mean *he'd* lost *her*.

"Well, a bad dictatorial asshole shits on everyone who loves them."

She bent forward, sucked his nipple into her mouth. He didn't understand a word she said, but he let her have them because in the only remaining brain cell he had, he understood she needed them.

"But a good dictatorial asshole," she went on after freeing his nipple from her succulent mouth. "A good one does everything in her power to protect the people she loves. Of course, she'll be a bitch sometimes when she doesn't get her way, and she'll issue orders before she thinks. But she'll never do anything to hurt the man she loves. She'll cherish him till the day she dies."

He wanted his hands free. He wanted to touch her. He wanted to understand what she was saying.

"A very good dictatorial asshole friend of mine taught me that." She flattened herself against his chest, rubbed her

nipples to his, slid her hands out along his arms. Her hair
covered his face. "I've been so afraid of losing myself with
you, of letting you be the man, the strong one." She eased
back far enough to capture his gaze. "I thought you'd try to
crush me. So I decided to do the crushing first. But I was so
wrong about you. You're not like . . . that other man. You
never could be. You're too good for that. I think I knew
that, too, and that's why I fought even harder. I always
thought falling in love meant giving up a piece of myself."

He closed his eyes, shoved his head back, and let out the
breath he'd been holding. "I love you, Kirby. I'll never
crush you. I don't want to change a thing about you or
make you give up anything. You're all I've ever wanted,
just the way you are."

Taking his face in her hands, she put her lips to his in a
gentle kiss. "There hasn't been a day in the past year that I
haven't thought about you, haven't wanted you. But I didn't
want things to change between us. I was afraid it wouldn't
work out. Maybe it won't, but I want to take the chance."

"Untie my hands."

"Your wish is my command." She pulled the knot loose
on one wrist.

Jack took her hand. "Not a command, just a request."
Then he let go.

She undid the other knot, her hot, hard nipples branding
him as she leaned over.

The scarves falling away, Jack wrapped his arms around
her, and rolled until he was on top. His hips moved against
her, his cock thrusting high and deep. He stopped before he
lost control.

"Do you love me, Kirby?" He waited, tensed, because
she hadn't actually said it yet.

"Yes. I love you."

"Then everything will work out. I promise. Because I'll
never do anything to hurt you, I'll always love you and
cherish you till the day I die."

He sealed the vow with a kiss. "Now that we've got that
over, may I please fuck the hell out of you?"

"Yes." She laughed, a light musical sound unlike any other she'd ever gifted him with.

She brought her legs to his waist, tightened her hold, and pulled him deep into her body. Then, putting both hands to the top of his head, she rubbed her palms across his scalp. "God, your bare skin makes me hot. Now do me."

He did. And he would. For the rest of their lives.

For **Jasmine Haynes,** storytelling has always been a passion. With a bachelor's degree in accounting, she has worked in the high-tech Silicon Valley for the last twenty years. She and her husband live with three cats, Boneyard, Louis, and Eddie, as well as Star, the mighty moose-hunting dog. Jasmine's pastimes, when not writing her heart out, are hiking in the redwoods and taking long walks on the beach. Jasmine also writes as Jennifer Skully and JB Skully. She loves to hear from readers. Visit her website at www.skullybuzz.com; e-mail her at skully@skullybuzz.com; or write to her at PO Box 66738, Scott's Valley, CA 95067.